An
Unexpected
Apprentice

An
Unexpected
Apprentice

Jody Lynn Nye

A Tom Doherty Associates Book
New York

TOR®

AN UNEXPECTED APPRENTICE

This book is printed on acid-free paper.

A Tor Book
Published by Tom Doherty Associates, LLC
175 Fifth Avenue
New York, NY 10010

www.tor.com

Tor® is a registered trademark of Tom Doherty Associates, LLC.

Library of Congress Cataloging-in-Publication Data

Nye, Jody Lynn, 1957-
 An unexpected apprentice / Jody Lynn Nye.—1st. ed.
  p. cm.
 "A Tom Doherty Associates book"
 ISBN-13: 978-0-7653-1433-8
 ISBN-10: 0-7653-1433-9
 I. Title.
 PS3564.Y415U54   2007
 813'.54--dc22

2007006145

First Edition: June 2007

Printed in the United States of America

0 9 8 7 6 5 4 3 2 1

To my wonderful mother-in-law,
Jeanne Fawcett,
a wizardess in her own way

Acknowledgments

I would like to thank everyone at Tor Books, especially Brian Thomsen for his encouragement and friendship, Tom Doherty for his guidance and good advice, and Patrick Nielsen Hayden for his professional support and faith.

Chapter One

he merry piping stopped.

Tildi Summerbee looked up idly from the book she was reading, which was propped on the carved shelf beside the huge bubbling stew pot.

How strange, she thought, lifting the stirring spoon to her lips for a taste. Her youngest brother, Marco, usually played his flute all the way home from the fields as he, and the rest of her brothers, and the farmhands headed toward the big old house. Teldo, Pierin, and Gosto would sing along.

That was how she knew without looking out one of the round windows that it was noon, and that they were coming in for lunch. Now, at the beginning of June, the first crop of Daybreak Bank Farm's sweet-smelling hay had to be cut. The work was hard, and it made her brothers hungry. It was a big job to feed them and their farmhands on an ordinary day, but even bigger at the times of haying and harvest, when hosts of neighbors came to lend their strength so that the expanded workforce could swiftly clear field after field. By the week's end, all the hay around Clearbeck would be cut and drying, its sweet scent wafting in through the open windows, along with a fair bit of chaff.

She didn't mind sweeping up. At least there wasn't a mess of mud to scrub off the floors. The fine weather kept the ground dry. It was perfect for cutting hay.

A long wisp of her soft brown hair drifted down from her modest white cap and over one eye. Tildi tucked it back into place.

Where were they?

She strained one leaf-shaped ear to listen for the distant music to begin again. Instead of the friendly chatter of men and women she heard faint frightened shouts and cries.

One word rose above the others, and was repeated over and over.

"Thraik!"

Tildi threw open the nearest window and raised her eyes to the heavens. Her heart tightened in her chest. The greatest terror in her life had come again.

Against the expanse of pure blue she saw the black shadows swooping and diving. The torsos of the airborne devils resembled her people, the smallfolks, except that the monsters were four times their size. The thraik's green-black skin glimmered as though it had been painted with grease. As did the wings, each a fan of long, yellow, spearlike bones with dark greenish skin stretched between them. Their faces were death's-heads, the skin barely painted on the gaunt bones. Sharp yellow teeth crowded their jaws, giving them drunken, evil grins.

A huge thraik floating high on the air opened its maw and emitted an earsplitting shriek. The sound echoed on and on. Tildi gasped as she saw what was going on beneath it.

In the field below, a hundred yards away, a flock of thraik circled and struck at a tiny band of smallfolks. Marco had cast aside his flute and was defending himself with swipes of his scythe from a huge devil that slashed at him with its talons. Marco's sunbrowned, round, normally cheerful face was set and pale. His fluffy brown hair was slicked to his scalp with sweat. Tildi knew what was in his mind. *Not again!*

Five times over the seventeen years of her life the thraik had returned to the Quarters. The winged monsters appeared in the sky from nowhere, and descended to maim and kill whatever they could find. Usually they attacked farm animals, swooping down too swiftly for the landowners to stop them. Once in a while an unlucky smallfolk not fast enough to get to shelter had become their prey, torn apart or carried off. No one knew where they roosted, since no one had ever returned to tell. The horrible beasts didn't remain in any place for long, but their visits wreaked tragedy.

In her mind's eye, Tildi saw the same horrible sight, an event ten years gone.

Waiting for their parents to return from town, she and her four brothers had been standing in the doorway of their house when thraik fell out of the sky, like black, rotting leaves. Tildi remembered screaming a warning to her mother and father. The devils swooped down upon the cart containing Bernardo and Gelina Summerbee. Her father had smashed at the beasts again and again with his walking stick. The beasts had not seemed to notice the blows at all. The largest thraik had tucked Gelina under its arm and hoisted her right out of the cart. Heedless of his own safety, Bernardo fought to save his wife, driving the creatures back, but they had the advantage of flight. He slashed at two hovering before him, but another dropped behind him and clasped him around the neck. Bernardo kicked and thrashed, but the thraik effortlessly lifted him up into the air. Struggle as they might, the elder smallfolks were helpless to break loose. Tildi remembered stumbling after her elder brothers, running desperately, trying to get to her parents. The monsters flew up out of reach long before Gosto and Pierin reached the cart. The children leaped, screaming and yelling threats at the thraik, begging them to bring their parents back. The thraik ignored them, and vanished through a tear in the sky. Tildi's last vision of her mother had been Gelina's frightened eyes staring back at her children as the sky swallowed her up.

Tildi saw that moment in her nightmares, and she was seeing it now. Not again! Not her brothers! She clutched the windowsill, wishing she could do something.

Marco thumped his opponent in the chest with the butt of the scythe. The thraik was knocked backward a yard or two in the air. It let out a tearing cry and flew at him, all four limbs reaching for his flesh. Marco braced himself. He brought the blade around in an arc. It bit through the thraik's wrist. The creature shrieked as its left hand tumbled away. Blood sprayed from the limb, covering Marco in a black mist. The smallfolk spat, but he brought the scythe up, ready to defend himself again. The thraik opened its wings and rose high over the young man's head, angling for a new strike. Tildi quaked with fear for his safety.

Beyond the slashing wings and whipping tails behind, Tildi could see the rest of her brothers and the farmhands fighting for their lives, wielding hoes, billhooks, rakes, even sticks as makeshift weapons. Tildi dropped her spoon and sought about for a weapon. She seized the poker from the fireside. They would not die if she could prevent it! What if she was a mere female? They were her family. She must help.

"Mistress, what should we do?" Mig and Lisel pleaded. Tildi had forgotten about them. The smallfolk sisters were daughters of the Summerbees' farm manager, Mirrin Sardbrook, who must be out there somewhere with the thraik. They clung to each other, trembling, their large brown eyes round with terror. Tildi could see they would be of no use at all.

"Bar the windows," Tildi said crisply. "I'm going to go help my brothers!"

Another shriek split the air. Tildi left the girls and dashed outside. She raced up the footpath and plunged into the swaying, chest-high hay grass, wielding her poker.

"Get back in the house!" her eldest brother Gosto shouted, waving her back. He swung a reaper twice as tall as he was at a black-winged creature hovering over him. The thraik lunged down. Gosto slashed the long blade across, severing a wing tip, but a talon caught the flesh at the corner of his eye. Red blood beaded down his cheek, mixing with black ichor. He grimaced. "Tildi, go! Take the field women with you!"

The thraik hovering over him turned to scream at her.

Trembling, Tildi stumbled to a halt and gazed up at the dark-winged beast. She had never seen her enemy so close before. It was huge, and ten times more horrible than it had been from a distance. The lumpy skin looked as if it would creep, maggotlike, under her fingers if she touched it. The thin bones in the wings seemed ready to tear free from the fragile sails, but that fragility was an illusion. Nothing about a thraik was weak. She had seen one snap the neck of a dray horse like a candy stick. The beast's sinuous neck undulated from side to side. Its round, heavy-lidded eyes were the color of dried blood. As soon as its gaze settled on her, a gleaming, irregular golden shape like knotwork appeared in the dull brown-red orbs. Her hand brandishing the poker sagged as if the thraik's stare was enough to drain the strength out of her body. She thought she heard it speak to her inside her mind.

You're next. It left Gosto, lifting ominously into the air like a storm cloud, and began to glide toward her.

Never, Tildi vowed. She would never let her family fall prey to them again! To her own surprise, she broke free of the glamor of terror. She raised her poker on high, and pressed forward toward the thraik. Her short legs threshed with difficulty through the high hay grass. Tildi shook with fear, but she would not turn back. She braced the poker in both hands to strike.

Just before the thraik descended, a heavy body landed on her, bearing her backward to the ground.

"What in hell's imagination are you doing, silly girl?" hissed Mirrin, the Summerbees' farm manager, the father of Mig and Lisel.

"Saving my brothers! Let me go!"

She struggled to get up, but the big man held her limbs pinned. He smelled sharply of sweat and fear.

"What can you do, girl? You're no warrior! Aargh!"

Mirrin stiffened. The thraik landed heavily on his shoulders, pressing the breath out of both smallfolks. The swaying head lowered, and Tildi cowered from the terrible, glowing eyes glaring down at her. She couldn't move. Mirrin cried out as the horrible creature pawed at him with its talons, digging to reach the girl beneath. Tildi was terrified to see cloth and flesh alike rent in furrows by the sharp claws, but Mirrin would not give up. At the cost of his own pain, Mirrin shifted from side to side to defend Tildi from it. The girl pressed her head into the grass, turning her head to avoid the talons, making herself as flat as possible. The thraik grew tired of the game and pushed a stinking palm into Mirrin's head, holding it down and out of the way, and stretched its other taloned hand past his shoulder, reaching for Tildi's throat.

Quick as thought, Tildi sank her teeth into the web of flesh between the long fingers. The thraik screamed. Tildi fell back, gagging on the bitter ichor. The thraik lifted clear, still howling its outrage.

Mirrin rolled off, and lay on his back, panting, as other smallfolk ran in to attack the beast. He was covered in blood. Tildi scrambled to her knees and spat the dirty, burned taste of the thraik's flesh out of her mouth, then bent to tend to Mirrin. He pushed her away.

"I'm all right. Go back to the house. Now!"

"I have to help."

His voice rasped hoarsely. "You're in the way, girl! Away!"

The thraik descended again, avoiding the farmworkers. It reached for her. Tildi dodged it, seeking the fallen poker in the long grass. Mirrin sprang up and clung to the creature's leg, weighing it down long enough for Tildi to escape. The thraik screamed. Tildi found her poker and half-ran, half-stumbled toward the fray.

"No, girl!" Mirrin shouted behind her. "Go back!"

Tildi paid no attention. All she could see was her second brother, Pierin, at bay against a towering thraik that dipped and bobbed at him, lashing out with its claws. She ran to help him. She fetched up short, nearly falling over an outflung arm. The battle had claimed casualties. Her eyes filled with tears as she recognized them. Jinny, an older woman who had lived on the farm since Tildi's father was a boy, lay dead on the ground with her throat gashed to the backbone. Nevil, the dairyman's boy, was huddled in a tight ball, rocking and sobbing with pain. Tildi couldn't see what was wrong with him, but there was a lot of blood. She dithered for a moment, wondering whether to help him, but the thraik seemed to be ignoring him. Pierin needed her.

He and a field woman, Franne, fought off the beast with harvesting hooks. The thraik's claws flashed with rusty redness. It was missing a foot, and dark blood ran from tears in the thin wings, but it had taken its revenge on the smallfolks. A gash in Pierin's scalp ran with blood, and Franne tottered to the left to favor the wound in her right leg. Tildi surprised that monster from behind, whacking it at the base of its spine with her poker. It let out a shriek and spun in the air, looking for its new assailant. The distraction gave Pierin a chance to draw back his scythe. He plunged it as high as he could reach. The curved point sank into the creature's back. The thraik let out a shrill, tearing cry and sagged. Its wings flipped upward. No longer able to hold itself in the air, it plummeted. Tildi jumped back just in time to avoid having it collapse on her. The ground shook with its weight. Franne limped forward and hacked at the dead beast with her reaper like a predator savaging its kill. Tears ran down her plump, lined face.

"Don't waste your time!" Pierin shouted, almost right in her ear. "Go take shelter! Take Tildi with you!"

Franne ignored him. She raised her arm again and again, hacking at the fallen thraik with a grim-set jaw. To her there was nothing else in the world. Tildi and Pierin tried to pull her back.

"Look," Pierin said urgently. "Mattew is in danger!"

That was Franne's son. Her face didn't change.

"Her mind's away with the elves," Pierin said grimly. "We can't leave her."

"Pierin, look out!" Tildi cried, pointing.

A thraik lifted away from the trio of smallfolk attacking it and made for Franne's unprotected back. Together Tildi and her brother struck at it. The thraik curled its tail in annoyance and snapped at them. Pierin swung the scythe. The winged beast flapped its wings and lifted straight up. Pierin brought the long pole around again. The blade just missed the creature's tail tip that time. It hissed at him. The other smallfolk stumbled and threshed over the unmown hay to help.

The largest thraik let out another cry that pierced through Tildi's whole body like needles. Her arms and legs felt weak. The poker slipped in her hand.

Pierin faltered, too. His scythe trembled and dipped for a moment, just long enough for the thraik to stretch its long neck past his guard. It seized him by the shoulder with its teeth and lifted him up into the air. Pierin cried out. The scythe fell from his hands. Tildi screamed.

The others slashed at the ugly beast, leaping up to get in a strike at it, but it rose swiftly out of reach. Tildi jumped up and down, trying to grab its leg.

"Put him down, you monster!" she shouted.

The shrill cry of the lord thraik tore through Tildi's hearing once more, driving her to her knees with the pain. Many of the smallfolk clapped their hands over their sensitive, leaf-shaped ears.

"Aargh!"

Tildi spun. Her eldest brother Gosto struggled in the claws of another thraik. With a triumphant look on its obscene face, it spread its wings and flapped upward.

The smallfolk snatched up rocks and threw them at the beast. It dodged away from them, screaming. Gosto kicked and pushed at his captor. Blood and smudges of dirt could not disguise the pallor of his face. His life was through. He knew it, and so did all of his kin. Tildi refused to accept it.

"Bring him back, you monster!" she screamed.

The beast grinned down at her.

"Save yourself, girl!" Gosto groaned. The translucent wings wrapped around him, hiding him from Tildi's view.

"No! Gosto!" She flung her poker at the beast. The iron rod missed its mark, tumbling end over end to earth. The creature rose high into the air, clutching its prey.

The smallfolks were powerless to save one of their own. Stunned, they watched the bundle's struggles grow more and more feeble. Gosto's strength was no more than a sparrow's against a wolf. One last kick, and the figure concealed in the sheer sails went limp, his head hanging back.

"Gosto!" Tildi screamed.

Shrieks brought Tildi back to earth. More thraik still threatened their lives. Gosto was lost, but the rest of them were still at risk. She scrabbled around in the trampled grass for fallen rocks, a scythe, a rake—anything.

"Back, hellbeast!"

A few paces away, Teldo, the brother who was only a year older than she, stood facing a hissing beast, holding a billhook in one hand and a ball of green fire in the other. Tildi blinked. For the last two years Teldo had been studying magic out of books bought from traveling peddlers and shops in the human village where the smallfolk took their crops and other goods to sell. The making of fire was one of the first spells he had mastered, yet Tildi had never seen him able to create more flame than could be used to light a candle. Necessity must have driven him to reach deeper inside himself than he had ever done before.

The thraik did not seem impressed to see a smallfolk wielding fire, no matter what color. It stuck its long neck out and bared its teeth at him. Teldo heaved the fistful of fire. It struck the thraik in the middle of its chest.

To everyone's astonishment including the thraik's, the fire adhered to the greasy flesh and began to burn. The thraik yowled in surprise. It tried to scrape the fire away, but only managed to spread it to its claws and forearms. The flame spread up the arms to the shoulders. It screamed in agony, tossing its head. The lord thraik howled an answering cry.

Teldo, his face drawn and looking decades older than his eighteen years, held his palm upturned. Tildi knew he was trying to will another ball of flame into existence. The burning thraik did not wait for him to add to its pain. It opened its great wings and flew away. Teldo looked grimly triumphant.

But the threat had not departed—in fact, it had doubled. The lord thraik shrieked out an order. Two of the black-green beasts flapped away from the smallfolks they had been attacking, and homed in upon

Teldo. His mouth moved. Tildi could not hear the chant, but she knew the words. Teldo had taught her what he knew and encouraged her to practice. Another green flame bloomed in his hand. He held it out, keeping it between him and the circling thraik. They kept their distance, darting their long necks at him. Teeth snapped close to his wrist. Teldo faked a throw at the nearer beast. It hissed and retreated a yard. He could only attack one of them, and they knew it. He threw away his reaper and held out his hand, palm up. He meant to make a second flame.

He needed help. Tildi held out her hand and desperately said the ancient words to herself.

Ano chnetegh tal, she thought firmly, willing the spell to work. *I create fire!*

Her hand remained cool. Not even a flicker of light bloomed in her palm. Had she gotten it wrong? Come now, she knew how to do this! She thought the spell again, begging for a boulder-sized blaze, one that would consume every thraik at once. From the bottom of her soul, she invoked every whit of power inside her. She pictured the thraik withering away. Nothing happened.

Light crackled into being in Teldo's other hand. He glanced down at it. The moment's distraction was all that the terrible beasts needed. Two of them swooped down on him at once. He threw the mass of fire at one of them. It shrieked, bleeding gouts of green flame, but the other was waiting behind. It took him by the back of the neck, and lifted him up, struggling, as if he was a kitten carried by a grotesque cat.

"Help him!" Tildi cried. She invoked the spell again. A minute fire bloomed on her palm. She threw the pathetic dot of flame at the retreating beast, then followed it with all the rocks and stones she could find. The beast rose into the air. Teldo seemed to reach out to her. Tildi stretched out her arms as if she could drag him back.

A handful of farmworkers had one of the smaller thraiks at bay. It hissed and screamed, bending its snakelike neck. Marco, possessed of dead aim, kept hitting it in the eyes with sharp stones as the others battered at it with flails and rakes. It was seeping black blood from a hundred wounds, and becoming more unsteady by the moment. The lord thraik let out a bellow, and all the remaing thraiks descended upon the smallfolk en masse. Tildi and the others ran to help. The beasts plucked two of the smallfolk out of the group and flapped upward into the sky with them. One of them was Marco.

"No!" Tildi screamed.

The leader, high above their heads, tilted his ugly head back and let out a scream that rose up and down the scales. A tearing sound made Tildi's ears ring. A black gash opened in the sky. The thraik flew through it, bearing their prey. It sealed, leaving the world soundless.

Tildi stood staring at the empty sky.

Mirrin came over and put his hand on her shoulder. Tildi hardly felt it. All her consciousness was focused upon that spot in the blue expanse. It had closed up like a door, and her brothers were on the other side! With all her heart she willed herself to follow the winged demons so that she could drag them back. Her brothers! Her brothers were gone! She couldn't believe it. Her hands were in tight fists against her chest. Her eyes flooded with unshed tears. She couldn't draw breath. Mirrin wrapped an arm around her and pulled her to him, burying her face in his torn tunic, patting her back as if she had been one of his own daughters.

"There, there, little one."

At his kind words, the pressure loosened. Tildi fetched in a deep gasp and began to cry. Mirrin patted her shoulder absently as she wept. The farmhands came by to touch her arm, offering sympathy. The kindly words bounced off Tildi's hearing. Over and over again she saw the thraik carrying her brothers away through that scar in the sky.

One by one, the farmhands helped one another stagger off the field and down the hill toward the farmhouse. They carried the bodies of the dead into the shed at the rear of the house. One of the unwounded ran for the road, to tell the families the bad news and to come fetch their loved ones. Tildi had no bodies to bury. They would be eaten by the thraiks, torn apart in the invisible nothingness behind the sky just like her parents had been.

Mirrin let Tildi weep herself into empty gasps, then guided her gently into the hands of the women, who surrounded her. They took her hands and turned her away from the torn field. Tildi let herself be gently towed down the slope and into the house. Lisel, with a gravity greater than her years, took charge of her and helped her to sit down on her little stool at the foot of the table.

"I'm so sorry, Tildi." There were tears in the girl's voice. Somewhere in the back of her numb mind Tildi recalled that Lisel and Pierin had been courting for a month or two. She lifted her eyes to Lisel's and tried to find the right words, saying that she understood that the girl shared her misery. Her lips trembled so much she pressed them together. Lisel ducked her head and went to serve the men.

"There, Tildi," Mig said, briskly setting a bowl down on the table. She put a spoon in Tildi's limp hand. "Eat. It'll help."

The heavy smell of the stew turned her stomach. Tildi shoved it away from her. She couldn't look at the people gathered around her. She knew they were staring at her, wondering if there must be some kind of curse on the Summerbee family, to have all but one of them carried off by the demons. Tildi knew there couldn't be any reason but chance. Her brothers must have attracted the thraik's attention because they fought harder and more bravely than anyone else. The scene played itself out in her mind over and over, always ending with the thraik lifting into the sky as lightly as snowflakes falling up instead of down, belying the horror they had just wrought. Nothing, *nothing* that Tildi recalled her brothers doing could have provoked the thraik unusually. Oh, why couldn't she have saved them? Not even one of them?

Mirrin cleared his throat as the hands finished their silent meal. "There'll . . . there will surely be an emergency village meeting this evening in Clearbeck, Tildi. You'll be there."

Tildi nodded without looking up.

Chapter Two

he meeting hall that served Morningside Quarter was a high-peaked wooden structure with a huge brick chimney at either end and a tall, ornately carved and painted double door in the center of the south-facing long wall. It stood at the top of the common green in Clearbeck, the village closest to Daybreak Bank, situated nearly at the precise geographical center of the Quarter. Smallfolks liked things to be precise and neat. A grand hall like that stood in every one of the Quarters. Tildi had only seen one other, when her family had gone to a wedding in Nightside Quarter, the province that overlapped the north arrow of the compass, as Morningside lay on the east. The Quarters were not exactly a fourth of a circle each, since there were five of them, but the smallfolks stuck by the historic name in spite of the mathematical disparity. The master archivist in the Noon Quarter claimed that "quarter" was meant

in its definition of "somewhere to live," and people settled for that explanation. Nor was the outline of the province exactly round, but it was as close as nature provided.

Smallfolks set great store by nature, even if they did like things neat.

Tildi usually looked forward to monthly meetings, often promising the next one to herself as a reward for the endless tedium of daily work. This was usually the time when everyone shared all the news: marriages were announced, traveling troubadours from every land in Alada performed and told stories, and projects to benefit the Quarters were discussed and organized. Meetings were lively affairs, with food and drink served throughout, and often music and dancing afterward.

Tonight, though, everyone was solemn.

Tables laden with food stood against the walls, but no one helped themselves. Two of the families present were clad in full mourning, and their eyes were still red from weeping.

Tildi sat stiffly alone on the cloth-draped bench reserved for her family. She was the only one left of the Summerbees. Her friends shot her sympathetic glances, but none of them dared leave their husbands' or fathers' sides to be with her.

Smallfolk tradition prevented the girls from going off without permission, even such a small distance. It was only common sense, Tildi had been lectured all the time while growing up. Girls weren't as strong or as fast as boys. Plenty of dangerous creatures lurked about the Quarters waiting for such a tender young morsel to happen by unprotected—and not all of them were wild animals. That was the rationale her mother had given her for why the custom continued even in cultivated places where there was no reasonable threat. The explanation did not satisfy her, but such matters could only be discussed in private among her companions where the boys couldn't hear them. Disobedient girls would be made to stand up at meetings with a slate around their necks that read SHAME.

Her brothers knew Tildi's thoughts. Gosto felt questioning the ancient ways was insubordinate, but the others were more moderate in their views. Teldo, at least, agreed with her. Unlike most of their peers, none of them would ever have humiliated her by turning her in as long as she behaved herself like decent smallfolks in front of the elders.

Mirrin, though he worked for the Summerbees, was an elder of the community. Admirably and generously, he kept his two jobs separated, and only exercised his authority when he was in meeting. He'd heard her spout off, as he put it, and let it pass. When she was a child he had scolded her for such views, but not since. She appreciated his forbearance, which she knew was due to the fact that the Summerbee children were orphans. He would never tolerate that kind of behavior in his own well-schooled daughters. Both Mig and Lisel kept their eyes aimed modestly toward the floor whenever Tildi glanced their way. All she could see was the top of their white-capped heads. Behind the Sardbrook bench, her friends Joybara and Nolla Coppers smiled but didn't move. A quick tilt of the head in the direction of their very conservative father showed Tildi why. His choleric face was the same shade of red as his hair.

Not that Tildi spent the time entirely by herself. Many of the young men stopped by briefly to chat with her. The first was Dyas Holt, the youngest child of the local butcher. He was a bit slow-moving, but kind and considerate. Tildi often danced with him at meetings, the other girls complained he stepped on their feet, but she was quick enough to get out of his way. Tildi was good friends with his six sisters and Aine, the girl married to his elder brother.

"Evening, Tildi," Dyas said solemnly. He hovered over her, just a little too close. She pulled her feet up a bit and concentrated on keeping her nose out of the lavish embroidery on his pale blue shirtfront. She recognized it as his best tunic, which usually came out for Year's End parties and weddings. The finery reminded her once again, as if she needed it, that ornaments and decoration were forbidden to her now. She would be in mourning for a year. Her dark blue dress, the plainest thing she owned, had a white sash to compliment the sleeves and neck of her white chemise that peeked out at wrists and neck. Her neat, soft leather shoes were plain, too, tied with simple black ribbons.

"Evening, Dyas," she said with a cordial nod.

"My sympathies on your loss. My family's, too." Dyas stopped short and turned red. Tildi understood. It was hard to think of what to say after a tragedy. She owed a visit of condolence to Jinny's family.

"Thank you, Dyas."

Dyas struggled for something else to say. His big, kind face contorted. Any moment now he would sputter out something awkward and retire in confusion, as he always did. Tildi usually offered a subject of conversation that he could take up with ease, but she didn't feel up to making the effort.

"Are you troubling the poor lass, Dyas?" asked Gorten, sliding smoothly up beside him as if cutting in to a dance. The weaver, about Gosto's age, came from the western quarter of the Quarters. He specialized in linen fabrics, so every woman in the southern quarter knew him well. He was quick-witted and a trifle cruel.

"Not at all, Gorten," Tildi said quickly. "He came to offer his sympathies."

"Why, so do I, Tildi." Gorten picked up her hand in his long fingers and bestowed a light kiss upon it. He was tall for a smallfolk, about half the height of a human. "What a terrible thing. Why, it could have been anyone, but *all* your brothers! They were fine men. You did not deserve such ill luck. Is there anything I can do to help?"

"I . . . I hardly know yet, but thank you for asking."

"My father and I will be over to help finish the haying tomorrow," said Jole Bywell, coming up with his twin brother Nole. Their family owned the land that ran along the western border of the Summerbee fields. "Our sisters are cooking up pots of food so you don't have to trouble yourself at all for us."

Tears sprang into Tildi's eyes. She leaned forward to clasp their hands. "That is so kind of you both."

Nole looked abashed. "It's just the neighborly—"

"I will help with the cutting, too," Gorten said suddenly, interrupting him.

"And I," added Dyas, pushing forward.

"Aah!" Tildi gasped, as he trod on the foot she had just set down.

"Tildi!" She looked up to see the frustrated, swarthy face of Ronardo, the herbalist's son, peering at her between the solid shoulders of the Bywell boys. "May I speak to you after the meeting? Will you wait for me? I'll walk you home."

"Thank you . . ."

"Nonsense, she'll come with us," Jole said cheerfully. Ronardo let out an explosive breath as if Jole or Nole had elbowed him in the stomach. "Our way lies with hers almost all the way back."

"But—" Ronardo said. He was interrupted by the sound of the mayor clearing his throat.

The Bywell brothers winked at her in unison. "We'll see you later, lass." They dragged Ronardo off with them. The others retired to their family benches as the elders stared at them with impatience.

Tildi shook her head. She had been grateful for the expressions of sympathy, but she wasn't a fool. It occurred to her that the young men weren't so innocent of purpose as they appeared. Gorten, for one, had danced with her at meetings only when the pattern put them together temporarily. Otherwise he preferred the company of Shanee or Rowan, both plump, fair-haired, and blue-eyed, whereas Tildi looked like every Summerbee in the family tree, small and lightly built, with light brown hair and big, round, brown eyes. No, she understood their motive.

As the eldest male, the big farm had belonged to Gosto absolutely with his brothers as his tenants. Under normal circumstances, if something happened to him, the valuable Summerbee property would pass to the next brother in line. The elders could also decide to divide the property among one or more of the brothers. Now that they were all gone, the property was a single lump, and a desirable one, which would now go to whichever lucky man Tildi chose to marry. She nodded grimly to herself. Most of her visitors had been landless second sons whose prospects suddenly ascended from tenant or journeyman to landowner. Her authority over the land owned for hundreds of years was temporary until a male with the right to give orders could be put in charge of it. Mirrin would be its steward until then.

There had been some mixing and playful wooing in the past, but none considered serious since neither they nor she were considered of an age to marry, but now that she was the sole survivor of her family they wanted to declare their interest. Tildi felt alarm rising at the prospect. Must she choose a husband tonight? The possibility existed, since the land must be farmed. As an orphan she was under the direct authority of the mayor and the council of elders—their protection, they called it. She had no right to refuse if they demanded she marry. Names and faces spun through Tildi's mind. Who among her male peers could she stand to live with from that moment on for the rest of her life? And not just her own age group was keen for such a prize: she observed a few of the tradesmen who owned no land eying her with interest. Horrors! She wasn't ready to make a decision like that so swiftly. By no means was she ready to settle down. She had dreams—many of which had flown away with her brothers.

At that sober realization, she sat back with her hands in her lap. How her world had changed in just a few hours. Her mind whirled, trying to make sense out of the chaos. She needed time!

"Sit down, everyone. Let's not make matters wait. Sit down!" Mayor Jurney shook the gold chain of office that lay on his shoulders. During the majority of his hours not devoted to council activities, Edyard Jurney was a physician. He was a thin, stooped man, with prodigious black brows that overhung observant, dark eyes. As a doctor he was dry in manner, not unpleasant to deal with, but demanding. If one was his patient, one didn't dare not get well. He had brought back so many oldsters from the brink of death he was considered a miracle worker by some (others, particularly relatives cheated for a time out of expected inheritances, whispered darkly of sorcery). Therefore, when he was elected mayor, few disagreed. And, to be fair, as acrimonious as politics got, his rivals for the office had little to complain about. Few of his pronouncements proved to be ill thought-out.

Like the best of his profession he had little imagination, which meant he had no patience either with children's fancies or such affairs as magic. He had openly disapproved of Teldo and his studies, but as long as Gosto, as head of the family, permitted it, Jurney had nothing to say about it unless Teldo committed a crime.

"All right, order," Mayor Jurney said. "I hereby open this meeting." Everyone obediently bowed their heads. Tildi tucked down her head and studied her folded hands. "We ask for the bounty from those forces who give all blessings, Mother Nature and Father Time, whom between them encompass all existence."

"Give us your blessings," the assembly recited.

"So mote it be. Secretary Mazen, announce the date."

Everyone glanced at the smallfolk scribe who sat at the foot of the council with pen and ink on a stool at his side. Mazen taught the upper grades in the local village school, and was an artist by inclination.

He carefully drew the rune for the day, season, and year in ochre-colored ink on the top of the page in the huge annal open on his knees, and turned it toward the assembly.

"This is the ninth day of Haymonth, in the year of 15,268 since creation began," he said, his clear voice reaching to the rear of the hall.

Tildi nodded as she translated the complicated mark. Those lines in the center described the month and the season, half-spring, half-summer, and the tick marks were the day itself. The year formed a wreath around the rest. It was a pretty design. Each sign stood for a letter, a word, or an entire phrase. Workaday words were the simplest, for speed in setting them down on paper, probably a throwback to when they had had to be carved in stone or wood. More complex concepts required more complex pictographs. She remembered thinking before she could read that a page of text looked like a garden of flowers, each a complex blossom. Or . . .

With a feeling of shock, it occurred to her it looked like a simple version of the design she had seen in the eye of the thraik. *The golden mark had been a word! But how was that possible? Thraiks weren't intelligent, not as smallfolks counted intelligence. Surely they could not read. And what did it mean?* Tildi tried to bring back the memory. *What had it looked like?* She remembered what she could of the configuration of the design. Her mind's eye followed all the complicated whorls and crooks, as intricate as the tiny pattern on the tip of her fingers. The configuration was unfamiliar to her, so it wasn't a word or phrase she had ever come across before. Did that mean that the thraik had been looking for something specific, and thought she was part of it? She had been saved when others had been carried off or killed. Would it come for her again? She was called out of her worried reverie by the sound of her name.

". . . Tildi?" Mayor Jurney said, with a touch of impatience. He must have said it a few times.

"I am sorry, Mayor," she said, sitting up straighter. "My mind was elsewhere."

"Hmph." He pursed his full lips. "Well. That's understandable, girl. It's been a hard day for you. I wish you to know that until matters are settled for you, you can count on everyone in the quarter to assist you in any way you need. You have our deepest sympathies. That's official. And personal, from all of us, I might add." He gathered nods from the rest of the council.

"Thank you, Mayor," Tildi said. She had to press her lips together so she wouldn't begin to cry. One could depend on smallfolks, she thought gratefully. They were a conservative breed, rule-bound and suspicious of outsiders, but healthy and hearty and willing to throw themselves into work to help friends and neighbors.

"You're very welcome. Now, about the business of what occurred today, can anyone give a good report to those of us who did not witness it?"

Mirrin rose to his feet among the elders sitting on the padded benches along the back of the dais. "I can." He paused.

Tildi felt hands on her shoulders. She glanced up. The miller's wife, Derina, looked down kindly on her. "There's no need for you to sit and listen," she whispered. "We'll just go out for a moment until they've finished."

"I can endure it," Tildi said stoutly. "I was there, Derina."

Derina shook her head and put a firm hand under Tildi's elbow. She escorted the girl out of the hall and nodded to Mirrin from the threshold. The door boomed solidly closed behind them.

Tildi sat on the edge of the hard bench with her arms folded, stolidly ignoring Derina's attempts to draw her into conversation. Out of the corner of her eye she could just see the pale circle of the woman's face under her white cap. The moon, just a day past full, hung in the eastern sky. She stared at the white disk until a black afterimage swam in her eyes. How did they think that not making her listen to an account of what had happened would be worse than living through it? She was the one who had to go back to an empty house! She clenched her jaw until it hurt.

At last the door behind them opened. Tildi rose with dignity and stalked back into the hall, avoiding Derina's motherly hand.

"I've heard that those thraiks are attacking more than ever," Arnot Driever was saying from his seat at the left side of the dais. "Like they've gone wild."

The mayor nodded. "I'd heard that myself. The bards have said the same has been happening in the lands of humans, elfkind, and others. I thought we could be spared. Secretary, when did the thraik last attack here in the Morningside quarter?"

Mazen wound the book back on its spindle. "Two years and three months, Mayor."

"Uh-huh. We'll have to take precautions, in case they come back again. We will be more prepared. Build burrows where we can run to earth if needed, set up a warning system so we can come to one another's aid. . . ."

"What good does all that do?" Thom Holt demanded, rising to his feet. "There's nothing much we can do to protect ourselves from them! Look what happened! Three killed! Dozens wounded. Four strong lads in the prime of life carried off to be eaten—"

At the sudden gasp of outrage from the assemblage, Holt shot an ashamed look in Tildi's direction. "My apologies, lass, but I have to state the facts. I've heard the same as Arnot Driever, that the demons are raiding more places. They hardly ever killed people before, mostly animals, until now."

Driever, the wine merchant, nodded firm agreement.

"They got Gosto's parents," Sotheny spoke up.

"That was years back," Mirrin said. "Spare the child the repetition of that story."

"Probably aiming for the horse," Holt said firmly. "They're no more intelligent than a wolf."

"That's intelligent enough," Sotheny argued. "I've set up trap after trap to get the pack that's been threatening my herds for years, and I've never caught one single wolf."

"He ought to check the sheep in Wilnam's field," a voice muttered behind Tildi. "Not all wolves have ears and tails." Tildi found a smile trying to force its way to her lips. Everyone seemed to know about Wilnam except Sotheny. It was part of an ancient grudge match that went back decades. He always declared that he'd give them back if he was asked. Of course, he never was.

"Still, it looks unlucky," Sotheny said. "All four boys—the family's about wiped out!"

"It's not wiped out," Tildi protested. "I'm still here."

"But no male heirs," Mayor Jurney reminded her gently.

"I know, but I am a Summerbee! My ancestry is just the same as theirs."

Mayor Jurney frowned at her. Tildi quailed at the thought of displeasing the elders, but she stood her ground. Gosto and the others would want her to. Yet, she was at a disadvantage disagreeing with the council. Three disadvantages, if one counted being under the age of majority *and* female, but they ought to let her have her say. To her chagrin, Jurney went on as if she had not spoken.

"We'll send notice to the other quarters asking for other descendents of the Summerbee line. Unless another male relative comes to the fore, we will have to consider the family extinguished, leaving relicts and property."

Tildi opened her mouth in outrage at the word *relicts*, but a quelling glance from Mayor Jurney made her shut it.

"That brings up an important point," Migel Sundstrand said. "The property must not suffer. We've already discussed helping to get the hay cut, but there are other crops ripening, and orchard fruit to be picked soon. Not to mention some fine cows that need to be milked daily."

"Yes, indeed," Jurney said, nodding. "A man ought to step in to run the farm as soon as possible. That means marrying the heiress, of course, not taking it over outright. That's not legal," he added, with a glare at the man to his left. "Any recommendations on who would be a worthy steward, who would take good care of that land?"

Tildi rose to her feet. "Mayor Jurney, I protest! My brothers haven't been dead six hours! I can't make any decisions so soon!"

Jurney looked at her with deep sympathy. "I know, my child. We are very sorry for your loss. We know that you are too young to make a decision like this now."

"Well, that's a relief," Tildi said, sitting down heavily.

"Therefore, as your elders, we are making it for you."

"What?" Tildi yelped, springing up again. "Mayor, you can't mean that. Choose a husband *for* me?"

"Sit down, girl," Derina hissed, putting her hands on Tildi's shoulders.

"Please, I have to speak," Tildi said, twisting away. "This is not like deciding what to do with a bolt of cloth or a horse! Can't you give me time?"

"Now, I think Lucan is the best choice," said the smith. "He's strong, never complains, and he keeps track of what needs to be done. Methodical."

"You would recommend your own boy," Migel Sundstrand snorted.

"I can't just marry someone just like that!" Tildi shouted, trying to be heard over the discussions breaking out all over the room. Jurney gave her a sad, paternal smile.

"Better this is settled right away, to give you some stability. It'll be good for you to have someone in the house. You wouldn't want to be alone like that, Tildi. It'll be for the best, I promise you."

"But, Mayor, may I not speak for myself?" she protested.

"Well, not to promote my own interests, but I have considerable experience—" Migel Sundstrand began.

"Oh, come on, the girl deserves a young husband."

The smallfolk man drew himself up. "I am not yet in my dotage, you whelp. There are considerable benefits to wedding a man of experience."

"Experience losing a fortune," the baker said, with a bored wave of his hand. "This is a wealthy property of respectable age, and we would hate to see it dispersed out of carelessness."

"Carelessness!" Sundstrand exploded.

"This is wrong," Tildi said, marching down to stand directly in front of the council.

"I know," Wilnam said, snapping his fingers. "Bardol. He's the younger son of Georg Bellfield, the stonemason. He's strong as can be. He moved to the Eveningside quarter to find work. He can be back here in three days easily."

"Bardol!" Tildi said, her voice rising. "He's a troll. I won't marry him."

"The ideal solution," Sandro Cartner said. "A strong man."

"That'd be a good idea," the others agreed. "That's what we need here. And it'll be good to pry him out of that mountain hole he's living in. It's barely a hut, do you know? He hates it. It's so far away from civilization that it takes him half a day to get to meeting. Every time I see him he's angrier."

"Well, his brother ought to have treated him better, but there's only so much business in that town, you see? I'm not saying I agree with the decision, but it was either a decent living for one or a poor living for two."

"I think it's a disgrace," Elina Driever, the merchant's wife, put in. "The boy ought to have gone for a journeyman elsewhere, if there's no work where he lives, not hide himself away."

"Smallfolks belong in the Quarters, woman," the miller said sharply. "I admit the lad could have shown some more initiative than he has. What do you say, Mayor?"

"I agree with the proposal."

"I protest!" Tildi said. "I don't want to marry Bardol!"

The mayor paid her no attention. "The motion is seconded. All in favor of Bardol? Ah. Well, that's decided. Any more business? Well, then, who wants to start the singing? Tildi, you've got a good voice," the headman said kindly. "How about you? Give us a ballad, girl."

Outraged, Tildi remained silent.

"All right, who else will sing for us?"

The headman paid little attention, but went on to the first raised hand. "Monci, good! Did you bring your lute?"

Before any of her would-be suitors could ask her to dance—not that they would, now that the prize had been withdrawn—Tildi excused herself from the room. Derina glanced up at her as she made for the door. Tildi nodded and pointed subtly. Derina nodded understanding. Tildi went out into the night and headed toward home. What of it if the miller's wife was deluded into thinking she was going to the necessary? She was in no mood to dance or socialize. No one certainly expected Jinny's family to be rejoicing this evening. Feeling as if she had been run over by a wagon then flayed with a spoon, Tildi followed the scant moonlight to the path leading home.

For a moment, setting out in the open, she glanced nervously at the swirled silver dots on the black sky. What if the thraik came back? In her misery she would have welcomed the sudden relief. Let them come, and carry her off, too!

Bardol!

Tildi wrapped her light cloak around her and held it tightly furled. How could she go from being among the most comfortable and well-situated smallfolk in the whole of the Quarters that very morning, with her books, brothers, and studies, to an unwilling bride with no family to look after? She trudged across the common by the faint light, hoping no one would come out of the hall and see her leave. Even deprived of the chance for a fortune, some of the young men would insist on escorting her out of gallantry. She did not want company at the moment.

Bardol!

Among the young men in the Quarters she could have thought of half a dozen who would be good stewards of her family's holdings. A couple she might not have minded getting to know to see if one day one would suit her as good husband material. But this! It harkened back to the bad days of the early recorded smallfolk history, when lads and lasses were paired for desirable traits, like so many horses or sheep!

Bardol. The very thought of marrying him made her shudder. He was strong and hardworking, yes, and not even bad-looking, in an over-muscled, brutish way, but from what she recalled of him, all good things were always his idea. He did not brook competition in any thing. And all ill that befell was never his fault. Mirrin, for one, wouldn't stand for an employer like that. He and his daughters would find another family to work for, and Tildi would be left alone in her big, old echoing house with a lout.

It wouldn't even be her house any longer. She stamped down the path, as if grinding this injustice into the gravel.

To live and die by the harvest and the turning of the seasons—too dull, but it was a burden she bore gladly for the sake of her beloved brothers. All that they had had would now pass to a non-Summerbee, some stranger who would put his mark of ownership on the land and on her. She would have to bear her unwanted husband countless brats, and have no one who respected her grief. She'd have no one to play music for her, to laugh at her little ways, or to teach her magic. The hole the thraik had torn in her heart had widened so much that she gasped suddenly from the pain. Where were they now? Had they died swiftly? Were any still alive? Oh, merciful Nature and Time, let it have been quick! She dashed away tears that rolled down her cheeks.

The furious energy that had driven her feet homeward was draining away, leaving her feeling despairing and longing for familiar things. *Let me be near home,* she pleaded.

Chapter Three

t last, there was the tiny golden light of the lantern she had left burning hanging from the porch post. She took the bronze cage, each screen wrought into the form of lilies and irises, down from its hook, and let it light her way into the big dark house.

She had never been anywhere so silent before. A dog barking in the distance was louder than her footfalls. Tildi crept to her own room and lighted every lamp and candle. The flickering flames made the room feel not quite so lonely. Though the night was warm, she wrapped herself in the quilt made for her by her mother and huddled in her deep armchair. There ought to have been voices, laughter, and Marco playing something he had composed on one of his collection of flutes or guitars.

She missed her brothers so much.

She missed her parents.

Tildi let herself cry, alone.

The women and men would be at the meeting for some time to come. After a shock like they had all had that day, there would be a great need for the relief to be found in song, drink, and the company of one another. Tildi had no one. Her practical streak took over and informed her she had better get used to it. That fact would not change. She had to take care of things as they came. Perhaps life ahead would not be as bad as she feared. In any case, the only way to go was forward.

She changed into her nightdress, braided her hair under her nightcap, and settled in beneath the light summer coverlet. A few pages might help her to sleep, but her mind refused to translate the ornate runes into letters, syllables, words, concepts, or phrases. One after another she rejected all the books that lay within reach of her bed. She was too angry to settle down.

Tildi imagined the quilt she was helping the neighbors make for the upcoming wedding of their dairyman's daughter. The girl loved red roses, and had embroidered them on every part of her trousseau. The quilt's pattern was of stylized roses the size of Tildi's head, in five shades of red thread on a green background. Red as blood, blood on green grass. She sat up and clutched her eyes to clear the image from them.

Sleep would not come, not when she was haunting herself. Impatiently, she kicked her way out of bed. Tildi rejected the notion of a cup of cocoa or a glass of warm milk with honey. The sweetness would gag her. Wine or whiskey wouldn't help, either. She must not think of the coming wedding, or she would get no sleep at all. Some kind of task would take her mind away. Something mind-numbingly tedious.

She took on the task of gathering up and clearing out her brothers' things to make way for Bardol's, and any relatives or hangers-on he brought to Daybreak Bank with him.

Tildi started in Gosto's room. This had been their parents' chamber, suitable for the head of the family. All the Summerbees' treasures were there: the silver candlesticks that had been a wedding present to her grandparents; embroidered quilts made by several generations of talented needlewomen; shiny, thin, but durable dishes from some far-off land that Papa had bought from a peddler to please Mama when Gosto was born. All those things were to have been kept for the day when Gosto took a bride, but it had been too soon. At twenty-six he was considered too young to settle down, though he had proved himself a worthy successor to his father, taking up the task of managing the farm ten years before. Why, he had been a mere boy, a year younger than Tildi was now.

Of his personal effects there was little. Gosto collected no extraneous belongings. There was little but his best clothing, kept freshened for meetings and special occasions, and his second-best clothing that he wore to spend evenings in the tavern with the other boys and their mates. He was muscular in build, the biggest of her brothers. Stocky Bardol might want these garments, as much as it griped Tildi even to think about it. She folded the clothes and laid them back in the chest at the end of the bed.

Pierin's room was another matter. He was so slim that no other grown man could fit his clothes. It would be best if Tildi offered them to one of the neighbors whose son had hit the weed-stalk stage, growing too long for his trousers by the week. He had several sets of best and second-best clothing. Pierin loved fine fabrics as much as any woman, and liked embroidery and other finery. He had been a charmer. Pierin could do anything with animals. There wasn't a pony he couldn't break in an hour with a gentle conversation, nor a bull he couldn't take to cow. He'd never been butted by a goat, unlike the rest of them, who bore their bruises. He had a similar talent for bewitching smallfolks as well. Tildi smiled, clutching one of her second brother's fancy waistcoats to her breast. Half the room was filled with gifts from pretty girls, "Just because." Though he was a second son, he would have had no trouble at all when the time came to finding a wife—or six or seven. Thank Time and Nature that the smallfolks' custom confined a marriage to two people!

Marco had no garments that could be offered to other families, since he rarely got anything new. Any clothes that reached him were four-times hand-me-downs that had survived Teldo's carelessness. Luckily their mother had raised them to buy the best and sturdiest cloth. Marco did not mind dressing in worn shirts and trousers. He cared little for finery, but he could not resist music manuscripts or strange instruments. Marco had been a gifted musician. He could play anything he picked up. Tildi touched the collection of pipes, drums, fiddles, and horns. She plucked the lowest string on the short harp in the corner of the room, letting it fill the chamber with its melancholy twang, as if it could evoke her baby brother's presence. She hated to let the collection go, but it would be a tribute to him to donate it to the schoolmistress who taught the younger children, and hope they would be used well in Marco's memory.

It took a special effort for Tildi to push herself over the threshold of Teldo's room. Her mother had joked that the two of them were twins born a year apart. "The longest lying-in in history!" she would say with a laugh.

Tildi and Teldo were alike in nature, too. Each had a bookish bent and boundless curiosity for the nature world. They demanded to be read to, long after their younger brother had moved on to playing tunes on his first pennywhistle, and had an insatiable appetite for new books to read. Mama hadn't minded. She borrowed whatever texts the neighbors had, and had first right of refusal for children's books with all the regular peddlers who made their way semiannually through the Quarters.

Some said that Mama had married beneath her, Gelina Bellwood wedding Bernardo Summerbee, a farmer. She had been a scholar's daughter from Cedarbrake village in the Evenside quarter. She had never seen it as a lack, however, and had thrown herself into her husband's work with the greatest of goodwill. She seemed glad that her third and fourth children inherited her intellectual gifts, and gradually ceded ownership of all her books to them as she became too busy to read them.

Among them had been a treatise on magic. It was so old it was a yards-long piece of parchment wound onto a pair of spindles, not pages between covers as her schoolbooks had been. Page-books were a new invention, only a hundred or so years old, according to the aged aunts and uncles of the village. One very elderly aunt claimed she recalled when they first came to the Quarters, a human invention, of course, but not a bad idea, made looking for a recipe much easier.

Teldo had devoured the book of magic, demanding to know more, badgering the troubadours to tell him tales of great wizards and great workings. He found their stories too light on details for his taste. Mama always sought for more histories and accounts. Once in a while she was lucky, presenting her purchases to him like a queen bestowing an honor. Papa didn't hold much with magic, but as long as Teldo did his small chores, only those that were expected of an eight-year-old boy, he didn't mind how Teldo spent his spare time.

Once their parents were gone Teldo had thrown himself into his studies. He and Pierin soon began to make regular selling trips with their goat's fleece-combings and their prime tree fruits down to the human-run port city of Tillerton. After one very successful venture he began a correspondence with a human who ran a bookshop there with a bent toward esoterica, who held manuscripts on approval for him, to be paid for out of his share of the sales. Teldo began to do his farmwork as quickly as he could so he could get back to his magical studies. He often indulged his curious little sister in secret, because she showed an aptitude for spell-crafting, and he did pick up on more refinements when he taught her what he knew. He ran far ahead of her—but only to start with. Over time she had practiced her little bits of magic. She could make a small fire. She did it now, as a sort of tribute to her lost brother. She wouldn't let his teachings die. How she wished she held the power of the great wizards whose stories in which they had reveled! If she could have sent bursts of flame from her hands and burned the terrible thraik from the sky, she would have done it in a heartbeat, and never mind the cost—for cost there always was. Teldo had cautioned her that magicking exhausted the body, and some workings ate away at it. But she could do little things. Teldo was proud of her, as she was of him.

Only one time did she dare to show her friends what she could do. They shrieked at her not to do that, that she'd get in trouble. *Magic is not for the likes of us!* After that she'd been careful to keep her secret, and talk only about the subjects that interested her friends: new clothes, new embroidery or knitting patterns, stories told by the traveling bards, and who was going to marry whom. She never again trusted them with the knowledge she gained. She could only share her triumphs with Teldo.

More copious even than Pierin's "trophies" were Teldo's papers. He made notes on every facet of magic that he studied. They were full of erasures and scratched-out lines where he had learned something more from another source that contradicted what he had learned in the first place. He had letters from apprentices in human cities, their correspondence paper the size of placemats. In them they discussed the smallest techniques to death. Teldo would read these avidly over and over, then reply. He could write and craft beautifully, and used his skills to attempt to render the spells that he read about. He had been studying runes from old manuscripts Mama had bought from a traveling peddler from the bigfolk lands many years ago. One in particular was his prize possession and the basis of his collection.

That beautiful parchment was very old, but the material was still supple and pure white, obviously prepared by the best papermaker. The signs on it had been rendered in the most gloriously ornate style, furnished with curlicues and other fancies of calligraphy, in every color including bright gold and silver. There weren't very many symbols on it, just nine, but they seemed very full of meaning. Struck by its beauty

Mother had bought it from a peddler for her precocious children. The peddler had sold it cheap, because it hurt to hold it. Nobody to whom he had displayed it, not even collectors, wanted to touch it for more than a moment. Intrigued, Mama bought it, but she couldn't decipher it, nor could anyone else in the village to whom she showed it. It piqued the curiosity of the two children. Mother brought it inside wrapped in the edge of her apron to keep it from getting dirty, and put it on the table in the midst of their schoolwork. It hurt to handle at first, but the longer Tildi and Teldo tried, the less it pained them. The symbols sort of looked like the words for *tree, stone,* and a few others that they knew, but not precisely. Teldo kept it as a curiosity, a special treasure, and never gave up trying to figure out what it meant.

She remembered well when Teldo discovered what they were, if not their specific meaning. A few years ago he had become wildly excited, saying that its signs were like some in the magic books he had been studying.

"These runes are what the world is made of, Tildi," Teldo had instructed her, his voice solemn. She had asked him to tell her more but he couldn't explain more than that. Mother had studied the parchment as well. All the family had seen it, touched it, wondered over it, but only Tildi and Teldo continued to peruse it after the others' initial curiosity wore off.

On the small desk underneath the window Tildi found Teldo's pride and joy, the letter from a human wizard named Olen in the vast city of Overhill. Smallfolk had little use for magic in their prosaic existence. Teldo had applied for an apprenticeship with Olen, and had been accepted. Soon, he would have been going away. He had often told her he wished he could take her with him, but as she was merely a girl, there was little chance of that. He always said she couldn't possibly understand enough about the great workings or the universal truths to be a true wizard. She scoffed at him, telling him he got it all out of a book, and if he could have picked it up there, so could she.

"But you don't really understand them," he had argued.

"All right, then," she had countered, "why are the stars smaller than the sun?"

He had no answer that satisfied either one of them. But here was the parchment that was sent to him by the great wizard. She ought to write to Olen and tell him of the tragedy. Teldo would never now be able to take up the apprenticeship, Tildi thought sadly.

But she could.

The thought crept in unbidden and surprised her so much she stood gazing for ten minutes at the letter in her hand.

No, she thought, putting it down. She had no hope of getting permission from the elders even to ask the wizard if she might take Teldo's place. Even if they had any respect for magic, they would insist that she would be useless, even dangerous as a mage. Why, she might have hysterics and let a demon loose upon the world! Instead, she must remain there and see that Bardol didn't destroy her family's ancestral holdings.

But why? the annoying little voice in her mind demanded. *The moment you say "I will," the holdings won't be yours any longer. You'll be a chattel, thrown in with the estate as a makeweight. Bardol likes you as little as you like him. He could even beat you, and no one would cry against him for it.*

That truth was so painful that Tildi sank onto Teldo's writing stool to think about it. She had nothing of her own left here at all, nothing but a few clothes and books and a few mementos of her parents.

So why shouldn't she go? She was as passionate about magic as Teldo. Perhaps not as advanced in her studies, but that could come in time. Probably the wizard had no real idea as to Teldo's abilities. If . . . if he thought she was Teldo, he would take her on and let her learn. All she had to do was get to Overhill and present the letter. It was a radical idea to travel such a long distance, since she had never set foot outside the Quarters in her life, but she was good at finding her way. Once she had passed over the hills into the human realms, someone ought to be able to direct her to Overhill. Teldo had talked about the road over the Eastern Hills that divided the land of the smallfolks from the human realm beyond. She could remember almost everything that he and the other men said about the journey. How hard could it be, beyond a few days' walking?

For the first time since the tragedy she started to feel hope. She began to look around her with renewed interest. She must pack what she meant to take with her. What should she do first?

Oh, but how could she leave the Quarters? Human ways were not smallfolk ways. What if she couldn't find decent food, or if the living space offered her by the wizard—even if he did accept her as her brother—left no room for privacy? What if their practices were indecent or dishonorable? What hints she had had of the culture from reading Teldo's correspondence told of lives very different from the ones smallfolks led in the Quarters. She would have no recourse but to return to Clearbeck—and Bardol.

The little voice inside her head grew excited at the prospect. What if the culture is different? What if you cannot abide by the wizard's rules? Find another place! You'll learn more as you go along. There's more to know outside the boundaries—a world is out there! She could see it for herself. Teldo would want her to.

The thought of her brothers brought back the morning all over again. Tildi began to cry, harder than before. She was mourning not only their death, but the death of the pleasant life they had had here. Not one thing was left the way it had been at the moment she had awakened that day.

And now she would change, too. Instead of being someone's sister, she would be herself, by herself.

The wizard Olen expected a male apprentice. He would never accept a mere female, so he must believe that she was Teldo. She must make herself look like her brother as best she could. The family had always remarked upon how much the two of them looked alike, leaving aside the obvious differences of gender and height—but the big folk rarely took them seriously. Gosto was always annoyed with his trading partners' assertion that little folk were small enough to put in their pockets, so Olen would not be likely to notice small details that would give her away to other smallfolk. The inch or so between her height and Teldo's wouldn't be noticed. As for the rest, that was easily disguised. Surely the wizard didn't expect to see her without her clothes! She wore cosmetics only for feast days. The only thing that would give her away was her long hair.

The more she thought about it, the more that seemed like the only solution. This wizard, perhaps, represented a new beginning for her. She must grasp the opportunity and make the necessary change.

In the dead of night she blocked all the windows in the big, empty house with the storm shutters. Anyone stopping by would assume that she wanted her privacy on her first night alone. They would be sad, but they would understand. She gathered up the fine shears from the sewing box, two looking glasses, a multibranched candlestick, and all the determination she had in her soul. Glancing up and back along the main hallway that intersected with the short passage that led from the front door, she wondered where she could have the most privacy.

The stillroom was the obvious choice. It had solid stone walls with no windows through which a determined well-wisher could peer in. Tildi carried her burdens down the winding flight of flagstone steps that led from the cupboard behind the central chimney, and locked herself in.

Undoing the ties of her white cap, she set it aside with reverence. It symbolized the tradition of hundreds of years of her people, tradition upon which she was turning her back, but only because it had turned its back on her first. The face that looked out at her from the looking glass seemed trepidatious. Was she betraying all she knew? Shouldn't she do as hundreds of her foremothers had, and give in to the commands of the male elders?

No.

She knew from the bottom of her heart that what they required was wrong.

The long plait of hair fell down her back. Tildi felt for the spot where it met the nape of her neck, and brought the scissors around to it, with her eyes squeezed shut so she wouldn't have to see the first devastating cut. Her hair had not been clipped since Jole Bywell had slopped leather glue in it when she was six. Cutting through was like sawing off her arm.

The severed braid fell over her wrist like a garter snake dropping out of a tree. When she opened her eyes, the sight astonished her. She looked so much like Teldo, albeit Teldo in need of a good haircut, that tears began to run down her cheeks again. Tildi brushed them away with her wrist. He was gone forever. The only memory of him was here in her face. She'd do honor to that memory as best she could.

With the two glasses arranged so she could see behind, she trimmed what remained of her hair in the same style she used to trim Teldo's. She managed to achieve detachment from the task at hand, peering critically at her work instead of thinking that it was happening to her. She parted her hair on the side and combed the length over the side of her head. A snip here and there to cut carefully around her delicate ears, making sure it was even on both sides, and she was finished.

There, she thought, turning her head to catch every angle in the two glasses, it looked just like her brothers' hair did. After all, she cut theirs every month. When she was finished, she noticed the ends of her hair, freed of the weight they'd carried all these years, beginning to curl up on their own. The curls changed her face subtly, making it not entirely hers. Her reflection was that of a stranger, some cousin of the Summerbees. She was certain now that no one in the Quarter would know her at a distance. If she was observed by a neighbor they would assume that "he" had heard the news and had come to help his orphaned cousin. Alas, the Summerbees had no kin that lived close by. Even the ancient great-uncle of her mother's had been gathered up by his many descendants and taken back into the distant downs in the warm Quarter to the southwest.

She wondered if she ought to draw in light hairs on her face, and decided against it. A boy her size would just be beginning to see changes in himself, and she could always argue, if pressed, that "he" wasn't old enough to grow a mustache yet, with a proper expression of chagrin. No, she must not speak to anyone. In spite of the startling change, the people hereabouts would know her voice. She had to get away before the first light, or trade her loneliness for a prison she couldn't break. They could keep the land, and all that went with it, if they insisted, but she would not be part of the package, please and thank you.

Until she departed, she kept her white cap tied on so that no unexpected visitor would see her barbered hair and ask awkward questions. She set about gathering up travel provisions, plus a few comforts. One of the boys' rucksacks ought to hold what she needed. She hauled it down into the stillroom, keeping an ear out for visitors.

Her boots were unsuitable for mountain travel, that she knew, but Teldo's were barely two sizes bigger than hers. If she wore two pairs of stout socks they would fit just snugly. And clothes? For a moment she was shamed at having to travel as a boy. Still, she couldn't put herself into danger if others saw an unescorted girl. She retained her own undergarments, chemises, and drawers, but took what clothes of Teldo's that were closest to her size.

She started to put the cap into the pack, took it out, put it back, took it out, and at last stuffed it down into the corner of the pack with her braid folded up inside it. Anyone who found that would figure out in an instant how she had disguised herself, and there would be a hunt after her in hours.

Soap, a comb—ought she bring a razor for show? No, she told herself. Don't waste the space on it when there were so many useful but heavy things that must be left behind. A stout knife, though, would come in handy. Pierin's had been brought in by the farmhands that afternoon from the field where he had dropped it. Trying not to remember how the shiny, green-black residue got there, she scrubbed off the thraik blood, honed the blade sharp, and found a makeshift scabbard for it. She threaded it into the belt around her waist holding Teldo's pants up. It weighed a surprising amount, but she'd be a fool to go without it. She took a few utensils that the boys swore were vital for sleeping in the wild, such as a jack for holding a kettle over a fire, and a long metal spoon that would not burn and could be used for stirring or eating. A pot for cooking and making tea. She rummaged through the pantry for food that would last several days, for who knew how long it would be before she reached a farm or an inn? A bottle of well water. Salt and a few herbs, to make camp food more interesting. Some physics, a roll of bandages and fleabane from the medicine cupboard. Fishhooks and a line. A jaunty cap and a warm cloak over all completed her wayfaring clothes.

All of Teldo's magical impedimenta must come with her. She might need it, and Bardol would certainly throw it out the moment someone let on to him what it had been used for. Teldo hadn't much: a wand he had been carving out of alderwood; an ornate brass pot that he mysteriously referred to as a "cauldron"; a couple of rings and amulets. He'd paid such high sums for the latter that he had begged Tildi, his only confidant in matters magical, never to reveal to Gosto what they had cost. Teldo had never learned what they were for, but perhaps the wizard could translate the runes that decorated them. Most of the space in her pack she stuffed with his papers, most especially the leaf of the book they had never been able to read, his texts on magic, and his correspondence. Tildi folded up the letter from the wizard, Olen, offering Teldo the apprenticeship and tucked it into her bodice. If she reached Overhill with nothing else in her possession, she must have that.

A bit of space remained. In her most practical heart she knew she ought to pack in a few more pairs of socks or a warm scarf. She found herself drifting around her brothers' rooms. Why not take a memento of each one? No one else might like to hear the stories of how they had made this or found that—nothing was more boring than someone else's family history—but it would be like bringing them with her. She already had Pierin's knife and Teldo's wand. Marco had a small pipe he had made from a river reed. With it he could play tunes as light as birdsong. Those went into the safest corner of the pack. It was more difficult with Gosto. In the end she took one of his handkerchiefs. They were large, practical, and entirely masculine, but softened by many washings into a texture like kidskin. How often she had tucked one into his overall pocket as he went out into the fields. They would come back filthy with soil and sweat, or torn from being used to help haul up a fence post, or covered with blood where they had been used to tie up a cut hand or wipe the face of a newborn lamb. These handkerchiefs were like a diary of Gosto's day.

Ruthlessly, she turned out the strongbox that Gosto had kept under a loose floorboard beneath his bed. The family's small treasures were also kept there. Tildi removed the thin gold band that had been her mother's wedding ring and her grandmother's before her only worn on feasts, and all the hard coinage, leaving just enough money to pay Mirrin's and his girls' wages. It was still her money for three more days. By the time any pursuer could have guessed where she'd gone and caught up with her, she ought to have taken up her apprenticeship to the wizard Olen. Chances were that they'd no longer wish to bother with her, and the mayor and the elders could do what they liked with the farm. They would anyhow. Tildi simply wouldn't have to be a party to it. Pity she wouldn't be able to watch the alarm raised when she was noticed to be missing. By the time the girls and the farmhands returned to the house, she would be gone. No tea made. No breakfast laid out. No water pumped up for baths. No washing hanging out. No mending in the basket. No sticks broken for the fire. No bread rising in the bowl near the fireplace. . . . Once Tildi began to enumerate all the household tasks she did out of love for her brothers and had no intention whatsoever of doing for her unwanted intended, a long journey alone overland to an apprenticeship sounded like a week off with time to read in bed!

She left the strongbox unlocked on the big table. After raising the hue and cry about her disappearance, Mirrin would figure out what it meant. Let Bardol and the council work out how to pay the farmhands thereafter. He could mortgage the crops. Time and Nature knew they were more than worth the cost.

By the time Tildi had completed all her preparations she was hungry again. Blessing the kindness of smallfolks, she tucked into the funeral meats with good appetite. The leftovers, of which there was a good plenty, would make a fine lunch for her puzzled farmhands.

A lightening in the sky showed pale gray through the crack between the storm shutters over the round, east-facing window in the kitchen. Tildi rose and donned her pack. She knew she had been putting off the final moment, but no time remained for dithering. She must go now, or accept her fate.

Divided between sorrow for her loss and excitement at the prospect of the new and unknown, Tildi pulled the door closed behind her.

Chapter Four

bird's warble broke the hush of night as Tildi crossed the threshold.

False dawn was not long away. The dark plum sky, with a few straggling specks of stars, began to grow silver above the treetops as she looked out over the garden gate along the track that led southeast, away from town. All of her male relatives had taken this road, to go trading with the humans on the other side of the Eastern Hills, leaving the females at home to wonder what the rest of the world was like. It was her turn to see, but only if she lent speed to her feet. Any moment now someone was going to pop out of one of the three houses that lay in sight of the Summerbees' front door and order her back, demanding to know in the meanwhile what she had done to her hair, and why was she wearing her brother's clothes? Had she gone mad? *It was all that reading of fairy stories, Tildi Summerbee!*

If only she could go back to yesterday and keep everyone inside, so that when the thraiks descended, they would find no prey. Her heart clenched with sorrow, but she had to move on. The day was dawning, and soon she would be discovered.

The hardest step she ever took was passing through the gate to the road. On this side lay the familiar, the safe, the known. On the other was the unknown, laden with who knew what dangers? She reached out to open the latch, but her hand kept dropping down to her side.

If I don't do it now, I never will, Tildi told herself. *Go. Now. Hurry!*

A rooster crowing at the Bywells' farm precipitated action. Before she knew what she was doing, she'd unlatched the gate and stepped out. It swung shut behind, hitting her in the heavy pack on her back. Tildi was knocked forward a pace.

Well, if that's not an omen, nothing is, she thought with wry humor, regaining her footing and reseating the pack. She glanced nervously up and down the road. She reassured herself. *I'm a boy,* she thought fiercely. *I'm a boy! Remember that! I cannot be sent back to an empty hearth, for that's not my fate. I am a man with an office to take up, and people to meet, lands to explore, sights to see before I do.*

The thought made her walk straighter, with a longer stride. There. Even her body believed it now. With a glance over her shoulder at the old farmhouse for farewell, she marched as quickly as she could toward the east and the graying sky. A few fat puffy clouds touched with orange and pink at the eastern edge anticipated the arrival of the sun.

In the distance, a dog barked, and a few more roosters raised their hoarse cries. Tildi enjoyed a tender moment of longing for the life she was setting behind her. Dawn was a time of day she normally loved. As the one in charge of getting everyone else in the house up, Tildi rose at the first fingerling sun ray to peer over the ring of hills that surrounded the Quarters. She loved the freshness of the pure, newborn light, the cool sweetness of the air. Unless the weather was very cold, she always threw open the big windows to let in the scent before she started the fire to make the morning tea. Around her she scented the faint, sweet, tangy aroma of wood-smoke, as dozens of women like herself, and a few men, rose to the same task that would get their households up and moving. She could use a cup of that good, strong, sweet tea now. How tired she was! She was not accustomed to staying up all night, and grief bent her spine with exhaustion.

Well, she'd best make speed now. Once she was out of any danger of being seen by her neighbors she could find herself a comfortable place to make camp. There she would be able to make herself a meal and take a nap. She bent her back to her pack and trudged gamely along the road. The rucksack's weight wasn't so overwhelming as to keep her from noticing the spring flowers peeking out at her on either side. Tildi admired the pinks, yellows, and purples, drinking them in to keep in her memory forever. With some difficulty because of the pack, she stooped to pick a small handful of the fragile blossoms, still damp with morning dew. She tied the stems together with strands of grass, and tucked the fragrant posy into the breast of her borrowed shirt. She would miss all the beauty of her home. If only things had not had to change!

Get on with you, Tildi Summerbee, she thought severely. *The future has to make itself now.*

She looked back over her shoulder toward her home. The trees and fences were lit silver-gilt by the light of the rising sun. Tildi felt her throat tighten with grief and longing.

Farewell, she thought sadly. *The last heir of the Summerbees is leaving in search of her fortune.*

She turned away, rasping up the empty road in the unfamiliarly rough pants and boots.

From their property's edge the land sloped upward in gentle, forested hills for several more miles until it met the foot of the eastern range that guarded the sunrise side of the Quarters. The massif was called the Eastern Hills out of modesty. The peaks were rounded at the top, but they stood as high as proper mountains ought to. Her smallfolk ancestors seemed not to have much imagination. The rest of her homeland was ringed by other ranges with, alas, equally prosaic names: the Northern Tors, the Southwesterns, and the Sunlit Hills that connected the long Southwesterns to the Eastern Hills. Her homeland lay in a kind of bowl that protected it from the rest of the world, but within those boundaries it rose to a dome shape, cut by many rivers and dotted with lakes and marshlands. In almost the precise geographical center was a high tarn known as the Eye Lake. Generations of schoolchildren, Tildi included, had been assured that from the air the water bubbling up from the vast underground streams was so clear that one could see through it down to the center of the earth, though none of them knew how the teacher or the author of the schoolbook had made that discovery. The five streams that flowed down from that lake divided the land into the five Quarters.

Beyond the protective mountains to the south was an ocean. According to the schoolmaster's map the Quarters occupied a small part at the south center of Niombra, the biggest of the world's five continents. Beyond the steep cliffs that terminated the Eastern Hills lay the main river, the Arown. It flowed down all the way to the main trading seaport, protected by a wide, bean-shaped cove protected by natural seawalls.

The Tench, the southeastern river that delineated the border between the Morningside and Noon Quarters, also reached the seaport, cutting underneath the Sunlits and emerging on the other side at the head of a picturesque waterfall high on the cliff face. The natural tunnel cut by the stream was wide enough and high enough for three smallfolk to walk abreast on either side if the river was not in a flood stage. The smallfolks made use of the handy shortcut to bring their goods to market in Tillerton. A cart drawn by a pair of ponies could make their way beside the torrent. Humans never came that way. The echoing tunnel was just low enough that the big folks would have had to walk stooped over for miles. Several attempts to raise the roof had been abandoned for fear of bringing the mountains down upon them.

There were other terrors. Gosto used to scare his smaller siblings with tales of centipedes as long as his arm that haunted the tunnels. Their fierce pincers could nip off a finger. The ceiling was hung with bats that drank blood and ate eyeballs. Ants plied the roadway in silent, armored masses. They carried off shoes after mistaking them for prey, and Nature help the smallfolk who fell behind his fellows when the ant armies were afoot! Tildi always shivered to hear those stories. Once the terrifying journey in the dark had ended, descent to the port city was by way of a causeway cut into the cliff so narrow that the off pony was always walking with one hoof hanging off into thin air. Gosto had been a wonderful storyteller, and was looking forward to telling his tales to his own children as he put them safely to bed. Tildi knew how the seaport looked, how the people spoke, and how many ships went hither and thither from his descriptions.

Teldo had only been interested in the city for what new wonders it could furnish to his deepest passion, magic. The seaport was home to sailors and sea witches, each with their own stories of magic, which Teldo had brought back to a rapt Tildi. One of the sea witches had sold Teldo the book of study she now carried in her backpack.

Tildi hoped to see the port one day, but her path took her in a different direction. Olen lived in Overhill, many miles to the northeast. Perhaps in the future her master would send her to the seaport on an errand, or perhaps she would travel with him, on a flying chair or a horse that could travel a thousand yards in a step. Who knew what wonders lay in the years to come?

So many lands lay around the Quarters, and lands beyond those, places she knew only from their names on maps. The lands immediately beyond the Arown were good farmland, the teacher had instructed the smallfolk children. *Not quite as good as theirs,* Tildi thought with pride. The Arown's river valley flattened out in a series of long terraces that often flooded, constantly washing away the best of the topsoil.

Beyond the Arown lay more mountain ranges, then the hot countries where nothing at all grew. According to the schoolroom map, they were all sand except in a few green oases. The sky was reputedly a deep blue without a single cloud. She couldn't imagine living where there were no trees or grass or rain. The beasts there were strange, too. Each of them had a natural water reservoir within its body to sustain life in between oases.

To the north lay most of the noble kingdoms of humankind. Three were the oldest known, their origins going back more than ten thousand years, predating the earliest written records of the smallfolks, before the dawn of the written word. Overhill lay in Melenatae, the most southern of the three, and possibly the oldest of them all. *Think of that,* Tildi told herself. *I am walking back into history, when I never dreamed I would be traveling at all.*

To the west and northwest lay more human kingdoms, but according to her lessons those territories in the high mountains were reputed to be shared by dwarves, whose realms were belowground. Tildi thought she had never met a dwarf, though Pierin insisted she had. Dwarves were reputed to be insular and unfriendly and did not welcome travelers. A story one visiting troubadour had brought to a meeting fire told of a cold winter's journey where he could smell good food cooking all around him and heard music coming up from beneath his feet, but he never could locate the way in to the dwarves' hall.

South of the ocean was Niombra's nearest neighbor, Sheatovra. She always loved hearing stories from Sheatovra. Men lived there, but so did many strange creatures such as werewolves. A peddler who came through the Quarter once brought a square of rough hide he said came from a werewolf he had slain with his own hands, but Gosto and the other men scoffed at that. No ordinary man, especially not a peddler, could kill a werewolf.

The forest loomed closer with every step. Tildi found she was trembling as the great trees rose over her head, blotting out the rising sun in a mass of shadow. She had never gone into the wild woods alone. If the stories were true any of a dozen large predators were waiting to pounce upon a small and defenseless morsel like herself, waiting to tear her into quivering shreds. Anything that behaved like prey, Pierin had warned her, was likely to be stalked. He had bragged that he always walked with confidence even if he didn't feel it. She must take his advice and do the same. She worked his knife loose from its sheath on her belt and held the gleaming blade up for a talisman as she approached the forest's edge. It was a small glimmer of blue-white against the sinister hulks of the dark, gnarled trees, too little to protect her against a threat. Tildi felt as though both it and she would be swallowed up in a moment. The gloom had a presence of its own, one imbued with a forbidding consciousness that focused upon the smallfolk that approached it. Who was she to challenge the territory of these most ancient of creatures? How dare she attempt to travel out of her proper sphere and into the country of wild things?

"Walk with confidence," Pierin's voice seemed to say.

Tildi clutched the memory as tightly as she did the knife, and strode forward under the canopy. At that moment she missed her brothers more than she could hardly believe. In the face of her grief, fear lessened, as though she only had room for one overwhelming emotion at a time.

Once she was within the forest the gloom seemed to lessen. The trees emerged from the black-brown mass as individual shapes. For a moment Tildi fancied she could see the word for *tree* drawn upon each in faint strokes of ink, a trifle darker than the bark. Each rune was just a little different, as though the trees were telling her their names. It didn't matter that her tired eyes were playing tricks on her; the fancy lessened her fear of going forward. She was meeting new acquaintances, that was all.

A shrill whistle overhead made her crouch in place and clutch the knife hilt harder. Thraik! Her heart pounded. She ran to hide behind one of the huge trees.

No, it couldn't be thraik, could it? Tildi wondered, scanning the faint blue beyond the canopy of leaves. They'd have attacked her before she entered the forest. Its crown was too thick for the thraik to see her now. Could they detect her presence in some other way, using their own dread magic? The whistle came again, and developed into a warbling song that rang through the otherwise silent forest. She recognized the call of a woods cuckoo. Tildi relaxed, shook her head at her own fancy. There were no eyes in the sky over her head; just a bird or two coming out in the early dawn to seek its breakfast. She wished it a good day's foraging. Her sleepless night was making her imagine things. Fie on her fancies!

Tildi focused on the middle distance, trying not to mind the straps of her heavy pack cutting into her shoulders or how the boots slid around on her feet in spite of the double socks. The air a few feet before her seemed to twinkle. Tildi put it down to a shaft of sunlight peering through the leaves overhead. Then, into that very place dropped a spider the size of her palm. Tildi gasped and jumped back. It was as if the spider had sent a message ahead of its arrival, warning her to avoid walking into it. How extraordinary! She had never known that this forest was such a magical place. How selfish of Teldo not to have told her about it. Yet it explained why the smallfolk elders were so insistent that young people not come here alone. They disapproved of anything that smacked of sorcery. There must have been an unspoken pact not to pay attention to the enchantments they found in the great forest, seeing as how they had to pass through it to reach the rest of the continent.

What she had read in Teldo's books said that a magician must always be honest in dealing with the unseen, or it could consume him. Tildi paused. What if she did something false in error? Would she have a chance to make it right again, or did fate come upon one in the next heartbeat?

Tildi let out a snort that echoed in the stillness. She had a long way to go, and if she kept scaring herself she may as well go back to the Quarters and accept whatever fate the elders had in mind for her. She had chosen this for herself, and no matter what came of it she had that comfort. If a real threat arose she would deal with it then. Her practical nature overrode her sense of loss and fear. Instead, it would be wise to concentrate upon her surroundings. All of this was new, as good as opening a birthday present every few feet. That ought to be enough for any respectable smallfolk to go on with.

Resolved, Tildi fixed her gaze on the farthest point of the road she could see, took a deep breath of the leaf-scented air, and marched onward.

Chapter Five

I f a fisherman should chance to look Nemeth's way as he crawled out of the sea, he might think he was looking at a strange kind of huge fish with a gasping mouth and bulbous eyes all but staring out of his pale, domed head. But the shape of the blue-scaled body was all wrong. It was flat between the dorsal and ventral fins instead of from side to side. Where one would expect a tail fluke was a long ribbon of muscle like the belly of a snail, and one of the side fins appeared to be deformed with a long bulge. The gills behind the rudimentary ear holes spread open, the red membranes suffering as they strained to gather oxygen in this too-thin atmosphere. He lay still for a long time on the shore amid the other flotsam: decaying seaweed, weather-beaten chunks of timber, dead fish, and dying crabs. He, too, was dying.

Nemeth had lived a long time this way. To pass along the seafloor he had exchanged lungs for gills and feet for a rippling pseudopod. It was necessary. He could not expose himself to potential attackers or thieves, but it had been a horrible existence. He had hated what he had done to his body. The changes affected his mind, reducing him from the thinking creature he had been to a monster from which he would have run away from on land. Anything with eyes would have. Yet it was the simplest form of which he could conceive that would suit his purpose. Necessity had set a whip to his back. He had outdistanced what pursuers remained, but he never thought he could outrun all of them. He did not have time or the imagination to form himself into something that would preserve his humanity intact yet allow him to do what he did, to live in near darkness in the twilit depths, breathe water, and survive upon the forage he could find near the seafloor. Now he did not know if he could turn back. His tongue still felt coated with the livers of the creatures he had eaten. He had killed with his own hands for food: pale white fish with bulging eyes, giant shrimps that were more bitter than the seawater he had breathed day in and day out, crabs like spiders whose long, spindly legs caught in his teeth like strands of corn silk.

Corn.

It had been a long time since he had tasted corn.

Nemeth grasped for the memory of corn. Fish thoughts were good only for survival. He must get used to thinking like a human again. Yellow. Corn was yellow. The way it looked growing in a field was . . . pretty; the horizontal sweeps of green stalks with gold tassels waving in the wind. Its milky sweetness on the tongue was the next thing he recalled. It helped dispel the bitterness of the shrimps. He clawed back each vision, each sound, each taste. Clouds. Clouds rolled through the sky above his head. They were the same as the last time he had seen them—how long ago? The color of the sky beyond them was called . . . blue. His lidless eyes watched the white patterns change, but black crept up around the perimeter of his vision. He did not have much time.

Runes lay all around him, on every leaf, every grain of sand, each fish in the sea. Another wrapped him about like a cocoon, defining him in every way: his shape, his history, his future all expressed as one symbol. It was deformed. Nemeth hated the sight of it. He had been forced to see it every day since he began this journey. Now he must repair it before he suffocated on the hot beach. With difficulty, he called up the memory of the one rune he knew better than any other. For months he had concentrated on every stroke, every detail, every nuance, in order to recall it without error. Now he must summon it or perish.

The sigil appeared in his mind's eye. He admired its perfection. This is how he ought to be. With an act of will he expanded it until it was large enough to surround him, glowing with such golden light that it washed out the pale sunlight. He could feel its hot power coursing through his body, as though the lines were connected to organs and blood vessels, a design more complicated than could be conceived by any ordinary mind. Where the living rune did not match the rune in his mind, he must make it match. A line here needed to be straightened out, a flourish lengthened. Other parts must be erased. As though he was scrubbing out a mistake on a document, he corrected the symbol. Around him, the pattern altered, and he felt himself altering in response.

The first part to grow back was his eyelids. Thankfully, after so many months of inescapable light, he was able to close his eyes. No matter. He did not need to see to complete the transformation.

Behind his ears he could feel the gasping slits close. Inside his chest lungs came into being and expanded, lifting his rib cage almost painfully. Nemeth gasped and coughed. The fins at his side grew slowly into arms, and the scales fell from them, littering the beach with their blue shimmer. He rolled over on one side in the coarse sand, feeling for the burden that he had carried all this time under the left arm. It was there, no longer a part of his physical body, but as close as his soul. He relaxed a little, patting the bundle as if it was a faithful dog. So all was well. He would soon be himself again.

Patiently, he endured the continuing pain. Soon he had legs, toes, fingers. His tongue marked the blunting of his teeth, and he nodded approval. One painful surge as his prominent nose, which had receded into his face, regrew all at once.

That nose had endured humiliation in his past, as had the rest of his person. Such disrespect would never again be his part. The bundle in his arm would ensure that his would always be a name to reckon with. He summoned clothes. It had been months since he had had shoes on, but they could not be more painful than walking the seafloor on his belly.

Nemeth waited until the transformation was complete, and crawled to his feet, careful not to drop his burden. How much he had suffered to gain it! How much privation and pain! *The reward would be worth all the trouble,* he thought, and a bitter smile bent his lips. The book was his. From the moment he held it in his hands, nothing could harm him or deter him. It was rightly his, and its powers belonged to him. If any could guess his purpose, kings would send armies against him. Mages would call up the most powerful forces in existence. All their efforts would be useless. The power lay in his hands.

Eyes were upon him. Nemeth recalled the last time he had felt every being looking at him. They were laughing, laughing at him! Though it was so very long ago every detail remained fresh in his memory. They were the goads that drove him when the book's guardians attacked him. They were the extra strength upon which he drew when his spells proved too weak to withstand theirs.

He would show those who had humiliated him that they could not treat him with such trifling disdain. He would cause destruction on the very site of his disgrace, and bring the world crashing down upon his tormentors. As long as he was assured of that, he did not care what became of him afterward. Since the very day he had learned about the book's whereabouts, he had begun to make his plans. The preparations had cost him dearly—but he had already lost all. Gaining the book would restore to him all that and more. He had nothing to lose in the essay. That knowledge was a shield and a weapon against those who would stop him. But he had succeeded at drawing forth the book. How it had been kept hidden for so long he did not know.

Nemeth hugged the hide-wrapped parcel to him again, as though he was embracing a precious child. He felt a great urge to open it and enjoy its beauty, for it was a beautiful thing. He looked around. This was not a proper place. He must find somewhere more suitable. He could pause in his journey for a moment to refresh himself by turning through a few pages. Nemeth could see the entire book in his memory, every word. It unrolled through his dreams. The stories it told led him on nighttime journeys beyond the confines of his poor human brain, into the realms of other beings, living and never-living. It took joy in its own creation, and shared that joy with him. It was a part of him, or was he a part of it? Of that he was uncertain, though he felt it had preserved his sanity during the months it had taken to walk from Sheatovra to Niombra.

The sun beat down upon him. He had done without its scrutiny for a long while, and disliked it peering into his business now. He shook his fist at the sky, sending a curl of hate in the sun's direction. His power had not risen to the level where he could snuff out the blazing orb, but it was only a matter of time. All creation would wither at his hand, if he chose. He smiled, and the movement hurt the newly grown skin of his cheeks. He would decide later what would befall the sky and the rest of the world.

Behind him a bubbling growl attracted his attention. From the surf a pale tentacle as long as his body uncoiled. The claw at the end, dripping with blue poison, felt for him. Nemeth watched dispassionately. The creature hauled itself out of the surf, its cone-shaped body rearing up ten feet high, muscular tentacles digging into the sand. It was mud-colored except for the red fleshy lips drawn back to show endless rows of translucent, sharp white teeth, and the bright, flat, golden eyes each the size of Nemeth's head. It turned one eye toward him, and the slitted pupil widened. A deeper growl issued from its throat, and the poisoned claws whipped around to point at him. The beast lurched up the sand, anger giving it the speed it would normally lack without the water's support.

The ugly beasts had been following him for some time. He had killed many, but always another came to take its place. It was as if they did not care what had happened to the others. Perhaps they did not believe that the same fate would overtake them. Ah, well.

In no hurry at all, Nemeth sat down upon the sand and unwrapped the book. He did not have time to remark upon its beauty as he would like to have done. He unrolled it to the page upon which the beast appeared. The book always seemed to assist him in finding the right place, the complex runes almost glowing with joy that he wished to behold them.

The monster's claws reached for his head. They were only feet away. Nemeth summoned a thread of magic, and set a stroke down through the monster's rune that split it in two. He looked up.

The creature wailed, a terrible sound that echoed down the curved coastline. Before Nemeth's eyes the reaching pseudopods fell away as the monster's body parted neatly in two halves from snout to tail. The pupils in the flat eyes widened until the golden irises were a mere rim.

Yes, Nemeth thought, as the twitching hulk poured guts, brains, and blood out upon the sand. *You all believe me an easy target, but I command the book's power now.*

Buoyed by triumph, he rolled up the book and wrapped it in the soft leather cover. He rose and stepped over the quivering claw. It would take some time to die, and he could not be bothered to watch it. Seagulls were already circling overhead, drawn by the smell of fresh flesh.

"Feast well, my friends," Nemeth said, turning his back on his fallen prey. They were the first words he had spoken in over eight months. His voice sounded strange to him. "I must be on my way."

A bit unsteadily at first, Nemeth set out northward. He had so much to do. So much time had passed in gaining his objective that his work was years behindhand. No matter. He would take care of everything.

Where he went, the grass changed, the trees burst into bloom or withered. A wraith flew overhead, but with a sign from the wizard, it fell from the sky, burning. He hated thraiks. Their very creation was an abomination against nature. When he reached his destination, he would wipe them out without regret.

Unsteadily, he rose to his feet and set out northward.

Chapter Six

oes this path only go up?" Tildi asked herself, shouldering the pack once more to conquer a particularly steep stretch. Here the hard-packed trail had been cut into terraced steps, each with a squared-off log at the edge to prevent the whole thing from disintegrating into a mass of mud when it rained. She was accustomed to hard work, but the endless slogging on foot was a new and not very pleasant experience. Pity the nomadic peddlers whose job it was to walk the continent day in and day out, no matter what the terrain and weather!

After a climb that made the muscles of her thighs ache white-hot, she stopped at a ledge about the size of the farmhouse's kitchen. She dropped the pack and let it fall in between the knobbly roots of her host, an oak tree whose branches stuck straight out over the path. Gratefully she flopped down beside it. Her heart was pounding. She undid the cloak clasp so that the folds of cloth slithered down behind her back, giving her a pad against the rough bark. Tildi settled back with a sigh of relief. It was odd to feel the cool air at the back of her neck where her hair used to be, but it was an advantage in this hot weather. She pressed her palms to her cheeks to help cool them off.

She now regarded the big oaks and beeches as kindly elders instead of the sinister monsters she had thought them when she first entered their domain. It seemed like half a day since she had left her home, but by the twinkle of the sun through the treetops it could not have been more than two hours. She judged it to be late midmorning. The pain in her legs receded to a glow of healthy effort, but her feet in the too-large boots felt hot and sweaty. She took off the boots and both pairs of socks and examined her feet. They were pink from tip to heel, but there were no blisters yet, she noted with relief.

This burrow in the shelter of this tree was very comfortable indeed. How many of her neighbors and relatives had stopped in this very place for a snack? She undid the fastening of her pack and got a drink of water and a bite of bread and cheese from her provisions. Squirrels and chipmunks ran up and down the boles of the smaller trees to either side, angling to see if she was dropping anything they might like to eat. She brushed off her lap and flung the crumbs toward an empty piece of ground. The bolder squirrels dashed in to get them, and fled up the trees with their less courageous fellows in pursuit.

She stoppered the now-empty bottle and slung it on the outside of the pack. A faint trickling sound in the distance told her there was a stream nearby where she could refill it. She hadn't yet passed over it, so it must still lie ahead. By her reckoning it would be the Grayling, a small stream that fed off from the Yellowtail, the river that divided the Morningside Quarter from the Nightside Quarter. The Yellowtail would still be far ahead. She wouldn't see that until she was level with the Northern Tors.

Long before that she expected to have passed over the notch through the Eastern Hills and to have met up with the high river road. The way to Overhill lay along the Arown. That was the main route humans and others used to visit the Quarters. Teldo and Marco said it was an easy road, well maintained and well signposted. They had often discussed the benefits of this pub or that inn along the road, but Tildi had no real notion of how long it would take her on foot. Her brothers were often gone for a week or more on business, and were somewhat vague on how many days they spent in the towns they visited. The precise itinerary was not important: they went; they returned. Tildi never expected a full travelogue, but at the moment it would have come in handy.

This early in the day she did not expect to meet any other travelers coming into the Quarters, nor, she hoped, coming up behind her from the village. As much as she longed for sleep, she wanted to find a particular kind of stopping place, one that was on a level, with thick woods to either side of the path so she would not be seen. As she continued her walk, on a steadily increasing slope, she saw signs that others had rested here, even camped for the night, based upon the rings of head-sized stones with a residue of gray ash inside.

About midday she heard a heavy rhythmic sound coming toward her. A horse or pony, moving at a plodding walk, scraped the packed-earth road. Her keen ears told her it was ahead, not behind. The others were not coming to take her back, not yet. If it was one of the smallfolk traders returning from a journey she must hide at once; she couldn't risk word of a lone traveler outbound from the Quarters at just the time Tildi Summerbee had gone missing. As quietly as she could, she stepped off the main path and retreated into the brush, letting the twigs swish back into place.

Within five minutes the other traveler appeared. It was a young human male. He had long hair tied at the nape of his neck with a leather cord. He rode a multicolored horse that was half again as tall as one of her brother's plow animals. Strangely enough, nature had marked the mare's master as oddly as it had herself. The human's hair was a mix of colors, caramel and white streaks running through the dark tresses at the nape and one temple. Weatherworn packs were tied behind the saddle and behind both knees over the horse's flanks. Tildi would have assumed that he was a peddler but for the soft leather case held to his back by a strap that crossed his chest. By its shape Tildi guessed it held a jitar. A minstrel, then. By tonight he would be in Clearbeck, and a meeting would be held to hear his news and dance to his songs. She sighed with regret.

The noise of her breath, tiny as it was, brought the man's head up with a start. He pulled the horse to a halt. He scanned the area with keen, bright eyes the color of hazel leaves. Tildi held very still. Providing they weren't caught out in the middle of a field her kind was good at hiding from predators. Smallfolk seemed to pull themselves into a hole in the air. It was reputed that not even their scent escaped. Only fear could make her reveal herself, and a traveling bard was nothing to be afraid of. After an interval, the young man decided there was nothing to see. He flicked his reins, and the good horse began once again to make his way downhill, grunting as it trudged down each terraced step. Tildi waited until the pair was out of earshot before allowing herself to relax.

She prepared to hoist her pack and go on, but her legs had finally decided they had had enough. She bent her knees underneath and tried to stand up.

She sat down. Her thighs were as wobbly as a new colt's. Tildi braced her hands against the rucksack's straps, and discovered her shoulders winced at the notion of taking the pack's weight again.

Perhaps it was time for a rest after all. She glanced around and discovered that beyond the brush at her back was a tiny, grassy meadow shaped like the open palm of a hand. Sun dappled the raised northern edge, and a fire ring occupied the center. A few logs, green with moss, had been stacked up against the big, motherly-looking beech tree at the side. It looked so inviting that Tildi decided it was the very place she was looking for: well secluded from the road but close enough that she could hear travelers approaching. The only thing that gave her pause was the crescent-shaped slice of sky beyond the circle of the tree's crown. The thraik could come back while she was asleep and carry her off. The thought chilled her soul, but her exhausted feet told her they just didn't want to go looking for a better spot. She surveyed it and came to the conclusion that if she huddled just beneath its roots she would be invisible from above. Tildi carried her pack to the far edge of the clearing. She flattened out the flap end to use for a pillow.

Tildi hoped no wolves would come and sniff her out, nor wild dogs, nor any of the other things that the elders had always warned against— were they right to be so cautious?

Their mother had once taught her a protection charm. Teldo had laughed at it as having no magical power behind it, but Tildi had always found comfort in it.

> *Nature guard me while I sleep,*
> *From all who fly or walk or creep,*
> *Ward the earth and guard the sky,*
> *May I wake safely by and by.*

The drowsy rhyme went around and around in her mind, becoming less and less coherent. Tildi thought in the distance she heard a faint shrieking of a hunting thraik. They could smell magic, she knew, but she felt too heavy to move. She tried to recapture the rhythm of the charm, and soon the noise receded. No night monsters would come now. She pretended the cloak above her head was the four walls and roof she had left behind at Daybreak Bank. The shrill, faraway whistle pursued her into her dreams.

*T*he snap of a twig brought Tildi out of a sound sleep. She sat up and clawed the all-enveloping cloak away from her face. The light in the clearing had diminished by two-thirds, and Tildi could no longer see the sun peeping through the leaves overhead. Footsteps on the path now hidden from view receded, heading in the direction of the Quarters. It must be some lonely traveler seeking to find a bed in Morningside before night set in. Tildi realized she had better bestir herself if she didn't want to spend the night in the clearing. She ought to have a few more hours of daylight. She was glad to know that her hiding place had been a good one.

It had been warm during the day, but the evening that high up on the hillside was considerably more chilly. A good meal would warm her up from within and give her the heart for a second hike. Tildi chose a meal for herself from her cold viands, cutting a slice of chicken pie and counting out a few pieces of dried fruit onto a flat rock that would serve well as a table. A cup of tea would taste very good with those, she decided. She poured some of her water into the small kettle and set it just inside the ring of stones that lay near the flat rock. Clearly some practical earlier traveler had decided to set his cooking fire near to his serving area.

In spite of the warm weather it was damp underneath the trees. Tildi had to forage to find the driest sticks, and an abandoned bird's nest for tinder. Then she felt in her pack, working her hand carefully past the roll of Teldo's papers to the small cache of tools at the bottom. Her heart sank. She had no flint and striker to make the fire.

In her mind's eye she went back over how she had packed the rucksack, and hoped she was mistaken about the omission. But, no. The black square of flint and matching steel she used at home was still on the shelf above the hearth.

Cursing herself for a fool, Tildi looked around for a rough flint among the rubble that formed the surface of the road. With a few tries she was sure she could strike a spark using the blade of her knife. Unfortunately, none of the stones in her vicinity looked like flint nodules. She wondered how far it was to travel back to the nearest smallfolk holding, then laughed bitterly at herself. She could hardly walk in and ask, "May I buy a flint block from you? I . . . er . . . lost mine somewhere." She would be worrying the whole time whether the farmer, or more likely, his wife, would penetrate her disguise and send her back to Daybreak Bank in disgrace.

Annoyed, Tildi shoved the pack away from her with one bare foot. The heavy sack rolled over the root behind it and rustled to a halt, its contents shifting noisily. There was plenty of paper in there that would make good tinder, if she had a means of making a fire, but she would never burn any of Teldo's lessons or books.

She grinned to herself, half sheepishly. She had the means to light a fire, if she could manage it. Fire was the simplest of the magics, Teldo had always told her, though it had never felt simple. To reach deep within herself to bring forth the spell always made Tildi feel like she had to turn herself inside out. She was ashamed that she had not been able to help Teldo in his ultimate need. Intellectually she knew how; she had even done it in practice several times, but the skill had deserted her while under pressure. The last time she had attempted to create a viable fire she had failed, and her brothers had died as a result. It was hard to summon up the confidence to try again. But Teldo had believed in her. She must try. Perhaps it would be easier now, when no one was looking. She held out her hand over the mound of tinder and concentrated.

She still felt held back. Should she be allowed to make magic for such a homely purpose, then? In the books she had read magic was only to be used for great purposes, to save lives or defeat great perils. Yet, Teldo often practiced his spells. Was it really permitted? She found she was waiting for someone to give her permission to proceed.

Well, there was no one left to ask. She had no family, and she had just cast away her claim to a place in decent society by cutting off her hair and running away in boys' clothing. She had no intention of waiting until she got to her new master to ask him if she could make a cup of tea, please and thank you! Time and Nature knew he wouldn't want to be bothered by such silly, minor questions, so she'd surely have to answer it herself. The absurdity made her laugh, and unlock the tight place inside from which she had to evoke the magical power. Even before she began to properly think the words, a green glow erupted from beneath her outstretched hand. The spark leaped from her palm to the leaves. A white curl of smoke arose. She regarded it with pleased astonishment. It worked!

"I did that," she said out loud, her voice a surprise in the quiet woods. "Oh, I wish Teldo could have seen!"

She sat beside it and watched. As the green flame consumed the pile of leaves and fluff it expanded and warmed in color to a more normal yellow-colored fire. Tildi warmed the pot and brewed the tea. It tasted better than any she had ever made. She sipped it appreciatively, holding the bowl up between her hands to warm her cool cheeks.

Yes, it would be good to practice the skills before she arrived in Overhill. The wizard Olen would surely want to see that the smallfolk he was taking to apprentice was worth the trouble. He would no doubt have many such tests for her. She hoped they weren't too hard. In her experience the boys who apprenticed themselves to a trade needed little more than a reasonably good wit, willingness to learn, and a strong back, not expert knowledge of that trade. The secrets would be imparted to them once they signed the contract. Surely magicians weren't that different as masters from, say, smiths, who had lore of their own?

She had no idea how much farther it was to the crest of the pass, but she knew that just beyond it was a tiny town owned by humans. The main feature of Rushet was an inn that catered to every race in the world. Gosto had told her stories of drinking beer in its cheerful pub with centaurs and elves as well as humans.

The flames flickered brightly. Tildi found it amazing how just having a fire in a cozy place could make it feel as though she was safe at home. The thought that she had no home made her sad again.

Light dwindled around her with distressing haste, and the temperature crept distressingly lower. Night must be fast approaching. Tildi pulled both pairs of socks on again and tied up the boots. She brushed the crumbs off her little table and tied up the backpack over her cloak. She would just warm up the last cup of tea, and she would be on her way. She reached for the kettle, and a yellow hand stretched past hers toward the fire.

Tildi jumped back in horror, dropping the kettle. Water splashed into the fire, making it hiss. A glowing mask leered into her face. It seemed to float on the air above the campfire, as did the two skeletal claws now reaching for her throat. Tildi let out a muffled shriek. She threw at it the only thing she had in her hand, the half cup of tea. The specter recoiled. It looked shocked.

Tildi scrambled backward, fumbling for the knife at her belt. The ghostly being gnashed a mouthful of yellow stumps at her. She brandished the gleaming blade. The creature floated toward her, an avid, hungry look on its face. Tildi thought that it was the last moment of her life. She slashed at the creature desperately with the knife. Her blade passed right through the specter's body. It paused, its ugly mouth open in a rictus. It was laughing at her! She scooted backward, holding the knife outward, but the specter swooped *through* blade and arm. Its temperature scalded Tildi's skin. She whimpered and snatched her hand back. The specter raised a claw and swiped at her. Tildi fell back, clutching her cheek. The scratch burned red-hot. Tears filled her eyes.

"Please leave me alone," she begged.

The specter grinned again, moving closer and closer until her hair crackled from its heat. No weapon she had could stop it.

The campfire popped, shooting sparks outward. The creature stopped. It turned away from Tildi, fixing its hollow eyes upon the yellow flames. It floated back toward the dancing light until it hovered over the circle of stones. Fed by an invisible breeze, the flames roused and licked upward. The creature's body took on the same glow as the fire and began to grow. Its hollow eyes rolled upward. Tildi watched, frozen like a frightened rabbit. The creature fed upon fire. She crept toward the edge of the clearing, glancing back to make sure it was paying no attention to her. Only a few feet from the undergrowth and the road now. She mourned for the loss of her pack, but better to lose her possessions than her life!

Snap! Her knee came down upon a twig, shattering the silence. She glanced back. The fire demon's dreamy gaze focused upon her again. Eyes pinpoints of white-hot light, it flew at her. Tildi sprang up and dodged toward her pack. She could use it as a shield. The monster, perhaps divining her motive, harried her from this side and that, until she found herself driven toward the fire, now a pillar of gleaming gold.

The specter dived at Tildi. Its claws caught in her shirt. Tildi batted at it, her hands passing through its hot substance. She was helpless to keep the talons from ripping the cloth. *Fool,* she chided herself. She should have run for it when she could. With a yell, she tripped over the stone ring, and huddled down in as small a bundle as she could make herself. She did not want to die! What could she do? Burbling noises told her the kettle still sat steaming away on its make jack suspended in the middle of the fire. Tildi almost raised her head in surprise. The tea!

The monster had recoiled from the cup she threw at it, though it had no fear of her knife. It was a creature of fire—it must abhor water. She sprang up, grabbed the kettle, and splashed its contents at her pursuer.

The campfire went out with a loud sizzle. White steam rose from blackened ashes. The specter drifted to a halt, its mouth widened in horror. It let out a wail, the first noise she had heard it make, like a rusty hinge screeching open. Its yellow light faded away, like the wick of a lamp running out of oil. Tildi found herself staring at the empty clearing, the kettle in her hand.

A wet drop fell onto her wrist. She looked down and saw a dark dot on her pale skin, followed by another. In a moment, her eyes accustomed themselves to the absence of the firelight, and she realized that her cheek was bleeding. A handful of grass would do to pack the scratch and stop the flow, but first she meant to ensure that the fire was out! Tildi poured all the remaining water from the kettle and her bottle over the sodden logs, then kicked dirt onto it for good measure. She would rather go thirsty than let a single ember feed that horrible creature. Then she gathered up her pack and made all good speed getting out of the clearing.

Chapter Seven

he moon known as the Pearl was rising in the east, just a day past full. Tildi noted the sigil that seemed to be limned upon its round, white perfection. The rune was not as distinct as it had been when she first noted it, at the eastern edge of the Quarters, but was still clear enough to read. The other moon, the Agate, because it was not as beautiful as its younger sister, showed a glimmer more like a wet river pebble, but it, too, displayed its name on its dull surface.

She had been walking for three and a half days. The scratch on her cheek from the fire-demon had stopped bleeding long since, but under her cloak, Teldo's shirt was ripped. She was very annoyed about that, but she had not wanted to take the time to repair the tears until she reached a safe place. The first night she had stopped to camp, she had heard a chilling cry overhead. She looked up and saw a shadow against the moonlight. It was a thraik, hunting in the dark. Had it been looking for her? She did not want to find out.

She longed for a hot bath and a real meal, and someone to talk to. As she had promised herself, she had practiced her spells while she had walked. She could now ignite a green flame in her palm every time she tried, but she could not extinguish it without dousing it with water. Fortunately, there was plenty of that along her way. Practicing kept her mind off how much her feet ached in the unfamiliar boots, or how much the pack straps rubbed the skin of her back and shoulders.

With every mile, the oaks and beeches gave way to thinner-skinned trees like rowans, silver birches, and hornbarks. The latter picked up what little sunlight was left and exuded a warm glow that helped light Tildi's way. She had bathed in and drunk from miniature waterfalls that flowed down along both sides of the ridge protecting the Quarters from the rest of the continent, and eked out her food supply with spring berries and a fish or two caught in the mountain brooks. She had slept in fox dens and the hollow places underneath the roots of enormous trees. Dreams of thraiks and fire-demons had disturbed her sleep, waking her in the night, though neither had appeared in truth. She had been desperate to reach the edge of civilization. She had had no real idea how far it was from smallfolk habitations to the first human village. Gosto's tales had always skipped over the details of how long and how far. He preferred to tell humorous stories of drinking or trading or dancing.

Once over the forked granite pass, she had noticed how differently everything had smelled. Unfamiliar plants grew along the roadside, and straggly cone trees clung to the mountainside. The slope on the eastern side of the mountains was much gentler than on the west. She was glad of it because the pack's weight tended to nudge her forward with each downward step, putting strain on her knees. Shallow steps had been cut into the spaces in between the loops in order for travelers unencumbered by carts or animals to travel. She could tell by the height of each stair that smallfolk had built them. The humans who had visited the Quarters could take these two or three at a pace. She kept an eye out for thraiks, but they never passed overhead again.

The rutted road that led her northward had been flanked on one side by the rocky escarpment that hid her old home from her. On the other side, it was a steep drop into the life's blood of the continent of Niombra, the river Arown. It was larger and more impressive than she had imagined from her geography lessons. From one horizon to the other the

Arown looked like a broad field of dark blue-green glass. Its surface rippled like hard muscles under smooth skin. Here and there a rock interrupted the flow, sending arrow-shaped waves downstream to rebound against the banks and back again, overlapping themselves like warp meeting weft in a loom. The river, too, had its rune, a gigantic image that appeared to float just beneath the surface. Tildi sensed power in it, like lightning made liquid.

The runes now were very distinct in all things, much more so than she had noticed west of the mountains. They almost glistened in their intensity. Tildi shook her head in wonder. Magic was everywhere she turned. Were the Quarters themselves under a spell to shut out the magic of the outside world? It would not surprise her a bit.

The cliff edging the river path had receded steadily beside her until she was walking out in the open beside green fields bounded by low hedges, stone walls, and split-rail fences. The fence posts were much higher here than at home. If she bent at the waist she could walk underneath the lower rail, and it would take a boost up for her to climb over it. The upper rail was just out of her reach.

The animals, too, were in proportion to the fences. What she thought had been a sheep, newly sheared for spring, had bleated at her through the rails. When she had tried to feed it a handful of grass, a woolly behemoth fully the size of a Quarters' cart horse, had trotted up to glare at her. The lamb, for so it was, had abandoned her and gone to stick its head under her flanks to nurse. Tildi gawked at them. It had never occurred to Tildi that the animals humans kept would be in proportion to them. It seemed unnatural. True, she'd seen humans' enormous horses, when peddlers and musicians had come through the Quarters, but she had never really thought about other animals. In fact, here came a black-and-white sheepdog to round up the two stragglers and bring them back to the fold. Its head was as high as her own. She literally did not fit into this world.

Tildi clicked her tongue at herself. She knew there was no going back, and no use in worrying about the fact that everyone and everything was taller than she was. Spirit was needed to rise above such petty things as physical appearance. *I am a man now*, she thought boldly, *a man making his place in the world*. No one would know about the quailing little girl underneath. With that attitude she marched on toward the chimney pots that were in sight among the trees.

The light was almost gone by the time she reached the picket wall surrounding the town. A big man wearing a brown tunic half-buttoned over a not-too-white shirt and a pair of dun-colored breeches was heaving the gate shut. Alarmed, Tildi hurried forward and she slipped in under his elbow.

"Hey, now!" the man said in surprise, and looked around. "Who's there?"

"Down here," she said. Her voice squeaked. She lowered it. "Er, down here."

The puzzlement cleared from the man's face, and he smiled. "Ah, smallfolk. Come in! Well, you're already in. I was about to lock up for the night. There's thraik abroad."

"I know. They flew overhead two nights ago."

"Ah," the man said, nodding. "They're out your way, too, eh? It's dangerous times for all of us. Welcome to you to Rushet."

"Thank you," Tildi said.

"Best get about it, then," the man said. He pushed the gate the rest of the way and snapped down a catch, then lowered a heavy bar on a hinge to a set of four brackets that spanned both of the doors. "There, now."

It seemed to Tildi a mighty flimsy barrier to protect against thraik, or against human robbers, for that matter, being made only of wood. But even as the thought went through her mind, she was overwhelmed by a strong feeling that she need have no intentions of attacking this town. She couldn't possibly succeed.

Now, why would she think that, she wondered, then enlightenment dawned. There must have been a magical compulsion laid upon the picket wall to protect the little town from thieves and other threats once the gate was closed and the circle completed. She shook her head. What would the elders think if anyone told them to use magic to guard the village? But why not? Such threats were undoubtedly commonplace on a main road like this one.

The gatekeeper dusted his hands together. "Good night to you, then. Fair journeying, eh?"

"Good night," Tildi replied. She opened her mouth to ask the way to the inn, then realized she was looking at it. It was the next building after a large stable yard where ostlers were walking horses and backing coaches off the road.

Rushet was not a large place. The main road was paved with cobbles. Besides the inn and the stable, she saw a smithy, and beyond that a covered marketplace. On the other side were permanent shops, by their signs a tailor, a baker, and a grocer, all with residences above the premises. The pickets marched around behind the buildings, giving her a measure of comfort. The fence couldn't keep thraiks out, of course, but she would be among other people again, and that gave her confidence.

Though the size of everything continued to amaze her, she was pleased to see how little a human town differed from those belonging to smallfolk. One could tell who was house-proud and took care of their property, and who wasn't; who was popular, to judge from the wearing away of the graveled path to each door, and who seldom had visitors. The baker did a good trade, even at this late hour. People were still passing in and out of the shop with covered baskets. Indeed, the smell of good bread wafting on the evening breeze only reminded her of how hungry she was, and how tired she was of eating stale food out of her pack. She hurried toward the inn.

That establishment was freshly whitewashed and painted with murals of contented-looking farm animals, its wooden beams were sound and well varnished, and its sign was welcoming and cheerful. It wasn't subtle in its approach, either: the place was called the Groaning Table. The sign showed a huge table beginning to bow in the middle from the platters of food and jugs of wine heaped high upon it, with fruit and loaves of bread all but spilling over the edges. The inn was spruced up with big pots of flowers along the street side, and was brightly lit both inside and out. Polished brass lanterns hung on either side of the door, which stood hospitably ajar. Tildi squared her shoulders and marched inside.

Tildi blinked at the sudden brightness. Two huge brass lamps with eight jets apiece hung from the beamed ceiling, spreading pools of light over two long tables, and more lamps were set in sconces against the plastered walls. A dozen or more customers sat on benches flanking the heavy, aged wooden tables. They all glanced her way as she came through the door. A few registered surprise, but that must be, Tildi realized, looking around, because she was the only smallfolk in the room. A dog as large as a Quarters pony came up to sniff her, nose to nose, until its master gruffly called it back.

"Welcome, lad," a plump young woman wearing a broad white apron said, leaning down to smile at her as she passed by carrying a tray full of empty tankards. Tildi stepped back. She'd never seen a female fully twice her own height before, nor one who wore such immodest clothing. The girl's neckline was cut down to . . . well, you could see quite a lot of her chemise and the lushly feminine form beneath it. Her head was uncovered, and her hair, wavy brown and streaked with sunlight, spilled over her shoulders. Unable to point with her hands full, she aimed her nose toward the counter. "That's Wim behind the bar. I'll be by in a moment to serve you."

Better to take control of the situation at once, Tildi thought. *I'm a boy!* Steeling herself, she marched up to the counter where a plump man with greasy skin and fluffy red hair clinging to the sides of his bald head peered down at her with cheerful curiosity.

"Greetings!" she boomed, making her voice as low as she could muster. "Can you give a fellow a room for the night?"

"Ah, is that the way of it, *young man?*" the innkeeper asked, putting down the beer he was pulling and leaning forward with both hands planted on the board. "Of course we can find you a place. Can't we, Danyn?"

"Sure as sunrise," the young woman said, sweeping back again to pick up the filled glasses. She plunked them on her tray, slopping a little of the foam. "Comfy and cozy, as good as if you was in your own home. S'pose you might be wanting a bath, too?"

"Oh, yes!" Tildi said fervently, already feeling the blessed embrace of hot, soapy water. "I mean, that I would."

"I'll make sure the boiler's full, then," the girl said. "Nice hot water." She sashayed around Tildi, sweeping the tray up to miss her head, and vanished into the back room.

The innkeeper grinned down at Tildi. "There, you see? Now, I'm Wim Cake. Never could find a woman to marry named Ale, so I had to make do the best I could with a Miss Pound. Good enough, eh? What do we call you then, my lad?"

"Ti-Teldo Summerbee," Tildi stammered, aware that the roomful of patrons had turned to look at her. She wished he didn't talk so loudly. She didn't want anyone taking too close a look at her. So far, she had fooled the innkeeper and his barmaid, but what if any of the customers had keener eyes? "I've come all the way from the waterfall today. I'm on my way to Overhill to become an apprentice. I have my papers right here." She patted the side of her pack with a nervous hand. *Why am I talking so much?* she thought desperately, and bit the tip of her tongue between her teeth.

"Ah! A grand profession. Well, settle in and have your supper. You'll not find finer food on this road from Tillerton to Overhill!"

"True, true," the patrons said.

"Nor pay so much for it," one tawny-skinned man said, with a humorous look toward his fellows. "He's got a captive market, here. Charges just what he likes."

"What a liar," Wim Cake said, flicking the end of a drying cloth in the man's direction. "We'll not cheat you here, young *gentleman*."

"That's good," Tildi said, and felt she must say something else. "We smallfolk like a fair deal."

"And who doesn't?"

"Now, wait just a moment," said the man at the bar. "It wasn't three months ago that a smallfolk fellow, not that high"—he gestured two and a half feet off the floor—"but with a square chin like a mattock, came here and bargained me for a packet of embroideries not half the size of my hand. You can't say that was fair, now, can you?"

"Did you buy it?"

"Well, the quality was mighty good. . . ."

The other patrons laughed.

"Then stop laying your tongue to slander," Wim Cake said mildly. "He was a good trader, and you accepted the bargain at the time. You only recall now that it's more than you wanted to pay. If he managed to talk you around, then he's smarter than you were. A good fellow, comes through now and again," Wim added, as an aside to Tildi.

Gosto! Tildi thought fondly. It had to be. And that packet could have contained some of her own work, along with that of half the village matrons.

"What'll it be then?"

"A half of your best beer," Tildi ordered, bringing out a silver coin. "And perhaps one for my friend, to show that smallfolks are honest. And one for you, Mr. Cake?"

"Thanks, little one," the man at the bar said, a sheepish expression on his wry face. "Maybe I was hasty talking down your kinsman."

"No offense taken," Tildi assured him.

"Well, thank you, young sir," the innkeeper said, pushing a few bronze coins over for change. "Sit down and enjoy the beer. My wife's brewing is too good to drink standing up."

Tildi started to turn, and found herself wedged between benches, thanks to the bulk of her pack. Wim pointed to the wall, where a few other rucksacks and bags had been stowed beneath the window. She backed carefully away from the bar and shucked off her burden. What a relief it was to be rid of the weight! She felt at least three inches taller.

A couple of humans made room for her between them at the table on the bench facing the counter. She sat down on the base of her spine, sticking out her belly and throwing out her knees like Gosto did when he was making himself comfortable.

Danyn, the barmaid, set down a foaming mug before her with a *clunk*. Tildi thanked her, then regarded the metal cup with dismay. This was a half? It looked like the two-pint pots that the granddads used during outdoor festivals so they wouldn't have to go back to the kegs as often! With both hands she hoisted the cup and took a deep swig. She set it down carefully and wiped the froth off her lips with the back of her hand.

"Ah!" she breathed out gustily, in imitation of Pierin after a long day at work. "Good brew. Couldn't have done better myself."

"Do much brewing yourself?" the barmaid asked curiously. The other patrons glanced at her, too. Tildi quailed internally. Girls must do the brewing in human families, too. She wished she didn't have to pretend she was a boy. It was so easy to make mistakes! She forced a grin to her lips.

"Er, a bit. My mother thou—thinks we should all know how to do all the tasks on the farm. I sew and weave, too. We all do."

"Ah, you're a farmer, are you?" Danyn asked.

"No, I'm a scholar!" Tildi insisted. "I'm going to take up my apprenticeship in Overhill. My eldest brother's the farmer."

"Oh, fine," Danyn said, with an outrageous wink at the other patrons. "Well, then, I should ask for my tip in advance. You scholars are notoriously cheap."

The customers roared with laughter. Red-faced, Tildi felt in her purse and handed over a silver penny. Danyn shook her head over it.

"You're generous. Must be the farmer blood in you. But you'll need your money for books, my dear." She handed it back. "Copper will do for now. If you ever write scholarly books and you make your fortune in gold from a king, come on back and buy us all a round." She reached down and pinched Tildi's cheek.

"Ah, she likes you," said one of the dark-skinned men, who were all sailors from Tillerton.

"She's nice," Tildi said sheepishly, feeling her face burn. The men nudged one another and chuckled.

Humans were kindly, she thought, as she drank her beer. Not at all what she had feared of such gigantic beings, though their regard wasn't without its dangers. The drunken fellow on her right, with a pale belly peeking out between the buttons of his soiled blue tunic, kept slapping her companionably on the back while he talked. His blows were enough to bounce her off the table edge.

The tall, skinny man at the end of the table went on with the story he'd been telling when Tildi had come in.

"And my captain said there must be sea serpents out there," he said, holding out his raw-skinned hands as far as they would stretch. "What else could bite a halibut right in half like that? Dead afore it hit the nets!"

"Did you ask the mermaids?" asked a woman alone at a table in the corner. Tildi glanced at her over the top of her mug. Her long dark hair was unbound, and she had golden skin, but what set her apart from the rest of the company were her ears. Between the silky tresses of hair, pointed tips swept gracefully at a backward angle. She was an elf! Teldo and the others said they had met some in the human kingdoms. She didn't look that much different from humans . . . but there was a quality about her, something elusive that Tildi couldn't put her finger on.

"My captain don't like to talk to them mermaids," the skinny man said, shaking his head. "We after the same catch, you know."

The elf caught Tildi staring at her and fixed large, dark eyes upon her. Tildi blushed and bent her attention to her drink.

"I heard the big fish are like their sheep," Wim Cake said, from behind the bar. "To them, you're rustling!"

The skinny man signaled for a refill. "And what have you got on the stove, eh?"

"Mutton stew, boiled chicken, some ham," Danyn said, coming over to replace the fisherman's empty mug with a full one. "No fish." Skillfully, she avoided his grab at her skirts, and turned to Tildi. "You will be wanting to eat some supper, too, Teldo Summerbee," she said, then clicked her tongue. "And what happened to your shirt, little one? It's all burned on the shoulders. Drying your washing too close to your campfire?"

Tildi glanced down at the black marks. "No, I . . . I was attacked by a creature in the forest, a fire-demon." She took a hasty drink as she realized everyone was looking at her.

"Eh?" asked a bent woman with deeply tanned and wrinkled skin, peering at her with sudden interest. "A fire-demon? What kind of creature is that?"

"Well, it was like a light shaped like a man," Tildi said. "More of a fire than a light, I mean. But it was a bright shape."

"And that's all?" the old woman insisted. "You can't just say something like that and let it rest. How did you meet it, and how did it come to burn you? Tell us all! I want to hear it."

"We, too! Tell us the tale, smallfolk!" the fishermen chimed in. "Is that where you got the mark on your face?"

"Síyah, a tale, a tale!" A fat man with golden skin and long black hair like the elf's seized her around the waist and hoisted her up in the middle of the table. She windmilled her arms to keep from falling over. The man steadied her, and gave her a slap on the back. "There, now everyone can hear you."

"A tale, a tale!" the patrons chanted.

"Er . . ." Tildi hesitated, looking around at the circle of eager faces. She didn't want to make a spectacle of herself, but all these men were demanding she comply. She felt she must obey their wish. "Er, I was hiking in the forest. It's at the eastern border of the Quarters. Where my people live."

"We know that," the old woman said encouragingly. "Some of us have been in the Quarters."

"Have you?" Tildi asked awkwardly, trying to recall if a human woman had ever visited her village. "I . . . uh . . . stopped for a rest. I made a campfire," she began. It would be wise not to mention making the fire spell, so she devised the existence of a flint and steel, and described having a little trouble getting her campfire started. At first she was sorry to disappoint them with such an ordinary narrative, of an outdoor picnic, but they were good listeners, and she could tell they anticipated something exciting. So she clawed back every detail from her memory, making it sound as lively as she could, throwing in every leaf and tree, every twist and turn. When she reached the part where the demon hand had reached through her chest toward the fire, the audience as one gasped and sat back. She showed them the burn on her face, and told how it had come about. With growing delight she realized that she had as good a story as any Gosto had ever told, and it was all hers. It had happened to her, and no one else! By the time she got to the point where she stamped the earth down over the ashes of her campfire and ran away, the audience roared its approval.

The eldest fisherman slammed his mug on the table. "Well told, little one! What an adventure! Danyn, a drink for the smallfolk!"

"Are you certain the *heuren* didn't follow you?" the elf asked. The others turned to look at her.

"Well, she killed it, didn't she?" the old woman asked.

The elf didn't disagree, but her quiet question left Tildi feeling nervous again. She climbed down and wriggled her way into the place beside the stout man.

"A refill, anyone?" Danyn asked with a smile.

"One for me," the wrinkled one said. "And another one for Teldo."

"Aye! Here's to Teldo, the bravest smallfolk we've ever met!" shouted the tawny man at the bar.

"You're a brave one, for certain," Danyn said, placing two more mugs of beer and a steaming bowl of stew down before her. "Well, I'd be proud to mend the shirt of a hero like you. Slip it off and hand it to me."

"No!" Tildi yelped, grabbing the hem with both hands, as if she were afraid that Danyn would strip it off her right there and then.

Danyn's eyebrows went up. "Why not?"

Tildi felt her cheeks burn. "I mean . . . uh, I don't have another. Not until I reach Overhill. I'll make do. But thank you for your offer. Truly." She raised one of the gigantic cups, but she kept one hand on the fabric of her tunic. "Your health!"

The others laughed. Danyn winked at them. "Modest, too, as well as brave." She dropped a kiss on top of Tildi's head. "Tell us some more stories of your homeland. We have a few come and go, but only rarely. Mostly they go to the south and the seaport to trade."

"That's true," Tildi said, feeling a trifle more relaxed. "It's just closer by. What would you like to know?"

A lot, it seemed. The queries flew at her from all sides. The Groaning Table was a busy place, and it had filled up over the course of the evening to near bursting point. Word seemed to have spread that she was there, and everyone wanted to know all about smallfolk. In between bites of the excellent stew, Tildi did her best to answer everything, without giving too much away about her own life. Everyone had a question or two, about the food, the sport, the beer, women, music, and dancing.

"We dance a lot," Tildi admitted, pushing the bowl aside at last and returning to the beer. "During meetings and at festivals, at Year's End and weddings, of course."

"How about singing?" asked the stout man. "Give us a lusty song to drink by. Go on, lad!"

"Yes! Sing! Sing! Sing!" chanted the crowd.

"I . . ." A *lusty* song? Tildi knew some that her brothers liked, but she had never sung them in public.

"Go on, then!" He grasped her by the collar and stood her on the table.

"No, I really shouldn't." She tried to climb off, but the stout man had a firm grip on her shirt. Was she destined to spend the entire evening on the table? "Please, let me sit down."

"Are you refusing, after we showed you such hospitality, runt?" demanded a truculent patron at the end of the board. He had arrived very late, and seemed to have started drinking before he got there.

"No, indeed, I'm not that good a singer," Tildi protested with a calm smile, hoping he would calm down. "You just wouldn't enjoy hearing me."

"Smallfolk snob," sneered the thinnest of the seamen, peering at her with red-veined eyes. He had hardly lifted his nose out of his mug all night, and was far past the stage when Tildi usually took the beer jug away from a potentially disruptive visitor. He sprang up, and a knife appeared in his hand. "Too good to offer cheer to us big folks, eh? Little unnatural runts."

Everyone seemed to be shouting at once, most of them at the fisherman, whose friends immediately leaned over and pushed his arms down. The innkeeper reached under the bar. Tildi assumed he had a stick or a riding crop there; many of the innkeepers in the Quarters had something to get the attention of angry drunks. The cheerful mood in the room turned suddenly menacing. Tildi was afraid. She dropped to her knees to crawl off the table.

Someone pulled her by her arm across the table. Mugs overturned and spilled their contents onto the laps of patrons, who jumped up, swearing at the sudden flood. Tildi found herself face-to-face with a pimply blond man who was screaming unintelligibly at her. His breath smelled of stale beer and onions. Gasping at the stench, Tildi pushed at him, but he was much stronger than she was. Another pair of hands seized her legs and hauled her across the tabletop. The blond man let go, and Tildi curled into a little ball, covering her head with her arms as her body crashed into more dishes. She had been so grateful to get to the inn. She wished she had spent another night in the forest.

Just as abruptly as it had begun, the feeling of fear drained away, to be replaced by a calmness. Tildi felt at peace. She uncurled and peeked out from between her hands. The patrons had stopped shouting, and were slapping one another on the back. That seemed unnatural to Tildi. She glanced around, and saw Wim Cake spreading a cloth over a lumpy object before he put it back underneath the bar. A rune shone through it, one she did not recognize.

Danyn and the boy-of-all-work, who would have looked to Tildi to be ten years old if he hadn't been almost two feet taller than she was, swept in with mop, bucket, cleaning cloths, and a huge pail of sawdust. In no time the tables were cleared, and Wim Cake was pulling another round for the table. Danyn handed her a rag, and she blotted her clothes with it.

"Sorry, small one," the stout man said. "Don't know what I was thinking. My apologies. Danyn, give this little one a fresh drink on me."

"No, don't trouble yourself," Tildi said. "Truly. No more for me."

"But I insist!"

"Well . . ." She hated to refuse a gift from a human man, for fear of offending him.

"He doesn't have to have any more beer if he doesn't want it, Paldrew," the publican said, thumping on the bar to get their attention. Tildi pulled herself erect and tried to look alert, but the beer and exhaustion were taking their toll on her. Mr. Cake appeared to be surrounded by a haze. "Well, *young man*, you've had plenty of adventure for one day, haven't you? Perhaps you'd like to get some rest? We have no empty room your size, and I'm not going to put you in a room with us big folks. You'd get walked on when these drunken louts stumble up to bed. But we have my daughter's bed from when she was little. The potboy will put it in the corner room for you. I'd hate to have someone roll over on you in the night, so you can have it to yourself."

"Many thanks," Tildi said with relief. "It sounds perfect to me, but I'd also be longing for a bath. And a chance to wash my clothes." She held out the sleeves of her sodden tunic.

One of the publican's red eyebrows rose on the creased forehead. "Aye? Well, the bathing room's generally empty *from half-past eleven until just before midnight*, if you want a soak before you go to bed. If you've been on the road a few days that'd be a treat."

"Indeed it would," Tildi said fervently.

"Aye," the barmaid said. "Then you'll have one, if that is what you wish. I'll make sure the boiler's full. Half-past eleven, mind. That's when the room will be empty. Am I not right, fellows?" Danyn asked pointedly. "No one is ever in there then." Tildi glanced at her fellow patrons.

"Aye," they chorused.

The drinkers could hardly look at her. *They must simply not be comfortable around smallfolk*, she thought. *Or bathing.* But she could hardly think of anything else but scrubbing the road dust and the sudden deluge of beer off her skin.

"Well, then, it still lacks a half hour 'til then. How about having a song?" the man at the bar said, nodding at the big clock. "We'll all sing, so no one can hear a false note, eh? Do you know 'The Sailor and the Dolphin Lass,' smallfolk?"

Tildi did. It was a slightly ribald tune about a lonely fisherman who sees a smooth-skinned form floating in the water and decides it's his own true love. After some determined and cleverly phrased wooing, the dolphin accepts him as a suitor. The Tillerton men produced from their dirty rucksacks a squeeze-box and a metal flute. The eldest started the beat off with a one-two-three tap on the table, and his companions began to play the lively air. The rest of the room joined in.

> *Oh, I have been on rolling seas forever and a day,*
> *And I would seek a lusty lass to join me at my play,*
> *The kind of girl who's not afraid to sit upon my knee,*
> *With whom a lonely sailor lad won't miss the rocking sea!*

It was an immodest song, but Tildi didn't want to be the only one sitting silent. *Teldo would sing,* she told herself firmly. She couldn't manage the humans' range, but joined in an octave above their voices. By the time they got to the verse about the wedding, with humans on one side and the dolphin's family on the other, Tildi was laughing with her fellow patrons.

"That's a fine voice you've got there," the fat man said. "High and pure, like a girl's."

"I'm no girl!" Tildi protested, alarmed.

"Ah, of course you're not. That's just how your kind sounds, ain't it? Thin little pipes. No offense, *young man.*" He shared a grin with his fellows. "One day you'll grow a beard, and your voice will change. No hurry, is there?"

"Right," Tildi said with mock seriousness. She slapped the table in emphasis. "My voice will change the very day I grow a beard. Count on it!"

That suddenly struck her as inordinately funny. It'd be true that if she could grow a beard her voice would drop, and one was just as likely to happen as the other. She laughed heartily at her own witticism, and her new friends joined in. The first pot of beer was empty, so she began on one of the remaining two, oops, three!

"Good beer, this," she said, after a deep draught. "Herbs in it, give it a spicy flavor. Must ask the brewer what she uses."

"Aye, she'll tell you with pleasure," Wim Cake said. "My wife is always glad to talk about her work."

"Have another on me, smallfolk," the old woman said. "You're a nice little creature."

"Thank you," Tildi said, beaming at her. She waved the mug, which slopped a little. She wiped up the spilled beer with her sleeve. "You are all very nice, too." They cheered her. She toasted them all.

She decided that big folk were rough but friendly. She never did get a chance to meet many in the Quarters, except during meetings. When her brothers took produce or handwork down to the port city to sell, they never took women with them, and when human peddlers came through, she and the other women stayed away from the hard bargaining. Gosto would bring her cloth, needles, and other goods to have a look, far from the summing eye of the visitor. She'd send beer and cakes out with a brother if the dealing went well. Often she had just a glimpse of the human travelers through the shutters. To be among so many made her feel as if she had gone back to her childhood again, when everyone towered over her. Still, they offered her drinks and larded their language with salty expressions, not the way they would treat a child in company. She hoped no one had noticed how much she was blushing at the rude jokes. On the other hand, she knew she was getting rather tipsy. She wondered how she could ask the genial Mr. Cake to give her a milder brew.

"One more song!" the fishermen called.

Tildi suddenly felt cold. Eyes were boring into her from some quarter. She glanced idly around at her new acquaintances. The elf was staring at her. Those deep-set, dark eyes were peering into her very soul. In spite of all the beer she had drunk Tildi was as sober as a cat now.

"I . . . my voice is worn-out, good folks. Thank you for a fine evening. I think I'll go up for my bath now."

She climbed down from the tabletop and went to retrieve her pack from the pile near the window. Danyn gave her a grin and waited before she was halfway up the stairs before calling out, "Give me a shout if you need me to wash your back now!"

The men in the bar laughed heartily. Tildi breathed a sigh of relief. It meant that her disguise had fooled them all. She bolted the door on the bathing chamber. The boiler was, as promised, full. The bath was enormous and furnished with huge white linen towels and a round cake of soap that smelled equally of lanolin and lavender. Tildi slid into the steaming water and had a good long soak, thankful to get all the dust of travel out of her hair. It was much easier to deal with her locks cut short. No wonder men rarely grew their hair out. Since she had experienced the novelty, it was difficult to think of going back to long tresses that either had to be plaited or tangled, tore out when combed, and got in the way of every task she undertook, not to mention as a lure to every kitten ever to sit in her lap. She rinsed and wrung out her beer-soaked garments, then, wrapped in her cloak for a dressing gown, she found the lumber room, its door standing hospitably ajar, with a candle burning inside.

A bed just the right size, spread with a light quilt, had been set up among the stacks of unused chairs and tables. Tildi spread her washing on the protruding legs. At the top of the house it was much warmer than below. Most likely everything would be dry by morning. She surveyed her accommodations. The single candlestick sat on an upturned pail beside the bed's pillow. There was also a bowl and pitcher set before a small looking glass on a box near the wall. *Almost as good as home,* Tildi thought sleepily. The Groaning Table was as good at hosting guests as she would have been herself. Humans were kindly, and not as stupid as smallfolk traders made them out to be.

She sorted through her pack for a fresh chemise to use as a night-gown, and her soap and comb to have them ready for the morning. But they were not where she expected to find them. She blinked at the packet of Teldo's papers and books, which were stuffed down among the personal items. Surely she hadn't left them in that place, where they might get daubed with soap or insect repellent. She realized with a shock that her pack had been searched. Who could have done it? *When* was no problem: the bag had been out of her sight against the wall all evening long. But who? And why? Nothing was missing. Her bag of money contained exactly the number of coins she had had when she left home. What were they looking for?

Perhaps the searcher was waiting until she was asleep to rob her. There was no lock on this side of the door. With some difficulty, Tildi hoisted a heavy, human-sized wooden chair and hung it on the iron latch to prevent it being lifted. It wasn't much of a protection, since it could be shaken loose with a couple of sound kicks to the door, but it gave her a feeling of security.

She lay down and watched the candle make shadows on the ceiling. As tired as she was, the questions nagged at her mind. The bed was comfortable, she was clean and nearly dry, but she couldn't relax. She was safe, wasn't she? Wim Cake and his employees would come running if she screamed for help, she was sure of it.

Her practical nature demanded that if she wasn't going to sleep, she might as well do something useful, such as mend her clothing. She pulled off the maligned shirt and in the light of the single candle looked at the black rips in the shoulders, even more bedraggled from the constant rubbing of the pack over the last day and a half's walking. What a ruin of good fabric! She could make the torn places look like pleats, but those would be uncomfortable under the rucksack's straps. Better to fold them over and stitch them flat, no matter what it ended up looking like. She caught a glimpse of her pale reflection in the little glass and snatched the discarded shirt up to the breast of her camisole.

Then, interested, she took a closer look at herself. Her dampened hair was settling into soft curls, making her look more like Teldo than ever before. How she missed him! Could it only be a few days since the thraiks had carried him and the others away?

While she sewed, she recounted the evening to herself. She thought of the avid looks on the faces of the humans in the room, enjoying her storytelling and her singing. Suddenly, she was filled with shame. The beer, much stronger than what she normally drank at home, had made her uninhibited, and she had forgotten herself, performing in public like a clown. No smallfolk woman should ever have put herself on show like that in mixed company! What if word got back to the Quarters? She'd never be able to show her face in decent company again!

Ah, well, she thought, tying off the thread and biting it off between her teeth, *they weren't going to want to bother with a girl who had run away to be a wizard anyhow.* She would just make sure not to push herself into the spotlight again like that. But it *had* been fun. She understood why Gosto loved telling his stories. There was an . . . energy in it. It felt almost as good as making spells. When they worked, that was.

A thread of moonlight peeped in through the shutters, and Tildi reminded herself it wasn't that many hours until dawn. She could still hear voices down in the bar, including one upraised in off-tune song, and some loud splashing and swearing that told her the bathing room was again in use, now that it was past midnight. She wasn't alone. The people below were her friends, now, most of them. She would just have to accept that whoever went through her belongings would remain a mystery.

She dreamed that the thraik were searching everywhere for her, and they had paid a sheep to search her pack for her brothers. Across the face of the moon was a rune, the same one she had seen in the lord thraik's eye.

Chapter Eight

ildi all but crept down to the main room the next morning before sunrise. Most of the other guests were snoring heartily in their rooms, but she was wide-awake.

"I'm sorry for the spectacle I made of myself last night," she said to Danyn, while the serving maid dished up a plate of eggs and sausage for her.

"What?" Danyn exclaimed, leaning back with hands on hips. "Why, you were fine! It's not every guest that can come in here with a fresh story that no one has heard before. Except for that elf, of course. She never acts surprised at nothing. 'Course, she might be a thousand years old. No one can tell with elves. They could be the same age as your grandmother, or older than the mountains. Did someone say something to you?"

"Er, no. I just hope I didn't give offense."

Danyn grinned, her widely spaced white teeth brilliant. "You are the most inoffensive thing to come through here ever, I might just say. You're going to need to grow a little gumption if you're going to stick up for yourself with your fellow students, is what I think."

"Oh." Tildi had never considered whether Olen might have more apprentices than herself.

"Would you like me to fix you some provisions?" Danyn asked. "It's two days on foot to the next inn, maybe three for someone your size." Tildi nodded eagerly, and Danyn moved over to the bar, where she filled a bottle with beer and smacked a cork into the neck. "Three more beyond that to Overhill, but you won't have to worry once you reach the Eagle, just over the border into Melenatae. It's a busy road, and there're guest houses and inns in plenty past the province marker and on near where the road forks for the city. Now, it's the left fork, remember. The right will take you into Rabantae, and you're not going that way. It's well marked. You can't miss it."

"I'm grateful," Tildi said. "I couldn't have asked for better directions."

"Ah, well," Danyn said with a grin, handing her the bottle and a wrapped packet. "I meet a lot of first-time travelers, and they never know what it is they *should* ask. The experienced ones can always tell me they know already. Good journeying to you, Teldo Summerbee. Whatever it is that you're going to—or going away from—I hope you accomplish what it is you wish." Tildi felt for her belt purse, but Danyn shook her head and held up the coins Tildi had given her the night before. "Keep that generous heart of yours beating now."

"My thanks," Tildi said, touched by the girl's solicitousness. She stowed the food away and shouldered the pack resolutely.

"Come back to us when you become a famous scholar," Danyn called to her.

Fortified with a good breakfast and fresh linen, she felt prepared for what might be a five-days' hike. Tildi marched out into the thin light of dawn, touching the lintel for thanks as she departed.

She was reluctant to leave the relative safety of the Rushet inn. More than the night before, the sky seemed infinitely open and empty. If the thraik in her dreams was to return, she was vulnerable. Still, now she knew the measure of time it would take her to reach her destination. Five days was bearable.

Other folk had roused and were preparing to depart for the north at the same time as she.

Few of the guests were preparing to depart then. The three fisher-men had gone to bed with a wineskin apiece to keep them going through the long hours until dawn, and Danyn had had no idea when she would see them surface. The fat man, a carter, had declared the night before that he was staying on until after lunch. No hurry, he had said, as his load of copper ingots wasn't likely to rot, and he prefered to travel in the day and avoid thieves. The old woman was waiting at the Groaning Table for her son-in-law to come over on the ferry from the other side of the Arown.

Tildi started off alone; others caught up to her, but with their long legs they soon outdistanced her. The last of her fellow patrons gave her an apologetic glance over his shoulder and a wave as he loped out of sight. Tildi, burdened with her pack and much shorter legs, shook her head and bent to covering ground. No matter; she would have plenty of company at the next coaching inn, and her magic studies to occupy her mind when she reached Olen's home. If the road stayed this empty, she might even get in a spot of magic practice.

"May I walk with you?" A voice startled her out of her reverie. She glanced up into the honey-colored eyes of the elf. "I am Irithe."

"Yes, of course," Tildi said, surprised but pleased. "Glad to meet you."

"Are you sure? You are new on the road. You ought to know that you can't trust every fellow rambler just because they seem to be going in the same direction as you are."

"I . . ." That was unanswerable. Tildi had been inclined to trust Irithe just because she *was* an elf. But what would one of the woodkin want of her? "I'm sure you're right."

"But you wish to stay by me anyhow."

"I've run into thraiks and—what did you call them?—*heurens*," Tildi said. "I'd say they were a common enemy of anyone who traveled these roads."

"So you think of the common defense against more powerful ene-mies," the elf said. "Curious. But not everyone will have your altruistic outlook. I just give you my advice, for what it is worth. I've lived a long time not trusting too readily."

"Thank you," Tildi said thoughtfully. "I wonder why you want to give me such a warning, when I am a stranger, and, as you say, you have your own outlook."

"Because you have secrets," Irithe said. She smiled. "You are ill-equipped to protect them unless you protect yourself."

"Secrets!" Tildi exclaimed. "I have no secrets!" It was an impulsive outburst, and even as she made it she knew how feeble it must sound. She did have secrets. She did not dare to ask her new companion which ones she had discovered.

"How about the apprenticeship to which you are making your way?" the elf asked, keeping her long stride slow so Tildi could stay level with her. "I noticed how careful you were never to tell anyone you were going to study with a wizard."

"How . . . ?"

The elf regarded her with large, solemn eyes. "You reacted to Wim Cake's peacemaking spell, not by calming down, but by looking around for the source. That's not the reaction either he or I would have expected of those like you. He's not a magician, as you must have surmised. He only knows that uncovering the amber stone stops brawls. Fortunately, those were simple folks with us in the inn, and none of them paid attention. Because you have faced thraiks and *heurens*, do not underestimate the danger posed by people who are frightened."

"With so much magic in the world, why would people be frightened of it?" Tildi asked seriously.

Irithe smiled again. "Because they do not see it, and if they did they wouldn't embrace it. Keep that in mind, too. You must have been very sheltered where you grew up not to know that."

"I did know it," Tildi said softly. So humans were very much the same as smallfolk after all. If that was the case, then she must never let anyone know she was a girl.

"Don't let anyone ask too much of you. You're inclined to give freely, but it might not always be the right choice. I noticed that when you offered Danyn silver. Err on the side of caution. The askers will expect a prudent response, and you won't be giving offense. Remember, some secrets are worth keeping, even at the cost of your life, and others are not. You will learn to tell the difference, if you live so long. Truth is the best path, but there are many kinds of truth. That, too, you will learn."

"I'm grateful for the reassurance," Tildi said, though she was troubled by some of the elf's words. She would have a lot to think about later.

"Good. Then let us enjoy the fine weather."

They walked together for two days. Tildi asked Irithe questions, which the elf might or might not answer. She just looked at Tildi when she asked about the animal that ran by them one afternoon that looked like a deer but whose head was larger in proportion than seemed normal. The elf frequently outpaced her on her long legs, leaving Tildi alone with her own thoughts, but made conversation with many humans they met along the busy river road, when they stopped to buy or trade for food or a place to sleep. Tildi had never met anyone like her.

On the morning of the third day, they passed a milepost that said IVIRENN on the near side and MELENATAE on the other.

"What is Ivirenn?" she asked Irithe.

"That is the human name for your homeland and the provinces around it. Humans have a great penchant for naming places and things that do not belong to them." The thin lips tightened in an expression as close to a smile as she ever wore. "I leave you here, meadow child. Good fortune go with you."

"And with you," Tildi said. "Thank you."

Irithe nodded. She walked up the slope and into the trees at the left side of the road. The branches rustled around her, and Tildi lost sight of her at once. Their mother had said the elf folk were one with the trees. They could hide among them like branches, and never be seen unless they wished to be.

Well, that was a wonderful experience she never would have had if she had remained in the Quarters, or Ivirenn, as she must now think of it, being a woman of the world. She settled her pack on her back and began walking toward the white haze hanging in the air. From the border it was at least two days' walk to Overhill. How vast must the city be if the smoke from its chimneys could be seen that far away!

Many more wayfarers had joined the road. Humans taking their rest on the wayside hailed her with a friendly shout.

"Good day for walking, friend!"

Joining in the spirit, she shouted back.

"A fine day!"

"Going far, little master?"

"To Overhill. Where are you bound?"

"To Tillerton! You've just missed the spring wine festival! Pity you weren't two days earlier! Do you want a drink?" Several of them held out bottles.

"Thanks, but no. Farewell!"

"And to you, little master!"

Tildi waved and walked on. She had never known any society but the one in which she had grown up, so she was surprised to discover a kind of fellowship among those who traveled from one place to another. People met and chatted as if they were neighbors, offering news from the places where they had been, gossiping about common acquaintances, the weather, the latest outrages, though it was hard to tell until she listened closely if they were over serious matters or not.

The world was full of celebrations she had never heard of, kinds of people she had never seen, animals as big as houses. Everywhere lay fresh wonders. And more magic than she had ever dreamed: the mystic runes that existed only on paper in her homeland seemed to be everywhere now. In fact, they were so commonplace that no one ever commented upon them. No one, that was, save for Irithe.

Travelers on this big main road all troubled to acknowledge their fellow wayfarers, whether by a solemn nod or a friendly hail. Tildi had seen no other smallfolk thus far, so she continued to be an object of curiosity among those who passed her coming or going. A wagonload of passengers bound for Rushet warned her of a blind patch a few miles ahead where the road turned sharply to avoid an ancient oak tree. The place was a notorious hideout for brigands who jumped out at lone travelers.

"Especially one your size," they assured her.

"Brigands?" Tildi asked, alarmed.

"Get in with a big group," advised a woman, peeling an apple with a small knife and feeding the slices off the blade to a man lying with his head in her lap. "Safety in numbers. There's strange things abroad, you know."

*B*y the time she got to the dangerous stand of woods, the brigands were not in a mood to attack smallfolk or anyone else. Six rough-looking humans were among a crowd pointing and gawking at a stinking, black hulk that lay among smashed trees.

"It fell down here several hours back," a short, freckle-faced man confided to Tildi as she came up to get a look. "No one knows what it is—or was. Horrible, isn't it?"

Tildi shed her pack and scrambled up onto the seat of a nearby wagon and peered down at the mass of rotting flesh, from which the crowd was keeping a healthy distance. "It's a thraik," she said in amazement.

"How would a pip-squeak from the country know that?" asked one of the men she presumed to be a brigand temporarily reformed by fear, lifting an unshaven face to hers.

"Because they attack my country," Tildi shot back, surprised at her own boldness. "I've seen them. I've *fought* them."

"Aah," the man said, waving a hand disbelievingly.

"What happened to it?" asked a woman.

"It just came flopping down on us," the unshaven man said. "Landed flat on Harn, there." One of the men sat on the side of the road, looking dazed. He was covered with black blood, and some of his own. "He's out of his wits. Been that way since it happened. We had to move it off him. It was greasy. It . . . fell apart when we touched it." Tildi realized that the thraik seemed to have been split in two pieces. Her heart almost stopped in her body. What could possibly have done that to a *thraik?*

"It had to have been killed before it fell out of the air then," another traveler said reasonably. "But how?"

"How indeed?" echoed Tildi's confidant. He turned to her. "What a monster! I never thought to see one, alive or dead. You always hear of them flying around, but I've always been lucky enough not to be near when they do. Are you going far, smallfolk?"

"To Overhill."

The man looked pleased.

"Why, I'm going up the Arown toward Rabantae. I can go as far as the confluence of the rivers. I'd be glad if you'd like to ride with me. I want to hear more about these beasts from one who's seen them up close. My cart's this way. Will you come?"

Tildi nodded.

The freckled man waited until she had jumped down and retrieved her pack. They left the gathering crowd staring at the dead thraik. Tildi kept looking back in its direction until the road had wound, concealing the scene from sight. It could not rise up from the ground and come after her, not cut in two pieces like that. What beast or power could possibly destroy a foe that took almost everyone in the village to stave off?

Benrum Pattersley, for that was her host's name, was driving a load of chickens in wicker cages from a nearby farmstead to a city in Rabantae. The cart had little room for anyone but himself. Even the seat held six cages roped together. He made a little space for her behind him.

"You can talk to me, then take a rest, if you want one. And if you would like an egg or two, no trouble. Just see to it that my chickens come to no harm, eh? Sometimes boys like to poke sticks at them from the roadside, or try and pull their feathers. I don't hold with that kind of mistreatment. Now, tell me all about these thraiks. . . ."

Benrum was a good listener, who seemed to know just how and when to ask a question, and the trip went swiftly. She was grateful that he asked nothing about her personal life, preferring the sensational tales she had heard about the black-winged monsters. He liked to talk himself, and Tildi found him to be an engaging companion.

The big-boned mare hauled its squawking burden slowly up a long slope of the busy road until they came to a fork, where the road divided at sharp angles to the northeast and northwest.

"Down that road is Overhill," Benrum said, nodding toward the right-hand road. He gave her a hand down with her pack. "It's been a pleasure, Teldo Summerbee. I wish you well."

Tildi stretched up her small hand to clasp the poultry man's big, rough fingers. "The same to you, Benrum Pattersley. Good trading."

The freckled man tipped her a casual salute and flicked the reins. The draft horse shuffled into a lazy walk. Tildi brushed off chicken feathers and went in search of her new master.

Chapter Nine

he town was built on both sides of a branch of the river, here a wide, placid blue stream upon which boats of every size plied their way up and down. The river valley lifted at its edges like a pair of huge hands cupping the town, out of which the river spilled northeast to southwest. At piers in the center of the metropolis, cargo was being unloaded from three-masted boats with their sails furled tight. Tradesmen hoisted bundles into wheelbarrows and wagons. Outward from the busy port area she counted roofs and treetops and the rainbow of many gardens, some square and some in irregular shapes. She hoped her duties would allow her to explore the city. She had never seen so many colors of leaf, nor of roof tile. Roses as big as her head lolled over garden gates. She could have made a bathtub out of the dock leaves that clustered at the base of the enormous trees.

Everything was so huge, she was overwhelmed by it. She walked around gawking at it all. Most of the buildings were made of stone, not wood or plastered brick like they were in the Quarters. They ought to have blotted out the sky, they were so big, but as she lifted her eyes toward the rest of the town it seemed to fall into proportion.

The townsfolk didn't seem surprised or upset to have a smallfolk in their midst, but she found it daunting. *Heavens, it's like being a child again,* she thought, as she dodged a huge terrier who came up to her waist. A cat nearly half her size wriggled, *pounced,* and came up with a struggling rat as long as her arm. A nearby man with a red, pockmarked face praised the cat, and gave Tildi a crinkled grin.

"How may I help you, small stranger?" he asked.

"I'm looking for . . ." She paused. Wizards might be better respected in human circles than they were in the Quarters, or at least she hoped so. Otherwise, the kindly man's smile might turn to a scowl. She'd have to risk it. She was hopelessly lost. Even the street signs were far above her head. "I seek a wizard named Olen. Have you . . . ever heard of him?"

The grin grew wider. "You're having me, right?"

Tildi shook her head.

"O' course I've heard of Olen. Been here since before the city. You could say it grew up around him." His own words seemed to strike him as funny, and he shook with laughter. "Mmmph, mmmph, ever heard of Olen! Ah, little one, I haven't had the finest day, but you've improved it for me a mile!"

Tildi gave him a quelling glance, the one she used on Marco when he raided the sweets before supper.

"Ah, yes, of course. And you want to find him, do you, er, boy?" the man asked.

"I do."

"Good, then, good." He put a big rough hand on her shoulder and steered her to the downhill side of the road, which had a waist-high, whitewashed wall to prevent accidents. She could just get her chin over the top edge. "Go down to that tree, the pale gray one down there. You'll find him."

Tildi peered out at the mosaic of treetops below, until she picked out a round spot that as a courtesy she could call pale gray when compared with the green or yellow-gold of the surrounding foliage.

"He lives near that tree?" Tildi asked. That set the man off again. He tried to speak, but his face kept convulsing in merry chuckles. Shaking her head, Tildi shouldered her pack and trudged down the road to the next gate leading downward. Teldo would probably have gotten the human's joke.

Ah, but then she had it! The letters she carried had the return address of "Silvertree." That must be the name of Olen's great house, named for the tree in his garden. It lay about two-thirds of the way down this side of the city.

She turned down the next flight of stairs, only to find they were too high for her to descend them while carrying a pack. Grudgingly she returned to the cobblestoned road that spiraled downward through the several levels of the city. It was by far the longer way to descend, but at least the slope was one she could manage.

"At this rate I'll need to check into an inn halfway down," she said ruefully.

Each turn took some time to negotiate. Tildi began to feel accustomed to the scale of human habitations, and almost at home with the people themselves, for all they were as tall as trees. They lived just like smallfolk, going between their shops and houses with their burdens and their gossip. Tildi listened frankly as people chatted or argued loudly over the noise that filled the endless street. A crowd of gigantic children ran out of what had to be the local school as a tower bell tolled out the noon hour. In the Quarters, smallfolk children would be finished with their lessons for the day so they could help with the vital fieldwork. Here, perhaps, they went to assist fathers and masters in stores and workshops while the girls went to assist their mothers at home.

She found it curious that, except for a few who wore hats to protect them from the hot noon sun, most of the women and girls went bareheaded. Their hair floated loose or was tied up in nets, buns, or plaits. Their dresses, too, seemed just to cling to their shoulders, leaving necks and the top curve of bosoms bare. It was clear from the way that the men treated them that this was considered respectable dress. She found herself blushing on their behalf. Her red cheeks earned an indulgent chuckle from the women she passed, who thought she was a callow stripling seeing the big world for the first time.

When a gap overlooking the river valley presented itself, Tildi peered down the hill to make sure she had not gone off track in her search for the silver tree. She was pleased to see it was directly below her current of vantage point. It loomed up so large that it could not be far now. Narrow lanes bordered it front and back. If she missed the one path, she should easily be able to locate the other.

As she descended, the bright green blobs of foliage divided into individual tree crowns, but the silver globe never did. In fact, it seemed to be larger than ever. Tildi realized that she had not properly taken in the scale of it, when on one of those tiny paths that ran near it, she saw a wagon drawn by four draft horses disappear underneath the lip of the circle, like an ant running under a leaf. Silvertree must be one immense single tree, bigger than any in the Quarters or possibly any other in the world.

A sound like an intake of breath made her jump and turn around. This stretch of road was the site of a public fountain, with water trickling out of pitchers held by white stone statues of slender young women barely draped to save modesty, and a public garden, the gate of which was well overhung with thick, dark-green leaves. Someone was watching her! The humans walking up or down the street seemed unconcerned beyond mild curiosity regarding the smallfolk in their midst, but Tildi had the uncomfortable feeling of eyes on her back. It couldn't be a thraik. Their arrival was never subtle. Harshly, she quashed, at least for the moment, her fears of being swept up into the air and torn to pieces. Was it a more ordinary peril? A cutpurse, or worse? Compared with these humans she was a child, in both size and strength. She started out walking again, and listened carefully. Footsteps paced hers, slowing when she slowed, stopping when she stopped. She began to walk faster, and noted that the sound increased in tempo.

Now that she had become more proficient at creating the magical fire, she felt it would be an effective defense, should her pursuer turn out to be mortal. She thought the words, concentrating upon her left hand. The tiny ball of flame winked into being. She closed her palm around it. It no longer burned her if she willed it not to. The tongues of flame licked out between her fingers as if reluctant to be imprisoned. She would be safe where she went. Once in a while the people making their way along the steep street glanced at her curiously, but no one frowned or looked threatening. After a mile or so she was prepared to put the feeling down to imagination, but she could not explain the echo in her footsteps. She sped up. There was no time to be lost in reaching Olen and safety.

. . .

One more hairpin twist of the roads, and Tildi at last saw the great pale dome of leaves rising above the houses and shops of Overhill. She hurried toward it, ignoring the ache from the tops of her shoulders where her pack rubbed, the holes in her socks that let her feet be eroded by the inside of the heavy shoes, and the stealthy presence always just out of sight behind her. What would the wizard's house be like? Could it be a sprawling mansion, all knobby towers and little gardens like the fine manor three levels above? Would he live in a tiny cottage underneath the grand sweep of leaves? Nothing in his letter even suggested what she was to expect.

When she reached the ornately wrought gate, she let out a breath of astonishment. Silvertree was not the landmark to designate the wizard Olen's home; it *was* the wizard Olen's home.

Silvertree was more than a mere woodland plant. It was nearly the size of a smallfolk town. Its thick, silver-green crown, growing in a dome shape from pale gray branches many feet or even yards thick, covered more than a city block. The trunk itself was more than a dozen times as wide as Tildi's farmhouse, and the cross-section of a branch could conceal her home and barn. This was a marvel, the king of trees, the absolute of trees. It stood within the grounds of a huge park. Other trees clustered about it, looking rather like chicks pecking around the feet of a hen.

Tildi had never seen anything even a tenth as large. The biggest tree in the Quarters wouldn't have made a toothpick beside it. Its roots must have reached all the way down to the center of the world. One would never know when it rained. The leaves were so dense that what light penetrated was tinted the palest greeny gray. It ought to have looked bilious, but Tildi found it as beautiful as a jewel. It was a wonder, beyond the range of Gosto's tales or any bard's imagination. This, she hoped, would be her new home.

Tildi washed away the wizard-fire in a small public fountain that bubbled in the square opposite the gate. People coming and going along the street paid no attention to the glorious tree. They were used to seeing that marvel daily. She hung onto the gate with both hands to study the house, for house it was. The living quarters were sized to the inhabitants, not to the scale of the giant tree itself. Round or oval windows scattered about its surface resembled tiny knotholes, and little balconies were half-moon-shaped bumps on the satiny bark. The front door was a high, pointed arch in between two vast roots that humped up to either side of pale blue stairs. Figures in livery trotted up and down, going about their business.

The grounds had been lavishly planted with beds of flowering plants that were separated by bushes trimmed into lacelike sculptures and joined by bowered arches. Brightly colored blossoms as large as her head nodded on stems edging the wide path. The path itself consisted of the palest blue-gray flagstones, smooth as skin. There were outbuildings around the perimeter of the estate, but they were artfully concealed among shrubbery and behind high hedges. The clang of a blacksmith's hammer and the whicker of horses could be heard, but neither anvil nor animal could Tildi see.

The gate itself was as interesting. More than twelve feet high, the portal looked as though it had been wrought intricately of metal, but she identified it as a kind of stiffened vine or wood. Instead of being carved, it felt as if it had grown, and was still growing. She sighed with awe. This was a marvelous place.

The gate thrummed under her hands. Tildi staggered back as the flowing lines divided in the center and drew back like parting curtains. She gawked at the opening for a moment, then realized that she was being invited in. Hastily, she bobbed a curtsey, the pack making the gesture awkward.

"Thank you," she said, though to whom she had no idea.

*T*he path felt as long as the trek from the edge of the city. As soon as she was past them the gates swung silently shut at her back. Tildi trembled, wondering who was watching her from the tiny windows set in the tree trunk.

When at length she reached the great doors, they swung inward. In between them, like a tree himself, stood a huge man in pale gray livery. Thick, ruddy hair had been forcibly scraped back into a queue, leaving his thick, ruddy face free to glare at her. His nose took up most of his face, and his beady black eyes had to peer around it. Tildi swallowed deeply. He stepped forward to loom over her.

"Arrr?" he said, a cross between a question and a gurgle. "State your business?"

"I..." Tildi tightened her fists out of sheer nervousness, and the parchment crackled in her hand. The noise reminded her she had the right to ask. She straightened her back, and thrust her chin up. "I must see the wizard Olen. I have business with him."

"Do yer?" the man asked. Was that the suggestion of a twinkle in his eye? "State your name."

"T-Teldo Summerbee. I have a letter from him bidding me to come here."

"Do yer?" the man repeated, holding down a broad hand for it. Tildi hesitated. "I'm no' stealing yer correspondence, smallfolk. I work f'r the wizard. M' name's Samek. G'e here."

Very reluctantly, Tildi surrendered Teldo's letter. The large man turned smartly and marched away, leaving the door open. She peered inside, not daring to proceed further without permission. She didn't feel the same magical compulsion against entering that had been around Rushet. It was the sheer awe that the tree castle, for this was no mere house, engendered in her.

In a moment not one, but two equally gigantic men in livery appeared. The top of Tildi's head was level with the hilts of the swords they wore on their hips.

"Please come with us," they said in unison. One of them relieved her of her pack and handed it to the other.

Goggle-eyed, Tildi followed them. Once inside, they gestured for her to precede them. Uncertainly, Tildi ventured along the polished floor. They moved so silently that she had to glance back occasionally to see if they were still there. They nodded for her to go on.

The hallway, as broad as her farmhouse kitchen and about eight times as long, had a gorgeous polished floor that appeared as though it was made of a single piece of wood. Of course, she chided herself. It was cut into the wood of the tree! This elegant entry terminated in a broad, smooth staircase covered with a gorgeous carpet patterned with millions of tiny flowers stitched from every color under the sun. The first tread seemed too high, but the second step was just the right height for her, and so were all the rest. Could they be adjusting themselves to suit her smaller reach? It wouldn't be impossible, in the house of a great wizard. It was a long way up, but she had had several days of hauling a heavy weight up and down slopes. Her cheeks were warm by the time she got to the top landing, but she wasn't breathing hard. The footmen hurried ahead of her to open the white-and-silver paneled doors at the end of the corridor. Feeling like a clod of mud at a wedding, Tildi marched past them.

She found herself in a study filled floor to ceiling with bookcases on every wall. A globe of the world sat in a handsome chestnut-colored stand with models of the sun and both moons hovering around it. She felt a faint twinge of surprise to note that the daystar cast light over the portion of the globe it was near, and the two moons appeared to be playing a stately game of tag around the belt at its center. No wires or threads supported them. Just under the window was a crystal table with spheres of crystal standing upon it, catching the afternoon light. Each transparent orb was a different color. As she watched, the hues deepened or paled. She wondered what they were for.

The noise of a throat being cleared brought her attention to the center of the room. Before her stood a great carved chair whose upholstered back soared up and curled back over on itself like a parchment scroll. Seated in the chair was a lean human male with weathered hands and face, long white hair, and a silky beard that started under high cheekbones and fell down past his waist. Tildi could not even begin to guess his age. He was clad from neck to ankles in a soft silk robe with wide sleeves, almost exactly the same color as Silvertree's bark. His eyes were the most exceptional thing about him, piercing, bright green, with long, black lashes and curling gray eyebrows like storm clouds. He was tall for a human. Even seated he looked down upon Tildi.

"Well, I'm Olen," he said. "What is it you want?"

"I . . ." Tildi's mouth went dry. The wizard held out the letter. She pointed at it, all her assured and practiced phrases deserting her. Words rushed out. "Yes, that's me. I'm here to take up my apprenticeship. As you offered. To learn to be a wizard. Too."

"I see." Olen regarded her owlishly as if she was an interesting specimen of insect. "Didn't know you were a *girl*. I thought Teldo was a boy's name."

Tildi started in alarm. "I'm not a girl, I'm a boy."

The green eyes narrowed. "Nonsense, I know a girl when I see one. I may be old, but I'm not blind. Or . . ." he offered, a bit more gently, "perhaps you were raised not knowing the difference? Children with an inclination toward magic are often backwards in other ways."

Tildi felt her cheeks flame with embarrassment. This must be one of those times to take Irithe's advice to let go of a secret. Above all things she did not want to anger the wizard. "No, sir. I know the difference."

Olen's eyes widened again, and the hint of a smile lifted the silky mustache. "Good. Then let's not have any more argument on that front.

Life's confusing enough, and magic requires precision. You must know that from your reading. Ah ah ah! Who brought that inside?" He glared suddenly. "I do not like that kind of thing here. Silvertree dislikes them."

"What?" Tildi asked, turning around hastily, but she saw nothing.

"Why, this creature," Olen replied. He spread out his fingertips and pointed. Beside Tildi the air began to glow. An outline etched itself in tongues of red flame. She jumped back.

"The *heuren!*" she exclaimed.

"Ah, so you've seen it before, have you?" Olen flicked his hand and the creature rose in the air and revolved slowly before him. "You know its name?"

"Irithe told me. She is an elf. I came part of the way with her, from Rushet."

"Did you? How interesting. They rarely find smallfolk interesting. Nor humans, for that matter. You must be a remarkable young woman. Or she is, having the patience to speak with outsiders. I don't know if I've ever met her. Must check my daybook. Oh, no, I can't have that."

The *heuren* had flared out suddenly, its flames threatening to engulf them both. Fearing another burn Tildi dodged away from it. Olen did not flinch at all. He closed his hand slightly, and it receded to its original size. Tildi watched with fascination. Containing the creature seemed to give Olen no trouble whatsoever. She was determined to learn how to do that.

"They're nasty little things, no soul at all," Olen said. "It's a fragment of a natural consuming force, and as such is attracted to certain kinds of destructive power. How did it come to follow you, of all people?"

"It appeared in the forest above the Arown when I made a fire. By magic. To make tea," she added, as the wizard's thick eyebrows rose.

"A most practical enterprise," he said gravely. "Did you draw wards before you cast your spell? Create a protected space for yourself?"

"Er . . . no. I didn't know I needed to do that." Tildi felt her cheeks burn fiercely. That was a bad answer. It struck her Teldo probably did know to draw wards, and how to do it. "I was just making tea. I poured water on the beast, and it went out. I thought I killed it."

"Ah. It takes a bit more to kill a *heuren*." Olen closed his fingers and the fire-demon winked out like a snuffed candle. "As thus. But you could have avoided it altogether, you know. You must always remember to draw wards. You know the basic spells, I presume?"

"Er . . . they're in my lesson book." It was an equivocation, less believable than asserting she was a boy since it was delivered with no kind of conviction that she had actually read the lessons, but Olen accepted it. Tildi was relieved.

"Of course. In the meanwhile, I will draw wards. Watch me."

Olen raised one of his long hands and pointed toward the wall of the window. *"Crotegh mai ni eng."* The pale sunlight seemed to dim slightly. He repeated the gesture toward each of the walls of the room, the chant varying slightly with every direction. Tildi promptly forgot the words, and hoped that Olen would not be angry if she asked him to repeat them later. The runes were very like the ones she had seen in the gates of Rushet, and in Master Wim Cake's peacemaking charm. No wonder the *heuren* had not dared follow her there.

"Very well, that will shield us from most magical invasion," the wizard said, nodding to her. "Show me this fire."

Tildi had never been more nervous in her life, nor had anything hung upon her performance as at this moment. She had danced and sung before people, she had demonstrated embroidery, weaving, metalwork, cooking, all without embarrassment or fear of failure, but making magic had so long been a private thing between her and Teldo that it was difficult to open the circle to one more person, and that person held the key to her future. This should have been Teldo's apprenticeship. He should be the one standing in Olen's study, performing with much more confidence than she felt. She was there under false pretenses. Yet, if the thraik had not come, she would have been content to stay at home with her other brothers, and wished Teldo all the success in the world. Still, from beyond, he had given her one last gift, an opportunity. That she must work to make it come true on her own.

This is for Teldo, she thought. Boldly, she held out her hand, palm up. Olen watched her from under his curling eyebrows. Tildi felt panic in the pit of her stomach. What if the magic wouldn't come? Her fears were only that, fears. *Ano chnetegh tal!* As she thought the ancient words, the green flame flared up in the middle of her palm. She was pleased to see that it was larger and brighter than her earlier efforts. All that practice had done her some good. She looked up at Olen. He looked pleased.

"I see. Very curious that it is green. Say aloud to me the words that you used."

Carefully, Tildi recited the spell. Olen nodded. "Again, please. I want to listen." He closed his eyes and put his chin in his hand, stroking his mustache thoughtfully with thumb and forefinger. He had her repeat the phrase again and again. Every time she said it the flame grew larger than her palm and threatened to pour off it like a handful of pancake batter. She tried to catch it in her other hand, but to her non-spell flesh it was just as hot as real fire.

"Master Olen," Tildi began, as a gout of it dripped down between her fingers, lambent honey about to drip to the floor.

"Say it again," the wizard said, waving his fingers. "There is something in your pronunciation. I wonder if it's the product of how you were taught to speak, or just the shape of your palate. It should not be coming out green."

The blob of flame dipped down, stretched into a filament. Any moment it would let go.

"Master Olen!"

Olen opened his eyes at last. "Oh, look at that," he said. "Tal cretegh!"

The flames went out just before they reached the rug. Tildi let out a sigh of relief.

"A most interesting phenomenon, and one that I will look forward to studying with you, Teldo."

Tildi flinched. She could not see herself going through the next several years being called by the name of her dead brother. She held up a finger. The green eyes fixed upon her.

"Well?"

"Um, it's Tildi, not Teldo."

"Not Teldo?" the wizard echoed, sounding puzzled. "I was sure I could read your language. I thought I was corresponding with a Teldo Summerbee. Ah, these old eyes." Olen peered at the letter of invitation and turned the sigil this way and that to make sure. Tildi knew that the rune was formed correctly, and hoped the wizard couldn't read her mind. Her personal tragedy was something she would keep to herself. "Ah, well, but smallfolk culture is not my primary study. There are a finite number of wizards in the universe, powerful and connected to the infinite, and we have many matters that consume our valuable time."

"I won't take up more time than you are willing to give, sir," Tildi said, alarmed. "I will be grateful for anything you will teach me. I have come so far. I can't go back. Please, sir, I will cook and clean for my place. I know you must be disappointed to discover I am only a girl. . . ."

Olen seemed genuinely taken aback. "No! What a silly idea. Where did you get it?"

"Well, the men in the Quarters do all the important jobs, and wizardry is certainly one of the most important occupations I know of, but I thought, I have . . . some aptitude for magic. Perhaps it is like brewing or gardening, that if I have the talent I can do it. I will do my best for you."

Now Olen was amused.

"I've never heard wizardry compared with gardening; brewing, now there's an apt simile. I shall have to share that with my correspondents. Hm. *I* don't mind a girl as an apprentice, Tildi—Teldo. Your assumption is correct: if you can do magic, then you are meant to do it. Your sex does not matter. The talent is present in so few we must nurture it where and when we can. You have an exceptional natural ability. You were right to come." He held out his long hand. Tildi extended hers, which was swallowed up in the warm, dry clasp. "Very well, I accept the terms of your apprenticeship as offered. Welcome, Tildi. You will not find me a bad master."

Tildi was overwhelmed with joy. "Thank you! Oh, thank you! I will do whatever you wish!"

Olen shook his head. "You will learn to do what is *right*. That is far more important. You will learn to make the distinction. There may come a time when you may contradict me."

"I would never do that, sir," Tildi said nervously. Contradict a master wizard on a subject of magic? It was not at all like telling off one of her brothers when he tracked mud into the house. "But I shall try, sir, I promise!"

"Hmmph, yes. Save your energy for your lessons. Perhaps we will start at once. I presume you can read human runes."

"Yes, sir. A little. A little dwarvish, a little elvish. Not much else."

The eyebrows rose again. They had a life of their own, Tildi decided, like the globe and its revolving spheres. "Hmmph. I thought you were better educated than that, from your letter. Still . . . show me."

He reached around to a small writing table that sat beside the crystals and retrieved a sharpened quill for her.

"Show me the rune for *tree*."

Pen poised in the air, Tildi looked around for an inkwell and paper. Olen blew out the corners of his mustache. "No—you must know how to draw the runes without using ink. The line is enough."

Tildi stretched her memory backward. Teldo had taught her lessons in scribing while he was learning it, with the aid of a book he had purchased and the leaf their mother had given them with the runes upon it that glowed. *Tree* was a rune she had seen with many variations since she had set out from the Quarters, but Olen would be satisfied only with the classic. Really, if she thought closely she should be able to recall it. She thought she must be hesitating far too long, but Olen sat patiently, not hurrying her at all.

The root of *tree* was the same from which the rune that opened the sky came from. In the books about the origins of the world it shared characteristics with the underlying reality of . . . reality. In fact, it wasn't that different from the word for *real*. But where to start? She hardly knew which stroke to try. All the words she knew jumbled together in an incomprehensible mass in her mind's eye.

Behind Olen, on the wall, a silvery rune shimmered into existence. It said *tree*, or rather, Silvertree. Was the house deliberately displaying it for her to see now, to jog her memory? The tree must be a thinking being, like a human or smallfolk. Tildi could not take the time to reflect upon that concept, not unless she wanted to tell Olen his own house was helping her cheat on his little test. With a grin she raised the pen and touched it to the air as if writing on a piece of paper suspended there. A silver line followed the point as she drew it down. *Tree* could be written in a single stroke. Tildi bit the end of her tongue as she did her best to follow all the loops and turns that described the roots and leaves, the water it drank, and how it tied the earth to the sky. It felt right as she drew it, and to her delight she knew just where to stop.

Olen's large eyebrows had been drawn down, too, but they began to rise like clouds. "Not too badly done. But that is a specific tree, isn't it? I recognize Silvertree's name there. I want just the essence of the species itself. Reach more deeply into your knowledge and see if you can separate what is specific to Silvertree and what is general about trees."

"I'm not sure if I can. If I could only look in my book—" Tildi started toward her bag.

"Why? It's a simple word. You've seen it in storybooks. You went to school, you said so in your letters. Drag it up from your memory, by force, if necessary." The look of mild amusement in the green eyes took some of the sting out of the sharp direction. "Don't be afraid of me, girl. I'm the safest thing you will face in your career as a wizard. If the first lesson scares you, then you have chosen the wrong calling. Go on. Go back to your earliest days and think." Tildi closed her eyes.

She was hesitant about calling up any memories of home, as if they would bring the horrors of her last day to her. It was best to follow Master Olen's instructions, and think forcefully, ignoring that which she did not want to see. In her mind she called up the picture of the slate in the village classroom, and the schoolmaster's hand as he wrote upon it in white pencil. He drew the picture of a tree, then next to it a word. Yes, there it was. Why did she ever think it was hard to recall?

Tildi mimicked the symbol in the air. It looked rather like a very young schoolgirl had drawn it, but it was accurate.

"Now, draw beside it only the details that make Silvertree's different. Only those details, mind you!"

That was much harder. It was like picturing embroidery without the garment inside it, with all the crossed threads that usually remained hidden. When she finished there was a tangle of lines in the air. She blushed to look at them, but Olen seemed pleased.

"That's good, girl. You're teachable."

"Thank you, master," Tildi said, clutching the pen. "I'll do anything I can for you, sir. I am a very good—"

Olen chuckled and interupted, "I appreciate your eagerness, lass. Ah, here you are."

Chapter Ten

len turned and gestured toward the door. A plump woman with silvering brown hair done up in a braided bun on top of her head stood in the doorway. Her complexion was fresh pink and white, she had a pretty, pointed nose above plump, pink lips, and she had the lightest blue eyes Tildi had ever seen.

"This is Tildi Summerbee, my new apprentice," he told the woman. He peered down at Tildi. "Liana is my housekeeper. She will show you to your room, if she would be so good." He looked Tildi up and down again. "Perhaps we will take the legs off the bed for you."

"A pair of steps might be easier, Master Olen," Liana said with gentle patience. "It's a nice bed the way it is."

"Hmm?" Olen gave a dismissive wave. "Whatever you will. I'm not in charge of housekeeping. I have other matters I must attend to for now. Go ahead and see if you like your room."

Tildi put the pen down and hoisted her rucksack, which now felt to her as if it weighed no more than a feather. "I am sure I will, sir. You won't regret it, sir."

Olen was already engrossed in a closely written scroll. "I'm sure I won't."

"Thank you, master!"

Liana laid a large, pink hand on Tildi's shoulder and guided her toward the door. "Come on, child. He's not hearing a word you say. Tildi, is it? That's a pretty name. I'm sure Master Olen told me something different when you first arrived here, but he does not always tell me things clearly so I can understand them."

Tildi didn't say anything, but followed the housekeeper up yet another winding flight to the next level of the gigantic house. Her cheeks were red with shame, realizing that perhaps no one at all had been fooled by her disguise! Why had the people at the Rushet inn not said anything, instead of letting her carry on like a strolling player and making a fool of herself?

Because they were kindly folks, and they let her say what she wanted. Perhaps they thought she was a runaway apprentice looking for a better life. Or any one of a hundred stories she could think of. Could be they were talking about it among themselves at that moment, over a glass of Mistress Cake's excellent beer, trying to guess the fate the little smallfolk girl was running from. They must have been able to sense that beneath the bravado she was frightened to death of traveling alone in a strange land, and saw fit to smooth the way as they could. If she wanted them to think she was a boy, then they felt it was only kind to let her think they believed it. It did no harm. In fact, now that she was getting over the shame, it had made her feel more confident, and let her continue her journey without fear. The favor they had done her was immeasurable in its value. If in the future she could do the folks at the Groaning Table a good turn, she would.

Here we are, Mistress Tildi," Liana said, stepping aside so the smallfolk could step over the nut-brown threshold. "All yours."

It was indeed a nice bed, with a chestnut-colored counterpane, surrounded by pure white gauze curtains, in a beautiful room that would have done credit to the wealthiest family in the Quarters. Tildi forgot about the heavy pack she was carrying as she wandered in the chamber, hardly daring to breathe. The ceiling was a high dome, a rounded triangle in shape. Around the top of the walls, a pattern had been painted of green vines that tumbled down in each corner in a riot of leaves and small, perfect pink roses. The room was alive with the scent of them. Tildi touched one with her hand, and the petals yielded to her fingers, releasing more of their luxurious perfume. They were growing right out of the walls!

The rest of the space was crowded with furniture: a writing desk underneath the high clerestory window, a wardrobe of a rich, dark wood she did not recognize, a couple of chests, a washstand with a looking glass, and a pair of narrow tables flanking the bed. Candlesticks sat on the tables and the writing desk, and a large brass sconce with a crystal chimney loomed over her head near the door.

"It's a bit small to live in," Liana said, "but since you're a smallfolk it must feel big enough to you."

"It's . . . regal," Tildi whispered, trying to find a rich enough word.

The housekeeper laughed. "Well, then we all live like kings and queens here. This is one of the very smallest bedrooms, but it's traditional to keep the apprentice in here. The last one was a lad bigger than the master, and I would swear that his head hit one wall and his boots hit the door." She raised the gold watch to look at it. "It's five o'clock. There is bread, cheese, and some fruit on the tray there on the desk. Have yourself a little snack and a rest. Dinner's at eight. You'll dine with Master Olen."

Tildi looked at the generous tray and back at the housekeeper with puzzlement on her face. "But you didn't know for certain that he would accept me as his student."

Liana smiled down at her. "If Silvertree lets you in, then you'd almost be certain to be accepted. He takes her recommendation. She's a good judge of people."

Tildi stroked the silvery wall. "It's a she, then?"

Liana looked up at the high ceiling. "I suppose not, as we count things, though she bears seeds and fruit, so I think of her as a her. She's got her feelings, you'll come to find. I had a lot of things to accept when I came to work for a wizard. I'm sure your house is full of wonders, as well, you being a student of the infinite arts."

Tildi shook her head. "Not at all, and never anything like this. My home is so different than the way you live. My people don't like magic." *Or girl wizards*, she thought to herself. "Everything I've seen since I left home is different. I like some of it very much, but a lot of it makes me uncomfortable."

"I think that defines Master Olen's household," Liana agreed. "You may never know the meaning of what's going on, but you can't let that haunt your mind a bit. Dinner at eight. You've no clock, but you'll know. Take some time for yourself. Your bathing room is just to the right. You don't have to share with anyone. The tub is big, so take care climbing into it. Take your time. It's a lot to absorb all at once, I know. There's a wardrobe for you. Linens are inside it. Leave your laundry in the covered basket. It will be gathered up with the rest of the household's. If you need anything, ask for it. Welcome, Tildi."

She sent a kindly smile over her shoulder as she departed.

Tildi's meager belongings filled only two shallow drawers at the bottom of the grand wooden wardrobe and two hooks in the cabinet. It was just as well, because she would have needed a ladder to reach the hanging bar. There was room to store a hundred garments. Her clothing, which had seemed respectable enough in the Quarters, seemed ragged and faded in the gorgeous bedchamber. She took out what few items were still clean and unworn, and bundled the rest into the woven basket. Everything in her pack smelled of the road, especially her. She ought to take advantage of her own bathtub before dinner, and put on her best clothes to honor her master. She hoped he would like her.

With the greatest of care, she stowed her books and papers in a small chest clearly intended for that purpose that stood beside the writing desk. Soft light shone through the window above it. Tildi glanced up, bemused. Something had changed in the last few moments. She was sure that the window had been higher off the floor. Now she could look comfortably over the sill into the gardens below.

Tildi patted the soft-colored wall. "You are aware, aren't you? You can change your insides as you please. Thank you. I've met some very fine trees since I left home, but you are the most amazing of them all."

The smooth wood warmed under her touch. Tildi almost imagined that it bulged out slightly to accept her touch like a cat arching its back.

At the bottom of her dusty pack were her brothers' token possessions. Tildi lifted them out and sat on the floor with them in her lap. Tears pricked at her eyes as she turned them over. They were precious to her, almost the only reminders that she had from home, and the only ones she really wanted. Beside them was another small white parcel. Tildi unwrapped it. It was her cap and the braid she had shorn off. Automatically she smoothed out the white linen and started to put it on, to regain a seemly appearance.

No, she thought firmly, setting it aside. She could never go back to the way things were. It felt as if it had been a lifetime since she had left the Quarters, not a mere ten days. So short a time had passed to encompass so many changes. In that time she had been stripped of family, home, name, even gender, and taken on an identity and a dream that were not her own. Should she throw away the cap and braid?

She made as if to drop them in the basket, but hesitated. It was too soon to make such a final choice. Tildi rolled up the cap with the hair inside it and stuffed it into the back of the drawer at the bottom of the wardrobe. Her brothers' possessions she put into the drawer of one of the night tables, to keep those memories near at hand.

A chiming like distant birdsong made Tildi drop her comb on her nightstand in surprise. That must be the dinner bell. She followed the sound out of her room and down the long, curving stairs to the ground floor. Now that daylight had fled, the interior of Silvertree was illuminated by sconces that shed a soft, golden light.

A luxurious, hot bath had done much to soothe her nerves, which felt rubbed almost as skinless as her feet and shoulders. By the time she had returned to the room, others had been at work, ensuring further comforts. A pair of steps had been placed to make it easier for her to climb into the tall bed without a scramble. The night tables had been pushed much closer to it, and a soft rug now covered much of the floor. Other furnishings, including a tilting mirror, had been placed where she could use them. The writing desk had been replaced with one more suited to someone of her height, and her clothes were neatly folded upon a low chair. Lacking a single dress among her hastily assembled travel wardrobe, she was forced to don the neatest shirt and trousers she had, and hoped that they would be suitable for dining with a wizard.

Panting, she fetched up in the grand corridor. There seemed to be dozens of rooms, but she could see no one to ask for directions. As if in answer to her thought, a sconce light flickered at the post of one on her right. Delicious smells wafted through the cracked door. Timidly, Tildi peeked inside. Floods of light gleamed from a dozen hanging lamps off a tablecloth whiter than snow. There must have been a hundred chairs set at the huge table, Tildi noted as she entered. Olen, seated alone at its head, waved her over.

"Sit down, young Tildi," he said. The corners of his long mustache lifted in a smile. Tildi climbed into the chair he indicated to his right. A large pillow had been placed in it to bring her up to the level of the table, but leaving room for her to rest her heels on the seat.

"Where are all the other people?" Tildi asked, nodding at the forest of chairs.

"Elsewhere," Olen said vaguely, with a wave of his fingers. "It will just be the two of us this evening. We will talk a little about your duties and your education."

Mostly he told stories.

Tildi found herself held rapt at Olen's description of dire battles between wizards and unbelievable monsters, coronations of great kings and queens, the birth of phoenixes and the flight of dragons. A stream of servants in pale gray and green slipped in and out of the room silently, offering food from priceless, gold-trimmed dishes, and departing without a word, but Tildi paid little attention to what she ate except to note that all of it tasted wonderful. Gosto could have taken lessons from Olen, and had enormous fun swapping tales over a glass of his excellent wine.

The wizard was an excellent host. He made sure that she had anything she needed, and her glass was never empty throughout the long meal. There must have been magic at work, for though she drank many glasses, she was as awake and aware as if she had had a long, restful night's sleep. Many of his stories were humorous. Tildi laughed at them, and he seemed to share her pleasure, but she sensed a watchfulness in him. That was to be expected, since she was a newcomer, but there was more to the mood than that. When he was not launched upon one of his anecdotes he had a careworn expression that made his face look aged, like a shriveled apple. Something terrible was troubling him. A man with his many responsibilities couldn't help but feel their burden, but this seemed to be a deep-felt problem on his mind all the time. She had seen that look on her father's face the year that drought almost destroyed their crops.

"Master Olen," she began, and blushed when he raised his great eyebrows at her. "You seem preoccupied. May I help in any way?" she asked.

"You will be doing enough," Olen assured her. "But thank you for your consideration. Your empathy does you credit. I am sure your family must be ruing your loss."

She smiled sadly. If only they were.

He flicked his long fingers, and servants seemed to rush from everywhere to clear the table. Tildi started to gather up her own plates, but a large man in a formal coat appeared at her side and gently but firmly took them out of her hands.

"But, I want to help," she said.

"You're an apprentice," Olen said. "Let my servants do their job, and you do yours." He rose. Tildi stood up to climb down from her perch, but a gentle force surrounded her, and before she could do more than gasp her feet were touching the ground. She gaped up at her master. "I'll teach you that in no time, if you study hard. Shall we begin early tomorrow morning?"

"Oh, yes, sir!" Tildi said.

"Good. Good night to you."

Without another word he turned and strode away, robes flapping in his wake. Tildi frowned. In anyone else she would have found his departure to be inexcusably rude behavior, but she could not help recalling the look of deep concern in his eyes. Giving a grateful smile to the servants, she went up to bed.

Chuff!" Tildi smothered a sneeze in her dusting cloth.

"You're not going to let a little dirt get in your way, are you?" Olen asked, a trifle gruffly. He sat on a wooden chest with his hands on his knees and his head bent to avoid the ceiling.

"No, master," Tildi said.

The small, dim room, shaped rather like the inside of a gourd, was full of boxes. Seated on the floor, Tildi pushed aside the rosewood coffer through which she had been searching, and pulled another to her.

"You're the only one in this house who can creep underneath that overhang without banging your head every other minute," Olen explained. "I'm over twice your height. It's best if I sit here out of the way. I'll let you know when you have found what you're looking for."

"I understand." Tildi opened the small, brassbound chest, and found it to hold a single scroll nested in crushed velvet. "Is this it, master?" she asked, holding up a scroll.

He peered through the dancing dust motes, lit up by the single, irregularly shaped window. "No. It ought to have a black ribbon around it."

Tildi shook her head and put it back in its box. Before she closed the chest she dusted the edges and polished the lock plate.

"There is no need to do that," Olen chided her.

The next box, rough-hewn out of timbers but still airtight enough not to let in any dust, contained a mix of bound books and scrolls. Tildi began to sort through them in search of the black ribbon.

"Only the scrolls, mind you," Olen said, tapping his fingers on his knees. "The ancient form of the book. I'm not sure that it's been bettered by these page-turn books. With a scroll you must read it in the direction that it is going, no hustling back and forth and getting things out of order. No. No. No," he added, as Tildi held up one book after another for his inspection. "None of those."

"Have you ever thought of labeling the boxes, master?" Tildi asked.

"Why? To shorten the search? I enjoy the challenge of the journey of discovery. In my hunt for a hidden resource I often come upon treasures that I have forgotten that I have. Such serendipity has frequently stirred me to make an intellectual leap that I would not otherwise have made. Don't you think that is better than thinking like a clerk?"

Tildi didn't remind him that she was the one engaged upon the journey of discovery, not he. She flipped up the lid of a small, time-darkened box.

A sour smell rose from the interior. She leaned back, coughing, with her nose wrinkled. Olen chuckled.

"Ah, yes. The smell of the ages, which means 'here is mildew, and a history.' Is there a book inside?"

"Yes," Tildi said, dashing dust from the surface of the box with her cloth. Oddly, the book's smell was not of mildew or dust, but reminded her of the clear scent that came after lightning. She conveyed the black-bound scroll to Olen, whose green eyes lit avidly.

"Come, sit by me." He shifted to make room and helped her up to sit beside him on the sea chest. He unrolled the book so she could see the first pages. He patted the open scroll. "This is the first book that I ever came into possession of that explains the runes of power without going off into recriminations or storytelling. I have admiration for this unknown teacher, for teacher she must have been. And an artist as well.

"You know the basic runes we use for writing. Writing is an ancient art that describes the physical world around us in a few lines. But it is more than that. You use the simplified runes to express what you see, but in its purest form, the rune is the object. The two are connected. If you have the true rune before you of a person or a thing, what you do to that rune, happens to that person or thing. That is the basis of magic, the manipulation of those names to affect the physical reality."

Tildi was fascinated.

"See here. This is the origin of all creation. The first image is the simple circle, the most all-encompassing symbol that contains all matter, all energy, all thought. You can deduce from this image, as the artist who compiled this tome did, that they are all one. It is when they became differentiated that they began to lose contact with one another." Beneath the circle were three more symbols. Each had characteristics of the ring, but were all very distinct. In fact, when Tildi peered more closely at them, she realized that they were very complex, showing, as her first drawing of *tree* had, what had changed from when each was part of the circle. The artist who had drawn them must have been a very good observer. "It was a student of what became magic who discovered the links. He did not so much reestablish them, as redescribe them. From that revelation came more study."

The subsequent pages showed general runes. Tildi let out a pleased exclamation. She recognized all of these: tree, river, flower, sky, and, of course, fire.

"Yes," Olen said. "This section does resemble a reading primer for very young children. This is the distilling down of every image to find the very basic elements that these things have in common. Therefore, these runes direct energy to and from an entire class of objects, such as all trees. The early mages found that one had to be very general in order to direct a change in all of anything. In fact, since one mind's influence is so diluted by attempting such an alteration, a general spell has no effect whatsoever. It is when you wish to enchant a single object that your power is the greatest, for then your attention is focused upon it. You can work upon its name, its single designation, and get results.

"You can do magic without runes, but to understand what it is you do, you must study the image behind them. This is matter put into thought, or thought from which matter or energy arise. That is why you must truly know the name of something before you alter it, and once you know the name, you know much more than what it is called."

Tildi stared at the runes. "So if I know the name of something, I can change it?"

"No. And yes. Once you know the name you have the key. There-after you must study to understand the nature of the object. Though you may see the rune, you will not necessarily know which strokes correspond to which characteristics. That comes over time, a lot of time. Some things are easy to change. Others are not. That is something apart from whether or not they ought to *be* changed. The balance of existence is maintained because there are reactions that come alongside every alteration, and the wise ones, such as we pretend to be, must take that into consideration. You can simply go ahead and alter or interfere with an object through its rune, if you are willing to take the consequences. Like the Shining Ones, or so they called themselves," Olen said tersely. "They did not care, and see what trouble it's caused?"

"Have I seen some of that trouble yet, master?"

"They created the thraik."

"Created!"

"Indeed, yes, among other things. It's the eternal scope of their meddling that both astonishes and appalls me." At her puzzled expression he chuckled. "It's not something I expect you to comprehend in its entirety now, or for many years, but you will. You will. I merely wish to stress that magic is easy for those who have the talent, or the opportunity. Judging whether to do that magic is not."

"I had heard," Tildi said slowly, echoing something that Teldo had once told her, "that the ancient runes are what the world is made of."

"That's a very simplified expression of the process," Olen said. "Who told you that?"

"My . . . my brother."

"Well, he did not precisely mislead you, Tildi. Indeed, that was a very penetrating thought from a layman. I'm rather surprised that he didn't apply for an apprenticeship, too." Tildi didn't reply, and Olen did not notice. "If you think about these runes as a representation of each facet of existence, then you could, in fact, say that they are what the world is made of. You certainly have access to those elements through the runes. Like in the Great Book."

Tildi prepared to jump down again. "Shall I look for that one next, master? I'd like to see that."

Olen arrested her with one long hand. "It is not here, Tildi. Please to creation that it will never be anywhere where one can see it. Though the rumors trouble me—"

He stopped himself. "Never mind. We are flipping ahead in the pages, and that is just what I said we would not do. It is best to do, not just to describe. Let's take this book down to my study and I'll demonstrate some simple applications that you can work on. I am pleased with your aptitude, and your application. Indeed, your energy makes me feel tired. What are you doing?" he asked, as Tildi headed for the remaining three chests she had not had time to clean.

"It won't take a moment, master," she said, setting to industriously with her cloth. Along with the broom she must see if she could get hold of some brass polish, or a lemon and some salt.

"Stop dusting that," Olen ordered, waving a hand at the box she was polishing. "It will only get dusty again, and your efforts will be wasted."

Tildi had heard similar logic over the years from her brothers, and ignored it. She finished cleaning the tops of all the chests. "There! Much better. I could come up here and attach labels so that you know what is in each," she offered.

Olen just shook his head. "Please don't. Now, if you will let me reestablish authority, let us go down and work on the practical applications of rune manipulation."

The lessons were always electrifyingly interesting, even basic studies like working on identifying the parts of runes that indicated specific sections of an object. By the end of the first day, Tildi could cause the leaves to fall off a plant. By the end of the week, she could pick out a specific leaf, but she despaired of ever reattaching one, let alone learning all the intricacies of every rune ever drawn.

When she was not studying, she explored Silvertree. The house was grand, with corridors that ran into one another, intersecting in odd corners. Many of the rooms were square or rectangular despite the round shape of the trunk they had been cut into, or perhaps grown into would be a closer truth.

"An ancient forest once stood all around Silvertree," Olen explained one day, in answer to her questions. "If you could see into the earth—teach you to one day," he added, patting her on the shoulder, "you'd see the remains of mighty roots wider than whole blocks of this city. This is the only one left here." Olen patted the wall. "One day both of us shall pass into memory. Silvertree gives a seed now and again. None of the saplings are as grand, as of yet, but give it ten or twelve thousand years, and we'll see, we'll see."

"Who are the other people who live here?"

"Only I and my servants live here, Tildi. Silvertree attracts visitors, and I enjoy having them. Musicians, artists, other mages, craftsmen, scholars, priests, philosophers, lords and ladies, and common folk of every race. They come here for the peace, and the intellectual exchange. Nothing so organized as a school. Properly speaking, you are my only student here. I often learn from my guests, and they from me, but it is a free exchange. We have many concerns, some of which I will discuss with you in time, as well. We keep an eye on the world, you see. We study it. I can't think how long it has been going on, but many years. Centuries, perhaps."

Tildi felt her eyebrows climb her forehead. "How old are you, master?"

Olen's gaze drifted to the ceiling. "Not sure at the moment. I'll have to consult my daybook. I can't say I recall when Silvertree sprouted, of course."

"Of course not." Tildi laughed.

"And why 'of course not'?" Olen asked, snorting.

"But you just said that it would take ten or twelve thousand years to grow this big!" Tildi replied, wide-eyed.

"You've got to stop thinking in terms of limits. How that will hold you back in years to come! Of course you must understand the function of limits. I know others who took the concept perhaps a little too far, and they *delimited* themselves. Yes, hmm."

Tildi looked up at him hopefully. It sounded as if he was going to tell her another story, but he sucked in his lower lip with a hiss.

"Go on, Tildi. I want you to give the matter some consideration. We'll discuss it later. I have much I must do."

Tildi went away to her room to practice not thinking within limits. Everything that she did was defined in some way. Everything she thought was based upon what she knew from something else.

When she was studying, her room seemed to become more cozy, and the light more intense, though not brighter so the notes danced on the page as if brought to life, but with a character that made them easier to see and absorb. It felt as though Silvertree herself was encouraging her to study. She began to see more than the similarities between runes, she saw their differences. Something struck her as she was looking at the sigil for tree, and fished out Teldo's precious manuscript page, which they had never been able to comprehend. Yes, she was sure of it. One of those symbols contained the base sigil for *tree*. She tried to find other symbols that matched the other lines and curliques, but she realized she just didn't have the vocabulary yet to translate it. One day she would.

When she was not studying, she found herself down in the servants' hall. The guests who were staying at Silvertree over those months included humans, a few elves, and a hairy-eared woman that Tildi thought must be a werewolf. They greeted her pleasantly, but in her shyness she could find no opening to begin a conversation. Olen encouraged her to join them at dinner. She tried once or twice, but felt completely out of place among these educated, cultured, and above all, big people. None seemed interested, though, in making friends with a young and humbly raised smallfolk girl. They tried to make her feel welcome, smiling at her at meals and asking for her opinion. She appreciated the effort, but often choked on her shyness, unable to speak up for fear of humiliating herself. She ended up gravitating toward the homely sounds coming out of the kitchens.

Chapter Eleven

ne morning Samek looked up from the silver vase he was polishing when Tildi appeared at the door of the white-painted dining hall.

"Can I do f'r ye, girl?"

"Oh," Tildi said, feeling so lonely she didn't know how to express it. She had been drawn by the sounds of clinking dishes and cheerful voices, and finally dared to come in. She approached the big, coarse-haired man. "You don't have to do anything for me. Can I help you?"

He flicked the cloth and turned it over. "Gorra, yer just starved fer sommat to do, arrren yer? Hae yer no' lessons enou'?" he asked.

"I do. I just wanted to be useful."

She reached for a polishing cloth and a silver cup. The butler shook his shaggy head. "Nae, don' do tha'. The housemaids'll think they've no go'a do ennythin' anymair. Come on down and sit wi' us here."

Tildi hopped up on the bench across from him. The room smelled of salt and lemon juice, rising bread, soap powder, drying herbs and sausages, and, she was fairly sure, a whiff of beer from the big man opposite. It was a little early to start drinking, in her opinion, but he was so nice she didn't want to offer a scold.

If Liana was surprised to find her master's new apprentice sitting on a heap of folded towels, chatting with the butler, she didn't show it. She came in with a basketful of bright red mushrooms and sat down beside Tildi, offering a friendly smile before setting to work peeling and paring them into perfect slices.

"A dot of butter here and there, bake them, and they'll be delicious," the housekeeper said. "Have you ever eaten Kolsh mushrooms before?"

"No, I haven't," Tildi said, with interest.

"They're sweet and juicy and not like any you've ever had. They come from the forests far to the northwest. Olen put them in the garden many years ago. They're at their finest now, while the weather's hot, not like the white-and-brown ones that are best in spring and fall."

"How many years ago?" Tildi asked. "Liana, how old is Olen?"

Liana chuckled. "I don't know. I think he is as old as time. He's lived the calendar around and partway back again, I think. That way he's just remembering things, which makes it more accurate than trying to see into a future that hasn't happened yet."

"Is that possible?" Tildi asked, reaching for a knife to help. Liana whisked it out of her reach.

"I don't know. You're the apprentice wizard; you tell me."

The other servants came through, carrying baskets and heaps of linens. When they spotted Tildi, they hesitated, then came forward and sat down at the big table. Tildi guessed that Samek or Liana had made a surreptitious gesture to them to behave as if nothing was out of the ordinary. She was almost desperately grateful.

"Cloudy today," one of them observed.

"Out of the ordinary for this month," said a footman, taking the bowl of silver polish and a rag from Samek, who started tucking the cleaned items into a box lined with linen towels. "Would it be fine this time of year where you live, Tildi?"

"Yes, it would," Tildi replied, keeping her hands firmly folded in her lap. Her fingers itched to be doing *something*, but it was no use. Olen's staff weren't going to let her help with a single task. "We get a few hard storms during Blackberries, but it's clear weather from now until then.

We're farmers. We welcome the long growing season. It's good for grain and our orchard."

"Aye, my old dad's a farmer outside 'er Jaftown," said one of the scullery maids, chopping up onions at the far end of the long table. "He counts on this month to dry out the fields."

Tildi relaxed. This was the kind of conversation she was used to having, not high-flown discussions on the position of the stars. Someday she might be comfortable with those, but in the meantime, she felt as if she had come home.

"Peaches are my favorite," one of the housemaids said, with a dimple in her cheek. "Peaches, and you can keep everything else . . ."

"Tildi!" Olen's voice shouted. It seemed to come from everywhere. Tildi looked up.

"Oh, he's in one of his moods," Liana said indulgently. "Go on. He's in his study."

Tildi sprang up and headed for the stairs, but her master was on the way down. He had on a tall, dark hat, and he swung a cloak around his shoulders. One of the footmen followed him with a tall staff with a luminous orb on top. "Get your cloak. Hurry."

Tildi dashed up the long flight and all but tumbled down them trying to get her cape on while she ran. Samek must have followed her up at Olen's shout. He stood at the door, in a posture of exaggerated attention, and waved her out. At the bottom of the grand steps, Olen was swinging into the saddle of a horse whose coat was the same shade as Silvertree's bark.

"Easy, Sihine. Hurry, child. The Madcloud is coming this way."

Tildi looked up at the sky beyond Silvertree's canopy. As the staff had said, it was lightly overcast everywhere but in the southeast, where a dark blanket gave the light a horrible green hue.

A groom swept her up and placed her on the back of his saddle. Olen's cloak closed over her. Tildi felt the horse give a mighty leap. She clung to the wizard's back as Sihine's powerful muscles under her swelled and relaxed, but she heard no footfalls on cobblestones. She could hear Olen's voice, but any meaning was drowned out by the flapping of his cloak in her ears and the whistling of the wind.

After an eternity of semidarkness, the horse's hooves clattered suddenly on stone. They trotted to a stop.

". . . Can see it properly from here." The cloak swung aside, and Olen looked down over his shoulder at her. "Did you hear a thing I was saying?"

"No, master," Tildi said. She looked at the landscape. Towers and the tops of evergreen trees protruded above a thin layer of gray mist. The only shelter they had from the sudden chill winds was a leafless tree behind them. They must be very high up. Over them the sky was a sickly gray-green, and a wind was stirring the thin grasses under her feet. "Where are we?"

He slid out of the saddle and helped her down. "We are on the east side of the river valley above Overhill. This is wild country, a band of marshes and forests between the city and the farmlands. I am hoping to intercept the Madcloud and direct it away from Overhill."

"What is the Madcloud?"

"What? Hasn't it ever attacked the Quarters? It's a lightning storm that travels about of its own accord, often sailing right into the teeth of prevailing winds. It is a most destructive force. You've never seen it?"

"Thank Nature, no!"

A blinding stroke of white erupted in the distance. Tildi jumped. Olen counted quietly to himself until a distant crackling boom was heard.

"Still a way off. Good. Gives us time to prepare." He dropped into his lecture mode, and peered at her under his large eyebrows. "Now, Tildi, you may guess that a wizard receives many requests, among which are pleas from farmers to change the weather. It's raining too much, it's not raining enough, they want more sunshine, and, of all things, they want me to put off the sunset in harvest times! Do you know, one of the most dangerous temptations of power is not to avoid doing wrong, but to do all the things people want you to. Not only are few paths ahead of you good choices, but not every path you do take is the right one. That's to be expected. You're fallible. Good judgment will keep you from making terrible mistakes. You must learn to say no when the time is right. You'll be better off refusing to take an action if you are not certain of all the potential outcomes."

Tildi frowned. "How could I know all of them?"

"You can't! But you should know as many as are reasonable. In that you may take the advice of others you trust to be as wise or wiser than yourself."

"That's *everyone*."

"Do you see, you have justified my faith in you," Olen said with a chuckle. I have met so many who always know best, you see. Most of them are dead."

"Dead?" Tildi blanched. "That would put me right off trying!"

"It shouldn't," Olen said, taking her by the shoulder and turning her firmly. "A judicious attempt, guided by wisdom . . . Look, here comes the cloud. You can see its rune within it, can't you?"

"Yes." The clouds that she had seen once she had left the Quarters usually had faint, light-colored sigils somewhere on their surfaces, changing and shifting just like the clouds themselves, but this was a violent display of colors at war with itself. It made Tildi feel a little queasy just to look at it. Lightning shot out of the roiling black mounds in all directions, like an injured cat striking out at anyone who might try to handle it. Tildi felt a hunger in it. It wanted something badly. But what could a cloud possibly want?

"The rune is spinning out of control. This is an entity without purpose. It was set going for no particularly good reason except that the incredible fool who made it, could," Olen said, with a grim set to his jaw. "What is it doing here, of all places?"

"Doesn't it just wander, like all weather?" Tildi asked.

"To start with the second half of your question, that is a misconception. Weather does not wander. It has many reasons for going where it does, and doing what it does. If you are so inclined, I will send you one day for a couple years' apprenticeship in Levrenn with my friend Volek, whose specialty is weather-witching. But we do not have time for a lesson in that at this moment. We are concerned with a storm that does not wander, the Madcloud. Many have studied this phenomenon over the centuries. It seems to go where it is attracted, though no one has yet divined to what. I believe it to have a tropism for natural power, yet I don't know what could have drawn it here: nothing has changed in this area in many months. I would have expected it to go toward the volcanoes in the north, or south if a tidal wave arises." He shook his head. "We have no time to speculate. It will pass over the city if we do not redirect it."

"Can't you . . . ?" Tildi held up her hand and closed it the way Olen had done to extinguish the fire-demon.

The wizard's curling eyebrows rose high on his forehead, but he didn't scoff at the question.

"Tildi, a *heuren* is a mere speck of power. This cloud is a powerful spell, combined with a force of nature. To destroy it would upset the balance of nature, to be undone only by a host of wizards, or perhaps one of the Makers. I hope one day it will simply rain itself out, over the ocean or mountains where it can hurt no one. In the meanwhile, the best that we can do with it is drive it away."

"Is it safe?" Tildi asked, as a lightning strike blasted apart a scrub bush clinging to the mountain. Rocks, dislodged by the bolt, rumbled downhill. Other rocks were knocked loose. Birds, disturbed by the fall, flew squawking into the sky.

"*Safe?*" Olen exclaimed. "Of course it is not safe. A wizard must always do what must be done. There is no choice. Our responsibility is to undertake the jobs that we can take. Yes, we may be killed by this storm, but what are two lives against all those in Overhill? You don't strike me as one who shirks a job just because it is unpleasant."

"No, that's true . . ." Tildi mused. But turning a storm? "It's taking a great risk."

"All magic is risk-taking, Tildi."

"I don't like to take risks. Well, not many," she said, after a moment's thought.

"You took many risks coming here, didn't you? I know something of smallfolk, you see," Olen said, bending down and putting a hand on her shoulder. "You thought I might not accept you as an apprentice because you're a girl, isn't that right? But you came anyhow. I honor you for that. It shows the proper chance-taking character."

Tildi wanted to say that wasn't exactly the way it had happened, though he was right about his conclusion, and she was so relieved that she didn't want to throw in the many other facts that had gone into her decision. Still, her conscience troubled her, and she opened her mouth to confess that it wasn't she who had applied to him for an apprenticeship in the first place.

"No time!" Olen snapped out. Tildi closed her mouth. Her private griefs would not concern him. He brandished his staff at the storm. "Here it comes. Do you have a wand?"

"No."

"Must see about getting you a wand. Are you carrying a pen? No? There, draw your knife. You know how to create wards now. Draw them as large as you can. Picture them filling the sky. You must protect the city. Keep that in your mind. It will inform your wards."

Tildi pulled her knife out of the sheath at her belt, but held it up uncertainly. This mere wisp of metal—how could it stave off a force of nature that was the size of an entire valley? The Madcloud came closer. Red lightning shot from its underside. Far below them, underneath the mist, Tildi heard shouting and the crackle of flame as unseen woods caught fire.

"Begin!" Olen boomed. He held out his staff and began to chant. *"Fornai chnetech voshad!"* The disk touched the sky and thick silver lines began to flow from it as the wizard swept his arm across, up, down, and back. The lines formed into a gigantic word-phrase that said "Protect!" on their side. Tildi knew that the reverse, the side facing the oncoming storm, said something that approximated the word "Away!" in the strongest possible archaic terms. Hastily, she began to draw her own ward.

The lines she produced were puny by comparison, but as she began to picture them guarding the entire city of Overhill, they did grow. The rune, though seemingly limned on the sky in a spiderweb, spread out until it was at least half the size of Olen's. She threw every bit of knowledge she had into its formation, as if by the force of her mind alone she could make it powerful.

The storm advanced upon them. Its winds whipped at her hair, so that it clawed at the sides of her face like a wire flail. Tildi slitted her eyes. Olen's beard streamed around him like a wild creature. If he could ignore that, she could, too. Doggedly, she drew the rune over and over, to the north, then to the south. Each new symbol bonded with the ones on either side, forming a wrought-silver gate that looked too fragile for the job. Nearer and nearer the cloud came. The winds grew more fierce. Tildi's clothes were plastered to her body by icy cold rain. She could no longer see what she was doing, but in her mind's eye she created yet another rune of protection.

Go away! she thought at the Madcloud. *Go somewhere else!*

A warm weight dropped upon her shoulder and squeezed: Olen's hand. His hand on her shoulder gave her confidence. The lines she drew were suddenly thicker and more confident. The gate in her mind turned to iron, and began to congeal into a translucent wall.

Abruptly, the wind stopped. Having been braced against it so long Tildi staggered forward a step. The hand caught her and pulled her back again. She opened her eyes.

Her wall of runes was just as she had pictured it, as if it was made out of silvery glass. Just beyond it was a wall of a deeper silver hue. Against this double protection the Madcloud bumped and pushed as if it was a ram attempting to push open a gate with its head.

"It's no match for us," Olen said, patting her on the head. "It cannot pass. Now, to send it elsewhere to cause its mischief."

He spread out his arms, the staff held on high. The silver-gray walls stretched out like taffy until they were wrapped all the way around the gigantic storm. The Madcloud rumbled menacingly and spewed multi-colored lightnings out of the top, but to no avail. It began to roll away to the southeast.

"I think we'll send it all the way to the sea, don't you?" Olen said.

Tildi watched with awe as the silver curtain receded swiftly across the mist. "Whatever you say, master."

"Oh, you may make a suggestion, since you were of such great help. That was very good work! You will be a fine wizard. I think I will drop a note to Volek when we return home. I will see if he has an opening in the next few years to teach you weather magic."

"Not too soon," Tildi pleaded, proud in spite of herself. If this was true magic, she wanted to learn everything possible. How exhilarating it had been. She had been so frightened, but together they had cowed . . . a thunderstorm! What would they say back in the Quarters?

*T*ildi sat before Olen in the great saddle as the horse bore them down again to Silvertree's front gate. She wasn't sure she prefered being able to see. Sihine galloped down through the air as easily as if he was trotting down a hillside, but Tildi always felt as if she was about to tumble over the saddle bow and fall to her death.

"Where do you find a flying horse?" she shouted over the wind whistling in her face.

"Sihine doesn't fly," Olen shouted back. "I make the air solid under his feet. He has gotten very good at running on terrain he cannot see. Much more convenient than trying to stable a pegasus, oh, yes!"

Tildi felt a little thrill of excitement even as she clutched the saddle horn in a tight grip between her small hands. Pegasi, the fabled winged horses, did exist! They weren't just legends, as the storytelling grannies had insisted. Tildi could hardly absorb such a notion, on top of the ideas that clouds could move where they willed, and she, Tildi Summerbee, could wrap up a storm like a parcel. With help, that was.

Chapter Twelve

hen they arrived at the gate, a mud-spattered messenger was waiting for Olen, with an equally bedaubed horse breathing heavily through flared nostrils. Olen swung off the gray horse's back, and put the reins into the hands of a groom. The messenger all but stumbled forward and handed the wizard a tightly bound scroll.

"You look exhausted," Olen declared. "Get inside and let Liana take care of you. Tildi, take him down to her."

"Yes, master," Tildi said automatically, her question about Pegasi forgotten. The wizard took the steps up toward his study two and three at a time, breaking open the seals on the scroll as he went. He did not look happy.

Tildi took the man down to the kitchens, where Liana fluttered and clucked around him, bringing him cold drinks and a big platter of food.

Once he had emptied a huge mug of ale and wolfed down a chunk of cheese the size of his fist he gave Tildi a curious look.

"Where do you come from?" the messenger asked. He was a pleasant-looking fellow with very dark skin like the sailors she had met at the Groaning Table. "Sit with me while I eat, little lass. I'm sorry I can't return the favor. I may not say anything about my mission, so don't ask me."

"I won't," Tildi promised. "What do you want to know?"

"Tell him about storm-warding," Liana suggested. "This is a small-folk, you know. She is the wizard's apprentice. They've just saved the city, the two of them."

The man beheld her with such respect that Tildi felt herself blush. "Well, there's a storm called the Madcloud, you see . . ." she began.

Tildi found that she was content in Olen's household . . . not happy, but content. She missed her own kind, having a natter. She found she was able to think about her brothers with a tiny bit of detachment now. She was more at peace with their loss. She would never stop missing them, but she had come to a safe place now, and was going to live a life that they would have approved of. Master Olen's servants understood her need to make herself useful, she could tell they had been spoken to. She was given more respect, and a little distance.

"You'll be pleased later that we did," Liana always told her. "When you take the master's place, you'll have to give us orders, and it's better if we're not friends."

Tildi shook her head furiously. "Oh, that will never happen! I have many years of study ahead of me, and he's got other, much more advanced apprentices in the world."

"Journeymen and journeywomen now, and a few master magicians," Liana acknowledged. "But it could happen. You're conscientious, and that doesn't happen that often. Not in this house, anyhow. That's why I say, maybe you."

That conscientiousness was why she was so surprised when a thread of power took her by the ear and pulled. Tildi turned her head to see who was tweaking her, but there was no one there. The others in the servants' hall regarded her with puzzled expressions. She felt around the spot that was being pinched, and tried to make it stop. The invisible force pulled hard, and the spoon she was polishing fell to the floor with a clatter. She gave an apologetic shrug to Liana as the invisible force pulled her out of the door and up the many flights of stairs to Olen's study.

"Why are you not working on the runes I set you?" Olen scolded her.

"I was!" Tildi protested. "Well, I was, before lunch. Then I got to talking with the others downstairs, and they had so much silver to polish. I didn't realize it had gotten to be so late!"

"Housework?" the wizard exclaimed, his big brows drawing down fiercely.

Olen paced up and back, his hands clasped behind his back. The crystals under his window seemed to pick up his agitation, bubbling in bright, intense colors.

Tildi sat with her hands folded, inwardly terrified. Would he send her away? For polishing spoons? Her heart sank.

The others had warned her, and she had not listened.

At last the wizard stopped before her. He knelt at her feet and stared into her eyes. She sat transfixed, feeling as if the green orbs were boring deep into her brain. At last, Olen spoke.

"Tildi, did you ever think before you came here what it would mean to be a scholar? It means that study is your job. You can't go and turn out closets or stay the day gossiping when you are supposed to be concentrating on the subject on which I will test you later on. Oh, I understand the value of taking a break, if only to let your mind digest the large plateful of knowledge I fed it, but that ought to be an intermission, not a substitute for the day. You have a great urge to help others. Do not try to be so pleasing to other people's wants and needs. You must learn to put your own needs first and foremost. Do it for yourself, and let others do that which they can do. I tell you that what you are doing now can be of more service to others than any number of potatoes you can peel. It is not selfishness when I tell you how little time there is in life, no matter how long it is—even one like mine—to learn the secrets of the world's beginning and ending. You would be greedy for every minute if you understood. One day you will, and by that time you will no longer need me to teach you. You'll grasp for every wisp of knowledge you can hold."

Tildi felt overwhelmed by his words. He was right about her feelings, and right, too, about her neglecting her studies to do favors for the people in the house with whom she felt the most comfortable. It wasn't why she had come, not any of the reasons why.

"I am sorry, master," she said sincerely.

He patted her on the shoulder. "Don't be. Just turn that astonishing energy of yours back to where it ought to be aimed. Heavens, if I had the perseverance you do, I'd have my own continent."

Tildi felt ashamed. "I just thought that I could be of some use. I studied the lessons you set me until I didn't think I could figure out anything new about them—"

Olen spun on her, and his dark brows drew down. "*That* is never true. There is always something you can learn from study, even if it is only to memorize a sign so that you can draw it from memory. Please leave housework to my servants. You may not understand how important it is that you use what time you have here. Life is uncertain, never more so than when you are comfortable."

Tildi wrinkled her forehead. He did set such conundrums for her to contemplate. "I apologize, master. It won't happen again."

Olen put his hands on his knees and straightened up with a sigh. "I know you mean well. Good heavens, the house has never been cleaner! But have a care for your own future, won't you? Some day the world may turn upon what you do or do not know, and there will be no one left to ask."

*T*ildi came down before dawn the next day, her resolve in place to obey Olen's strictures more closely. She set her book down upon the big table, and took down her bowl and spoon from the low shelf. When she climbed up on the padded end of the bench she smiled at Liana, who was sitting at the table with her forehead propped up on her hands. The housekeeper didn't glance at her. Her usually neat hair looked frayed.

"How are you this morning?" Tildi asked her. Liana's head snapped up.

"Oh, there you are, Tildi. My apologies. I am working out strategy in my head, as if I was a general in the king's army! The master was up all night long, and he met me at the bottom of the stairs two hours ago with an incredible list of tasks I must undertake. He has called a great conference here, to take place in two weeks' time, and we must have everything ready."

"May I help?" Tildi asked, looking with alarm at the closely written roll of parchment under the housekeeper's hands. "I'm good at organizing feasts. I always helped at Year's End parties in the Quarters, and whenever someone in the village got married."

Liana covered it up with both hands. "No, you can't help. The master specifically told me to keep you at your lessons. Please be out from underfoot today. We have many guests coming in the next two weeks, and I have to muster the entire household to have the place ready before they come."

"How many?" Tildi asked.

Liana glanced at a handful of notes, then stuffed them into her apron pocket. "The master says thirty-seven will be staying, but a hundred and forty will dine here, for at least three days."

"A hundred and forty!"

"Yes. He is sending out two hundred summonses, but that is how many he says will get here on time. One good thing about working for a man who can see the future. Ah, well, we have the room for it all. He likes to have company, which is why this place has so many guest chambers, and the kitchens can serve double that number. I will say that he always knows how many, so one is never turned out of one's bed to make way for a guest, unlike other places I've worked before this. Though I've never seen him this concerned before. He did not confide in me what the conference is about. Perhaps he will tell you. Anyhow, go be at your lessons, will you? I need room to make plans."

Tildi bolted her breakfast and ran up the stairs to Olen's study. The wizard sat before the table of crystals, staring into them. Within them the images were still a confused mass to her inexperienced eye, but they worried her master, and that worried her. She waited for a moment for him to notice her, then cleared her throat.

"Master, Liana said that the household is preparing for a conference. What may I do to help?"

Olen turned to her. He looked weary. "Nothing at the moment. There may be nothing any of us can do, but we will try."

"What is the problem? May I help? Will you tell me?"

"Not now." Olen waved a hand in sharp dismissal. Tildi must have shown her disappointment. "Forgive me, Tildi, but your expertise is too limited to be of service, and it would take too long to explain at the moment. Will you be patient? I have to explain all to a great many people, and I would rather do it one time and all at once."

To wait two weeks! This time Tildi hid her disappointment, but her curiosity was thoroughly aroused.

"I understand. Is there anything I can do in the meantime?" she asked.

Olen smiled, the corners of his mouth quirking his mustache. "No, no. Thank you for your courtesy. I will need you later, I promise you. If you don't mind taking lessons at odd times, when I can spare an hour from my watching, your education will go on, even in this dark time."

"Thank you, master!"

He waved away her thanks. "In the meanwhile, here is a text I would like you to study. Later we will discuss it. I hope." He thrust a roll of parchment at her. She unrolled the edge to find a page of the most complicated runes she had seen yet. She opened her mouth to protest that she couldn't make sense of them without help. Olen anticipated her outburst and forestalled it with an upraised finger.

"If you can't make progress with it, then work on your fire. I did a study on the spell you have been using, and your pronunciation of the rune." Olen started to chuckle to himself. "Imagine, using demon-fire to boil tea. Mmm-mmm-mmm. Do you know, that almost cheers me up." He turned back to the bank of crystals, and clucked over the mustard-colored mass that arose in the third one from the left.

Tildi escaped with the old book clutched to her chest.

Chapter Thirteen

onfined as she was to study, the two weeks crawled by for Tildi.

The housekeeping staff was under strict orders to keep her from helping, and plucked dust rags, brooms, and brushes out of her hands whenever they found her at any work other than her own. Plenty of activity was going on around her, and she itched to be part of it. Every corner of the kitchen was full of gigantic pots and stacks of trenchers and dishes. The twin footmen polished mountains of silver cutlery. The housemaids carried piles of linens up the stairs and made up dozens of beds in the guest rooms. Some of the guests would be staying in suites, the likes of which she had never dreamed existed outside of a fairy-tale castle. The rich, red brocade bed curtains alone in one grand room would have bought the entire contents of Clearbeck!

And every time she tried to help, she was shooed out of the room like an errant cat. She had never felt more useless in her life.

Despite his promise, Olen was too busy to spend more than a few minutes a day checking her work. Forced to apply herself, she learned to distinguish a hundred general runes, and manipulate a few simple specific ones, like that for a stone and a piece of wood that she found in the garden. She attempted to dissect the impenetrable, difficult runes in the page he had assigned her, and practiced warding. Despairing of ever being able to push thunderstorms around like Olen, Tildi sat despondently looking out over the gardens as Olen's grooms put up temporary stables for dozens of horses to supplement those hidden among the small trees at the perimeter of the estate. She wondered why the housemaids were carrying candlesticks and toilet mirrors into the nearest bank of stalls, but no one had time to answer her questions.

With her book in front of her, Tildi ate her lunch at the table in the servants' hall. Liana, beside her, sat poring over notes while the staff ran around them with heaps of linens and baskets of candlesticks.

"Mistress," one of the footmen said, dashing up, "we can't find the extra washbasins!"

Before Liana could put her finger on her notes to keep her place, Tildi piped up. "Second storeroom in the fifth attic."

Liana and the footmen both stared at her. "Master Olen had me fetch one for studying water runes," she said sheepishly.

"She's right," the housekeeper said, her smile lightening the look of concentration she wore. The footman ran off. "Well, you're not supposed to be helping, but I can't say I'm ungrateful that his current apprentice isn't as snooty as the previous apprentice but one. Lord of this land or that, that boy was. Ended up joining the Knights of the Book and leaving Olen in the lurch, wretched boy. As if he was worth a damn anywhere but washing retorts and scribing down spells."

One of the bells on the wall over their heads began to jangle. They both glanced up. "Front door," Liana observed. She went back to her lists, but the bell overhead went on and on. She smacked her palm down on the tabletop. "Where is that Samek?"

"I'll go and get the door, Liana," Tildi offered, jumping down from the pad perched on the bench.

Liana eyed her. "You're Olen's apprentice. Properly you should not." The bell rang again and again. She sighed. "I suppose you had better. I think Samek's gone off to get drunk, curse him. Crowds worry him. He prefers it when it's just the usual household ménage, but that's not his choice, is it? Go. Thank you."

Loud hammering from without alarmed Tildi as she flew toward the tall entry doors. Whoever sought entry was trying to hammer his way through the wood. She could almost see the timbers of the frame thicken as Silvertree protected itself from damage. Tildi reached for the round door handle, but whomever was on the other side had decided to resort to magic. Tildi jumped back just in time to avoid having the doors fly open in her face.

A woman peered down at Tildi. Her long white hair was braided and tied with glinting ruby and emerald pins. Her skin was a warm golden hue, set off by the pale green of her fine gown. Over that floated a white silk cloak tied at the neck with a ribbon. At first Tildi thought she was an elf like Irithe, but her ears were of the human shape.

"Hello, child," the human said kindly. Her large black eyes, as timeless as Irithe's with only the faintest hint of a wrinkle at the outer corners, widened a trifle. "Ah, but I see you are not a child. Are you new here?"

"My name is Tildi, honored one."

"Greetings, Tildi. I am Edynn. I apologize for bursting in, but as you can see"—Edynn gestured with the long staff in her hand—"the doorstep is becoming very crowded. I knew Olen would not want us standing in the street." Tildi gawked. Behind the old woman was a crowd spilling down the stairs and down the path, all most distinguished and clad in gorgeous clothes of brilliant colors and winking gems. They were too dignified to press forward, but quite a few of the people looked impatient and peevish. They were not precisely in the street, which was a distance behind them, but the courtyard was filling up fast.

"No, of course not," Tildi stammered, gesturing feebly at the hall behind her. "Please enter and be welcome. May I have your cloak?"

"You are not a door ward," Edynn said, divesting herself of her own outer garment. She undid the white ribbon, and the cloak lifted itself away from Tildi's hands, making for the endmost peg. "What is your place in Olen's household?"

"I'm his new apprentice, honored one," Tildi explained. The wizardess beamed and extended a long hand to her.

"Ah, then we are colleagues! Call me Edynn."

Tildi was abashed and gratified. She would not dare address such a grand lady by her given name, but she accepted the hand with pleasure.

The next person in the door was a younger, slimmer version of Edynn.

Her hair was as black as her eyes, and filled with golden pins winking with blue stones. Peevishly, she draped her ochre silk cloak over Tildi's outstretched arms and swept in, leaving the scent of a heavy floral perfume in her wake.

"Mother! This way."

Edynn's shoulders lifted slightly in apology.

"My daughter, Serafina." With a small smile, the older woman followed the girl through the towering doors and toward the stairs that led up to the great hall.

Tildi's arms soon became filled with the outer garments of the visitors who streamed into the foyer in Serafina's wake. Elegant men and women streamed in, laying cloaks, capes, and shawls on top of the heap. Some of the visitors greeted her. Many strode past without looking down. Tildi was too fascinated to complain. It was like watching a pageant or a wedding, with everyone wearing their very best to impress one another.

She had never seen jewels like those, or such fine clothes. As she made common homespun for work clothes on the family loom she knew a little about weaving. The visitors' garments were made of fabrics with complicated weaves and must have cost a great deal. A lot of the cloth looked coarse by her standards, but cut exquisitely, better than by any tailor who lived in Clearbeck. Some of it, she was sure, must have come from the Quarters. With a start of surprise she recognized the fabric in one swirling cloak as having come from her own village, made by Gorten. It was absolutely unmistakable. Tildi and her friends had lusted after that very fabric with the oak leaf pattern repeated over and over, with a touch of genuine golden thread as fine as hair that had been imported from over the sea. Gorten had been justifiably proud of the complex loom he had made, which could produce intricate motifs in five or six colors. She and a few of her friends had priced a length or two, but Gorten had been asking so much for it that it would have been a wrench even to pay for enough to make a sash. Not long afterwards the bolt had disappeared, no doubt in the pack of a passing peddler who knew he could find a market for it among the wealthiest patrons in the human lands. Linens, woolens, and even silks from the Quarters were known to be much in demand for their fine web. Now Tildi had the proof of it. She gave the fine tunic a fond glance before turning to the next guest over the threshold. Even being reminded of a story with an acrimonious argument in it made her homesick and glad at the same time. Though the cloak was covered up in the next moment by a shiny damask capelet in dark red silk, she felt contented to know it was there.

Humans, elves, werewolves in their dormant phase, and some stocky people she imagined must be dwarves, all passed into Silvertree's halls. The parade of guests seemed to be never ending. Every time Tildi thought she could withdraw and begin to hang up the cloaks in her arms, someone else whisked in through the door.

"Greetings, honored one," she repeated over and over, feeling like Olen's talking bird. "Welcome to Silvertree. Greetings. Welcome. Greetings."

One wag of a gentleman with bright blue eyes took off his peaked, feathered cap and plunked it down on Tildi's head. The brim went right down to her shoulders, encasing her head in a felt bucket. Now she was immobilized with the weight of her burden and she was no longer able to see. What was the polite thing to do in this case? If she had been at home she would have nodded off the hat onto the nearest bench, dumped the heap of cloaks on top of it and started firmly directing the men to hang up their own coats, if they hadn't the sense to figure that out for themselves. Her face was hot with shame. She didn't want to make Olen angry, but she did feel that she was entitled to some consideration.

"What have we here?" asked a pleasant tenor voice. "That's no place to put one's hat!"

The hot cap was removed, leaving Tildi, flushed and embarrassed, gazing up at her rescuer. A young man smiled down at her with bright yellow-green eyes. His long hair was a riot of color, white, chestnut, and black. Tildi was surprised to realize she had seen him before. He had been riding into the Quarters on the day she had left. Her thoughtful gaze brought an unwitting grin to his lips, which startled her into recalling her manners. He could not possibly have seen her that day. It was unthinkable for her to behave as though she knew him.

"Forgive me staring, honored one," she said, flustered. "May I take your coat?

"Thank you, little lass," the handsome youth said, swinging his cloak up out of her reach and hooking it onto a peg. "I'll hang it up myself. No need for you to climb a ladder just to show courtesy. Looking at the size of you I can't imagine what my fellow guests were thinking. Where is Samek?" He hoisted the armload of coats away from her and tossed it into a corner.

"He's gone to the stables, sir," Tildi said, scrambling to retrieve them and Samek's pride. What would her master say to her if his guests' things were damaged? Would he hold her responsible?

"You mean down in the wine cellar," the youth said, with a humorous nod. "Sampling the vintages before we do. Just to make sure we're not poisoned, and all. Oh, leave those alone, lass. Let Samek clear them up when he returns. I'll wager it's not *your* responsibility."

This young man was clearly a habitué of the house. He tossed his fine velvet cap toward a peg. It caught by the band and rotated almost a complete circle before settling to hang flat. He grinned at Tildi.

"Party trick," he said. "I've won many a drink in a pub betting I can do that. Very useful when one hasn't the price of a pint about one, and they won't accept a song in payment. I like to keep in practice, even when it annoys my betters."

That last was aimed at a regal man just behind him, who had a thick gold circlet holding down his curling yellow hair. This man's clothes were of the finest silks, scarlet and white, embroidered so finely that Tildi could find no fault, and he wore a single glowing yellow stone set into a medallion that hung by carved golden links about his neck. Behind him stretched a string of courtiers and soldiers, each wearing a badge of scarlet and white with the image of a winged horse pawing the ground.

"My lord Halcot," the young man said, with a deep bow. He swept his hand along the floor and came up in a graceful flourish. King Halcot seemed unimpressed.

"Magpie, what do you do here?" he asked.

The young man smiled at him impishly. "I am bidden to the council, the same as yourself."

Halcot snorted. "This was to be of the highest ranks only. I will speak to Olen about that."

Samek returned at that moment, just in time to catch the fur-lined cape that Halcot pushed off his shoulders before it hit the floor. He gave Tildi a sheepish look.

"You won't tell, will you, lass?" he asked, leaning close to whisper to her. She could smell the wine on his breath. His eyes were somewhat bloodshot.

"I won't have to, will I?" Tildi retorted. "Olen sees everything, and what he doesn't see the house will tell him."

"Aye, so yer right," Samek agreed sadly. "Sorry to leave yerr mindin' the door."

"It's all . . ." Tildi glanced out of the open portal, and forgot what she was about to say. Standing on the threshold were the most exotic creatures she had ever seen in her life.

With dark brown skin, large, lustrous eyes, and thick, flowing hair, Tildi might at first have thought that these tall beings were kin to the messenger who had visited two weeks before, but the resemblance ended at the waist, for they were only half human. The bottom half of each was that of a horse. Centaurs! Tildi had heard many stories of the fabled herds of Balierenn. Their eyes were large and lustrous. Not all brown as most of the ponies in the Quarters had been, but hazel-green, dark brown, black, and a rare dark blue. Their hair—or ought Tildi to say manes?—whether wavy or straight, was thick and springy, bound around the brow with fillets of leather or gold. The lengths were braided or woven, some with brightly colored ribbons and beads. One female's black-streaked hair had been divided into countless small braids each terminating in a faceted, glittering bead. Their horse halves were mainly black, but frequently striped, streaked, or spotted with a pure silver-white. One beautiful lady had silver hooves set off by jingling bunches of silver bracelets around her fetlocks. Their human halves were clad in fine silks, leathers, and velvets, breathtakingly embroidered in gold and silver.

Again, she found herself speechless, but Samek, having fortified himself for the occasion, did the honors.

"Wailco' to Silvertrree, my lords and laidees," he said with a bow. Tildi broke off her gaze, ashamed of staring. "Enter, pray."

"Thank you," the leader said, a handsome male with a deep chest, silver-shot, wavy black hair and beard, and an equine coat to match. He swept off a short silver cloak and placed it in Samek's upstretched hand. "I am Lowan. My sister, Rin. It would seem that we are just in time."

He nodded toward the ceiling, where brightly colored dust was swirling. As if it had understood that it had gained the visitors' attention, the whirlwind formed itself into the shape of an arrow that pointed toward the upper chamber.

The grand centaur and his retinue clattered over the fine wooden floor. With a sigh Tildi watched them go, admiring the swish of their beautiful tails, silky, wavy, braided with beads or tied with ribbons, and made for the stairs. If this was a grand council, then she would be in the way.

The cloud of dust had other ideas. Before Tildi could set foot on the first tread, a brilliant red ring looped around her waist, and the other pigments formed a rope that pretended to tow her in the centaurs' wake. She had no choice but to follow.

"Ah, there you are, Tildi," Olen called, as she made her way shyly into the room. The wizard sat in his high-backed chair, which had been set upon a small raised platform at one end of the huge chamber. The other guests turned to see whom he was addressing. Tildi felt her cheeks flame red. He held out his hand to her and beckoned.

She felt embarrassed about joining such illustrious visitors in her humble clothes, but she was too curious to let her natural reticence allow her to retreat. As she passed by each of them, many stared with frank, though friendly, curiosity. She held her back straight and walked with a seemly gait. If Olen wanted her there, then she belonged. Not that her twisting stomach believed it! As she passed the piebald-haired minstrel, he winked at her. He must have guessed what nervousness she was suffering.

Tildi had explored the grand hall some weeks before, when it was empty. The plain silver-gray wood of the walls was carved into scenes from Melenatae's history. It was interesting, but scarcely spectacular. Between Liana's careful preparations and Olen's wizardry, the great hall was now fit for any number of kings and wizards. The images had been limned with brilliant jewel colors and gilded in shining gold leaf, and acres of shimmering tapestries hung overhead. The pillars of the high-ceilinged grand chamber glowed with golden light, illuminating the whole room brightly and lending a warm sparkle to the visitors' ornaments.

The atmosphere was not unlike a meeting back in the Quarters, with Olen presiding in place of the elders. Beside him was a table heaped with papers, tied scrolls, and at least one of the crystals from the table in his study. Before him, instead of benches set in rows, upholstered couches and chairs had been arranged in small groups for each retinue. The golden-haired king in scarlet and white was in the tier nearest Olen's dais with a blond young man who must be his son and a handful of well-dressed noblemen and noblewomen. To one side of the Rabantavians was a cluster of black-haired elves surrounding a tall, austere woman in a simple blue gown, and on the other a semicircle of warriors in padded tunics with their swords laid across their laps seated behind their lord, a man with red-gold hair who looked younger than Gosto. The centaurs, tallest of all, congregated near the back.

"Now," Olen said to himself, as he gestured Tildi toward a small stool near his feet. "Where are those documents?"

"Are they in your study, master?" she asked, leaping up. "I will get them for you."

"No need," Olen said with an indulgent smile. "Please be seated,

Tildi. Ah, here they are." He unearthed a cluster of scrolls from the middle of the heap of documents and put them in his lap. Tildi sat down and put her knees together with her hands neatly folded. "Let us begin."

"Is this the representative from Ivirenn?" asked the chestnut-haired lord, clearly annoyed at the notion of Tildi being given precedence over him in terms of place. "I thought neither the smallfolk nor the dwarves could be bothered to attend this conference."

"Tildi is my apprentice," Olen said, raising his voice to carry to the rear of the hall. "As such, she belongs by me. Are there any objections?"

"None at all," the young man with the mixed-color hair said, his clear tenor voice rising above the murmurs.

"Never seen a female smallfolk before," added a man in one of the groups.

"Not outside the Quarters, anyhow," said a short woman with thick blond braids, with a smile for Tildi. "That's not the wonder you called us to discuss, is it?"

"No, Lakanta, it's not," Olen said, though he clearly appreciated her good humor. "Though we can talk about her later. She's a most interesting person, very worthwhile to know."

Tildi lowered her gaze to her knees.

"Let's get to it," said the man with chestnut hair. He kicked a chair out in front of him and swung his muddy boots onto it. He noticed Tildi's disapproving glance. "Don't like my carelessness, do you, little mother?" The lad, for he was a lad in spite of his outlandish size, exchanged smug grins with his cohort. Tildi glared at him.

"Stop annoying my apprentice, Balindor," the wizard scolded. "Pay attention." The heap of scrolls chose that moment to cascade off the table. Tildi sprang up to catch the ones she could. "Tildi, you need not pick those up. You pay attention, too. This is important. Will you take notes?" He waved his hand, and the papers tidied themselves back onto the table. The young man continued to gawk at her with amusement. Tildi knew who he was now: Balindor, and his sister Lindora, representatives of their father, Salindor, lord of Melenatae, the country in which Overhill lay. One would think a prince would be raised with better manners. Why, even the merchants and troubadours in the room were better behaved!

"My lords and ladies, I bid you welcome. To those of you who have not visited Silvertree before, I invite you to enjoy its hospitality. To the rest of you, welcome back. You will be looking around and wondering what such a varied group has come to hear. There are representatives here of several royal households, the guild of scholars, the fraternity of wizards, merchants, peddlers, craftsmen and teachers, bards and poets, of many different races. I promise you, what I and my fellow students of the world must reveal to you is of the greatest importance, to your safety and to the well-being of the entire world! Whatever your station on the outside, within these walls we are colleagues, and we must be allies, for the sake of all our futures."

On a fresh roll of parchment Tildi wrote as quickly as she could, hoping she got the list down correctly. Collective nouns were easy, but there were so many, and they were surprisingly similar in design.

"What's this I hear about a book, Olen?" Halcot demanded, one of the few guests whom Tildi could now identify by name. He tilted his chin back so his golden beard pointed directly at the wizard. "Hauled all this way when your messenger could have explained it in words of one syllable in my private study. I've got more pressing concerns within my own borders. We are still not at our full strength."

Olen acknowledged him with a polite nod. "My lord Halcot, your war has been over for two years. I respect that you are still rebuilding, but I need to warn you about the possibility of another war, this one waged across every realm. This summons has some urgency, because if my fears were true, then we are all in danger. If they were not . . . well, my lords and ladies, they are. I have had confirmation.

"It was a message from a fellow wizard in the south lands that has recently come to me that caused me to call for all of you. I could not tell the whole story to you in a mere message, my lord, and you will hear why. It takes a great deal of telling, and these here with you have the right to hear it as well.

"You will have heard of the legend of the Makers, the great wizards of a hundred centuries ago, who called themselves the Shining Ones. That was somewhat conceited of them," Olen added with a quirk of his mustache, "though their accomplishments most certainly allow them to claim great renown. We know some of their names, which are taught to every seeker who comes to learn magic, carrying on the oral tradition that gives those eight wizards a measure of immortality among humankind."

"Infamy," snorted the female centaur beside Lowan, her jade-green eyes flashing in her dark-hued face.

"I cannot dispute that, dear lady," Olen said. "Nor would I try. These eight wizards were very powerful and focused people. They discovered, after many years of study, that there is a vital link between a thing and a written symbol for a thing. They learned that, under the appropriate magical circumstances, to visit changes upon that symbol, or rune, was to visit the same changes upon the thing itself. Their studies, over many decades, not only confirmed their hypothesis, but allowed them to experiment upon the nature of reality itself."

"Perversion," growled one of the elves, a male with a perfectly young face framed by silky silver hair.

"Again, I cannot disagree with you," Olen said. "In light of the outcome. Wizards are by inclination observers, as many of you have complained when we have refused to perform functions that you see no reason to refuse. The reason we refuse is what immeasurable harm can come from meddling inappropriately. Alas, the measure of a true philosopher is whether or not he ever stops asking questions to take action. You would think that they would be content only to study what they had discovered. They were not."

"What did they do?" Halcot asked impatiently. Olen spread out his hands.

"Why, what any alchemist would do when given a number of reactive chemicals: they mixed them together to see what would happen."

"What is the problem with that?" asked Balindor curiously, hoisting his glass. "When you have a few good liquors you can make better drinks than with one."

"Yes, but what we are speaking of here are not liquors," Olen said patiently. "We are speaking of living beings. The Shining Ones combined species, to see what would live and what would die."

"Impossible!"

"Not impossible." Olen sighed. "Look around you. The world is full of the products of their imaginations. They came up with new kinds of plants, but also many, many kinds of animals. The very symbols of your houses are products of those studies. The pegasus race of Rabantae were horses given the wings of swans. The gryphon of Melenatae is a lion mated with an eagle. Countless others, successful and many less so. But the Makers did not even stop there. They began to experiment with themselves, and create new races of men bred with animals to produce *intelligent beings*. Centaurs. Werewolves. Mermaids. Dwarves. Borrens. Thraik. Smallfolk. They are the work of these eight wizards. Brilliant as it may have been, as viable as these species have become, the question still remains after all these centuries: was it right to do?"

"Blasphemy! How can that be true?" a hairy-faced man demanded.

Tildi noticed that his canine teeth were long and unusually sharp. Another werewolf. "We are natural beings, as old as humanity!"

"You are only as old as humanity because you are part of humanity, Timmish," Edynn spoke up from her place. "In the form your people wear most of the month. The three days of the full moon, your other part manifests itself. It was a less successful bonding than many."

"It's a lie," he snarled. "I will kill you for saying such nonsense."

"Truth," the wizardess said simply, with a sigh. "It would not matter at all if you did kill me. The truth would remain unaltered. Unlike Olen, I would rather have allowed this generation to go on having forgotten about its origins, as you have for thousands of years, and just faced the immediate problem at hand. I have studied this knowledge all my life, as have most of my magical companions here."

The other wizards in the room nodded gravely.

The Chief Lycanthrope, Timmish, was not appeased.

"The werewolf was brought into being to assuage the curiosity of the Makers—and disaster has befallen many because of it. You know your history. You know your behavior. There are tribes of your people whom you cast out because they refuse to control themselves when the change is upon them, isn't that true?"

Timmish was too offended to reply, but many of his people nodded to themselves.

"The alterations that the Shining Ones made caused many species to come into being. See all these symbols?" Olen began to draw them upon the air with his fingertip, and they hung there, shining in silver. "All of them descend from the rune for human"—he drew them on the air with a fingertip—"Dwarves, smallfolk, centaurs . . ."

Tildi studied them, astonished. She had noticed the similarities between the species' symbols before, but had passed them over as coincidence, thinking that all sentient beings must have something in common. She never dreamed that it would be because they were all variations on one general rune, that for *human*.

She was surprised to be able to consider the matter with such dispassion. In her belly was a cold lump of lead. Like the werewolves, she did not want to believe that her race had not descended from antiquity as she had been taught from childhood. How could it possibly be true?

"Elves, too? I'd heard that elves also were a product of the Shining Ones' work," Cadwallan said, from the second row. The elf marchioness in the front tier turned a scornful face in the noble's direction.

"The *legends* say yes—" Olen began.

"No!" the elf lady, Lady Urestin, snapped, interrupting him. "*We* created humans, back in the time before the skies were filled with smoke. It was a *joke*. Alas, it went too far, and you vermin were able to interbreed. Who could have guessed that a perversion of nature would do so? Do you see? The human rune is a mirror image of *elf*." She put out a hand and the rune hanging in the air before Olen turned around to face the other way.

"Why, so it is," Magpie exclaimed. "I never noticed that before."

"That means nothing!" Cadwallan exploded.

"Oh, yes, it does," Olen said. "I have always believed that elves and humans are complements to each other. Each has strengths that the other lacks. We have been both allies and enemies for millennia because of them. I am not saying that it is because one made the other, but that they are twins of Nature herself."

"But *we* are unique among species," declared Balindor, getting heated.

The marchioness regarded him with disdain. "No. All this is our fault. It *was* a jest. We should not have let it run this far, but there you are. We have a reverence for life, even that we brought into being as an error. Once born, we did not feel we could let it die. So it prospered and multiplied. And look at the trouble it caused. For that we are truly sorry."

"What?" Balindor was joined in his outrage by other humans. "No, humans created elves. Tell her, Olen!"

"You will never agree on the first part, my friend," the wizard said with a gentle smile. "And I cannot prove my thesis, either. I cannot give you proof, until the day comes when we can ask one of the Makers face-to-face what they did and did not do ten thousand years ago regarding elves and humans, but the others are all products of their endless curiosity."

"I don't believe it," Halcot said, stroking his beard. "Dwarves, centaurs, smallfolks, all made from humans? It's a fairy story."

"But that part is undeniably true," Olen assured him. "Tildi, show him your foot."

"What?" Halcot demanded.

Every face in the room turned toward Tildi. She felt her cheeks glow with embarrassment. Olen gave her an encouraging smile. Troubled as she was by his strange tale, she trusted her master. Shyly, she stripped off her shoe and stocking, and showed her foot to the room. Everyone burst into speech at once.

"She has no toes!" the dignified Halcot exclaimed, his ruddy face paling.

"How dainty," Magpie said, with a little smile for her. "Her foot looks like a lady's in a pale stocking."

Olen nodded, studying Tildi's upraised limb as if it was a curious specimen he had on display. "I believe that must have been the pattern for the design. All the muscles and bones are there to give her balance. They spread and ripple under the skin, but they are not separated into individual digits."

"But why?"

Olen settled into the attitude Tildi recognized as his lecture-giving mode. "Look how small she is, barely thirty inches tall! I have studied ancient documents that were the notes of the Shining Ones. A few survive, though there are not many scholars who have ever seen them, let alone have the skills to read them. I can show you the documents in which it is recorded."

He held up a much creased and rolled sheet of parchment, one corner torn or burned away.

"I regret that the language is difficult. Even a few hundred years makes a difference in how words are interpreted, let alone ten thousand. The diarist whose jottings I read reveal that the wizard whose work it was to breed human beings to the size you behold here, and combine them with a type of plant—which, as an aside, I must note that I have not been able to identify—as you might be able to tell by her ears, believed that their fingers and toes would be too fragile to coexist with nature. Further experiments, which sound horrible and inhumane to our modern ears, proved that these small beings could not live happily without fingers, but, as you see these dainty feet are not prone to stubbed or wrenched toes. Tildi has better balance than you, and better grip with the point of her foot than you have with your fingers."

"Really?" Magpie asked with interest. "Can you climb walls?"

"You have toes?" Tildi asked, faintly horrified. "Like animals?"

The minstrel let out a hearty laugh. He stripped off his big muddy boot and shoved his foot in her direction. The pale tan growths at the end wriggled at her. They looked like maggots in a piece of bread. The minstrel saw her disgust and laughed again.

"Ugh!" Cadwallan exclaimed.

"Please, highness, behave yourself in company," Olen chided mildly.

Tildi noticed that both Cadwallan and Magpie were startled at his scolding, and sat back obediently. Magpie tied his boot on again.

"You see, that could not have happened by accident," Olen continued. "Most creatures have some kind of pedal digit. All other humanlike beings do, except smallfolk. That was by intention."

The big centaur prince stamped his polished hoof.

"Come sit with us, little sister," Lowan boomed. "I have no toes, either. We are siblings in grievance against the human meddlers. As you see, we are descended from horses, but I defy any human to call our honor into question!"

"None would, my lord," Olen said, bowing to him.

"This . . . cannot help but change the way I see these people," Halcot said, shaken. "They are thralls of humankind?"

"Stop that line of thinking immediately," Olen said sharply, pointing a finger at the king. "You no more control them than you control the growth of any child. If you grant them their human roots, they are as autonomous as yourself."

"It could be natural breeding," Balindor mused aloud, studying her foot, but even Tildi could tell he didn't believe it. She had a lot to deal with in her own mind. Smallfolk not a natural race? Made of humans coupled with plants? How . . . terrifying. How . . . *confusing*. She felt as though she no longer knew herself. It felt as though her history had been stripped away. Hastily she put her shoe back on. Realizing he had been staring, Balindor gave her a sheepish glance.

"These Shining Ones must have been mad," he said at last.

"Madness or genius," Olen replied. "Yet some of their changes have proven to enrich the world, not besmirch it. Who can say what this world would have been like without the merfolk to guide humankind across the waves? Who would not have missed the wisdom of the centaurs, the indomitableness of the dwarves?"

"All this is undeniable, wizard," Cadwallan snorted, "but the workings of wizards long dead have little to do with us now. Get to the point. Why have you called us together?"

"There is a matter that concerns those of us who are alive today," Olen said. "The Shining Ones' studies, alas, did not end with their experimentation on the engendering of new beings. These wizards recorded all of their observations—the runes—into a single document, consisting of every object, being and feature of the world around them."

"They made a *book?*"

"They did," Olen said. "The Great Book was meant to be a reference. From the beginning it became clear that it was more than a mere book: it was a connection to all nature. At the suggestion of one wizard they amassed a single document that contained a description of all reality. It seemed to them to be the most useful and fascinating object to study, but they soon came to realize how vulnerable it made reality. Such a book is a powerful focus, like a burning glass. The runes in the book are exactly like the runes on which they performed their workings, but it had a further effect. Contact with the book causes one's rune to be revealed. Some of us can see them naturally, but near to the book itself, everyone can see them. The book unlocks one's reality, makes it possible to change one when the rune is visible."

"What could be the meaning of those changes?" the werewolf lord demanded.

"The runes describe living creatures. In fact, the entire book describes all of creation—everything. The runes alter slightly when the object does, say a child growing a tooth, or a tree losing its leaves in the autumn. If you studied a single rune over the years, you would see the differences over time. It is most fascinating to study a true rune."

Impatient murmurs ran through the assembled.

Olen smiled apologetically.

"Forgive an old scholar rambling on. If one did change a rune, it would be conceivable to improve its subject, perhaps, but also to pervert. We do not know all the ramifications of any change. It would require years of study to understand completely. We do not undertake such a task lightly. Few outside our order understand what a responsibility it is.

"The Shining Ones did understand. They realized what a dangerous thing that they had created in the Great Book. They argued about what to do with it. All of the surviving texts say the same thing. Knemet had fallen in love with his creation and did not want it to be destroyed. The others were afraid for posterity. What would befall existence if the book one day came into the hands of someone who did not have the well-being of the entire world at heart? By that time other wizards and magic-workers had joined the original eight in their studies. Many of these were understandably frightened by the power that had been unlocked by the creation of this book. The group divided into three factions: one under Knemet that wanted to keep the book and continue to study it, following wherever those researches led. One wished to destroy it, and one wanted the book hidden away so securely that it could never cause the twisting and rending of nature that they so feared. There was a terrible war among the Makers that shook the earth. Unable to agree or destroy one another, they went their separate ways. A century later they met again in battle, some wishing to destroy the book, others to continue their work with it, and one who wished to use it to rule.

"Knemet raised armies from inanimate objects and called down destructive forces—in other words, doing just exactly what the other seven feared might happen if the book fell into the wrong hands. In the end, he was defeated because the other two factions were so horrified by his actions that they joined forces. Dozens were killed, or changed beyond all recognition. That is why there is so little written matter left by the wizards. Much was destroyed." Olen's voice coarsened with emotion. "Whole countries had been ravaged by the battles. The wizards who had such a reverence for life had caused thousands of deaths."

He paused and poured himself a glass of wine. Tildi felt as though she could see the ruined countryside in her mind's eye, and shivered. She became aware of how still the room was.

"What did they do after the war was over?" Magpie asked, his voice breaking the silence as softly as distant birdsong.

Olen smiled at him. "The only sensible thing: they took the book away to the most remote location they could find. They secured it with spells and laid half a mountaintop upon it to prevent anyone from coming upon it casually. Then they set guardians around it. These protectors were gathered from the most powerful beings in the world, such as dragons, serpents, and lionelles, all bespelled to live as long as they were needed. These true hearts gave up their eternity to spend guarding that book. It is believed that even a few of the Shining Ones took up posts beside this mountaintop, changed beyond humanity. They saw it as their duty to see that the book never saw daylight again. They realized—too late—that it should not have existed in the first place."

"Why are we concerned about a magical book ten thousand years old surrounded by indomitable and immortal guardians?" Balindor asked, bored with the narrative.

Olen raised his voice so all could hear him. "The trouble is that the book is free, my lords and ladies. It is on the move. To what purpose I do not know."

Chapter Fourteen

ozens of voices burst out at once.

"Where is it?"

"Who could have taken it?"

"Why?"

"Why is the one obvious question, my lords and ladies," Magpie said over the rest. "For power, of course."

"But why are you concerned about this book, Olen?" Timmish asked. "What does it mean that it has been taken?"

Olen looked old and tired. "It could mean the end of all existence, my friend. That is why it was shut away in its fastness. And why it must be found and returned thence, before harm can befall it."

"Why? What does it matter where it is?"

"Because it's not immutable in and of itself. It is vulnerable. That was the one thing that the Makers discovered. If it *is* destroyed, all of that which is described within it is destroyed, too."

Everyone in the room fell silent.

Halcot shifted uncomfortably in his chair. "You have yet to convince me with your fairy stories, Olen. How can a mere book cause trouble? We have hundreds of books in my castle. Thousands throughout my kingdom! Not one has ever caused a problem. It's the people who read them that cause the trouble."

That evoked a chuckle from many of the visitors. Olen gave him a sad smile.

"My lord, I have reports here from brother and sister wizards. It does no harm now to tell you that the book was hidden in Sheatovra. I first heard from a wizard I know, Indrescala, who lives at some remove from that secret mountain. She sent me word of a poor farmer who came to her claiming that the cattle in his field had been cursed. My friend visited that field, and found that the animals had been transformed horribly, as if their flesh was clay and some child had decided to remold them but did not know how. The ones that were still alive were in terrible pain."

Tildi let out a gasp with the other listeners.

"The farmer said that glowing words appeared on each beast. Hence, you see, their reality had become within a hand's reach of anyone who might wish to meddle with it, and someone did. She wrote to me to see if I knew any destructive magic that could cause such deformation. It began to put ideas into my mind. I wrote to others of my order asking their counsel. I must tell you, we fought coming to the conclusion we did, but we had little choice, given the evidence."

"What if it *was* just a curse?" Halcot asked.

"The chances of that are so slim, and slimmer still when I tell you the latest dire news I have from the south. I received this only two weeks ago from Indrescala, and I did not hesitate a moment before sending for all of you." Olen raised a scroll from among the papers on his lap. "My lords and ladies, the guardians are dead. All of them. The mountaintop was breached. The book is gone."

"Well, why don't you just find it and put it back again?" the centaur lord asked with some asperity.

"We *have* been looking for it," Edynn spoke up. "All of us wizards, as well as our friends and helpers all over the world." She gestured around the room. The magicians bowed, but so did the more humbly dressed visitors, such as the troubadour and the merchants. "It is no trouble at all to conceal oneself from magical scrutiny. I can do it myself. This is much more difficult. I could even have caused harm to a herd of cattle half a world away. That is very difficult, but not outside the reach of my talents. It is the glowing runes that prove that the thief went that way. The book must have been close to the herd for that to arise upon the poor beasts. That means that whoever did it is not only concealing his passage, but the trail as well. We must rely upon keen-eyed observers to tell us where to follow."

"Why could you not scry out the path of this thief?" Halcot demanded.

"We have tried," growled Komorosh, shivering in his bearskin. "The pulses of the earth tell us nothing but that a great power walks upon it, but not where."

"How can you possibly miss something like that?"

Porrak, an older wizard in long brown robes, snorted. He had a long, gray beard that straggled over the breast of a worn, threadbare gray robe. "My lord, have you a spyglass?"

"Yes, I have. What does that have to do with it?"

Porrak pointed a long, broken, and chipped nail at Halcot. "Can you see all of a vista at once with it?"

"No, of course not. I can see what's in front of my lens."

"That is how it is with our magical farsight. We can see every inch of a landscape, but one inch at a time. I am sure in time we can spy out the thief's passage. Soon, I hope."

"Again, you say the thief," Lindora spoke up. "Who took this book?"

Olen shook his head. "Alas, we do not know."

"The thief must be a master wizard of the most high level," Serafina said, rising to her feet. "In order to penetrate the book's defenses, even to touch it, one must have magical safeguards that are out of the reach of ordinary beings. We fear, that is, my mother and I fear, that it could be one of the Shining Ones. Knemet may have returned."

"But he'd be centuries old!" Balindor burst out.

"That would mean nothing to them," Olen pointed out. "I'm a few centuries old myself. And they had the benefit of being able to rewrite their own runes to be rid of the pains and weakness of old age. There have always been rumors of Knemet walking the earth. No one ever knew when or *if* he died, you know. Nor most of his companions." He shook the parchment roll until it rattled. "It does not matter *who* took it, my lord. The important thing is to recover it before immeasurable harm can be done. We must find it, determine that it is the genuine article, and wrest it from its captor. On this the lives of every living being depends."

"Very well, then," Balindor said, smacking his palms upon his knees. "We are getting down to practical matters. What does it look like, so that if we encounter it we can, er, bring it back?"

"Ah," Olen said. He flicked his hand, and a thick roll of parchment flew to his hand from the spot on the table where it had been waiting for just such a moment. Tildi watched approvingly as Olen drew a couple of runes upon the air and set the scroll between them. It unrolled and hung on the air like a line full of washing, but glorious washing, a fair analog for the garments worn by the lords and ladies in the room. Each of the runes had been carefully drawn in golden ink, and decorated with many colors, rendering it as beautiful as an illustration. She studied the open book briefly before it began to move slowly over the heads of the crowd, allowing everyone to see it.

"This is a poor copy, but an ancient one," Olen said. Balindor stood up and put out his hands to catch the flying book for a closer look, then snatched his hands away before he touched it. "Oh, don't worry, it's quite safe. This one has none of the power of its original. The parchment is just that: parchment. I wish you could see the true book. I've seen it in visions evoked with the help of the ancients' diaries. Astoundingly beautiful. A masterwork. The Shining Ones were artists as well as philosophers of great ability. Here, see."

With a wave Olen created another book. The copy resembled it somewhat, in the way that the retelling resembles an adventure. The colors were more vivid yet. It seemed almost alive to Tildi. The visitors caught their collective breath. "Do you see? It is an integrated whole. Every part of it is lovely, well made, and well thought-out, and deadly dangerous."

Olen caused the book to spool slowly from one stick to the other. Tildi caught a glimpse of a rune she knew almost as well as she did her own name.

"Stop!" she cried, then blushed, ashamed of her outburst. Olen turned mildly quizzical green eyes to her. She was ashamed for bursting out in public, without the permission of her master.

"Go on," he said. "You have the right to speak, Tildi."

"I know that sign," she said, "or something very like it."

"You saw one of the runes in the Great Book? Where did you see it?" Olen demanded.

With every eye following her, Tildi dashed out of the grand hall. She hurried up to her small room. From Teldo's books she unearthed the precious leaf and carried it back past the curious faces to Olen. His brows rose almost all the way up his face.

"Do you see?" she asked, holding it out to him and pointing to the hovering vision. "It is the same."

"Why, so it is," Halcot said, coming up to peer from one to the other over the top of her head. "By the stars, it is beautiful. Pity there's so little of it left. Is this the fate of your so-called Great Book, Olen? Was it cut up and scattered around the world for people to find?"

"No," Olen said. "Ah, Tildi, what a find! Let me make certain." He beckoned, and the parchment copy floated back to him. He wound through it briskly, until he came to the page. "Yes, indeed. My soul, I never dreamed . . ." Tildi stood at his elbow, looking down at it. The single leaf practically glowed beside the copy. He gestured toward it. "May I?"

"Certainly," Tildi said, holding out the leaf to him. Olen made it hover in the air and turn about so he could see every angle, but Tildi noticed that he did not touch it.

"Yes. My word, a true copy. Where did you get this?"

"My—" Tildi stopped herself. She almost let the truth about Teldo slip. "My mother bought it for us from a peddler many years ago hoping it was a storybook. It's been in our household all this time."

"Ah. Is this what you learned the true language from?"

"No, sir. We couldn't read this leaf. I've got other books, plus a few other texts bought from traveling peddlers and from a shop in the Tillerton."

"You didn't go there yourself, did you?" Lakanta asked shrewdly.

Tildi met her eyes, much more comfortable to be addressed by a woman. "Oh, no. My brothers did all the trading outside the Quarters."

The blond woman nodded. "I thought so. Never saw a female smallfolk in all my days of trading. You're the first." She grinned, and Tildi smiled shyly back.

"So you couldn't read it," Olen asked.

Tildi shook her head.

"Indeed not!" snorted a large, black-haired wizard, wrapped in a heavy fur cloak despite the day's heat.

"Indeed, yes." Olen smiled. "Oddly enough, your mother's instinct was correct. It does tell a story. Masawa, I believe this is your speciality."

One of the dark-robed scholars came up to look at it and studied it with a smile on his face. "I believe, yes, this describes the giant yew tree that stands with its roots in the stone on a small island in the center of the fork of the River Moor. I've seen it myself."

"In *my land*," Lowan boomed.

The scholar turned to bow to him, one hand upon the breast of his robe. "Yes, my lord. The tree is ancient, older than you may dream. It was born more than six thousand years ago. Its whole story is here in one beautifully drawn rune."

Tildi examined the rune. For the first time she was able to see *tree* separate from the rest of the image, as well as *river* and many other general signs, including the one that depicted sixty centuries. If she had written out this tale, she would have used several word runes and a few individual signs to spell out unfamiliar words such as Balierenn. It was an art to combine them as this scribe had done. She was pleased to be able to understand a little of it, after so many years. If only Teldo could have lived to be here and know all this about his most treasured possession!

"It's a story that can be told in many ways," the scholar explained.

"And you handled this?" Olen asked, with a glance of respect at Tildi.

"Yes, we all did. It hurt a little at first. Tingly. Burning. But it was so pretty Teldo and I kept trying until we could."

"A mystery begins to reveal itself," Olen said, nodding. "There have never been many wizards among your kind. It's possible that this fragment of the Great Book, by mere contact, has unlocked talents in you that might never have come out in other circumstances. Time and Nature alone know what years with the book itself would have done."

Tildi was crestfallen. "I thought we . . . I mean, I thought I was *meant* to be a wizard."

"Tildi," Olen said gently. "It's a rare gift, no matter how you came by it. What you did, beginning at a very early age, might have killed a weaker person. You have increased your grasp of magic. That did not come by accident."

"Don't see what all the excitement is over a shred of parchment," Halcot snorted. "May I see it?"

"Certainly," said the wizard. "Go ahead."

The lord of Rabantae plucked the leaf out of midair, and immediately dropped it. His face contorted and his hands began to tremble. "Feels like fire," he gasped. "My hands!" Tildi sprang up to see if she could help. The king's fingertips were burned almost black.

The young female wizard bustled forward and spread her hand over Halcot's burned flesh. "Easy, now. Easy."

When she moved back, the skin had been restored to pink. "You're going to have to build those sword calluses up all over again, my lord."

"Thank you, Lady Serafina," Halcot said. His face was lined and drawn as he turned to Tildi. "The pain was terrible! How did you do that, young lady? You must be made of tough fiber."

"I . . . we didn't think much of it at the time," she admitted, with retrospective horror at what could have befallen her family. "It didn't do that to any of us. Not even once. My mother would have thrown it away if it had."

"Intelligent design," Olen said. "I told you, smallfolk were made to be tougher than they look. I must state, however, that the Great Book is many times more powerful than this."

The scholar clicked his tongue over the leaf. Tildi noticed *he* didn't try to touch it, either. "Where did the peddler get this?"

Tildi shrugged. "I didn't know. We don't see him anymore. We used to see him around planting, and again at harvest. It's been," she reckoned backwards, "about two and a half years since the last time he came. A nice man. Pretty close to our size, with big ears and a thick, blond beard and crinkly eyes."

"This comes long before the theft of the book, Olen," Balindor said. "Two and a half years!"

"There have been rumors that Knemet has been trying to find indications of the book's whereabouts for centuries, my lord prince," Edynn said. "It took him ten thousand years, but he seems to have found it."

"Now, Edynn," another wizard said, clad in red livery. "We do not know that it is Knemet who has stolen it."

"I cannot hold out hopes like you, Crispian," the white-haired wizardess said. Beside her, Serafina sniffed disdainfully. "It would take very powerful magic to have stolen it, not to mention an utter disregard for life to have harmed those poor cows. Do not forget them!"

Cadwallan shook his head. "I cannot pretend to understand the magical arts. Why would proximity matter?"

"Well, your majesty, lords and ladies," Olen said, "allow me to demonstrate. I can tell by my art that this is a true copy, made directly from the book itself. Even though it is not the Great Book, it has power because it was in contact with it at one time." He waved a hand, and sent the fragment to hover beside an unoccupied chair. "And when I put it near an object, you see how the rune appears."

To Tildi the chair's faint rune began to glow brighter.

"I don't see anything," complained Balindor, squinting.

"The rest of us can," Edynn assured him.

"I can, too," Tildi said. "I've been seeing runes like that on my travels, ever since I left the Quarters. In trees. Even in the sun. Do you mean it is my leaf that is making it do that?"

Olen's shaggy eyebrows went up. "This is very important. Very. It would mean that where the book passed, the runes are most likely rendered visible. We must discuss this later. No, highness, I did not expect that most of you could see them unaided. Here, my lord." He took the scrying glass off the table and set it on the floor. He held out both hands and began to mutter to himself. The glass grew until it was taller than Tildi. The image of the chair was inside the globe, the rune in it aflame.

"Ah, there it is!" Balindor exclaimed, as the symbol became golden to Tildi's unaided eyes. "And you say that every living thing has a rune within it somewhere?"

"Not just living things. Everything," Olen said.

"How is this pretty page dangerous?" asked a well-dressed merchant with a shiny, red face. "My scribes could turn out something just like this in a day."

"Your scribes could labor until the end of time, but without the talent to see and draw true runes they could not come close to evoking even a thousandth of the power that this book commands. Even this small leaf of a single copy is dangerous."

"Bah! Illusions!"

"Would you like to touch it?" Halcot challenged the red-faced man. "I assure you, the burns on my hands were no illusion. They still ache."

"Yes, but handling it is one thing. How could it *affect* something that it does not even touch?"

"The connection between the written word and the thing is made strong by proximity." Olen brought the leaf to hover beside a foot-thick candle in a huge bronze stand. "Watch. Do you see the rune within it?"

Tildi could. A simple glyph, gleaming coldly in the wax, broke through into ordinary sight. She had studied *candle*. There was little difference between the general symbol and this one.

Lindora beamed. "Ah! How interesting. It is not at all the same as the chair. Are the runes in all things so different?"

"Oh, yes," Olen said. "Just like the runes you use to read and write today, but flexible and self-altering. Each to its own design and good time, as well. All things change. People grow, age, die. Plants bloom and wither. Stone crumbles, metal is mined, worked, rusts away. The runes show the alterations as they occur. Behold. I will make it larger so that you can easily see the changes I will make in it now. Tildi, fire."

Tildi was startled out of her reverie. Fire? When she had been doing it incorrectly all this time? She looked at him with dismay. He gave her an encouraging gesture. Straightening her tunic unnecessarily, she stood up. It was a simple spell. She had done it dozens of times on the way to Overhill, and a thousand times since.

Don't make a fool of yourself in front of company, she told herself severely. *Ano chnetegh tal!*

All her practice proved worthwhile. The spell didn't fail her. She managed to cast a light between the tip of forefinger and thumb. The green flame flickered into life as if she had been all alone. She was so amazed that it worked that well she nearly let it burn her before transferring it to the wick. The wizards in the audience nodded their approval, and the nonmagical visitors seemed impressed.

"Do you see the change in the rune?" Olen asked.

They all leaned forward to study it.

"It has a little finger in the center of it now," Magpie observed.

"Yes. It's red and yellow," Merricot, son of Halcot, said with disdain. "A candle with a flame. We learned things like that in our reading lessons as children. This rune is fancier than most of the ones we use for every day."

"Now, see what happens when I change it."

Olen reached into the gigantic image of the rune. With a bold stroke, he enlarged the thin red stroke to a bold one. The flame at the top of the candle flared up into huge flame. The top half of the candle blew outward in gobbets of molten wax as if an invisible hand had smashed down on it.

"Now, my lords, imagine if that had been a human being or a centaur."

The room fell silent.

"One could kill, if you knew the glyph for a certain person," Balindor said.

"One could kill *millions*, without knowing who was whom," Olen pointed out.

"So, are we waiting for the end of the world?" Magpie asked.

"It's possible." Olen looked grave. "We must consider that such an outcome is possible."

Instead of being concerned, the young man grinned. "That's what you wizards always say. Doom and gloom and destruction."

Halcot turned a florid face to the minstrel. "You are irreverent, boy. Save your mountebank antics for an audience chamber or a music hall. If you were my son, I'd thrash you."

"Probably," the lad agreed, crossing his boots insouciantly. Tildi kept her face from changing, but she expected that the bard knew what was in her mind. If she lifted her eyes he grinned directly at her.

"Oh, stop, highness, he's winding you up like a clock," Edynn said, tossing her handsome waves of silver hair. "Impudent boy. If I were a hundred years younger . . ."

"If you were," Magpie said, with interest growing in his yellow-green eyes, "we could save the world together without all of these old men."

Her daughter looked from one to the other and made a horrified noise.

Edynn gave him an indulgent glance, and turned back to the matter at hand. "Olen, you must have a plan of action, or you would not have called us here."

"I have. I suggest a many-pronged attack. Most of you"—Olen gestured at the visitors—"will go home and mount a lookout for the thief. Be vigilant for reports of any unusual occurrences. Your wizards will be able to tell the difference between an ordinary magical outbreak and the passage of the book. Others, like myself, will continue our vision searches, through crystals, mirrors, and other philosophical devices. Yet, we must have some who will set out and look for signs of the book's whereabouts and pursue the thief to his lair. As you have seen, it cannot pass invisibly. Ideally, then, the book will be wrested away from that person, whomsoever it may be, and I am making it sound vastly easier than it will be, and placed back in a hiding place, with the best protection that we in these later days can muster, which yet a further group must prepare. Some of you in this room have been enemies in the past. I tell you that it is *imperative* that you should put aside old disagreements, in the name of our world's very survival. I can put it no stronger than that."

A few of the people glanced at one another, and exchanged curt nods.

Tildi, who was no student of history outside of the Quarters, wondered what Olen meant. Perhaps one day she would have time to learn more about it.

Masawa cleared his throat. "I notice, my old friend, that there are no representatives here from the Scholardom."

"Who?" Tildi couldn't help herself. Everyone looked at her. She blushed. She was forgetting herself. She would never have made such an outburst at a meeting. The scholar smiled at her. He did not seem to mind.

"It is an order of knights who have sworn themselves to the protection of the Great Book. They are very learned, and train themselves to the very peak of physical perfection so that they can serve it if it should come to them. I would have thought that you would have enlisted their help immediately when you learned of this theft, Olen."

"I am afraid," Olen said, "that we and the Scholardom would work at cross-purposes. I do not speak against them or their philosophy, though I do not agree with it. They would not see the urgency, as we do, of putting it immediately out of reach of the curious. I have broached the matter, in a subtle way, with an abbot of the order. In a hypothetical manner, of course. He became very enthusiastic on the subject, putting forth all manner of schemes to use it to correct 'aberrations of nature,' as their doctrine states it."

This phrase provoked an outburst from the centaurs and werewolf contingent.

Olen held up his hands for silence. "In other words, to let it fall into their hands would be to compound the problem. At present we believe that there is only one thief. We do not know who he or she is." He held up a hand to forestall another outburst from Edynn. "The fact that this thief has not immediately begun to use the book suggests that he or she has a purpose in taking it. Therefore we are under two constraints instead of one. We must find the thief before his or her purpose is set into motion, and we must keep this knowledge, and the book itself, from falling into the possession of the Scholardom. The second is by far the easier of the two, since all it requires is keeping our own counsel regarding what it is we seek. Alas, it is inevitable that the Scholardom will learn of our search, but I hope that by then we will have already accomplished our goal."

"Very well," Edynn said, standing up. "You need a party to seek out the thief. I will lead it. Who will go with me?"

Hands went up all over the room. Olen looked pleased. "I am gratified at your offer of service. Edynn, I believe you have your pick."

Tildi had been thinking hard since Olen had shocked her with the truth of her people's history. Like the werewolves, she did not want to believe it. How awful it was even to think that their ancestors were not truly smallfolk. She did not *want* to be the product of a curious wizard's experiment. She wanted things to be the way she had always believed, that smallfolk had been brought into existence at the beginning of all things by Mother Nature and Father Time. How horrified the elders would be to discover that their family tree might in truth *be* a tree. Only the ridiculousness of the notion allowed her to consider it without going mad. She hoped that the thief would indeed prove to be one of the immortal Shining Ones. She wanted to ask him very seriously what on earth he could have been thinking!

She had more to consider following the demonstration of the candle, and King Halcot's injury touching the page that her family had cherished for years. What harm the original, whole book could cause! It had killed so many beings, directly or indirectly. The cattle were only the latest victims. Still, she had a feeling that the chances were good that if she could handle the one, she could also manage the other, and spare injury to the very brave people who were putting themselves at risk, for the world's sake. She also felt that she owed something to the memory of her brothers, who had sacrificed themselves to save the other villagers that bleak day. It was in her nature to be useful. Here was a job that possibly only she was capable of. To offer her services was the least that she could do.

With regrets for the soft bed, daily baths, and regular meals, she put her hand up, too. It started trembling. Firmly she quashed her fears and held it steady with the other hand. Olen turned to her.

"Tildi," he said with infinite gentleness, "you do not have to volunteer for this task."

"Master, I do," Tildi insisted. Now that she had made the resolution, it felt like the most natural thing in the world. It took a good deal of courage to defy her master, but she must. She put both hands on his knee, and looked up at him, trying to find the best words to express what she needed to say. "You said that a wizard does what needs to be done. I don't *want* to leave here. I have been very happy, and you have been the best teacher I could imagine, but if I am the only one who can carry this book without pain, then I should go with Edynn."

Olen shook his head. "Tildi, there are other means to convey it to its next hiding place. Edynn and Serafina are as capable as I at levitating it."

Tildi felt a surge of desperation. He couldn't be refusing to let her go!

"But what if they can't? What if . . . if they have to take it away from the one who's got it? What if he won't let it go? I can do that. I *will* do it."

It was the least of reasons, filled with speculation, but Olen nodded, as if he could see what was in her heart. "Very well, Tildi. I honor your resolve." He raised his voice. "Nobles, ladies and gentlemen, I would go on this mission myself, but I am needed to help hold this city together if all things begin to crumble. Instead, I will send my new apprentice, Tildi."

Balindor sprang to his feet. "You're joking. A smallfolk? You should not be going," he told her directly. "Someone of rank ought to join this party. Someone who is trained to attack and defend! She will be helpless. You will not go, girl. I will."

Tildi quailed.

Olen tut-tutted and dropped a confident hand on her shoulder. "Do not think to order my apprentice around, highness, no matter what rank you hold."

"Why should she not go?" Edynn asked. "At present her reasons are better than yours, Balindor. She can see the signs. She has a sensitivity to the Great Book, which may be useful later on. She may not be able to wield a sword, but she is Olen's student. She is probably very learned in magic. I am glad to have her." Edynn gave Tildi a welcoming smile.

"How much magic could she know?" Balindor asked peevishly. "I thought you said she'd only been here weeks. You need someone strong. And big. No offense to you, smallfolk dame, but your size is against you in a test of force."

"This is not a matter for swords, my lord prince," Olen said patiently. "There is danger, of course, and I honor Tildi for offering to place herself in its way. It is no easy thing for me to send her, or to refuse you. Many others are perhaps as qualified as yourself to accompany Edynn, but you are needed at home. Who else but your family has the authority to call for searches in your realm? That is very important, more important than whether my apprentice has spent enough time with me to have learned magic."

"Yes, and perhaps I can teach her some along the way," Edynn added, with a sly look at Olen. "And she's got to learn magic somewhere, not as a side subject she picks up in between taking notes and washing floors."

"I do not *make* her wash floors," Olen snorted. "That's all her own doing. Buzz, buzz, buzz! I can't make her stop. I've never had an apprentice before who wasn't bone lazy. She's relentlessly tidy. It'll be peaceful to have you take her away with you. You may not thank me later."

He stood up. "My lords and ladies, let us adjourn for refreshment, and we can discuss who else will go with Edynn, and who will coordinate other watches after we have had a rest."

But no one else wanted to stop the discussion.

"Well, if *Tildi* is going, then I am going with her, and that is final," Lakanta announced. "Someone needs to take care of this child."

"What about your customers?" Magpie asked.

"Oh, I can find customers galore to sell and buy along the road. But hold, if anyone is going to the west, will you leave a message in Larchbrake for my cousin Dohondas to let him know I'm going out and about? He'll tell all my regulars for me—and doubtless steal them from me while I'm gone, faithless brat."

This last accusation raised a general chuckle.

"I will, Lakanta," a brown-skinned man in an ochre-colored coat said.

"Thank you, Sayrewald."

"But is this a journey for a mere *peddler?*" Merricot asked, horrified by the exchange.

"It's a journey for the sake of us all," Edynn assured them solemnly. "I will need more help than this if we are the ones who corner our thief."

"What about me?" Magpie asked. "May I be one of this party? I can handle a sword, and I can be entertaining along the way."

"No," Olen insisted, "you've got to go back to the northeast and warn the lords and wizards in Orontae and Levrenn."

"Orontae still has no wizard," Magpie said.

Olen nodded. "Ah, you're right. I forgot. Be discreet. Yes, tell them to expect the end of the world. In the meanwhile we will study and scry to discover how to recover and reseal the book in its tomb even if we have to fight a Maker to do so."

Merricot bowed to Edynn, and mockingly to Tildi. "You may count upon me for aid in any way possible. If our paths cross again, I am at your service."

"And mine," Balindor said, rising.

"And mine," Lindora added, with a graceful nod.

"I speak for Ivirenn," Cadwallan said. "Our strength is yours, should you need it."

"Someone of royal blood *ought* to go," King Halcot said.

"To do what?" Serafina asked, with a disapproving frown.

Halcot sputtered at the thought that anyone might question him. "Why, to protect you all. To take the book back to where it ought to go."

"We thank you for your offer, highness," Edynn said, with a graceful bow, "but this task is better taken in secret, not where we must go heralded by an entourage to prevent anyone from facing you. The delay might alert our quarry. You would not want that."

"Besides, my lord," Olen added, "strong leadership will be needed in your realm, should the book pass that way. Do not underestimate the value of the intelligence you can send back to us."

"I'll send my guards, then," Halcot insisted. "This little lass is valuable, if anything you said is true. If she offers any hope to help put the world back the way it ought to be. Captain Teryn, stand!"

A guard in helmet and supple silver mail sprang from near the wall where Halcot's contingent had been standing, and marched to the king's side.

"Sire," Captain Teryn said, in a clear, high voice. Tildi realized that the captain, fully as tall as the king, was a woman.

"You will accompany these people where they go. Travel in their company. Serve them as you would me. Take anyone you wish to aid you."

"As you will it, sire," the captain said, raising her hand in a salute.

Halcot turned back to Olen. "Then, what may I do, to raise 'intelligence' as you put it?"

"We don't want to cause panic," Olen said, "but word must be spread to stop the one who has the book. Put out word that an item of magical significance was stolen; that much is true and will be undeniable, once runes are spotted. We don't know where he is going, or what his aim is. We're blind, and we must go back to the only clues we have, such as the runes that Tildi saw along her road. If you hear rumors of such things, then send them to me. I will see that they reach Edynn. We must find out where he—"

"Or she," Serafina insisted.

"Or she," Olen echoed with a smile, "is going."

"Hmph," the king snorted. "If I was in the shoes, or fins, or talons, of someone carrying an object that everyone sought, I'd be heading where I felt safe."

Chapter Fifteen

I t is decided, then," Olen said, holding a scrap of parchment aloft before the assembled guests. "The number of this company will be seven. The wizard Edynn shall lead it. You have known of her of old. She is a most powerful and wise woman. Her daughter, Serafina, will accompany her."

Tildi glanced at the young woman, who stood looking balefully at the others as if daring them to disagree. She seemed to have the liveliest disapproval of anyone questioning her mother's judgment.

"King Halcot of Rabantae has offered the services of his captain of guards, Teryn, and one of her soldiers, Morag, as protectors on this expedition." Olen waved a hand at the side of the room. Teryn stood straight as a die, but Morag slouched so much that Tildi could not see the face under the long, straggly hair that peeked out from under the round metal cap and coif. "Edynn has also accepted Lakanta's offer to come along."

"I might be of some use," the peddler said with a cheerful smile. "I can mend things, and I can trade for what we'll need."

"She also welcomes Rin, sister of the Meadowlord, Lowan."

"I can intercede with those people who do not approve of humankind," Rin said, to the annoyance of the nobles present. "I wish to protect the interests of all nonhumans. I am an excellent tracker. Show me the signs to follow, and our thief will not escape us, I promise."

"And finally," Olen said, putting a hand on the head of his apprentice, "Tildi."

A good deal of murmuring accompanied her nomination, but no one demurred after the demonstration of the page.

Most of the others who wished to go protested at limiting the number of the company to seven. Every one of the scholars had wanted to be part of the group. The danger did not deter them. The chance to see the Great Book for themselves removed all fear. As for the discomfort and privation of the journey, one had said, only half-humorously, no one could live in more penurious conditions than a lifetime student. The warriors had argued that they were not troubled by the danger of the journey, and they ought to be considered for the honor of the task. The werewolf lord had also wanted to come for the same reasons as Rin. The elves conferred for a long while before finally suggesting two of their number. Edynn had turned them all down. They could not conceal how miffed they were that they were not chosen.

Tildi ate a meal that she did not taste, served by hands she did not see, as she listened, half in a dream, to the voices around her.

You volunteered for an adventure, her own inner voice said accusingly, breaking into her thoughts. Tildi tried to ignore it. *Were you so comfortable that you want to go back to sleeping outside? You could have spent the rest of your life here. Olen would never turn you away.*

It has to be done, she told herself.

But by you?

The more she thought about it, the more she realized that yes, it did. She had never shirked an honest task because it seemed too hard. If she needed help, she would ask for it. In the meanwhile, she had a skill that these educated, powerful folk did not. They needed her. *They do,* she told that doubting voice firmly. *I will go.*

After that, she listened to no more of the inner grumbling. There was too much to be done. She would have to pack, not that she had much to take away with her.

"Tildi, is it?" Lists forgotten, she looked up at the sound of her name to see the minstrel. He dropped down on the bench beside her. "I'm Magpie. I have been in your homeland many times."

"I think I remember you," she said, carefully. There was no way that he could know she had spied upon him on her way out of the Quarters.

"Yet, for all the times I have visited, I find I know little about your people. I never knew they were so brave, and their women most of all."

Tildi dimpled. "We do what needs to be done. Master Olen tells me that is also the way of wizards."

"I knew of the runes," he said. "I was one of the searchers that Olen sent forth to try and find signs of the book, but I never saw them. They are visible to you?"

"Oh, yes," Tildi said, and became very aware of his. It was a nice rune, though very complicated for a human, with a spiral pattern inside another spiral pattern at the heart. She remembered Irithe's admonition. *He keeps secrets, too,* Tildi thought.

"You are looking at mine," he said with a grin. "I'd like to see it."

"I . . . can't do what Master Olen did," she said apologetically. She wondered if he wanted her to go up and take the scrying glass off the wizard's table, or draw it on the air in silver, but after the explosion of the candle she was afraid something awful would happen.

The minstrel smiled at her, his teeth bright in his tanned face. "I'm not asking for magic. Can you scribe it for me? I would consider myself in your debt if you would." He produced a scrap of parchment and a pencil.

"Why, of course!" Tildi said, relieved. She took the pencil, and, ignoring the paper's own faint sigil, she carefully traced the lines that she saw in the young man. Weeks of working on Olen's assignments had trained her hand to be sure at reproducing the signs without error. One or two small details, and it was finished. "There you are. That's you."

Magpie took the little page from her and admired it. "Very interesting. Very. It's different from the sign we write for *man*, of course, but I never dreamed it would have so many other features. And this is like no one else's?"

"No one here," Tildi said. "Of course, I have not met many humans. I know little of them beyond what I have learned here. I never traveled before I came here to Silvertree."

"You handle us all with such aplomb, I would have thought you were used to being around us all your life," Magpie said. He tucked away the scrap in the breast of his tunic. "Thank you for this. I'll do you a favor one day if I can."

"You're very welcome," she assured him. He was really very nice. She regretted that custom had forbidden her from getting to know him when he had visited her village. "It's nothing, really."

"I could never have done it for myself, you see," Magpie said. "I'm grateful. Good journey to you."

"And to you," Tildi said. She looked up as he rose from the bench and noticed several of the other visitors standing around, as though they had been watching them. Many of them looked as if they would like to ask her to draw their runes, too, but they all glanced away hastily when she tried to meet their eyes.

*I*f Tildi had seen little of her master in the weeks before the conference, it was a good deal compared with the brief glimpses she got of him in the next few days. He seemed to be in all places at the same time, giving advice to the delegates, who would soon be going home, or in search of a fastness remote enough to secure the book a second time, should they be fortunate enough to regain it. She was aware of his scrutiny, though, always seeming to see his bright green eyes on her from across the room, where she was talking with one of the other chosen trackers, as Edynn chose to call them. She hoped that he would make time to see her before she had to go.

She need not have worried about her laundry, or any of the other small tasks necessary before setting out on a long journey. Liana and her staff were in and out of the small bedroom continually during those days, dropping off clean and mended clothing, new socks, a better made rucksack, a set of eating utensils appropriate to her size that looked like gold but were as light as paper, and other little conveniences.

A whirl of preparation filled the next few days. When Olen was not conferring with the delegates who would soon be departing to warn their people, he was stopping by Tildi's room with advice and items for her to put into her pack. She sat on the floor trying to fit everything into the new pack.

"This compass never fails," he said, handing her a small brass disk. "You will be able to read it even in the dark, even underground." He started to go out of the door, then glanced back. "I feel I have not prepared you enough to send you out in this manner, Tildi. I am remiss. I did not foresee you leaving so soon. I am afraid that my vision has been seeking out across the ages, and not giving attention to what is here in my own household. I am sorry to have neglected you."

Tildi jumped up and hugged him around the legs. "You have been so kind to me, master. I've learned so much. I hope it is enough."

The long hand touched her hair. "You have been a most interesting pupil. I will miss you. We will all miss you. Liana has been scolding me without cease for allowing you to go. If I can give you anything for your journey, it is yours. Edynn is a good teacher. I would give you three pieces of advice before you go. First, don't stop learning. I know you are on fire for knowledge now. Second, keep both your eyes and your heart open. One may tell you something that the other cannot see. Third, trust yourself. I believe in you. Otherwise you would not be going on this journey. And come back safely."

Tildi felt her throat tighten as tears started in her eyes. "I will do my best."

At last it was time to go. Tildi stood on the doorstep on a sunny, late summer day, taking affectionate leave of Silvertree, its master and staff. The footmen and housemaids stuffed what little room was left in her carry sack with small presents and sweetmeats. Silvertree itself had also given her a small keepsake: a twig the breadth of her thumb had fallen out of the branches and landed beside her feet when she had been walking outside alone. Not another leaf or twig had fallen, so she knew it was a deliberate action. She patted the wall one last time, and descended the steps into the courtyard at Olen's side.

Many of the guests had remained on to wish the party well. Halcot and his son had gone, but Cadwallan and the children of the Melenatavian king were still present. Komorosh, huddled miserably in his thick, shaggy fur cloak, towered above the circle of human and elf scholars, all talking excitedly to one another. To Tildi's delight, Magpie sat on a stone in the garden playing his jitar. When he saw her he began to sing.

> *'Tis the tale of Tildi that I tell,*
> *Out from Silvertree where she did dwell,*
> *Set she with a doughty force to look*
> *For that troublesome, fearsome, magical book,*

A centaur who is known as Rin,
A peddler of cloth and pin,
Two soldiers strong in armor guise
Serafina fair and Edynn wise.
But none so vital to the day
As the smallfolk with her vision fey.
Though mountains move and kingdoms fall
Stormclouds threaten, rivers crest,
She will set the book to rest.
Hail, Tildi! Hero of us all!

Tildi beamed at him. Even though her brother was an able, even in-spired musician, she had never had a song written for her before.

Magpie sprang up and bowed to her.

"A farewell gift," he said. "I hope to give you a similar welcoming gift when you return victorious."

"Let us concentrate our thoughts upon making that success," Olen said, guiding the smallfolk to where the rest of the party waited.

Edynn and Serafina stood by their horses, who were nearly identical white mares with dark noses and dark tips to their ears and tail. The sad-dles and bridles were silver and white. The only way Tildi could tell them apart was by the saddlecloths. Edynn's was a soft green, and Sera-fina's a vivid rose. Each of them could easily reach her staff, which was slung along the edge of the saddle by a couple of loops. Captain Teryn and Morag stood by their horses, glossy brown animals with black tails, on whom the Rabantavian white and scarlet livery looked very smart. Even the pack animal seemed dignified by the livery on his harness, though he was piled higher than his head with odd-shaped packages. In sharp contrast, Lakanta's short-legged little horse was an undistin-guished straw color, and the large, round leather packs on either side of its wide rump made it look like she was carrying a yoke of buckets. Edynn floated over to take Tildi's hand.

"Are you ready, my dear?" she asked.

"You are riding?" Tildi asked in reply.

"Yes. We may have to cover a lot of ground. Do you have a mount?"

"Er, no. I've never ridden a horse by myself in my life."

"Gracious, how did you come here?" Serafina asked, looking down her nose at the smallfolk.

"On foot, mostly," Tildi said, feeling her face flush.

"Well, no more," Olen said. "I've got one more surprise for you."

He signaled to a groom, who brought Sihine forward. "This child's saddle ought to be small enough for you. The stirrups are short enough for your legs. Try it!" The groom heaved her high in the air and set her down in the saddle. Sihine looked at her over his satiny shoulder and let out a contented *hwwwnnnh*. Gingerly, Tildi patted him on the neck. She looked down, and began to tremble. She was so high off the ground, and there was nothing to keep her from falling off if they started to trot. What if Edynn decreed they should fly?

"Olen, your mind must be wandering," Edynn said, walking over to look up at the smallfolk. "She can ride that way, but what happens when she needs to get down? Is your groom coming along with us? Did you include a rope ladder?"

"Of course not, Edynn," Olen said with some asperity. "But my apprentice needs a horse. Sihine knows her. He will carry her faithfully."

"Don't you have one more suitable for someone her size? A pony?"

Rin snorted. "A pony could not keep up with us if we had to retreat from some danger, Edynn."

"I cannot believe none of us discussed this matter before," Edynn said, shaking her head.

"There have been many more important matters," Rin assured her. "I, too, have been more concerned with where our book thief has gone to. How we will follow him scarcely entered my mind."

Serafina looked haughty. "Well, you cannot expect my mother or me to carry her. Our steeds are accustomed to our weight. One of the guards, perhaps?" She looked pointedly at Captain Teryn.

"Not my orders, honored one," Teryn snapped out. "I follow the instructions of King Halcot. In order to provide proper defense, we must ride as unencumbered as possible."

"It's all right," Tildi said sadly. "I'd rather walk."

"And why not?" Lakanta said, swinging out of her saddle. "Melune would be happier if I walked, as I often do," she added pointedly, looking up at Serafina.

"Oh, stop bickering," Rin said impatiently. "You shall ride with me. I should be honored. Come." She reached down one long brown hand for Tildi's. Before she knew it, the smallfolk was astride the warm, striped back in front of the band that held matching packs of red leather. Another band held a small pouch and a coiled whip around Rin's waist. "You can hold on to my mane." She pointed at her spine. The red silk blouse she wore parted to allow a narrow band of thick, wavy black hair more than a foot in length to flow freely. She stamped a hoof and shifted from side to side. Tildi felt herself falling, and buried her hands in the crisp tresses. They felt like washed sheep's fleece, a soothing and confidence-inducing texture. Suddenly, she was no longer afraid of being so high up. Rin smiled at her and flared her nostrils. "That's better, is it not? Your pack will fit in one of mine. Are we ready?"

There was no excuse left not to go. Tildi touched hands with everyone still in the courtyard, princes, wizards, scholars, and all. Edynn gave the word, and they trotted out of the courtyard. The last glimpse Tildi had as she passed the gate was of Olen standing on Silvertree's doorstep, waving her good-bye.

"I have never seen anything like that, Olen besotted over an apprentice," Serafina said, as they clattered over the cobblestones up toward the city limits. "He'd never have made that kind of mistake with one of those idiotic boys who usually come to learn from him."

"He is worried," Rin said. "As are we all."

Tildi said nothing. Serafina's words couldn't be meant to wound, but they felt to her like an accusation that she was putting more burdens upon the search party than they needed. Teryn and Morag rode stolidly at the rear of the party, not speaking, even to each other. Tildi tried offering them friendly glances, which were returned without any emotion at all. She felt lonely and unimportant.

"I agree with you, Rin," Edynn said. "I have never been as worried about anything in my life! We have no time to think about that. Tildi, you are the leader of this expedition. Take us back to where you saw the glowing runes."

Chapter Sixteen

iding a centaur was not at all like sitting on the back of Sihine, either before or behind Olen. Rin kept twisting her upper body around to talk to her, and she frequently made a comment when Tildi shifted. That there was no saddle between them also made Tildi keenly aware that she was wearing heavy shoes and coarse trousers.

"I'm sorry," Tildi said. "If I'd known I'd be on your back I would have asked for softer clothes."

Rin laughed, a musical whinny. "It's not your trousers or your boots, little one. You fidget like a fly. I swear to you I will not drop you, but it is difficult for me to concentrate on making my way when you move around so much."

Tildi let out a gasped apology, which made Rin laugh again.

"You are so serious! I have known this of the smallfolk. Ride with the rhythm, and you will find everything will go much more smoothly."

The centaur exaggerated her walk for the next few minutes, making Tildi tip from side to side. It was like trying to sit in a rocking chair that was also bobbing up and down. Tildi was all too aware that it was more than twice her height to the ground from where she sat.

Rin increased her pace a tiny bit at a time.

Gradually, the smallfolk discovered that her hips naturally rocked in the direction of Rin's forward foot. Before long, she let her spine relax and follow the centaur's gait. By the time Edynn spoke to her again she was able to reply without thinking about how she was going to hold on.

"The last time I saw the runes so bright?" she echoed Edynn's question. "It was not long before I came into the city. I wasn't paying a good deal of attention to the road. I was riding in a chicken cart—"

"Of course you were riding in a chicken cart," Serafina said with an impatient exhalation. Lakanta chuckled.

"Well, just because you wouldn't be caught dead or dying in one, Miss High Horse."

"Be kind to my daughter, peddler," Edynn said, a little smile on her lips. "She has not been out in the world much, and she has a great deal to learn."

"Ah, I see. Forgive me, then," the little blond woman said gravely. "I will always forgive youth and innocence."

That forgiveness seemed to upset Serafina more than Lakanta's displeasure. She sat on her horse with her back very straight, and met no one's eyes while they rode.

Tildi hid a small smile. Edynn's daughter was abrasive, but Tildi thought it wasn't so much to offend as deflect. She was afraid of something. Tildi could well understand that. She was afraid for herself and the rest of them. The more that she thought about it, the more she was astonished at herself for having put up her hand to volunteer. What did she know about the world beyond the one road she'd trodden from the Quarters? What did she know of magic and wizards beyond what she had read in storybooks? She had fallen lucky to have been in Olen's care.

Lucky, indeed. That was part of the reason she had put herself forward. She had been lucky since she was a child. Lucky not to have fallen victim to the thraik, not once, but twice. Lucky that the fragment of the book had come into her hands in a manner that allowed her to build up an immunity to its power. She would be selfish not to put her good fortune at the service of, well, the world. She almost blushed at the conceit of it all, but smallfolk had always gone by the adage that if you had the right tool for the job, you used it. If you were a weaver, you wove. If you were a carter, you drove. If you were a farmer, you tilled. *And if you were a Summerbee,* Tildi thought, changing the last line of the old song, *you filled the job that needed to be filled.* She told her knees that was the reason they must stop knocking.

*T*he sun blessed them as they traveled southward along the main road. There were many more travelers than before, all of them staring openly at the small group, and especially at Tildi. She didn't know whether her cheeks were flushing from the heat or the endless scrutiny.

Once they were out of sight of Overhill, Captain Teryn took the lead. She rode at the front of the party, her head held high and her hand on her sword hilt to forestall anyone who might approach them casually. Not that anyone would. Awe of the two robed wizards kept the eager children away, even if they would dare to pass the shining Pegasus of Rabantae resplendent upon Teryn's tunic. The stares flustered Tildi, but she remembered that she had an important task to perform. It was easier to shut out the curious gazes once she began to concentrate upon studying her surroundings, seeking any trace of the runes that had been so plentiful on her trip northward. Even the rune that had been gilded upon the glowing solar orb had paled into obscurity. She began to wonder if she had imagined them, and she had never thought of herself as the fanciful type.

"Any signs?" Edynn inquired after a few miles.

Tildi appreciated the senior wizardess's patience. They must all be thinking that the logic that had thrust Tildi into the search party was flawed. She had to produce some sign that she had not been mistaken, or lying. How could the runes have vanished?

Tildi held fast to Rin's mane as she squinted at the nearby trees. Nothing looked very familiar, but then, she had had a rooster to contend with, as well as all the questions fired at her by her kindly host on her previous journey.

"I see nothing here," Serafina said.

"They must be farther along," Tildi said, much embarrassed. The trees and fences all looked so *ordinary.* "I recall a big oak tree whose rune I could read very well. I saw plenty of runes, I promise you!"

"Did the carter see them, too?" Lakanta asked.

"I didn't really ask. I assumed he could," Tildi admitted. "I thought everyone outside the Quarters saw them. Everyone seemed so much more familiar with magic than we smallfolk are. I started seeing runes as soon I had crossed over the mountains, and I thought that it was an ordinary event, not worth mentioning."

"That goes along with what Olen and the other wizards suspect," Serafina said with a sage nod. "The book came from the south. It must have passed along, or close to, the road you, er, walked." She still didn't credit that anyone ever traveled between towns on foot.

"But how?" Rin asked. "No ship reports having carried a wizard with such a burden. It would be difficult to hide its passage. Where did he come ashore?"

"He or she would not need a ship," Edynn reminded them. "Whoever carries the book commands the waves, the wind, the earth herself. He could cause the water to be solid under his feet, then soften as soon as he had passed. He could have come ashore in the belly of a beast that he caused to hold him. I heard a rumor of a creature split in two, down south near Tillerton. That could have been his carriage, as heartless as that sounds."

Split in two! That brought a vivid memory back to Tildi.

"A thraik fell to earth, cut in half," she said, seeing it all in her mind and shuddering afresh. "It was a few days before I reached Master Olen's. It fell on a man. Everyone had stopped to look at it."

"A thraik, actually riven in half?" Lakanta asked. "Whew, a marvel! I've never met the warrior who could strike such a blow."

"It would take a wizard," Serafina said. "Thraiks are powerful, but there are spells that could do what you describe."

"Could our thief have done such a thing?" Rin asked.

"It would be no effort for the bearer of the book," Edynn said solemnly. "He would not even have to touch the creature, merely slice through its rune. He could have used a pen, a knife, or the tip of a finger."

They all shivered at the thought of such power. Tildi felt the frisson race through the hairy back under her legs, and Rin's thick mane switched nervously.

"And you didn't think to mention such an important thing to Olen?" Serafina asked, glaring at Tildi.

Tildi flushed.

"I thought he must already know about the thraik. He always seemed to hear news before messengers arrived with scrolls. He reads the glasses in his study."

She didn't want to talk about thraik, and was sorry she had brought it up, nor did she like the disapproving glance from Serafina.

"That wasn't the thought uppermost in my mind. I was about to undertake my apprenticeship, and all my attention was on presenting myself in the best possible manner," Tildi added defensively.

"I understand that, dear," Edynn said with an amused little smile, but Serafina wasn't going to let the subject drop.

"Didn't you think more of it than that?"

"I was glad it was dead," Tildi said firmly. "Thraiks have been in the Quarters many times in my lifetime alone. They killed my entire family. I'm the only Summerbee left."

The others fell silent at Tildi's outburst.

Rin broke the silence with a gentle *sn-sn-sn*.

"I am sorry for your loss, smallfolk," she said. "We have had many thraik incursions, and many brave centaurs have died. It would seem that all of us share that enemy."

"We do, too," Lakanta said. "The lost ones are named in our Day of Sorrow remembrance every Year's End."

Serafina had her lips pressed together.

"My apologies," she said, but the words seemed to come with a distinct effort. "I had no idea of your history. How far from here was the dead thraik?"

"More than two days' ride," Tildi said.

"But you *did* see runes after that?"

"Oh, yes, for a long while." The young wizardess looked around, and the disapproving set of her nose made Tildi begin to feel desperate. Would they take her back to Olen and tell him she had failed?

"Can we be sure that the book did not go back along this road?" Lakanta asked. "You only think that the thief came north. He might have started out somewhere quite different and gone south to Tillerton. We ought to travel there and see if we can find fresh clues."

"No. Why would you suggest that?" Serafina asked suspiciously.

"Do you want to miss this thief?" the peddler countered. "I thought the idea was to run him to ground, and swiftly!"

"Peace, please," Edynn said, more gently, holding up a hand to still the two of them. "Tildi's dead thraik is more recent than the beast found in Tillerton. That shows that it was coming northwards, at least at that time. We will see if we can pick up the trail from here, and hope that it does not die out past tracing while we pursue it. Our thief has had a long head start on us. Our other attempts to trace him have failed. Who knows where he is by now?"

Tildi interrupted them with a shout.

"Wait! That gnarled tree! I remember that!"

She pointed to an ancient oak at the top of the next hill. Its bark, instead of being combed neatly like furrowed earth, was twisted and puckered. "I remember it because it looks so much like an old man's face. Its rune was like a wart on the nose."

Lakanta laughed, gaining Serafina's instant disapproval.

"Is this matter funny to you, peddler?" the younger wizardess asked.

The small blond woman wiped tears of merriment out of her eyes. "Oh, child, let it be. Tildi made an association that helped her keep a memory. Can I help it if it's a funny one?"

Serafina, exasperated, looked at her mother for support, but Edynn was smiling, too.

"You did see it there, Tildi?"

"Oh, yes," Tildi insisted. She was sure of it now. The tree was as unmistakable as a face. "Rin, will you bring me to it?"

"My pleasure." The centaur broke into a smooth trot.

"It looks ordinary to me," Serafina said, bringing her mare's neck close to the centaur's flank.

It did look ordinary. The rune was still there on the "nose," but far less distinct than it had been.

"The marking is fainter than before. I guess they fade in time," Tildi said, dismayed.

"Yes, but no," Edynn said, as they drew nearer. "Do you see, Serafina? Watch!"

"Yes!" the young wizardess said, her eyes widening. The rune seemed to lighten slightly, making it more prominent against the dark bark. "Touch it, smallfolk."

Tildi brought her hand out to the tree. The rune paled still further.

"Bless me," Edynn said. "This is an extraordinary event."

"It's only the residual effect of her own exposure," Serafina argued.

"I think not, daughter."

"I see nothing," Rin complained.

"Wait a moment more," Edynn said. "Tildi, do you have your fragment of the book to hand?"

Tildi thrust her hand into her belt pouch. Olen had told her to keep the page near her, and not to let it fall into anyone else's possession. The moment she brought out the roll of parchment, the rune on the tree turned golden. "There! That's a little like the way I recall it."

"It is enough," Edynn said. She nodded slowly, studying the effect. "Remarkable."

"Remarkable indeed," Rin said, dancing forward and back to see it vanish and reappear. "All things do have their rune."

Lakanta swung off her pony and came over to look at it between the legs of the horses.

"I see it now," the peddler said with a satisfied nod. "I can see why your carter missed it. I might not have paid attention. It might look brighter to you, with your witch-sight."

"It's weaker than it was before," Tildi commented, tipping her head to study the rune critically.

"This is a much stronger evoking than was brought out by your fragment," Edynn said. "Draw back your hand."

Tildi obeyed, and the rune faded back to its normal bark color. Lakanta shook her head.

"It's gone, at least to me."

"To me as well," Rin said.

Edynn nodded. "Once the influence of the book has gone, the runes change back very quickly, just as the chairs and the other things in Silvertree did. With the Great Book it might take minutes or hours, instead of seconds, depending upon an object's sensitivity to power."

"The candle stayed blasted apart," Lakanta pointed out.

"Well, it had been physically altered," Edynn reminded her. "If I changed this tree's rune while Tildi held it unlocked for me, it would remain changed when we withdrew."

"This is going to make it hard to follow the thief's trail," Rin said. "If these are a month and more gone."

"Not if trees and animals retain a sensitivity to the Great Book," Edynn said, sensibly.

"Is that possible?"

Edynn said, "Let us see if it provides us with a distinct enough trail to follow." She smiled at Tildi. "Come along this way, child. We will see if we can awaken more traces with your help."

Rin shook her great mane. "It is going to be very slow, and we have no time to lose."

"Better slow and sure than to miss him altogether. Let us experiment."

With Edynn's encouragement, Rin trotted to the head of the party, alongside Captain Teryn. North of the old man tree were berry bushes. They, too, glowed into life when the leaf neared them. Their runes had changed, but so had the bushes, now covered in nearly ripe fruit.

Tildi kept her eye open for landmarks she recalled, and held out the leaf to them. If the faint runes awoke, they continued in that direction. Once in a while they disappeared entirely. Tildi glanced back now and again to meet Edynn's eyes. The elder wizardess smiled at her encouragingly, and urged her to continue.

Rin kept to the left side of the road. She and Tildi sampled the landmarks on the right side from time to time, but the stronger evocations were clearly to be had on the west edge.

"I believe your thief must have traveled at night," the centaur announced to the others. "I beg your pardon," she added, to an annoyed carter who had to swerve to avoid her. "Otherwise he would be walking in the faces of many travelers."

"If he stayed upon the road," Lakanta said. "The woods are thin here, and anyone could ride or walk just inside the tree line, if he chose. I'd want to stay out of sight, if I had just stolen the key to unlocking all of nature. I've gone that way now and again myself, when the company on the road looked a bit too rough for my comfort."

"We will see," Rin said. "Hold tight, Tildi."

Keeping the copy leaf in one hand, the smallfolk girl grabbed Rin's mane just as the centaur gathered her haunches and leaped over the berm that bordered the road. Tildi ducked to avoid a faceful of twigs.

"By heaven!" the centaur exclaimed.

Tildi sat up. Just off the main thoroughfare, she could see numerous small tracks winding in and out of the trees. Most of them had been made by animals, but a few bore thin wheel-ruts and hoof marks, the evidence, as Lakanta suggested, of those who wished their passage to go unnoticed. In fact, it would be possible for a few lightly laden travelers to travel in parallel, though over much rougher ground than the well-kept road behind them. It seemed to have been the choice of their unknown quarry, for as soon as they penetrated the screen of trees, runes burst into golden light.

"What is it?" Edynn asked, bounding up behind them. The others followed swiftly. "My goodness! Well thought-out, Lakanta. Yes, what a result! No wonder your kindly escort did not pay heed, Tildi. This is a trail, and more! I would like to see what it looks like when one is close to the book."

"It's still not half as bright," Tildi said.

Serafina let out an exclamation. "But don't you see what that means? If what you saw was more distinct than this, it means you had to have been right behind the book thief. If you were following prominent, bright runes all the way to Overhill, he could not have been far ahead of you."

Tildi's heart leaped into her throat.

"He . . . I . . . he could have killed me then."

"But he didn't," Edynn said, dismissing the speculation. "He didn't see you. And we do not know the radius of the Great Book's power. He could have been a good ways from you, just as he got ahead of Indrescala, who saw the cows, but not their desecrator."

"She might also have been right on top of him," Lakanta said. "I know the road she traveled. It's one of two on the west side of the Arown. The good road is on the east bank. The west road, up on that cliff, leads only from Tillerton. And from the Quarters, I beg your pardon," she said, bobbing her head at Tildi. "The other is a tow path down along the Arown itself, almost right on the riverbank, which I suspect is what the thief took. She is luckier than she knows. You would never have seen each other."

Tildi let out a sigh of relief. It had been enough of an adventure for her to have traveled on her own, for the first time. To think that she was within arm's reach of a powerful and merciless magician made her tremble in retrospect. "I'm glad," she said.

"Come, then," Edynn said. "Since we have all had a lucky escape, let us continue. Rin is right: we have no time to lose in catching up with our thief."

Now even Serafina was convinced that they were following the correct trail. Ignoring protests from Captain Teryn, Rin took the lead.

Astride her back, Tildi held out the rolled-up page like a wand, careful not to let it brush Rin's shoulder. The centaur ran onward, taking the coarse forest path as smoothly as if they were sailing on a pond. They whipped past sweet-smelling leaves and brushed aside hanging feathers of moss. Tildi could hear the others threshing along behind her. Now and again she caught a glimpse through the trees of the slower moving travelers on the main road, which drew near, then veered away again. Rin changed direction toward the brightest traces. If she missed one,

Tildi pointed it out to her, but she seldom went wrong. She was as good a tracker as she had claimed.

According to the failproof compass that Olen had given Tildi, they were moving nearly due north, but edging ever so slightly to the east. She tried to picture the map of Niombra in her mind, and could not guess toward which of the many countries and provinces he, or she, as Serafina had said, might be going. She hoped they could find their quarry soon, but she had no idea how they—two wizards, two soldiers, a centaur, a smallfolk, and a peddler—would be able to stop a powerful mage and take back the Great Book.

If what Edynn had suggested was true, then she had been close to the thief almost all the way to Overhill. Could she have seen him? She tried to imagine all the odd folk, both human and otherwise, that she had encountered along her way. The only one who struck her as truly odd was Irithe, but Olen had shown no interest in her. Why could the thief not have been an elf? She must mention it to Edynn when they stopped.

Rin was moving so swiftly that Tildi's whole world shrank to what she could see before her, a narrow tunnel of sight between the centaur's shoulder and neck, and the deep green of the forest crown. Rin kept her arms up so that branches and twigs didn't strike either of them, but the hiss of brushing by them and the thud of Rin's hooves on the earth were all the sounds she could hear. The glowing sigils flashed past them in a blur. The muscles in Tildi's arm holding out the leaf started to twitch, then burn. She propped her elbow upon her thigh, then gave up and tucked the parchment roll into the breast of her tunic, with enough of it sticking out to awaken the runes. She buried her hands in Rin's mane, glad to have something to hang on to. She didn't have time to think or be afraid. All she could do was watch the runes and make sure they stayed on track.

The shadows falling around them from the sun at their backs traveled from far to the left to some distance to the right before Edynn's faint voice cried for a halt.

Rin slowed to a trot, then a walk.

The trees around them were thinning out. Just ahead Tildi could see bright sunlight. Rin passed between two noble beech trees and stepped out into a clearing, where the trail they had been following split up into three shallow rabbit tracks that all went off in different directions over the meadow. The air smelled fresh and inviting. Tildi wiggled her shoulders, enjoying being able to stretch for the first time in hours. Teryn caught up with them almost at once, followed by Serafina. Edynn and the other two were too far away to be seen. Tildi listened to the crunching of their horses' hooves until they, too, emerged into the meadow. Half a mile to their right was the main road. Carters directing their plodding horses along the way glanced up at the sight of the seven travelers, but their curiosity faded quickly, and they were soon out of sight.

Chapter Seventeen

et us stop here, Captain," Edynn called. Teryn nodded. She scanned the area, then guided them to a flat, grassy sward in a hollow surrounded by tall grasses and wildflowers. Tildi looked down at them with delight. The flowers looked like the wild irises that grew in the Quarters, but they were almost the size of her head. "I don't know how far we are from the nearest inn, so I propose that we have a meal now. I apologize. I did not realize how long it is past midday."

"No harm done!" Lakanta said cheerfully. "I believe that it's a good three hours or more to the next inn along the road, if we were on the road. If I recall, it's the Stirrup Cup, a decent place, with good beer and good baths. We can surely make it before they lock the doors for the night if we keep up the pace we have." She swung down from her short horse and loosened the beast's girth. It immediately moved off to pull up mouthfuls of grass. "My bottom's rubbed raw, and I am sure Melune hasn't had a run like that since she was a filly!"

Rin reached behind her with one long, flexible arm, and scooped Tildi off her back.

"Time to get down," she said cheerfully. "I wish desperately to scratch my back!"

With that, the elegant chieftainess of the Windmanes collapsed onto her side and rolled over. Her human half lay upon the grass while her striped horse half writhed, all four legs in the air. Tildi laughed at the look of bliss on her face. Rin let out a breath of pure pleasure.

"Ah, that's wonderful! I haven't scented sweetgrass like this since I left home. Do you know sweetgrass, smallfolk?"

"We only get it dried," Tildi said, plucking a few short blades and holding them to her nose. "It is a popular herb used to stuff pillows to prevent bad dreams. I've never smelled it fresh before."

"Isn't it delicious?"

"Do you eat grass?" Lakanta asked curiously, sitting down beside Rin.

"Only if I am very hungry," the centaur replied, rolling over and rising to all four knees. "I prefer grains, but we can eat anything. What shall we be having?"

"I can help cook," Tildi said at once. If her ability to track the book was wanting, she would at least be able to hold her own with domestic duties. She sprang up to help, but her legs were so wobbly they gave way under her. Sitting down hard reminded her her bottom was numb from hours of jouncing. "I always cooked for my brothers."

The grim-faced captain shook her head.

"Morag will do mess duty."

The stooped guard was already unloading a cooking kit from the pack animal. Tildi tottered over.

She looked up into the face under the straggly hair, and was surprised to see that Morag was a man. He had clear, light, hazel-brown eyes, but the eyes were the only feature that seemed normal. For a moment Tildi wondered if he was from another race that had been created by the Shining Ones. His mouth was wide and flat, with snaggled, crooked teeth that held out his lower lip just far enough that he could not avoid drooling just a little. His nose was weirdly pinched, and seemed skewed off to one side. His cheekbones stood out prominently and pointed outward, almost obscuring his ears, which were crushed handfuls of flesh. Morag's ruddy skin darkened further, and Tildi realized she had been staring.

"I am sorry," she said. "May I help you cook?"

He shook his head, and the lank hair danced. "No," he mumbled. "Don' need." He clutched the iron cooking pot in huge, bony hands as if using it as a shield to protect himself from her.

"Whatever you say, but please ask if you want an assistant." The soldier dropped his eyes, refusing to meet hers. Tildi hurried back to the others.

Morag's twisted face revulsed her, but something in his eyes brought out the deepest pity. She knew of children born with twisted features. They often did not live long. Sometimes their minds were addled. Morag must be intelligent, or he would not be in Halcot's castle guard. She watched him out of the corner of her eye.

Captain Teryn licked a finger to find a spot downwind of the party and gathered dry wood from the forest. With an ax from the packhorse's bags, she chopped them efficiently and made a good-sized cooking fire. Morag cut up a large piece of meat from another packet, and arranged them to fry in the pot. He cut up onions and potatoes, set them to cooking with herbs he shook out of square bottles. Tildi watched him, always eager to learn a new recipe or two. The scent that rose from the pot, though, was not encouraging. Had he really put chili pepper and tarragon in at the same time?

Teryn came to them with a skin of wine and an armful of pewter mugs, including one of a size suitable for Tildi. When the captain had finished serving them, Tildi took the opportunity to beckon her over. She spoke in a low tone so it could not be overheard by the other guard.

"Captain, Morag seems very different than other humans I have met?" She made the question as polite a statement as she could. Teryn's thin lips tightened.

"He's a good man," she said tersely.

"I am sure of that," Tildi said in haste. Teryn set her jaw and stared out over the field, her clear blue eyes narrowing.

"He was normal before the war. You know of that?" She didn't wait for Tildi to answer. "Close to the end, a terrifying spell overtook some of us trying to cross into Orontae. They were twisted like broken dolls. Such a thing had never happened before. We thought their wizard incapable of attack spells. All of the others who were afflicted died. Sometimes, it might have been kinder—" she stopped herself, and scowled at Tildi. "He is a good man, and loyal. You need not fear him. Or pity him," she added fiercely. "His Highness holds him in esteem, or he would not serve in Meriote Castle itself."

"Oh, I am sure he is more than worthy," Tildi said. "Thank you. I apologize."

"She was in love with him," Lakanta said, as soon as Teryn was out of earshot.

"What?" Tildi asked, startled out of her thoughts.

The little blond woman made a half-rueful face at her. "She was in love with him. You can see it all over her face. And he might have loved her, too, who knows? How sad that he was crippled like that."

"That's a guess, peddler," Serafina snapped. "Do you have any reason to believe it's true, not that it is any of your business?"

"I don't know it," Lakanta said cheerfully. "Do you care to scry it for me? I revel in love stories."

The young wizardess took the suggestion as an insult, to judge by the look on her face. She turned her back on them, and faced her mother, who was sorting through a bag from her saddlepack. The blond trader winked at Tildi.

"Don't say anything," Lakanta whispered to her, then raised her voice to a normal level. "Well, Tildi, tell me about your home."

"It's an ordinary place," Tildi said. "The only excitement we have is when a peddler like yourself comes to town. Otherwise, we just live our lives."

"Sounds dull. But dull can be a relief. Regular meals, you know. Warm, dry bed, knowing where your shoes will be when you wake up in the morning."

Tildi laughed, but with regret. She had thrown away all of those things, not once, but twice. The first had been a decision made out of anger, grief, and panic, but the second was deliberate and thoughtful, or at least so she hoped. "What about you? What's it like to travel from place to place with a load of goods?"

"Oh, there's a touch of the dull about the life, too," Lakanta admitted, but her eyes twinkled. "But I get my fun out of it. You know, I never want to miss the chance to see new lands. You meet people, sometimes *very individual* people. Why, let me tell you about the last time I visited Tillerton. . . ."

Tildi liked her. She was glad that someone like her had been permitted to join the party. Serafina was haughty, like Doctor Jurney's daughter. Edynn seemed far above Tildi's station. Though she was kind, Tildi never dared think of having a natter like this with her. The two guards kept to themselves. Rin, now, Rin was an enigma. Tildi liked her, too, but she thought so differently than two-legged people, and she was nobility, as well. Lakanta was approachable, capable, and unflappable. She'd have made Lakanta a friend if they had been neighbors in Clearbeck.

The meal, when it finally came, was overcooked as well as peculiarly spiced. Tildi chewed gamely at her portion of tough meat and undercooked vegetables, wondering if Morag's creation was bad or just a recipe from a cuisine that she had never tasted. Out of the corner of her eye she glanced at the others' faces. To judge by their expressions, her first reaction had been the correct one. Lakanta, too, was munching energetically, trying not to make a face. Edynn cut her food into small bites and was eating them with a long fork while she read a sheaf of documents that she had taken from her saddlebag. Rin tasted the meat, let out a loud snort, and was chewing the vegetables with no evidence of enjoyment. Serafina was not even pretending to eat. She pushed away the blackened offering and sipped moodily at her wine. Teryn did not meet anyone's eyes. She and Morag finished their meals with despatch, then went about tamping out the fire and cleaning up the site.

Thankfully, no one found it necessary to criticize Morag's lack of skill aloud. He was undoubtedly doing the very best that he could, but Tildi felt there was no need for them to eat bad food all the way along their journey, not with her own skills available. She resolved that she would find a way to get Morag to let her help, at the very least to pull food off the fire before it burned.

Once base hunger was assuaged, she pushed the scraps around her small plate, looking forward to staying at an inn that evening. She had had good luck so far with food at travelers' rests.

"Who is Teldo?" Edynn's voice brought Tildi's head up with a jerk.

"T-T-Teldo?" Tildi stammered out. Her heart pounded.

"Yes," Edynn said, holding up a scroll. "Olen gave me the articles of apprenticeship when he passed responsibility for your education along to me. I read smallfolk language very well, and I cannot help but notice that the name on the correspondence is Teldo, not Tildi. Is that what you are called at home?"

Tildi felt all the blood drain from her body. What could she say? She knew in her heart that she must not lie to Edynn, but not only were they many days' ride from the Quarters, they were now many miles from Olen's home, even if she might be compelled go back once she had told the truth.

"No," she said at last. "It's not. Teldo was my brother."

"Was he? Why did you use his name to write to Olen?"

"I didn't." The terrible truth bubbled up from deep inside Tildi, as though it had been waiting months for her to let it free. "He did. He wanted to be a wizard from the time he was a child. He taught me the magic that I knew, but he was the real scholar in our family."

"I see. He was one of the family members killed by the thraik?" Edynn's tone was not accusing, but Tildi felt as though she had been caught stealing, which, if she thought about it, she might indeed be. She hung her head.

"Yes," she admitted.

"How did you come to bring his letter to Olen, then? Why did you not stay in the Quarters? You had a home there? Friends?"

"Do you know of our culture as well as our language?" Tildi asked, phrasing her words carefully. "The attack happened very suddenly. I have little value among my people. I couldn't inherit my family's property. The elders were planning to marry me off to a . . ."—there were no polite words suitable to describe the odious Bardol—". . . someone not of my choosing, and were giving me no option to refuse. I had only a short time to make a decision. I hope you and Olen will forgive me," she said, hanging her head. "I felt I had no choice but to leave, and Teldo's letter . . . he was never going to need it. I did want to study magic, but I thought that Teldo would teach me when he came home again. Once my brothers were dead that was no longer possible. I disguised myself as a boy, and left that very night."

She told the story as succinctly as she could. The others listened with solemn interest and not a little sympathy, but when she described her stay at the inn in Rushet, Lakanta burst into hoots of laughter.

"Oh, that's wonderful!" the little woman exclaimed, clapping her hands on her knees. "That's the funniest thing I'd ever heard in my life! Oh, they're a kindly group at the Groaning Table, they are. I'll have to tease Danyn about it next time I go through."

Serafina gave her a quelling look. "Her family had died violently, and you laugh at her?"

"If anyone had told me such a story, I'd laugh," Lakanta said. "I don't deny the terrible things she's been through. In fact, I think she's brave as a lion for picking herself up and setting out like that. Still, trying to drink her weight in beer and flirting with the barmaid? It's like something in a comic song!"

Now that Tildi started to think about it, she could see how ridiculous she must have looked. She smiled timidly at Lakanta, who beamed back.

Edynn nodded. "I, too, can understand why you borrowed Teldo's identity to get you safely to Overhill. Why not admit this to Olen? You showed the aptitude he requires, and a willing heart. He praises you highly. In fact, there were many times over the last days he considered refusing to let you go. You could have been accepted on your own terms."

Tildi felt more guilty than ever. "I did not know that until I began my apprenticeship, but a good opportunity never arose to admit it. I wondered how I could bring it up without making him disappointed in me. I was afraid that he would send me away. I don't excuse the lie. I did try to tell him, once or twice. I am sorry I let him believe an untruth. I knew I could earn my keep if he saw how hard I work. I only used Teldo's name so that he would consider me as a pupil, because I am only a girl."

"Never say that," Serafina said sharply. "Females are the half of creation."

Edynn's voice was gentle where her daughter's was harsh. "You could not know that this is not the custom of the rest of us, Tildi. Olen would have welcomed your confidence. He might even have chuckled about it."

"I know that *now*," Tildi admitted. "I have seen since that it is very different with human women. You are respected, and no one disagrees when you speak for yourselves." She regarded Edynn and Serafina with envy. If she had known of the differences in culture while she was still at home, she would have been more frustrated with her own situation than she had been, and that was a good deal. "Little wonder that the men keep us from asking too many questions of strangers."

"Humans are not perfect, either, Tildi," Edynn said gently. "There are many traditions within the race, and some of them hold life far less dear than smallfolk."

"I didn't know that. I'd never been out of the Quarters in my life." She had never felt more ashamed or ignorant. If the ground had opened up to swallow her at that very moment, it would have been a relief.

"You have much to learn," Edynn said, with a little smile. "I'll do my best to help you on the way to wisdom while we are together. Olen will say, as I do, that nothing you have done needs forgiveness. A little omission, as long as you have been honest in all your other dealings, is quite understandable. Shall we begin again?"

"Oh, yes!" Tildi exclaimed gratefully. Edynn rolled Teldo's letter up into a tight scroll and put it away.

"Very well. Let us make ready to ride again. Perhaps this evening there will be time for a lesson or two. Will that suit you?"

Tildi nodded, her eyes shining.

Edynn was not angry with her. She let Rin swing her up on to her broad back, and did not even notice how sore her seat was, now that the numbness had worn off.

She rode on the rest of the afternoon deep in thought. It became automatic to use her eyes to watch the runes and her hands to guide Rin, though the centaur hardly needed the guidance. Tildi was grateful not to have to speak. She had so much to think about. She felt almost as though she ought to turn around and ride back to Silvertree to apologize to Olen for deceiving him. One day she would. More than before, she felt grateful to have been born into the family she had, who had been tolerant of her dreams and her need to kick over the traces once in a while. Perhaps she was better suited to life outside the Quarters than she had known.

She wondered if Teldo had ever found a mention of smallfolks' origin in the books he read. She doubted it. He had never so much as hinted it. He liked to share any discoveries with her, and that would be too compelling to keep to himself. It still troubled her to think that she might be less of a being than the trees she saw around her, or the birds on their branches. Still, she was there, at that time and in that place, and she would make the best of it.

Beyond the meadow the forest closed in again, blocking the main road from view. The book thief seemed to have spent as little time as possible in the open. Tildi hardly felt the leaves that brushed her hair and shoulders, barely smelled the fresh sap from broken twigs, scarcely heard birdsong and the scolding of squirrels. Her determination to catch the thief was renewed, but how far away could he be? If only she had known she was following him. Now he had a month's head start, and could be half a world away. Tildi hoped fervently that he meant no harm, but if that were true, why not leave the book where it was?

Around her, the forest was a steadily fading blur as afternoon turned into twilight.

"We must stop soon," Rin said, dancing to a halt and letting the others catch up with her.

"But we can still see the runes," Tildi protested.

"The runes are visible, but alas, they do not light up the ground! I have no wish to break an ankle in a mole hole."

"You are right," Edynn said, peering around her. "If we were on open ground, I might say keep going for a while yet, but I won't risk any of us being injured. I want all of us to stay in the best shape possible. We don't know when we will come upon our quarry."

"Providing he is not warned we are following, Mother," Serafina said, with a disapproving little shake of her head. "If he's any kind of a wizard at all, and he must be."

"Ah, you're right, daughter," Edynn said mildly. "Once we are settled for the evening we shall see if he has lowered his defenses a little and allowed us a peep at where he is headed. You may assist, Tildi."

"Thank you, Edynn!"

The elder wizard smiled at her, making Serafina fume. Tildi guessed she was jealous of her mother's attention.

Lakanta's sturdy little horse was the last to arrive. The peddler blew strands of hair out of her red face. "Whew, my bumped backside! The inn is not far from here. I'll be grateful for a bath and a bed, and Melune is greatly deserving of a good rubdown."

Rin lifted her nose. "I smell food cooking, to the east of here," she said. "But they do not bury their refuse deeply enough."

Tildi inhaled deeply, trying to pick up the scent. "You've got a far better sense of smell than I do. I can only smell the woods, and me. Wait, you're right. There's spoiled meat off that way." She pointed toward the east, now plunged into twilight.

"It is not meat," Teryn said grimly. Making a hand signal to Morag, she took point, and rode out a good distance ahead of them through the thin undergrowth. Morag drew a sword in his knobbly hand and took the captain's place at the head of the party. Tildi leaned close to Rin as she watched Teryn scanning the ground between the trees. The guard captain stopped and shook her head. Automatically, Rin trotted toward her. Teryn held up a hand.

"It's a corpse," the captain called. "You don't want to get too close. It's nasty. Morag and I will bury him."

"I'd like to see him," Edynn said. She urged her horse forward. Rin followed. Tildi, curious but horrified, leaned for a look over the centaur's shoulder.

The captain made a gesture of resignation and made way for them. The body of a human male lay on its belly on the ground. He had long, thinning black hair and wore rough-spun clothing. Under the filth Tildi could only guess at the color, they were probably muddy green and brown, the cheapest kinds of dye. "Looks like he was running away from something." Teryn nudged it over on its back. It shifted with the slackness of a sack full of mud. Tildi let out a gasp and retreated behind Rin's silky back. The man's face wore an expression of terror that death had not erased. His hands and arms, up to the middle of his chest, were horribly burned, far worse than Halcot's had been after he had touched the leaf in Tildi's collar. Rin knelt down beside the body. Tildi caught a whiff of the corpse, and gagged.

"These surely did not belong to a man with such humble clothes," the centaur said, bringing a bright silver chain out of the corpse's belt pouch.

"I suspect that you are correct," Edynn said with a sigh. "And he chose to rob the very worst person possible. A man or woman, walking alone far from the main road, must have seemed like easy prey. See what happened when he tried to take the Great Book from its guardian." As one, they all turned to look at Tildi.

"He couldn't have died of the pain, could he?" Tildi asked. "He's not that badly burned."

"Not likely," Teryn said. "I've seen men hurt worse that this and live. He's dead because someone tore his heart out."

Edynn examined the corpse's chest. Tildi had all too clear a view of the shattered rib cage and the gap beneath. Her stomach squeezed, threatening to expel what was left of lunch.

"You are right," Edynn said at last. "I could do a working to reveal what happened here, but speculation can do as well. A brigand waiting in the shadows hears a lone traveler. Anything that person has may be of value, and you can be sure that our quarry would cherish his burden most carefully. The thief tries to take it away. The burns could have come from what may have been the merest touch of the book. He recoils before the book can consume him completely. Our thief could not stand another thief capturing his prize, and takes his attacker's life. So easy. Too easy."

Edynn looked up at the others, and her dark eyes were sorrowful.

"We must catch up with him."

Chapter Eighteen

raise to the Mother and the Father!
Praise to the Parents of us all!"

The daily song shocked Nemeth out
of his fitful sleep. He snarled at the dark
walls of his damp prison, and cursed his
foolishness in placing himself in such a
stupid position.

Outside the singing continued, more
voices joining in. That meant that dawn had come. He clenched his
teeth and peered out of the tiny knothole that served him as a spy window.

In the pale light, about thirty men and women clustered about the
enormous hollow tree in which he had lain hidden for more than a
month, their faces wreathed in joy. The fools. How humans could be so
stupid and superstitious made his mind spin. They saw a miracle to be

celebrated, and by heaven and earth, they were making as great a matter out of it as they could. Ah, well, he had been as stupid as they.

Undoubtedly he would have yearned for any kind of novelty, if he lived in as pathetic a village as Walnut Tree. He had drawn attention to himself, a terrible error in such a thinly populated place. Not himself, in truth, but the book's marked presence, impossible to conceal completely in the un-civilized wilderness, for so this appeared to him. He had so little experi-ence with anything outside of cities. It had been an age since he had lived anywhere but a capital. He was accustomed to having everything he might need at hand, or at least within an hour's demand. When he had set out to liberate the book from its hiding place, he had been able to travel as an ordinary man, stopping in inns and traveling in carriages and ships.

No one paid him any attention.

Nemeth could see in their minds that they forgot him the moment he was past them, and if they did not, he made it true, with a simple spell. He dined alone, took private rooms and cabins, and ignored his fellow beings. He had always prefered to pass unnoticed. He didn't like other people watching him. He always knew when they were thinking about him, and could often divine what they thought. It was not usually flat-tering, so he tried not to focus upon the specific details.

The other voices were awake, too. They had never left his mind, not for a minute. Nemeth clapped his hands to his ears to shut them out, but it was never any use. They were inside his head.

A gift, his parents had called it, and sent him to be trained by wizards. It was a curse! He heard voices from all over the world, from every species of being, including ones that no one else knew could think, like trees or stars. He could not call all of them intelligent, including mem-bers of his own race, humans. The nonsense that echoed around inside their skulls was gibberish, including some of what were known as the "best people." Most of the time the cacophony was an unmitigated and undifferentiated din, like being in the middle of the marketplace.

More and more, lately, he had heard his name popping up among the noise. They were talking about him. They were *looking* for him. Certain voices were always talking about him now. Some of them had reached out, with words of power that he knew well but had never had much skill at using, to try and find him, to compel him to come to them. He knew what they wanted! Nemeth snatched up the book from the crumbling floor and cradled it. They would not have it, not ever. Some of the voices were get-ting to be very familiar, and he did not want them to be. They swooped and dived around him like swallows catching flies, but had not touched him, yet, not really. He yearned to go where the voices could not find him.

They were even louder and more prominent since he had rescued the book—yes, rescued it, for all that one deep, slow, authoritarian voice kept telling him that he had stolen and was misusing it, and commanding him to bring it back. This voice was not like any of the others, who sounded weak and familiar, humans and other sorts. This one was different. In his heart Nemeth believed he was hearing the voice of Father Time himself. He would have thought that Mother Nature would have been angry with him, especially concerning the episode with the cattle, but this voice was distinctively male. Father Time, berating him for destroying His consort's creations? That did not come in any interpretation of the Origins that he had ever read, but those had been written by humans, not the creators themselves.

It did not matter if it was one of the architects of creation dinning him. Nemeth hated being spied on. He locked up his defenses tighter, drawing upon the book for aid. The voices dimmed slightly, giving him a measure of relief from their badgering. He had such a long way to travel. If he dropped his guard he could be intercepted long before he reached his destination.

At last the terrible singing was over, and the people outside dispersed. Nemeth relaxed against the inside of the tree. If he had the least idea a month ago that he would be trapped inside it all this time, he would have gone hungry a few hours longer. His human weakness was to blame for his predicament.

It had been impossible to travel back along the same roads he had taken south. The book lent its sheer power to everything around it, making even the humblest stone glow. Indeed, it was an excellent tool for study, but a poor one for stealth. Nemeth was forced to retreat into the byways. Luckily, there were many, more than he had ever dreamed, traveling as he habitually did on the main thoroughfares whenever forced to leave his fastness. He now found paths that led through forests and behind hills, to secret bridges and unexpected tunnels, providing him with shelter when it rained or when the cursed thraiks flew overhead, as they often did. What the byways lacked was a range of decent inns. He had never had to forage for food before, never. Below the waves he had eaten what he had to, when he could, but in his own environment of dry land, he was unprepared to deal with the lack of basic necessities. He starved for days. When the pain in his stomach and his head became unbearable, he stuffed anything that seemed remotely edible into his mouth.

The book could only tell him that these were natural things, not whether they were good for him.

He had eaten green apples as a child, but there was a difference between those and the ones he found north of the blasted mountain. That fruit had been hard and very sour, and had caused him hours of distress. He found berries, but never enough to assuage his hunger. He killed small animals or birds, then was unable to figure out how to cook them to edibility, never having had to learn the basics of housekeeping. That left him with no choice but to steal food.

His crimes began with a fish pie stolen from among half a dozen set out to cool on a rock beside a hut, in a tiny village of similar huts on the banks of a river. He knew that the pie was foul and badly made, but nothing had ever tasted so good. The dirty fisherwoman who returned to find some of her food missing abused one of the many brats running around for the theft. The boy denied it, of course; he was innocent. The woman didn't believe him, and slapped him about the head for it. No doubt he had plenty of minor peccadilloes to his name. Nemeth slunk away, the sound of the child's protests in his ears.

Traveling in the general direction of his goal, Nemeth journeyed from village to village, lurking out of sight in the most uncomfortable places until he could spot unguarded food, and making off with it, leaving the cooks to blame dogs, small children, or hungry husbands who couldn't wait for the evening meal. Nemeth knew from skimming the voices he heard in the air that there was always someone to blame. Most of the peasants were so magic-blind that they ignored the runes that appeared on everything around them. When one did notice, it drew attention away from the fleeing food thief. Nemeth's system had worked in both continents, up until he reached the smallest and rudest of habitations, Walnut Tree.

The minutes seemed to stretch out forever as he waited for his opportunity. At last, a woman sent her children running to find their father and elder siblings. He felt her yearning for a moment's gossip with her neighbor. Nemeth strengthened that longing, to the point where the woman emerged from her home and walked purposefully toward the next house, leaving the dinner to cook on its own.

As soon as she was gone, he dashed out of the shadows and into the house. It had been tiny, cluttered, and filthy, but on the fire was a bubbling, good-smelling pot. He had his hand on the handle when he heard the sounds of the children laughing and shouting as they returned from the fields. Nemeth had no choice but to run away without his treasure. As he emerged, he saw to his horror that the husband had decided to race his family home. The laughing man poised at the edge of the circle of trees and looked back over his shoulder. Blessing the distraction, Nemeth dashed to the only point of cover he could find, the great tree. He hid around the back of it until the family was safely inside, but he was not safe. More families were coming home. He must hide. But where?

The book in his arm seemed to urge him to look more closely. The tree's rune hovered just under his nose. He noticed suddenly that there was a flaw in it that set it apart from the symbols of other trees. He felt his way toward the flaw.

Nemeth's hand slid into a crack in the bark. To his amazement, he felt farther in. The tree was completely hollow. With the book's aid he widened the crack enough to let his body pass, then closed it again. He had gotten so much better at subtle manipulation. No longer was he blindly changing elements in hopes of finding the right alteration. He had had plenty of time, and mistakes, to learn the parts, while still traveling as fast as he could. His days of learning how to ken runes were so far behind him that it had all come as a shock to do it again.

He was just in time, for the next ploughman to come home let out an exclamation of wonder at the "sacred sign" that had appeared on the tree trunk. His cry brought all the neighbors running. They marveled over the rune, wondering how each of them saw just one, no matter where around the tree they stood. At last the headman had declared that it was a special marvel, bestowed upon Walnut Tree. Nemeth cursed himself for not retreating all the way out of the village. Of course the tree's rune had become visible.

A brave lad, urged by his friends, had put out a hand to touch it, but the liberty earned him a cuff over the ear, probably from his father. The women conferred, and decided that a miracle deserved a tribute of some kind. A few of the men proposed a sacrifice. There was a lamb or two of the quality they felt was necessary, but it always seemed the perfect animal for the task belonged to another farmer, who proposed somebody else's beast right back. With the long-neglected dinner on their minds, the women countered with a gift of already slaughtered meat, namely ready-made food, a share of what was already on their hearths. The men looked at one another and agreed this was wise. Nemeth felt his stomach squeeze in anticipation of that out-of-reach object of desire. Soon, the women emerged, bearing bowls or trenchers containing steaming stew, beans, porridge, or whatever happened to be on the menu for the night. It was more food than Nemeth had seen since he had left the south, a week's worth of meals. His mouth had watered.

It took hours before everyone had said all they had to say about the miracle of the rune. They even attributed the other enhanced symbols on other items within the book's range to the magic that had touched the walnut tree.

Nemeth waited impatiently while a few of the men came out with beer, toasted the tree by splashing it with the yeasty, sour beverage, before drinking the rest themselves and having a conversation that undoubtedly sounded learned to them in its presence. At last, after midnight, they had retired, congratulating one another on living long enough to have witnessed a marvel. Nemeth had waited until the sounds of voices had died away over the green, then crept out to collect his feast. He felt as though he had witnessed a miracle of sorts, as he ate his way through the offerings. So much food had given him a bellyache, but he didn't care. He was replete for the first time in months.

The townsfolk met the sight of the empty dishes with delight that their sacrifice had been accepted. They continued to leave food out every morning to appease the spirit of the tree. These were not the type of comestibles he would have chosen, but the women did their best with the ingredients they had. Sleeping inside the tree was better than sleeping in the woods. He kept the rough hollow clean by using its memorized rune to restore it to the state it had been in when he first crawled inside, as he did to maintain his garments and shoes. Once he had regained his health, he realized he must leave.

Such a goal was not easily attained.

From the moment that the "miracle" had occurred, the tree had seldom been without company. Even late at night a villager might take it into his or her head to come out at some odd hour and behold the amazing sight. Nemeth had tried to use magic to counter their untimely curiosity. More than once he put a compulsion on all the villagers to sleep soundly, gotten a few yards out of the village, then been chased back into his hollow by a nocturnal predator drawn by the scent of food. Safely inside the tree, he reminded himself he was the master of all creatures. He could kill any animal. But when danger threatened, such thoughts fled from his scholar's mind, driving him back to the primitive state ruled by fear. The tree afforded him protection. There was no answer but to escape by daylight.

Nemeth could have laughed at the absurdity of his situation. He had been trapped for a month, but now he had plenty to eat. He chafed for his freedom, though with it would come the freedom to go hungry once again. But he must go. He was becoming frustrated every day that his mission was delayed. There was more: in the last few days the voices in his mind had mentioned him much more frequently, and a few of them felt as if they were drawing closer. They must not be allowed to catch up with him.

The moment came that he had been waiting for all night. The village matrons returned from their cottages, bowing deeply every few steps. Nemeth eyed them warily. Did they have his breakfast? Yes! What a relief that they had never ceased to marvel at the wonder of the glowing sign on the tree. Now came the inevitable speculation on the meaning of the sign. If there had been a competent schoolmaster in their midst he would have pointed out that all it said was *walnut tree*, the eponymous sponsor of this blighted spot, not a message from Mother Nature and Father Time. Nemeth quelled his feelings of hunger and waited for them to go away. He had gone through the book for the correct signs to help make the coming day warm and clement so they would leave him alone. They must see that there was not a moment to waste in a potentially productive day. These farmers and artisans worked from the moment they rose until sunset, and if resources afforded it, celebrated in the evenings until their tallow dip candles or stinking oil lamps burned out. A fine day was a gift.

See that sunshine? he thought at them. *The tree gives you a gift, its last gift. Go away. Don't make me make you go.*

Indeed, he did not want to hurt anyone.

These people were not the objects of his coming vengeance. He was sorry, sorry, sorry about what had happened to the man near that little inn. Nemeth looked upon his imprisonment in this tree as a punishment for killing, but the brigand had sought to steal his beloved book. That must never happen. It was joined to him now and forevermore. He was a part of it. He liked to see the page on which his own rune appeared joined with the book, seeing his own place in the great scope of creation.

He was sorrier still about the cows.

It had been months ago, and he was still haunted by his clumsiness.

He had only been trying to help. The book's awesome power led him to believe that he could do anything. One cow had been on the ground, straining to give birth. The tendons in its neck were distended. The calf had breached, and both it and its mother were growing weak. He had stared at the rune, seen what he believed to be the block preventing the calf from emerging, and reached into his power to rewrite it. As soon as he had, his alterations had affected the entire herd. The animals seemed to come apart horribly before his eyes. He scrambled through the pages to find similar cow runes to use as guides. He had put the bodies back together as best he could. He was no herdsman or healer, with detailed knowledge of the species. He could not remember how they were, so he could not change them back. Thanks to the book, the poor creatures were still alive, but horrific to behold. He was so ashamed and horrified that he ran away. After that Nemeth realized the import of keeping the original rune memorized in case he failed at his design.

The book forgave him. With a guilty conscience, Nemeth turned to the page with the herd's runes. There they were, the poor beasts, changed but still alive. There was so much to remember! But the power was delicious and divine. He would never give it up, never. Once he had succeeded in his vengeance, he would find a place where he could study it all to his heart's content.

He was not sorry at all about the thraiks he had destroyed. He hated them intensely and always had. When walking the endless miles palled, Nemeth had tried to fly. The thraik appeared out of nowhere. They wanted the book. They could sense it. They would not have it, not now or ever. He cut them into pieces, destroying all of them. More would surely follow. Nemeth had returned to the ground, unwilling to make himself vulnerable, though he regretted losing the ease of flight. He created a shield to hide himself from anything that might spy on him from above. From the anger in the voices, it blocked their oversight of him as well. He felt smugness at their frustration.

The sounds died away. The clearing was his own, at last. Nemeth crept out, ate as much as he could of the food, and stowed away the rest in the leather pouch. He gathered up the book and prepared to bid the tree a relieved farewell, when voices, live voices, burst out, not twenty yards away. Hastily, he hurried back inside the trunk. Out of his peephole he saw to his dismay two old men tottering into the common. They sat down on a bench in the doorway of one of the houses and began to chat. Nemeth was desperate to leave. He could not remain one more day and keep his sanity. When their attention was distracted, he opened the book to the tree's rune, and urged it to move.

There may have been a mild protest from the tree's soul, but it had no choice but to obey. The earth swirled around the roots like swamp water, and the walnut tree shifted slowly and smoothly to the north, away from the spot it had been planted more than three hundred years before. Nemeth rode in his capsule of rotted wood as comfortably as if he was sailing on smooth water. The tree came to a halt about a foot from where it had begun. The rune displayed a kind of shrinkage about it, as if it had exhausted its energy in taking such an unnatural action. Nemeth let it rest. With luck, he could get it past the old men and close enough to the nearest house so that he could break out of his prison and flee into the woods before they had noticed.

Nemeth had not reckoned with a countryman's eye. One of the granddads looked up from his conversation, and his rheumy eyes went wide.

"Well, damn, loo' a tree!" He drew his companion's attention to the newest wonder. With more speed than Nemeth thought they were capable of, the elder hobbled to the edge of the village, and the younger came over to see the miracle up close.

In minutes, the entire population had returned.

Nemeth's heart sank. Making the tree walk had rendered it even more sacred in the minds of the villagers, seeing it as a combined miracle of Nature *and* Time. The vigil started all over again, more sacrifices were rendered, and the singing resumed. Quaking with anger, Nemeth cursed himself for his foolishness. He must take the risk and get out of the tree the moment that the common was empty, no matter what hour it was.

At last, that moment came. Long past midnight, the excited villagers had not ceased discussing the renewed marvel, but they were falling asleep where they stood, and the thin, new moon had already sunk into the west. A few at a time, they left the common, always looking back to see if anything new was going to happen. Nemeth held himself dead still, determined that he would give them no reason to return.

He opened the crack in the bark, paying close attention to any small noise it would make. Stepping out backwards, he drew his pouch and the precious book out afterward. As an act of will, the fissure snapped back to its original shape. The night was black. He would have to rely upon the runes to tell him where his escape route lay.

As he came around the tree, a couple of drunken men staggered out of the rough-hewn house that served the village as town hall and inn. One carried a candle, which cast the heavy bones of his face into relief. Oh, why, why couldn't they sleep after sunset like decent folks?

"Who be tha'?" the other asked.

"Dunno," said the one with the light. "Who be yer?"

Nemeth didn't reply. Keeping an eye on them over his shoulder, he made for the trees.

"Heya, he be stealin' our mir'cle!"

The rune! Nemeth glanced back at the walnut tree. The sigil had faded already to half the glow lent it by the book. He had no time to worry about it. The men were behind him, chasing the brilliance of the runes that surrounded him.

Unfortunately, they knew the land intimately, and though he had been there a month, he knew only the inner dimensions of the tree. Nemeth felt for steady footing in the deep blackness, scrabbling at walls and tree trunks with his one free hand. Clumsily the men pursued him, the one carefully cherishing his candle.

Nemeth saw a narrow path marked by the runes of two holly bushes. He made for it. Something rustled in the undergrowth, then fastened onto his ankles. He fell with a crash.

"I go' im!" called the second man. In the pitch darkness Nemeth could see nothing of the man but his rune, now glowing like the sun, as he sat down on Nemeth's chest. He reached for the cloth-wrapped book in his arms. "Why yer go stealin' our mir'cle, eh? Aaaah!"

The book took its revenge, burning the peasant's hands in an instant. Desperately, Nemeth kicked him off, and rolled over to stand up. The man wasn't giving up. In spite of his pain, he tackled Nemeth again.

"No, yer don'!"

By now the man with the candle had joined the fray. The tiny taper was snuffed out immediately, but the glowing runes of men, trees, and book lent enough light for Nemeth to see his attackers.

"Where yer come fro'?" the man hissed, his wounded arms folded across his chest. "Why yer steal our only treasure?"

"It's mine," Nemeth stated, his voice rising in alarm. "Let me go."

"No, it goes back!" said the first man. They dove at Nemeth. He struck back at them.

They screamed like dying sheep as the full force of the book exploded on them.

"No!" he shouted.

The noises had woken up the other villagers. Sleepy voices demanded to know what all the yelling was about. Lanterns and candles flared into light behind him. Nemeth got the merest glimpse of what remained of the men. He had only tried to throw them away from him. The book had . . . the book had killed them. He could see their runes shriveling as their bodies cooled. Nemeth started running, feeling blindly ahead of him with one hand.

"Why did you strike so hard?" he pleaded with the book, but it did not reply. It only seemed to nestle close to him like a child going back to sleep in the shelter of a loving arm. He was not used to handling such power. It frightened him. He knew he must get used to it, or it would master him. He was afraid, afraid of himself, afraid of the world around him, and afraid of the book. He loved it as he did his own heart, but it knew neither right nor wrong, only what it had within it, and was protective of itself. Mother Nature alone only knew what it would do to him if he attempted to harm it. He loved it, but it would drive him mad. He must accomplish his ends before it did.

"This way!" the headman's voice boomed. Snapped twigs broke behind him. Nemeth had no choice. He could not keep away from them for long if he stayed upon the ground. He used the book to harden the air, and ran upward into the cold sky. He didn't stop running until dawn began to stain the eastern horizon with red.

Chapter Nineteen

uddled in a corner between two panels of a carved wooden screen beside a rack of towels and a framed portrait of a narrow-faced matron in a black dress, Tildi waited her turn in the bathing chamber on the first floor of the Stirrup Cup Inn.

Tildi missed life in Olen's household. At home, and she was surprised to find herself thinking of Silvertree as home, she would have been able to take her hot, sticky body to her own bathroom, and not listen to the crowd of human patrons bickering about who left the floor awash or the low quality of the towels, nor be loomed over and threatened by tired men on behalf of their equally exhausted wives who were yearning, as she was, to take a few minutes' quiet soak in hot water to wash away the dust and aches of summer travel. If she was overwhelmed at home, she could retreat to the comfortable safety of the servants' quarters, to the uncomplicated friendliness of Samek, Liana, and the others.

As it was she could have used a nice hidey-hole to which she could retreat for a long think. She was surprised, and not a little shocked at herself, to realize how far life with her brothers had receded in her memory. She missed them dearly, but she had adapted to the loss and her new life. And there it went, changing again. If it wasn't for the cheerful presence on this journey of Lakanta, Tildi would have felt rather lonely.

Edynn awed her.

It was very kind of the senior wizardess to claim that she and Tildi were on equal footing, as students of the magical arts, but it was a polite fiction, and Tildi would have been foolish to take it seriously. She appreciated being included, all the more because Serafina clearly disliked her or her presence, or both. Rin was friendly, but seemed amused by everything Tildi did or said, not an attitude conducive to putting Tildi at ease. The guards did not speak to her at all unless addressed. They were following their absent lord's order. The merchant had declared she was on this journey to look after Tildi, and she was doing just that.

The stout little woman eyed the marked candle perched on a high sconce and rapped briskly on the door. "Time's up! Others are waiting out here!"

A grumble echoed from the bathing room. Lakanta waited until she had counted five, then flung open the portal. A potbellied man with white hair stood on a thick, braided mat, clutching a heap of clothes to his chest. Pointedly ignoring the chuckles and gibes from the rest of the patrons on the landing, he marched with dignity, still dripping, toward the room at the end of the corridor and slammed the door behind him. Lakanta ushered Tildi inside and dropped the latch. There were three tubs in the whitewashed room, plus a round bath Tildi's size.

"I thought that'd do for you," the merchant said, draping a thick white towel over Tildi's shoulder. "Let's get downstairs swiftly, if we can. I saw a joint of beef on the spit, and no one's asked for the spiced end yet."

This was a much different experience of inns than Tildi had had before. Lakanta had marched in and made all the arrangements for the party. The Stirrup Cup hosted all races, so Rin had a stall-like chamber outside the main building, sharing with one other female centaur who was staying at the inn. The finest chamber had been secured for the two wizards, but Lakanta had gone to the most trouble for Tildi. Upon learning that there was a bedroom built to house smallfolk, Lakanta had spoken for it at once.

"We'll share it," she said cheerfully. "We might as well take advantage of comfort while we can. I predict we'll have many nights in the open before we're through." The innkeeper had reminded her that there were only three smallfolk beds in it, but Lakanta had waved aside that inconvenience, saying she would push two of them together for herself.

The guards had insisted on sleeping on the main room floor with the humbler guests, all the better to keep an eye on the stairs. Tildi felt sorry for them, but Teryn had clicked her tongue.

"Do not trouble for us, honorable," she had said, using the title with no trace of irony. That was the end of the matter, and Tildi had known better than to broach it further.

She could see the two guards standing against the wall in the bar as they came downstairs, refreshed and clean. Rin waved to them. The centaur stood at the end of a table where the two wizards already occupied part of one long bench. Though the room was crowded, the guards refused to let anyone get too near the temptingly half-empty table. Lakanta winked at the man they had hurried out of the bathroom. He dropped his eyes to his beer as his wife gave him a suspicious look.

Edynn smiled at them. "I've ordered a pitcher of watered wine. You may share it if you choose."

"I like beer, but I'll enjoy your wine," the merchant said cheerily. She helped Tildi climb up onto the bench opposite Edynn, then rolled her hips onto it.

"We requested the small parlor for privacy," Serafina told them. "They're taking a very long time about preparing it. I hope it's suitable." She shivered delicately, giving a look of disapproval to the hearty travelers and customers quaffing down ale and eating the evening pie with their hands. Tildi thought the pub was a decently kept place, but didn't say anything.

At that moment, the tall, bony figure of the innkeeper came bustling over to them, wiping her red hands on her apron. "All ready, all ready," she said. "Please, honorables, won't you come this way?"

Teryn and Morag flanked the small group as they filed after the tall woman. They could not help but attract stares, Tildi thought, half embarrassed and half amused. Tildi was last in line. She glanced up at the soldier behind her and gave him a shy smile. His sad eyes met hers for a moment, then snapped up as if ashamed to take the liberty.

Through the remainder of their ride to the inn, Tildi had occasionally felt Morag's sad eyes on her, turning to see him hastily glancing away. Once she had gotten over her shock at his appearance, she was no longer revulsed, but curious and sympathetic.

"Have you had something to eat yet?" she asked him. He appeared to suffer her attempts at conversation like a horse did the approach of the veterinarian, with rolling eyes but hope that he could trust her.

"No'm, duty yet."

Tildi nodded, pleased that she understood him so well. "How long have you been in King Halcot's service?"

"Morag!" Teryn's voice cracked like a whip over their heads. Guilty, Tildi turned her attention to the narrow door where the captain stood at attention, hand on the hilt of her sword. Morag swung his heavy chin up and marched crisply toward her.

The innkeeper curtsied as Edynn passed through the door and handed aside a curtain that hung over the entrance to the private parlor. The folds of cloth dropped down. Serafina broke out of her dignified walk and dashed to part the curtains with her staff. Her mother turned to give her a mild look as she plunged into the room behind her.

"What's she so panicked about?" Lakanta asked, as the curtains swung closed again.

"Wizards' ways," Rin snorted. The centaur had to duck her head to fit under the lintel. Tildi and the merchant followed. Morag put his hand over their heads to hold the drape aside for them.

"Thank you," Tildi said, smiling up at him. His twisted lips seemed to form into the semblance of a smile, but it was a terrible sight, blocked almost at once by the curtain falling back. Tildi heard the heavy door close behind them.

"I asked him a sight of questions about his fate in the war while we were riding up," Lakanta said. "Captain Teryn there won't talk about what happened. Morag didn't answer me, but I think he might talk to you, if you asked him."

"Why?" Tildi asked.

"I think he thinks you might be able to help him, you being an apprentice wizard," Lakanta said. "Ah, this is nice!" Lakanta guided Tildi to a comfortable-looking chair covered with a cloth embroidered with enormous flowers.

"Me? I'm just an apprentice," Tildi whispered, as Lakanta hoisted herself into an upholstered chair high enough that her legs couldn't touch the floor.

"Well," Lakanta whispered back, though her voice would have carried right back into the main bar, as she stuffed cushions behind her hips, "Edynn and Serafina are too grand for him, though Edynn does see that the rest of us share the earth with her. You'd be about his last hope."

Tildi caught the others looking at them. She blushed. At that moment, the innkeeper shouldered her way into the room with her tray, and set down the pitcher of wine. To Tildi's surprise, it was accompanied by five very fine glasses, of a quality that wouldn't have been out of place on Olen's table.

"Mistress Golt," Edynn asked, "have there been any unusual guests in the last several weeks? Anyone stopping here that people remarked upon especially?"

"With respect, honorable," the innkeeper said, a humorous glint showing in her flat, dark eyes, "you all together are the oddest thing to walk in in a year. Can you tell me more of what this person might have looked like?"

Edynn leaned delicately forward, her hands tented. "Someone behaving in a secretive manner?"

"Ah, that'd be about half of 'em."

"Someone not in control of his magic," Serafina said, a trifle impatiently.

The bony woman sucked in her lower lip to think. "Ah, a wizarding type. Not anyone I saw, but a few of the boys claim there was odd goings-on here about a month ago. 'Round about when someone stole a prize ham out of my smokehouse. They said that magic was loose all over the place. I never saw a thing myself. I'm too busy."

A shout from the main room brought her head up sharply. "Oh, whatever now?" Mistress Golt nodded to her guests. "Do you require anything else, ladies? Accommodations all right? I'll send my boy in with your dinner right soon."

Edynn inclined her head gracefully. "We are comfortable, thank you."

With another nod, Mistress Golt retreated. Tildi heard more shouting, rising until Mistress Golt's voice rose above them all, then the noise in the bar fell to a more usual hum.

"He was here," Serafina said with some satisfaction.

"I think not," Rin replied. "Unless Tildi's page has failed, the traces do not come this far. I think perhaps the thief we found attempted three crimes, not two. I wonder if any other guests were missing goods, such as the owner of the silver chain."

"Yes, he was unlucky if he tried to steal the—"the merchant said.

"Shhh!" Serafina hissed. "We do not want to be overheard."

"What? This is a private room with two armed soldiers at the door!"

"There are other means of listening," the young wizardess said.

"Peace, daughter." Edynn poured some wine for them all. "Here, take some refreshment. Rin, were you able to glean any other clues about our quarry from the trail while running point?"

"He's a soft-foot," Rin said at once, downing her first glassful and pouring another. "Good grapes. He has chosen the simplest way, even if it meant changing paths often. He knows where he's going, though I haven't divined his destination yet. He's heading northeast, and soon he must cross the Arown."

"There are only six bridges over the river," Lakanta said, "though that's more than we can oversee alone. What about setting a magical snare for him?"

"I've tried and tried again," Edynn said with a sigh. "He is well hidden. I have not been able to detect where he has gone, nor have dozens of the finest mages alive today. I have not given up hope of conceiving some magic that will guide us to him. Let it be. I will send messages to other observers to mount a guard on the bridges. Tomorrow we will go back to where we left off, and hope we can find a fresher scent very soon."

Lakanta rubbed her hands togther. "Well, now that we've settled that, let us dine. I am ravenous."

"So am I. I didn't eat much of lunch," Tildi admitted, then cringed. She glanced at the door. No, there was no way that Morag could hear her.

Rin followed her eyes. She snorted, flaring her nostrils humorously. "He is a terrible cook, I agree. I can tolerate it for the time. He was undoubtedly a most faithful servant and brave soldier, and for that I will eat what he serves me."

"So will I," Tildi said bravely. She was thankful that at that moment the door opened, and a stolid teenaged boy came in carrying a heavy tray. With possibly days of inedible meals ahead of her, Tildi applied herself solidly to the platters of food.

"Tell us what life was like at Silvertree, Tildi," Lakanta said, around mouthfuls of delectable lamb cutlets. "It seems a marvelous place."

"It is," Tildi said. In between servings, she told them about her life as

Olen's apprentice. The others listened appreciatively, interrupting often with questions.

"About Silvertree," Rin said, helping herself to another plateful. "I have visited twice before this. I firmly believe that it has a personality. When my brother said something disparaging about its doorways, they all seemed to become smaller." She whickered in amusement. "He either had to admit that he had offended it, or claim that all the bumps on the head he got trying to pass through them were the result of his own clumsiness. My brother is vain about the grace of his movement. All of us are. It is a point of pride among centaurs."

"Oh, Silvertree does have a personality," Tildi said. "It . . . ," she was ashamed to admit it, but she had promised herself not to utter any more untruths, "it helped me on my first day when Olen was testing my skills."

Edynn smiled. "He must have known."

"I think he did, but he didn't say anything to me then. He was very kind about putting me at ease." Tildi felt herself relaxing in the wizardess's presence. A good deal about Edynn reminded her of Olen, especially her quiet wisdom and sense of humor.

"And well he would. He saw a good deal of promise in you, as do I. Should we be successful, and return to our normal ways of life, I predict a life rich in experience," Edynn said. "Ah, I envy you learning again all of the arts I have studied over the years! But we must not look too far ahead. Our task is more important. You have an important role to play in this drama. You undertook this task willingly, and for that many people have reason to thank you. With your aid we were able to follow our thief's trail, surely in a manner that he cannot have foreseen."

"Indeed," Rin said. "We have covered many leagues more than I would have thought possible in a day. If you had not observed the phenomenon of the glowing runes, I don't know how we would have been able to trace this path. If you wish for Olen's approval, you had only to see his face when you told him you could provide guidance. You may be the key to saving us all, smallfolk."

Tildi felt very humble as all of them, including Serafina, regarded her with respect.

"It's nothing," she said, dropping her eyes modestly to her plate. She felt as if she ought to say something profound, but couldn't think of a thing. "I want to help."

"Of course you do," Edynn said. "I promised we should scry for our thief. Have you ever tried Seeing before?"

"No, I haven't," Tildi said.

"Then it will be an experience for you. Serafina?"

The young wizardess took her goblet and poured a mere film of wine into the bottom. She swirled it lightly and set it down. Edynn opened a hand on either side of the glass. Tildi felt the warmth of power.

"Look into the glass, Tildi. Open your mind to the unseen. We seek a traveler with a treasure like yours. Help us find him."

Tildi concentrated as deeply as she could. The magic touched her, and made her feel as though the eyes of her mind were sharper and could see farther. For a moment she could see endless trees and branches flying, but that was probably a memory of the day, not a vision. She focused harder, and realized that all she really saw was the faces of her companions reflected distortedly in the glass.

"I don't see anything," she admitted at last. She was suddenly very tired. The day of jogging along on Rin's back had been more exhausting than she had realized. She looked at Edynn for encouragement, but the wizardess's handsome face seemed to swim in her vision.

"Alas, that is because there is nothing to see. He hides from us yet. Rest now, my dear. You will have plenty of time to prove yourself."

Tildi nodded. She felt, rather than saw, the hands that took her fork out of her fingers and lifted her gently out of the padded chair.

*T*ildi's bones were vibrated to their marrow by the time Edynn called a halt in the middle of the day. She lay in the bed of moss in which Rin had set her, ever so gently, and did her best to stomach Morag's inedible victuals. In her plate were some unfamiliar vegetables, crunchy green fingers and little white tubers that once probably tasted good, but all had been subjected to his merciless cooking technique and thoroughly scorched.

"It's no use, child," Lakanta whispered to her. "I tried persuading him to learn a few foolproof recipes from me, but he wouldn't listen. You'd think a soldier would understand about timing, or marching on his belly. Maybe he can't understand me."

Tildi thought he could understand very well. She caught a glimpse of the soldier's ears, red with embarrassment, as he scrubbed out the cooking pot with a scrap of knitted wire mesh. She was fond of Lakanta, and grateful for her endless good humor and knowledge of life on the road, but her penchant for thoughtless gossip would have gotten her thoroughly shunned in Clearbeck. She ate what she could, and scraped the rest under the moss when the soldier wasn't looking. She filled up on bread which Lakanta had bargained from the innkeeper upon their departure.

Serafina fluttered over and knelt down beside Tildi. She put her long hand on the smallfolk's forehead. Tildi sat up at once.

"Hold still," Serafina said impatiently. "We must ride as far as we can today. I will try to ease your muscles."

Tildi lay back and closed her eyes. The young wizardess wasted no words explaining what she was doing, but Tildi was fascinated to feel a sensation of warmth spread out from Serafina's fingertips and down through her scalp and into her entire body. She had not realized how tight her back and legs had become until they began to unknot.

She became aware of a hand, far less gentle, shaking her. She opened her eyes to see Rin grinning down at her.

"You've slept an hour. The others are impatient to be off. Are you ready?"

The sun had moved well along the arc of the very blue sky. Tildi jumped up, full of remorse, and brushed crumbs from her clothing. She checked her collar to make sure the precious page was still in place. Rin gave it a distrustful glance, and stamped a hoof.

"I only hope that that is leading us on a true path," the centaur said, as she helped Tildi mount.

Tildi hoped so, too. Edynn was sure, and she trusted Edynn, but what if their thief was setting a false trail for them to follow?

Chapter Twenty

y brother always wins the tourneys. He is the fastest among us. I am not far behind him, but he is a wonder," Rin said, turning her head again to address Tildi as she ran. She never seemed to run out of breath, no matter how long they ran. Her horse half perspired but lightly, adding a spicy aroma to the fresh scent of the air. Tildi admired her stamina.

They had left the Stirrup Cup several days before, and were still following the trail of runes north to northeast. The group stayed in an inn or farmhouse when one presented itself, but often enough, the glowing track led them far from a thoroughfare. When that happened they ate fry bread made from the stores of flour and grease in the packhorse's panniers and game snared by Teryn and burned by Morag, and slept under the stars.

Edynn's scrying was no more successful than it had been on the first night. The thief must be taking more care not to be seen, after the fatal attack upon the cutpurse. Tildi willed them to catch up with him, but part of her was afraid of what would happen when they did. It was a subject on all their minds, but no one wanted to raise it.

Tildi tried to picture in her mind what one of the Shining Ones must look like after ten thousand years. Would he still look like a human, or wizened and dried-up? The thought of the latter frightened her, but she was afraid to mention it lest Lakanta laugh at her fancies.

The path there, though not a well-used one, ran between a narrow river and fields that had been allowed to grow fallow. A veil of round-leafed, pale green weeds lay over the rich, dark brown earth, the scent of which made Tildi feel homesick. Fallen seeds from past harvests had sprouted into golden shoots of wheat and barley, with the occasional curl of dark green pumpkin vines spreading their huge leaves over all. Tildi assumed they were quite near another village, one that understood good land husbandry. She heard the splash of a waterwheel that probably ran the local mill or weaving looms. A stubby, square, stone milepost beside the lane was too covered with moss for Tildi to read. Rin continued her narrative, not noticing Tildi's inattention. "Many songs have been written about my brother by our bards. They say that he is the fastest warrior-stallion in two hundred years!"

"You must be very proud of him," Tildi said.

"He is my greatest rival!" Rin laughed. "Those songs should be sung about me! Did you never vie with your brothers for supremacy in anything?"

"Girls and boys don't compete with one another."

"How dull for them!" Rin said, and Tildi was beginning to agree with her. "By the Meadows, look at that!"

Tildi gawked.

"I believe we have found a sign," Rin said, trotting to a halt. She raised a hand to signal to the others, but they hardly needed it. The others came galloping up, staring at what lay beyond.

Within a space of ten yards, the runes they had been following brightened from a glow to a sunburst. A golden sign appeared on every leaf, every blade of grass, every rock. Edynn spurred her mare to Tildi's side.

"What has changed, Tildi?" she asked.

"Nothing." Tildi reached for the page and found it tucked as it always was, safely secured in her shirt's lacings, but something in the air itself felt different, not unlike Serafina's healing power suffusing her body. The plants smelled stronger, and the sound of their hoofbeats was louder, though not as loud as the pounding of her heart in her chest. "Are we . . . could he be . . . ?"

She did not need to finish the sentence. Captain Teryn and Morag drew their swords and trotted out in front of Tildi. Serafina pulled her staff from the slings that held it flat against her horse's side.

"I do not know, child," Edynn said. She held out her hands and closed her eyes. "If he is here, he is not aware of us yet. Let me listen a moment."

At that moment, they heard the screaming. Rin jumped at the noise, and a shiver ran down the hide on her back. Voices howled and yelled, then began chanting.

"Are they in pain?" Rin asked.

"No," Lakanta said, listening carefully. "It sounds like they're happy."

Edynn's eyes opened. "That's most unexpected. Well, let us see what it is that is making them rejoice."

"I advise against it, honorable," Teryn said.

"Then ride before us, Captain. You see the runes. Our path lies that way."

Tildi clung to Rin's mane, making herself as small as she could as the two soldiers led the way into the village. The shabby houses were tall enough for humans, but had almost as small a footprint, so to speak, as a typical house in the Quarters, barely large enough for a family to live in. Everything was much coarser and poorly made than at home. A cluster of men and women danced wildly in a circle, throwing caps and aprons into the air. Barefoot children in dirty linen shirts raced in and out under their parents' arms, shrieking with joy.

A big man with a linen cap tied on his head spotted the party and came running toward them. Teryn spurred her horse to block him, but Edynn urged her back.

"You come on a happy day!" the big man said, beaming at them all. "Welcome t' Walnut Tree, honorable ladies! Join us in our revel!"

"We thank you," Edynn said. "What is the reason for the celebration?"

His simple, big-jawed face was luminous with happiness. "We have a miracle, noble lady. Come and see our miracle. It returned to us!"

"A miracle?" Edynn allowed him to take the bridle of her horse. "Tell me about it?"

He beamed back at her. "A moon and a bit ago, our great tree bore a sacred sign, noble lady. None o' us could make out what it said, but it glowed like the sun! Then, one day, the tree *walked*, as if it was a real person. Walked a whole yard. D'you see?"

"You say that it *walked?*"

"I swear it, lady. From there to there, see?"

None of them could avoid seeing the huge tree that sat nearly in the middle of the common. Tildi paid little attention to the spot on the ground indicated by the headman. Instead, she stared in open amazement at the sigil emblazoned upon the tree itself. It was as bright as molten gold, but as Rin brought her closer, the rune became still brighter until it was too hot to look upon.

"Well, that is curious," Edynn observed mildly.

The villagers stopped dancing. They turned to stare at their visitors in wonder. They took in the two soldiers in livery, the wizards in their flowing robes, the centaur with her gleaming dark skin and striped hide, and looked back at the glowing tree.

"You must indeed be blessed by the Mother and Father," the man said in awe. The others ducked their heads, looking uncertain whether they should make a deeper obeisance. "It hasn't been like that since the day it went out."

Serafina nodded her head to them. "May I approach it?"

"Please yourself, lady!" the headman said eagerly.

The young wizardess dismounted and walked around the big tree. "This is indeed remarkable," she said. She stopped, and felt the bark with a slender hand. "It's hollow."

"It's more than three centuries old, my lady," a woman explained, bobbing her kerchief-covered head. "But the outside goes on livin'. It's one of Nature's wonders, so it is."

The power is here for you, a voice seemed to say inside Tildi. *It's yours. Claim it!*

"What is it, Tildi?" Rin asked quietly. "You are trembling."

Tildi could hardly find the right words. She looked around. "There was power here, more than I have ever felt anywhere."

"Is it something new?" Edynn asked, drawing close.

"Not completely new," Tildi said, thinking carefully. "I felt this way when I left the Quarters. In truth, I put it down to being out on my own for the first time, and when I discovered what I thought to be, well, everyday magic."

"So it is a good feeling? A euphoria?"

"It feels good to me, but it overwhelms me, too," Tildi admitted. "I feel . . . a kinship to it."

"No wonder," Rin said. "If this is the true book, you have felt a diluted taste of its magic all your life."

"I ought to be afraid of it," Tildi said. "I can feel it calling to me. I like it, too."

"It's tied through your fragment of the book," Edynn said. "Fight against it. It will overmaster you if you are not careful. It contains all the power put into it by eight experienced and powerful magicians."

Tildi took a deep breath, but the feeling worked its way past her defenses. *Why should you shut it out?* the voice asked her. *You have earned the right to it. Accept it. Use it.* Edynn was not blind to her struggle. She reached out and put a hand on Tildi's wrist.

"I should make you a shielding spell, but I am reluctant to break the link to the book. You are our only guide, Tildi. Can you bear it?"

"I will," Tildi said stoutly, determined to keep Edynn's faith in her.

Edynn smiled, and patted her arm. "No wonder Olen was so proud of you." Tildi was gratified.

Serafina came to her mother's saddlebow. "The tree is hollow. No one is in it, but I am certain that our thief was the source of this so-called miracle. I will tell these people that this superstition of theirs was wrought by mortals."

Edynn put her hand on her daughter's shoulder. "No, don't. Let them enjoy having a miracle. At least we have confirmation that he was here recently. Good sir," she said, calling to the headman. "Have you seen any strangers in this area over the last weeks?"

The big man returned to her at once. "No, lady. Just the blessing from the Mother. You've brought it back to us. We're grateful, lady, we are."

"Nothing has gone missing in all this time? No one has seen a thing out of the ordinary?"

He frowned up at her, impatient with her questions. "Nothing. No. Just that two men who died three days ago, struck down by the Father afore their time, just t' north o' town. That's why we're all here during what oughter be a workday. We was about to bury them. I think they must be curst. Maybe they're why the miracle left. That would explain the Father's hand on 'im."

"My husband had naethin' to do wi' mir'cle leavin'!" protested a middle-aged woman in a gray dress and cap.

The headman ignored her. This had the air of an ongoing argument. Edynn exchanged glances with Captain Teryn.

"Are they belowground?" the captain asked.

"No' yet."

"May I see the bodies?"

"Nae, y'll no' defile my poor husband!" the woman screeched. Another woman, probably the widow of the other dead man, joined her. The headman turned his back on them and led the captain away from the common. A few minutes later, they returned. Teryn came to Edynn and saluted.

"It's as the headman said," she reported, in her crisp manner. "One has a burn on his hand, and a red handprint in the center of his chest, matching the scorch in the shirt over it. If the mark is anything to go upon, we can stop looking for a woman thief. It's a man's handprint."

"What about the other?" Edynn asked.

"He just died of shock," Teryn said. "Not a mark on him."

"Our thief kills again," Rin said, drawing her dark brows down.

"If he was here only three days ago, we are close behind him," Lakanta said eagerly. "Let's be off! The trail will stand out as bright as day now."

"I agree with her, Mother," Serafina said, to the others' surprise. Edynn nodded. She raised her voice so all the townsfolk could hear her.

"Good people, we thank you. We are sorry to have interrupted the funeral. May we offer our sympathies, and hope that the Mother will embrace their return to the soil."

She started to turn her horse. The headman leaped to grab her reins out of her hand.

"You can't go," he said, panic in his eyes.

"You must all stay," the villagers beseeched them, surrounding the horses. "You must stay forever! You must share the Mother's blessing with us!"

"She, the wee one," cried a woman in a faded brown dress. "It's she who made the mir'cle return. Make her stay!"

The crowd swarmed toward Tildi. All the large people with their reaching hands terrified the smallfolk girl.

"Get me away," she pleaded to Rin. "Hurry!" The centaur stretched one strong arm around behind and enfolded Tildi tight against her. A toothless woman with raw, red hands grabbed Tildi's arm and pulled. Tildi shrieked, feeling herself slipping. The warm feeling distracted her. *Stay. Stay forever.* She let go of Rin's long hair and reached for the scroll in her collar.

"Stand back, I say!" Rin demanded. She rose onto her hind legs and flailed her front hooves. Tildi's legs flew out from under her. She scrambled for a handhold but she did not fall. She was secure in the centaur's mighty grasp. The shock put her back in her right mind. "Let us pass, or *I'll* give you the Mother's gift!" The people dodged around her. A big man tried to grab Tildi off her back. Rin kicked him in the stomach. He went flying backwards, knocking over several of his fellows. Others hurried in to take his place, unwilling to let the new source of miracles leave.

In a moment Rin was flanked by the soldiers. Teryn drew her sword and put the point of it under the headman's chin. Morag brandished a polearm. The villagers were taken aback by his strange appearance, but they knew enough to see he was a seasoned warrior. Edynn held up her staff, as did Serafina, and pointed it at the villagers.

"Do not be so foolish," the elder wizardess said to them. "You had the blessing for a long while? How long?"

"A month and a week," the headman said sullenly.

Edynn nodded. "Thirty-seven days. Then you were blessed far longer than many. I for one have never heard of such a thing anywhere, and I have traveled the world. Any of you?" she asked the companions. They all shook their heads. "Then you must celebrate what you had. You have the miracle here to prove it, a tree that walked! We are on our own pilgrimage. We must go. It would be wrong to keep us. Others have need of our services." Edynn fixed an appealing gaze upon him. The headman stared at her for a while, then backed away, gesturing to his people to clear the way. "Thank you."

With Teryn in the lead, they rode out of Walnut Tree. Tildi glanced behind her at the people, who had all turned to watch the light in the tree fade away. They had frightened her, but she felt sorry for them.

"Nine days' wonder," Teryn said. "They'll heal."

"So much for a night in a comfortable house," Lakanta said ruefully. "I was going to ask them for hospitality. Oh, well, I've spent worse nights in between doors than outdoors."

Tildi glanced back as the houses disappeared behind them. "I wouldn't have liked to stay there," she said. "We might have gotten shut up in that tree to keep us from going."

Edynn still wondered. "Now, why did the thief stay so long? Is he wounded? Ill? Is the book doing him harm?"

"See what its magic does to others?" Serafina said. "It must be making some kind of mark on him. Perhaps it finally took its toll."

Once the village was out of sight, Rin shouldered into the lead again. Tildi pulled herself together and straightened the roll of parchment in her shirt laces. The runes were bright as gold, and the rude trail they followed was narrow but level. They ought to be able to cover plenty of ground before nightfall. Tildi followed Rin's lead and ducked low to avoid a branch as thick as her arm that hung over the path at the height of a man's head.

When she straightened up, the runes were gone.

Deprived of her guideposts, the centaur let out a snort and danced to a halt. She swiveled her body so that she was facing Tildi.

"Where did they go, child?" she asked.

"I don't know," Tildi said, gazing around her in amazement. "I took my eyes off the trail for a moment, and it all vanished."

"Is something wrong with your page? Did that tree back there suck all the magic out of it?"

Tildi took out the leaf and unrolled it. It seemed intact, and as beautiful as ever. "It looks all right."

"Let us go back. We must have missed where our thief turned."

Tildi nodded and held the leaf at arm's length to bring out the maximum effect in the runes. Could something have happened to it in Walnut Tree? No, because within a yard or two, the brilliant glow broke out strongly again.

"What's the matter?" Edynn asked, as she and Teryn caught up with them. "Why did we stop?"

"We missed our turning, that is all," Rin said mildly. "Will you be our marker? Stay here."

Rin and Tildi described a large spiral, until they were riding in a circle a hundred yards across. No runes were visible except for the pale glow that Tildi was able to evoke from the leaf that she carried and on the trail that they had followed.

"The track goes nowhere from here," Rin reported when they returned to where the others were waiting. "It ends at this point."

"Perhaps he turned back in his own footsteps," Lakanta suggested. "He is still hidden somewhere close by."

"If he had, then the runes in Walnut Tree would not have gone out," Edynn said. "We are really not that far from the village."

"We'll go back and look," Tildi said.

"I will come with you," Teryn declared. She made a sign to Morag, who drew his sword and laid it across his saddlebow.

Even Lakanta's suggestion bore no fruit. They returned as near to Walnut Tree as they dared, but could find no evidence that the thief had turned off. Edynn received the news with a sigh.

"We shall have to find another means of tracing the Great Book later," she said. The lines around her eyes and mouth had deepened. "But for now I must rest. I'm just not as young as I used to be. Let us make camp here."

*E*veryone was subdued as they rested on the lee side of a low hill above a narrow stream. Tildi could see how concerned Edynn was. The elder wizardess sat on the blanket that her daughter set out for her and kept to her own thoughts. Serafina bustled around her like a sick nurse. She was worried because her mother was tired. Tildi felt sorry for her. She tried to help but the young woman rebuffed her. She returned to her own blanket, subdued. No one had an appetite for the ruined food that Morag set before them, and the water that Teryn was forced to use to mix with the wine was so heavy that everything smelled of sulfur. The two soldiers sat at a distance from them on the other side of the fire. The only sounds were the crackling of the fire and the faint gurgle of the stream. The sun set furtively behind a wreath of gray clouds. Tildi hoped they didn't presage an overnight thunderstorm.

"Does anyone know any stories?" Lakanta asked, a trifle too brightly. She was mending a crack in one of the company's cooking pots with a foot-sized bellows and a string of bright bronze metal.

No one answered her. Tildi felt dejected and lost. On a normal evening she would have watched the peddler plying her tinker's skills with interest, but she could not work up the energy even to do that. She plucked up blades of grass and tossed them into the narrow rivulet, watching their tiny runes spin in circles as the current took them. Her usefulness seemed to have come to an abrupt end. The Great Book had disappeared. She had been so hopeful when they rode into the tiny village. Ah, but so had the villagers, thinking that they'd been given the answer to their prayers as well. It worried her that she had been reluctant to leave the village, even though she was frightened. The feeling she got while near the walnut tree was heady, exhilarating. She wanted to feel it again—but Edynn had told her to fight it.

"I was asking," Lakanta said, in a more subdued voice than Tildi had ever heard her use before, "because of the story you told about how you came by that." She pointed at Tildi's scroll.

Tildi looked up at her. The usually cheerful little woman looked quite serious.

"My mother bought it from a peddler. I never knew his name. He was a nice man. I remember that he came through the Quarters about twice a year, spring and fall, up to a few years ago. Gosto always thought he was fair-minded about price. He was stockily built, small for a human, blond hair, round nose, and round cheeks. His beard grew a little grayer over the years, but he had a lot of energy." She cocked her head as she studied the woman beside her. "He looked a little bit like you, now that I think about it."

Lakanta smiled. "Most folks look like me where I come from. He was my husband."

"Your husband!" Tildi echoed.

The little woman chuckled. "Yes! You don't think anyone would marry someone like me? No, don't answer that. I am only joking. We loved each other dearly. We both fell into the merchanting life, though he liked to travel in the west most of the time, and I enjoy the east. We usually met each other somewhere in the middle, every few months or so. No one has seen him in more than two years. He and I had promised to meet in Lavender, in northwest Ivirenn, on Midsummer Day, but he never came. I wondered whether you might know what became of him. He would probably have visited the Quarters just before setting out to meet me."

Tildi leaned over and put her hand on the merchant's. "I am very sorry, but I don't have any idea what my brothers discussed with him on that last visit. We women were seldom allowed to bargain for ourselves with visiting peddlers. I rarely spoke with him."

Lakanta nodded. "Ah. The reason I ask, is that you say that the thraiks took all of your brothers. And your parents. I just wonder if it might be that the thraiks got him, too, him being in the open so much and having had contact with that leaf. Ah, I'm sorry. I have been wanting to ask since that day at Silvertree. You know how I talk, it's a wonder I haven't come bursting out with it before now, but I am so desperately worried about him." Her blue eyes were very bright. "Ah, well, I'm not trying to make you a partner in affliction."

Tildi squeezed her hand. "I hope it's not true. I hope you find what became of him. Could a message have gone astray?"

"We always sent *several* messages when we were going to be delayed," Lakanta said, dabbing at her eyes with the hem of her sleeve. "I just have to accept he's gone."

"I had heard of thraiks choosing their victims," Edynn said, speaking at last. "A scholar of the Shining Ones whom I know narrowly avoided being carried off. Since Lokfur spends most of his time buried in the libraries of the university town where he lives, he has probably been spared more often than he knows. It could be that others who have had contact with copies of the Great Book or certain runes attract them." The old wizardess shook her head. "But how can that be? The attacks should have ended with the theft of the book, when Knemet got what he wanted. It's still a mystery."

"Perhaps they do not all serve him," Rin suggested, sitting on the grass with her legs gathered up under her.

"If he is the thief at all," Tildi said timidly. "If it is Knemet, where would he be going?"

Edynn gave her a kindly look. "You seek to solve our own mystery? Ah, let me think. The Shining Ones were reputed to have had a hall of learning in one of the Noble Kingdoms, built for them by one of the kings. I wish I had Porrak here. He loves to quote obscure passages at one. No one really knows where it lies. It was destroyed during the war between the Shining Ones. Wizards have searched for it since then, but no trace remains."

"Could he be on his way to rebuild the hall? That is what I might do, if I had long-lost power given back to me. And he would know exactly where to go."

Serafina looked at her. "That's a good thought, smallfolk," she said. "But wiser heads than yours have considered it. Since the theft, scholars and wizards alike have been seeking the remains of the hall."

Tildi felt blood rush to her cheeks. "What I wished to ask was, did my leaf come from there? Teldo taught me some of the laws of magic. The Law of Macrocosm says that one thing that touched another still has a connection to it."

"Don't lecture me on the basics of ancient knowledge that you only know by hearsay!" Serafina snapped. "Macrocosm means that a larger thing is tied by magic to a small thing identical to it. You mean the Law of Contagion."

"Perhaps I do," Tildi said in a small voice.

"Now, daughter," Edynn chided Serafina from her side of the fire. "She might have called it by the wrong name, yet she may have the most practical notion I have heard." The senior wizardess was sitting up. Her dark eyes had a snap to them again. "Where were our minds when we were in council at Olen's? Why did we not just apply the Law of Contagion to Tildi's leaf? It is a true copy. It must *once* have touched the Great Book itself, if only for the scribes to compare a rune or two. The *man* has prevented us from following him, but the book cannot!"

"Eh?" Rin said, springing to all four hooves. Her large eyes glowed with excitement in the firelight. "What must we do?"

"It's a simple spell," Edynn said, as the others gathered near her. "Where is our map?"

Teryn had been listening. She sprang up and retrieved the map from her saddlebag on the ground near her feet. Wordlessly, she handed it to Edynn.

"Thank you, Captain," the senior wizardess said with a smile. "Tildi, come sit near me. We are about to improvise. Rarely do I have a chance to exercise two principles of magic at the same time, but it would seem we must. I hope they do not cancel each other out."

"What do you wish me to do?" Tildi asked.

"Ah, you will be doing most of the work, child," Edynn said. She tapped the girl's shoulder with a long finger. "We cannot touch that which you bear, and contact will be required. It will also be a good experience for you. Now, are you truly willing to assist in this? You have said that you felt the power pressing in on you. This will make the connection between your leaf and the Great Book stronger. It will have an effect on you; you must be prepared for that."

"I am. I mean I will," Tildi said at once, ignoring both the qualms that made her stomach twist and the insidious voice that urged her to seize whatever chance she had at the power.

"No, child, please take the time to think about it," Edynn said very seriously. "I'm not asking you to bake cakes for a feast. This will require you to reach into the depths of your being, and make yourself vulnerable to forces beyond your control. It may not work. You may come to harm, and though we will take precautions they may not be enough to save you. You could die in this effort. Magic is a risk."

Tildi swallowed deeply. "Do we have any chance of finding the thief without it?"

"Ah, there you have me," Edynn said, her voice soft. "I don't believe so."

The smallfolk girl summoned up all the resolution she had within her. "Then I must do it."

"Being useful again?" Lakanta said with a chuckle.

"We smallfolk pride ourselves on it," Tildi said lightly, but her insides were still writhing nervously. Edynn was not fooled by her tone.

"Tildi, I want you to understand how dangerous it is to undertake this task."

"I am not harmed by my leaf. I know it may be different when we find the Great Book itself."

"That is not what I mean. You have already said how attractive the power felt to you from the residue that we encountered in Walnut Tree. That concerned me greatly. To have the absolute ability that the book would give you is seductive. You must be stronger than any of us. There could be a backlash of power when we touch its aura. It may seek to overpower you!"

Tildi turned to face her seriously. "I know. Edynn, I am afraid of what could happen, but I will do it. I have reacted so often in the recent past, not acted after careful consideration, and if you had known me before I left home, you'd know it's not the way I usually am." Tildi shook her head. "I don't know how I'll manage if that happens. I know you will do what you can for me. All I can say is I'll try. A lot of people are relying upon me. I'm used to that. I've been running a farm household since I was very small. Let me try."

Edynn smiled and put an arm around her. "I forget you are not as young a child as you look. I would be proud to have your assistance. Come, let us begin."

Serafina scowled.

Chapter Twenty-one

dynn's style of teaching was not quite like Olen's, whose practice was more of the "study it yourself and ask me questions afterwards" school. Edynn liked to go side by side through the parts of a spell. Tildi was reminded of how Teldo had taught her to raise objects, one very small step at a time.

"First we must establish the identity of your fragment," Edynn instructed her. "Like everything else, it has its own rune. Do you see it? Study it closely."

Tildi unrolled the leaf and held it in both hands. She had not paid much attention to it, but the handsome section of parchment did indeed have its own sigil. It appeared to her to sit in the upper-left-hand corner of the page, appropriately, as if it was the capital letter of a document she was about to write. It was a complex rune. *I have. I am.*

"Mark it well. Unlike a page that is made separately, this one was part of a book. The rune is almost frayed there, and there." Edynn pointed to a couple of zigzags on the edge of the symbol. "Those show where it was cut, but I am more inclined to think, torn out of the copy. The stitching or glue is long gone, and the paper is smooth with age. See what it tells you about the parent book?"

Tildi nodded.

"But the parent has a parent, a progenitor. Through the rune I want you to reach back to this page's formation. Feel your way back to the day it was made. Be there with it."

Tildi stared at it intently. How funny that an object that had been around the house all these years had so many small characteristics she had never noticed before. Every detail seemed to burn into her memory.

Edynn touched her shoulder.

The rune seemed to open up like a flower, drawing her eye to look into its heart. She saw a blank page. A pen, gleaming snow-white and tipped in gold, touched down upon its flawless surface and drew the image of the yew tree. How deft the scribe, to be able to create such a complicated sign in just a few strokes. Brilliant color grew out from the golden lines, completing the image, that added in everything from the sky above it to the taste of the water the tree drank with its roots. Another parchment was set down just at the upper margin, with the same rune showing, but this one looked somehow more real.

Tildi's eyes widened.

"I see it," she said excitedly. "It's the Great Book!"

"Learn its rune. Touch it through the past history of the page in your hands. Can you?" Edynn's voice seemed to come from very far away.

Tildi put her left fingertip on the spot where the Great Book had rested. For the first time she noticed that there was warmth there. It was not quite the same as the feeling of magic, more a sensation of completeness that was satisfying in and of itself. How fascinating! There were voices. Tildi thought she heard someone say the word *ink* into her left ear.

In the meantime, Serafina was busy. She had spread out the map on the ground. It was a good one, measuring the height of a man and one-and-a-half heights wide. She smoothed her hands across the surface of the chart. Silver lines sprang into being along the roads and other features.

"Hey, now, that's a good map!" Teryn exclaimed, forgetting herself. "Don't ruin it."

"She is not," Edynn said. "It's an improvement, Captain. I promise you."

Each of the castles and towns indicated on the chart became more detailed as the pale sheen touched them, too. The silver lines ran off the edges into the grass.

"It's ready," Serafina said, the long oval of her face concentrated. Her mother nodded.

"Tildi! Can you hear me?"

"Yes," Tildi said dreamily. The voices were discussing which rune to add next. She could have told them to draw the temple that was just being built near Balierenn's great river. It would be most beautiful there, beside the tree's rune. She felt satisfaction as the lovely white pen came to rest in the spot she would have chosen, and began to write on the shimmering paper.

Edynn's voice was insistent. "Tildi, where is the Great Book now? Tildi! Show us on the map. Find it for us. Where is the book?"

Reluctantly, Tildi dragged her mind to the present. Her body wasn't her own, but she didn't mind. She trusted Edynn. She let go of the leaf with her right hand and stretched out her forefinger to the chart.

"There? In the south?" Lakanta said with dismay. "What have we been following then? I told you we ought to have tried the southern road."

"Wait," Edynn said softly. "Wait."

A gold light appeared on the map where Tildi had touched it. It spread out more and more thinly over the surface until it had nearly vanished. Then, a few faint gold dots winked into existence.

Edynn looked pleased. "I think these are other fragments of the book that Tildi herself carries, and possibly other copies as well. Here is ours. How interesting to see how many survive after ten thousand years. Ah, yes, there's the one that Lokfur was studying in Knerit. Look, there!"

Another dot, ten times as bright as the others, appeared in the upper-right quadrant of the map. It was also the only one that was moving.

"There he is," Edynn said with satisfaction. "Mother and Father, but you have led us a chase! Hmm, not the most hospitable terrain, is it? I know that area. The lands are broken from erosion, unsteady footing."

"He's hundreds of miles away, lady," Teryn said, measuring the distance between the first dot and the glow. "Seeing's not the same as catching."

"How right you are, Captain. But we know where he is now." She pushed the map back toward Teryn, who folded it so the section with the glowing dot was outward. "Tildi."

Tildi sat staring at her leaf. She was enjoying listening to the voices. They spoke an archaic version of human, but she understood most of their words well enough. Teldo would have loved to hear the scholarly discussion they were having about the merits of drawing runes. Was it better to use one long stroke, or a series of small ones?

"Tildi, come back to us now."

It was lovely in the scriptorium, with sunlight pouring in the windows. The narrow hand holding the pen made a light line.

"Tildi!"

Tildi blinked, and found herself staring down at the leaf in her lap. There, to the right of the tree, the long-ago artist had finished the temple rune, and several others. She knew now what they were. She almost snatched up the roll of parchment and embraced it.

"Are you all right?" Edynn asked. Tildi looked up at her. "You were very far away."

"Did it work?" she asked.

"Oh, yes. Thanks to you. In the morning we can get a good start going after our thief."

"Why not set out tonight while we can?" Captain Teryn asked. Morag appeared at her shoulder, seconding the notion with a vigorous nod.

"For one, the footing will be too difficult," Rin said. "You humans! You do not ask your horses, because you can't understand their answers, but they have more sense than you. For another, our wizards are all too tired for a long night's run. For a third, the thraiks do not need light to see us, but it would be to our advantage to see them, since they can appear out of the air."

"But he will be farther away by then!"

"Peace, friends," Edynn said, holding up her hands. "We will go in the morning when we are fresh. We can see where he goes now."

Tildi drowsed on Rin's back as they set out well before dawn the next morning.

Captain Teryn had tried to hurry them at their breakfast. Tildi ate what she could of the half-cooked cereal before the bowl was all but snatched out of her fingers. She had been too distracted to protest. She was troubled by her dreams of a thin, blue-veined hand turning a book on its spindle, and had awoken drenched in perspiration. It was a good thing that the map could tell them where to go. She was in no fit state.

How the wizardesses could rise up day after day and look as if they had just stepped out of a hot, perfumed bath into clothes made fresh for them by the best laundress in town, she had no idea. The soldiers, of course, had no trouble maintaining their uniforms in trim, and spent evenings polishing and cleaning their kit while they listened to the others talk about things magical. Even Lakanta managed to remain neat and fairly tidy after days of washing in streams and hanging clothes to dry from her saddle. Tildi knew that she looked like a beggar's brat by comparison, and studied the others in hopes of learning how to keep herself more presentable. No one in the Quarters would own her now. She was glad they were all hundreds of miles behind her. When she caught a glimpse of herself in a stream, she was ashamed.

Edynn had sent a message to Olen. The dove-shaped burst of energy had flown off silently to the south. It contained a charm of silence, to prevent the thief ahead of them from getting an inkling that he was being followed. They rode as swiftly as they could, over the hilly terrain of the river valley, but it was still slow going.

Rin made conversation now and again, as they cantered behind Captain Teryn. All Tildi wanted to do was think about the book, the one she had seen in the vision. She could still feel it. The power was there. It was warm, delicious, and comforting, like a cup of cocoa on a cold night. She wanted to take it into her own hands. She was sure it was not the same hand that she had envisioned during the spell to connect her leaf to the Great Book. It must be the thief's. How lucky he was.

That thought brought her out of her torpor. She sat bolt upright, blinking into the sunrise. What was she thinking? This wizard, whoever he was, had killed beasts and people and was endangering the entire world out of pure greed!

Rin felt her move and turned her head to see. "Are you all right back there, smallfolk?"

"Yes," Tildi said. "How far have we gone?"

"About twelve miles. The captain stares at our map as if she can will us to catch up with our quarry by mere thought."

"I wish we could. The only advantage we have is that he doesn't know we're following him."

The voices woke him from a sound sleep, but he already knew the moment he reached over to make sure the book was still beside him.

They had found him.

Some wizard had penetrated the layers of confusion and repulsion that he had drawn around him to stave off the spies.

How could that be? He had hidden his trail too well to be followed. He was surrounded in the glory lent to him by the book, which was obvious to anyone while he was nearby, but he knew from the voices that no one could follow him once he had passed from sight. But something had managed to pursue him where all the other voices had failed.

Nemeth rose from the rude bed he had fashioned for the night. He was getting used to changing objects with small alterations to their runes to make what he chose, so much easier than the traditional spells for transformation that took so much out of one. He had covered a lot of distance by taking to the air instead of walking. At first he had only hardened the air to take his weight, as his master had taught him. With a few modifications he had managed to make the air facilitate his travel, so that he was slipping along through the sky like a stone rolling down a greased chute. The process was far more comfortable than it sounded, but at the end of a day he was exhausted from having to maintain the spells. He had dared greatly, since the thraik were still appearing out of nowhere to seek him, but he was desperate to reach his goal swiftly. The inside of the fallen log he had found on his last stop had disintegrated to rotten fibers. It had been so simple to loosen the fibers more, until they were as soft as sheep's fleece and just as warm. It was so comfortable his body protested at being made to leave it, but he had no choice.

He commanded the wards to make themselves visible. The silver lines complied even before he finished the thought. They were intact. Then, how? How could someone have touched him? Even the thraik had been unable to detect his presence.

To his horror, he considered the book. He took it from the hollow log as tenderly as he would a sleeping child, and concentrated. A connection of some kind had been made to the book itself, joining with it on a primal, elemental level. Some distant mage had done this! Nemeth felt that the book had been violated. The link was passive at the moment, but it was strong, too strong for him to pluck out. He must enfold the book in secrecy to protect it. He began to draw a new set of wards. He spread his hand over the long scroll and recited the ancient words. Energy began to flow from his hands, enveloping the book.

The silver lines made a protective net, but it was incomplete. A nearly invisible thread protruded out from it, reaching toward the sky.

Nemeth passed his hand through it, and recoiled from the shock it gave him. It may have been thin, but it held the force of a raging river. He was powerless to cut the book off from this link.

Nor would the book accept his protection. The wards faded away as he watched. He would just have to make the spell stronger. Nemeth recited the words again, emphasizing the syllables firmly. Where they touched the thread the lines faded again and again. He could not cut the book off from the world. Even when it had sat under its mountaintop, it was joined to all things, living and nonliving. It was the soul of the world, right there before him, and the unknown mage had managed to tie into that connection. No matter where he took it, he could be followed. He felt betrayed and angry.

He could kill that wizard!

Nemeth's stomach rose toward his throat, and a sick taste filled his mouth as he recalled the burned bodies that had fallen at his touch. He had done enough killing. Naturally everyone wanted the Great Book, but it was his!

He forced himself to calm down. He must not retaliate. He had not been raised to behave like that.

His life before the book had been unimpeachable. He had been ethical. He was only a seer, only a seer . . . but the book had put unlimited power into his hands. The voices were talking again. They wanted the book. He must frighten them off, frighten away the mage who had broken through his protection, send them back where they came from. He did not want to do again . . . what he had done before. No, they must be driven back.

If he could not break the link, he must make use of it. It extended in both directions. Nemeth would make use of it. He would see who had done this seeking to spy upon him, and bring down upon them a warning. He did not have to know where the pursuers were. The book provided him with several models of beasts of terrifying mien that existed throughout the world. They would come into being where the wizard was. If he would not retreat, they would drag him into nonexistence. It wouldn't be Nemeth's responsibility if the wizard did not take the warning. If his deterrents did not work, then . . . death to them! No one would stop him from accomplishing his aims.

Carefully, he sent his sight back through the fine line, and began to draw new runes.

. . .

Rin trotted up the slope of a hill, then paused on a muddy patch to wait for Captain Teryn's horse to make the final jump up to the crown. The broad, green meadow was wet. The horse's rear hooves scrabbled slightly, scattering clods of earth before disappearing among a cluster of slender saplings. Rin gathered herself and made a single measured leap, landing easily on the grass among star-shaped meadow flowers that smelled sweetly when bruised by her hooves. Tildi's bottom bounced several times on the striped back. She was glad of a firm handhold on Rin's mane. Teryn glanced back, then continued on her way, glancing down now and again at the map in her hand.

"I wish that she would let us lead," Rin grumbled, settling her saddlebags more firmly on her hips. "I am faster, and more surefooted."

"I think she's happier if she is ahead of us," Tildi said. With the map guiding them toward their goal, she had been able to tuck the precious leaf away in her belt pouch with the other family treasures she cherished. "I feel safer with her and Morag to protect us."

"Bah. I do not need a human to defend me. Besides, I think that the wizard we are pursuing will be too much for them. It would be better for Edynn and Serafina to prepare. And you are more likely to know when we are close, aren't you? What do you feel now?"

Tildi thought about it. "I know that we are moving in his direction, that is, the book's. I have felt it more strongly since last night. Rin, I am afraid of facing . . . him . . . but I can't wait to see the book. In my vision it was so beautiful. I've never seen anything like it!"

Rin snorted. "It's only a book."

"Curse you, Melune!"

There was a crash behind them, and the peddler's sturdy little horse bounded up the hill by itself. Rin trotted to a halt. Lakanta appeared shortly, her cheek and hands muddy, her braids askew, shaking her fist at Melune. The errant horse cantered up to Rin with her ears set at a saucy angle. Tildi and Rin laughed. Lakanta stumped toward them.

Tildi felt a wave of warmth. Suddenly, white mist rolled up out of her belt pouch, blinding her. She batted at it, trying to clear the fog away. Tiny hands reached through the cloud and clawed at her fingers. Tildi cried out. Her voice was answered by a thousand shrill shrieks. Scaly, pale-gray creatures swarmed out of the mist. They dove at Tildi, teeth and claws aiming for her face. Tildi swatted at them. They raked her skin with their talons. She ducked and threw her hands up before her face, but they attacked her ears and hair.

"I'll help you, Tildi!" Lakanta bellowed, making a two-handed grab for one of the creatures. "Ow! They're fast little monsters! Something bit me!"

Rin snatched at the gray demons flitting above her head. They dissolved and re-formed just out of her reach, then zipped back to rake her skin with their needlelike talons.

"Guard!" shouted Rin. Teryn's head flew up at the warning in the centaur's voice. The captain thrust the map into her saddlebag and drew her sword in one swift motion. She galloped back to them and began striking out at the pale mist, grunting in frustration. Tildi flattened herself on Rin's back as the gleaming blade whipped over her head. From the rear, Morag came pelting toward them on his horse. He sprang down and stabbed at the creatures. They danced out of his range, shrieking louder.

"Get to safety," Teryn gritted, driving a half dozen of the fiends back. They gibbered and screamed at her. "Take the smallfolk out of this! I will overcome these beasts!"

"They are attacking *her*," Rin said. "What are they?" She took the whip off her belt and began to crack it at the creatures. They eddied back upon the air, then zipped in to claw at her face and neck. "What is this? I cannot hit them!"

Tildi crouched on Rin's back with her arms over her head. "Nature guard me while I sleep, From all who fly or walk or creep, Ward the earth and guard the sky, may I wake safely by and by," she muttered to herself. The simple words of protection were like throwing a glass of water onto a forest fire. The midge-demons stopped biting for one second, then began diving in again. She tried the words of the simple lullaby again. It had always protected her against childish nightmares, but it wasn't strong enough to stave off these. The pain of hundreds of scratches and gouges made her eyes blur with tears.

"*Ano chnetegh voshad,*" Edynn's voice rang out over the hillside, and Serafina's joined it. "*Voshte!*"

The silver symbol for "protect" appeared before Tildi's face. She was ashamed. She *knew* what to do. Master Olen had taught her how to drive away malign magic. She promptly sat up and began to draw her own wards upon the air with her knife, making them big enough to guard both her and Rin. Lacy walls of magic issued forth from the curling runes, spreading out to surround them completely. She sealed the last stroke. There, perfect! Those ought to keep out any evil.

To Tildi's horror the scaled beasts paid no attention to them. They zipped straight through her wards and Edynn's as if they did not exist. They almost *laughed* at her, as they took turns nipping and clawing at her. Tildi could see their runes in the center of their scaly foreheads. Something about them struck her as wrong, though she couldn't put a finger on why. She flung another ward at them. This time they did laugh, their shrill voices piercing her eardrums. Tildi was so furious that tears burned in her eyes.

"Crotegh mai ni fornai!" Serafina commanded, pointing her staff at the cloud. Wards sprang up before the little monsters, who swooped and dove around the lines in the air like linnets flitting through a trellis. She swept a hand at one. Her hand passed right through the fiend, which turned in midair and attempted to bite her.

"I deny you!" Serafina said. The fiend gnashed its pale jaws, and dove at her again. Several of its companions swept away from Tildi and the others to attack her. The young wizardess sat in the center of a whirling mass of beasts, unafraid. Her horse danced and whinnied, rolling the whites of its eyes, but she was unperturbed, and unharmed. "They're not substantial, Tildi! Close your mind to fear. Drive them back. They cannot follow. They are only seemings."

Edynn had come to the same conclusion. "They can only hurt you if you believe they can. Steel yourself. I know you can do it."

"Hah, is that all there is to it?" Rin demanded. She clicked her fingers at the swooping beasts and sneered. "Nightmares. They are for small children."

The gray creatures zoomed at her. They passed straight through her body and out the other side.

"See!"

Unable to affect Rin, they dove at Tildi. The first one bit her on the ear. Tildi knew that Serafina was right. She forced herself to think she was seeing nothing but clouds tumbling. They just *looked* like dangerous little monsters with teeth and claws. Ow! One closed those teeth on her thumb. She had to think harder, she realized, sucking the skinned knuckle. *Clouds*, she thought firmly, staring at the demons. *No power.*

"You cannot touch me," she said.

The creatures shrieked and flew at her. Tildi braced herself, but the expected pain did not come. Tildi crowed with triumph. The monsters tried again and again. Soon, they realized they had no more power over her. It was almost funny how frustrated they became.

Teryn got herself under control with the speed to be expected of a seasoned soldier and trusted officer. She stopped flailing at the insubstantial monsters with her sword, never having managed to hit one. She closed her eyes for a moment. When she opened them, the diving beasts zoomed straight through her.

The same was not true of Morag. No amount of cajoling by the others could persuade him that the fiends were not real. He slapped at them, growing more frantic. His eyes changed from their muddy brown to a gleaming blue.

"The madness is on him," Teryn said, alarmed, galloping to his side. "Morag, close your eyes. Close them now! That's an order! They can't hurt you if you don't look at them. Close your eyes."

The soldier did not seem to hear her. He waved his arms frantically. The spear fell from his hand and clattered on the ground. The fiends dived at him, laughing shrilly.

"They're everywhere!" he cried. "Help me! They want to kill me!" With a wild yell he wheeled his horse, and set spurs to its side. The animal leaped as if stung, and started galloping frantically over the rise. The packhorse, still tethered to Morag's war steed, was forced to run alongside. The cluster of demons swirled, gibbering, around his head.

"Morag, stop!" Teryn shouted. She swung into her saddle and cantered after him. The others followed.

Edynn aimed her staff at the fiends, chanting one spell after another. A beam of light burst forth, and one of the creatures burst apart in a puff of smoke. "That's done it! I understand their form now."

Tildi held fast to Rin's mane as they strove to catch up with the fleeing horses. Rin's muscles bunched and unbunched as she galloped faster and faster. Teryn, leaning low over her horse's neck, hurtled side by side with them. She glanced over, and the two exchanged a nod. They parted to overtake Morag on either side. Rin reached out and snatched the reins.

"Hold tight," she warned Tildi. All at once she leaned hard back on all four hooves, hauling back on the leads, pulling Morag's horse sharply to the right. It screamed and danced. Teryn, on the other side, put an arm around the struggling man. The flying creatures continued to bite at him, and their voices hurt Tildi's ears.

"Stop it, soldier!" Teryn commanded, her voice strained with worry. "They are but a dream. A dream, Morag!"

The white lights lanced around them, snuffing out one demon after another. Edynn and Serafina descended upon them like twin whirl-winds, robes fluttering, circling until the threats were gone. Morag sat with his head bowed, muttering to himself. Teryn spoke to him in low tones that seemed to soothe both the troubled soldier and the two pant-ing horses. Soon, she gave a nod and drew them back toward the rest of the group.

"My goodness," Lakanta said, riding up last. She went a few yards past the group and looked down. "Just in time! If you hadn't stopped him, he would have gone flying right over the edge of the bluff."

Tildi glanced in the direction the little peddler was pointing. Her heart leaped into her throat. They were on a steep escarpment that over-looked a river far down below.

"My thanks, honorables," Captain Teryn said stiffly. "Princess."

Morag murmured something that sounded like thanks. He could scarcely look up.

"I am glad to assist," Rin said graciously.

"This is my fault," Edynn said, sadly. "Our thief has detected us, and is using our own spell against us. I am out of practice in strategy. I would not have made this mistake in past years."

Serafina was businesslike in settling her mother's cloak about her shoulders. "Mother, it is not our fault. He is wilier than we suspected. We will be on guard against him now. I can set a trap upon the link so any more fiends he sends us will rebound again."

"But who knows if he will make a deadlier attempt upon us next time?" Edynn turned to the smallfolk girl. "This wizard has sent us a warning to withdraw. I cannot believe that he is incapable of more deadly spells and sendings. I cannot undo the connection between your leaf and the book, but I won't send you into greater peril for simple conve-nience's sake. We know in general which way he has gone. Let us with-draw to the nearest city and send you back to Olen. Others will assist me in the pursuit. The risk is too great for you to continue."

"He knows we are here behind him," Rin said grimly. "We must con-tinue to follow."

"Rin, you are a seasoned warrior, and I welcome your aid, but I have no right to throw this little one into danger that she is unprepared to handle."

"Don't, Edynn," Tildi said, alarmed. She didn't want to be sent back, not when she had talked herself into going! "I'm willing to take the risk.

I told you so, and I have not changed my mind. I have scores of my own to settle with him. I want to help catch him."

Edynn shook her head. "We'll stay closer to you. But now we have got an insurmountable problem," she said, looking down over the bluff into the river below. "How far are we from the nearest bridge?"

Teryn consulted the map. "I reckon it to be about thirty-five miles to the northwest of here."

"Yes, I imagined it was something like that. I put it to you that our thief did not go out of his way to take it. Nor could he have gained so much distance on us in an ordinary fashion. I fear we will have to fly, in hopes of catching up."

"Fly?" Tildi asked nervously. She had not forgotten her ride on Si-hine's back. "Is there no other way?"

Edynn was resolute. "If our quarry has become aware of us, and is willing to attack, we have no time to lose in catching up with him. He has killed, and he is making use of the book. We need to make haste. I believe I can support all our beasts on the air for at least a while each day."

Serafina looked worried. "Let me make the spell, Mother. I don't wish you to put yourself at risk of exhaustion. You will want to be ready if we come upon the thief." Tildi looked away, not wanting to embarrass Serafina by gazing at her with the admiration she felt. Once again she was impressed and touched by the solicitousness of daughter for mother. Serafina turned to her, the tender moment past. "And you can help, too, smallfolk," she snapped. Tildi opened her mouth and closed it again. Sympathy warred with annoyance, but sympathy won.

"I would be glad to," she said, keeping her temper under control. "Please tell me what to do."

Serafina, mollified by Tildi's easy acquiescence, taught her the spell to harden the air, so that each horse would find solid footing each time he or she set a hoof down. Tildi recited it several times before she succeeded. At last she was able to pat the air with her hand, and was pleased that it felt like solid ground under her palm. Under Serafina's direction, she laid the charm on Rin's feet and on Lakanta's horse, Melune.

"Are we ready then?" Edynn beamed at her two apprentices. "Let's go!"

She set her heels to her mare's sides and rode straight for the cliff's edge. Tildi held her breath as the wizardess stepped out into thin air. Instead of plummeting down to her death, she continued to ride out as though she was on an invisible bridge. Teryn took a deep breath, and spurred after her, followed by Morag and the packhorse.

"Here goes nothing," Lakanta said cheerfully. "Let's see how good your work is, Tildi."

"Race you!" Rin called. She burst into a running trot, easily outdistancing the stout horse.

"Unfair!" Lakanta's voice receded behind them. Tildi held tight to Rin's mane. The thundering of the centaur's hooves echoed on the ground, then there was no noise. Tildi screwed her eyes shut, hoping that her spell would hold.

"Oh, this is marvelous! Such nice firm footing, like running on loam! Look down there, Tildi!" she cried. "The trees look like puffs of green smoke!"

Tildi opened her eyes. She took one look down, and resolutely stared straight up. They were miles above the land. The river was a blue thread, and all the plants had blurred together into masses of green and gold. Her heart pounded so much she could barely breathe. She tried to feel what her brothers' delight would be at a treat like this, but all she wanted was to be back on the ground. The clouds above looked so soft. What would it be like when she fell?

"You can't panic!" Edynn shouted to her. "You must guide us, Tildi! Think! Where is the book? Don't look down."

Easier said than done, Tildi thought. With an effort of will, she pulled her chin down and squinted over Rin's shoulder. *Concentrate on the rune in your mind,* she told herself firmly. *Only on that. Only on that.*

A faint dot of gold glinted off to her right. "That way!" she cried, pointing toward it.

The others turned to follow her. Tildi kept her eyes focused upon the tiny point, and nothing else.

Chapter Twenty-two

agpie knelt on the cold stone steps before the winged throne of his father, who left him in that uncomfortable pose for a very long time while the king attended to other business. Behind him, gentlemen and ladies in waiting, clad in their day-to-day court finery, stood in rows between the gilded pillars that held up the round ceiling of the royal receiving chamber, resplendent with its lapis lazuli and white quartz mosaic of a gigantic eagle in flight over a green and fertile landscape. Though they undoubtedly had urgent business they wanted to bring before the king they also waited with the semblance of patience, but their knees were not wearing out.

At last, he felt a touch on his shoulder, and rose, silently cursing the stiffness in his legs.

"So you're back at last, are you?" his father demanded. "Well? What was the urgent summons in aid of?"

King Soliandur, lord of Orontae, looked his son up and down and shook his head in weary disapproval. Magpie had been given no time to change out of his dirty and worn riding clothes, and fervently wished he had a chance to wash his face, but the very young page who had scrambled to his horse's side when he rattled into the courtyard an hour before had pleaded for him to attend His Majesty at once. Magpie had long since stopped smelling his own odor, but from the wrinkling of his father's nostrils it must have been, well, breathtaking.

For the first time in a few months Magpie took the opportunity to study his father. He was still a fine-looking man, with a sharp profile and wise eyes surrounded by lines. Time and care had claimed an inch from his height, which in his youth was the same as Magpie stood now. His thick, dark hair under the circle of his crown was shot with more silver than it had been when Magpie had departed, and the lines around his mouth had deepened. The knee-length tunic, embroidered with the sigil of their house, and worn over loose trousers woven of silk and trimmed with gold, seemed just a little too large for him. Cares were eroding him, like water wearing away a stone. Magpie felt deeply sorry for him, and chose to ignore the disapproving tone. He put on the most responsible expression he possessed and straightened his back. In ringing tones, he addressed his father but pitched his voice to fill the throne room to the banners hanging from the tops of the walls.

"Yes, Father. I have much important news to tell you. I attended the conference as your emissary. Lord Wizard Olen sends his greetings, from one noble prince to another."

Soliandur, monarch of Orontae, lord of the High Lands, duke of the Wilds, protector of the first of the Noble Kingdoms of Humans, hissed through his teeth. He hated to think of his youngest son in any position of authority on behalf of the kingdom or himself. It took no imagination to understand that Soliandur was grateful that he had two older sons than the one he understood the least, and a handful of daughters, if it came to that. Magpie could disappear without a trace one day, and his father would be the most grateful among the mourners. Magpie's mother, who smiled at him from behind her husband's shoulder, often said that they were too much alike to get along. That was a comparison that Magpie devoutly hoped was not true. While he admitted that both of them overthought matters to the point where a lesser being would scream for mercy, he prayed that there was not so much bitterness and disappointment existing at the bottom of his soul. He continued.

"In attendance were representatives of the realms of—"

"Enough!" Soliandur said sharply. Magpie fell instantly silent, wondering how he had made a misstep this time.

The king looked around the audience chamber at the court, regarding them all with an expression that Magpie found all too familiar: distrust.

"We will talk in private. Come with me," Soliandur said.

Obediently, Magpie stood aside as his father swept down the stone stairs and off across the polished inlaid floor. His mother followed. With her light hair turning gently gray and her pale blue dress, Lottcheva was a shining silver presence that lightened her husband's angry aura. She paused to touch Magpie's cheek with her fingers.

"We'll talk later," she whispered. Magpie smiled at her. At least one of his parents was glad to see him safe and alive.

"Hem!" the prime minister cleared his throat to hurry them along. Magpie met his eyes and gave him a wry grin. He knew that Hawarti sympathized with him. They had worked closely together in the years since Magpie had attained his majority, and liked each other. Magpie would have been better pleased if his mother had said he had the same personality as the genial Lord Hawarti. He knew the same notion was in both their minds: it would be wrong to present the possibility of bad news in public. The king would not like it. He had lost his tolerance for bad news years before.

Magpie opened his stride to keep pace with the big man. Ahead of them, the pages and guards had had to break into a near run to stay ahead of the king. Doors flew open and curtains were swept aside as if by magic. The last door swung open half a pace before the king's foot crossed the threshold. The guards drew their swords and held them by the hilts point up before them as His Majesty passed, then swung around to follow Hawarti and Magpie into the small room.

Magpie looked around him. Little had changed there over the years. The king's privy chamber had been, in happier days, where Soliandur spent rest day afternoons reading documents sent to him by his regional governors and sister or brother monarchs as his children played on the floor about his feet, creeping underneath the priceless burgundy silk draperies or spinning the world globe in the corner. He had let them use the royal seal and glass desk ornaments as playthings, and given them quills and ink to draw on the back of discarded letters. Magpie always felt a sense of loss to have been banned long since from the chamber unless specifically requested to come. Since the war the room had become Soliandur's sanctuary. *If he had not been so proud,* Magpie thought sadly, *Soliandur would have been able to share his frustration and grief, and lessen the burden.*

His father waved the guards back as he and the prime minister entered the chamber. The king sat down in the gold-trimmed, tapestry chair at the handsome bronze and wood desk that had been his father's, his grandfather's, and his great-grandmother's before him. Hawarti took up his usual stance near the door, which the guards closed behind them as soon as Magpie had crossed the threshold.

"Well?" His Majesty demanded, not father but sovereign. Magpie was not invited to sit. No matter: he'd sat on his horse's back for more than a week returning home. It was a relief to be able to stand.

"Master Wizard Olen sends his compliments, majesty. There is a grave threat abroad in Niombra, and he wishes to have all lands advised of it . . ."

Hours later, his throat dry as leather, Magpie croaked out the last words.

". . . He begs you, your ministers and governors, watchmen, or any sane and trusted observer to send word at once if any of them sees anything out of the ordinary that could be a manifestation of this very dangerous book's power."

Soliandur looked displeased. He had not shifted his pose or changed his expression during the entire recitation, as if he was a statue instead of a man.

"And is that all?"

"All?" Magpie echoed, his dry throat rasping. "I hate to say it in such dire terms, my lord, but it's not a doomsayer's fantasy to say this book could bring about the end of the world."

The king waved a hand. "Olen has always exaggerated everything. And even if this book is dangerous, then what does it matter? Knowing about the book won't change anything, and won't help us in any way. All it can bring is more trouble."

"Sir, I have seen a demonstration of what the book represents. It is the most incredible magic—"

"There, you see, you have said the word yourself: *incredible.* I don't believe in it. Ah!" He held up his hand to forestall Magpie's protest. "And any other powers he may want to ascribe to it are obviously a collusion between himself and his apprentice."

"Tildi. But it's not a trick . . ."

Soliandur wrinkled his nose. "Of course, it's a trick! It's clear he wants it for himself, boy, and he wants to scare the rest of us out of wanting to do the same. That way, if we come upon it, we'll turn it over to him and be grateful to do it. Don't you see that? Can't you tell when you're being played?" A pained expression passed over the king's face.

Magpie refrained from saying that the king had not been played, he had played himself, and continued to suffer for it, long after most people had gone about their business. Because Magpie loved and respected him, he felt sorry for him, but kept that sentiment to himself. It would only make things worse.

"I . . . understand, my lord. I only report the events that occurred in the meeting, for your information. Whether you take action upon any of what I have told you is, of course, your decision. I only want to help."

"Help?" Soliandur echoed, with heavy sarcasm. "If you really wish to help, see if you cannot find it in your heart to visit your fiancée. There you may *help*."

"Has she sent word?" Magpie asked, his heart sinking.

"Of course she has sent word! Not that she should need to. What kind of unnatural man are you, when you make no effort to communicate with the woman to whom you have pledged marriage?"

"Father, because the matter is so likely to provoke overreaction in public, Olen asked that the conference be kept confidential except among trusted and thoughtful advisers. I didn't want to send a message that might have been read in transit, and would surely have been seen by servants or others after it was delivered, that would have included my destination or my task."

"And yet you were about to announce the event to the entire court, like a herald!" Soliandur spat.

Magpie bent his head. "You received me and asked me for my report in the audience chamber, Father." Soliandur frowned.

"Blame me for it, will you?"

Magpie glanced up at Hawarti, standing at His Majesty's shoulder. The prime minister sent him a look full of sympathy. There had been trouble while he was gone, and he was going to take the blame for it. Never mind; it was only one more stone in the load.

Magpie straightened his shoulders. "Forgive me. I should have insisted that I must tell you alone. You have other matters to concentrate upon."

Soliandur reddened. "Don't patronize me, boy." He waved a hand. "Go. If the girl has any sense she'll send you away, but it won't be because I let you shirk your duties. Go."

"Yes, my lord." Magpie bowed deeply. "I'll try to keep her from regretting accepting my suit."

"Go!"

Magpie strode back into the courtyard in search of Tessera, but the multicolored mare wasn't where he had tethered her. He searched the stables, dodging around grooms walking horses, until he found Covani, the stable master, overseeing the shoeing of a skittish mare. He asked about his missing horse.

"My lord, she was caked with sweat and dust," the master groom said, with a reproachful frown. He was a rangy man with wide-set brown eyes, not unlike his equine charges. "She's getting a bath and a sound rubdown, then out to pasture for a nice, calm feed. You've ridden her too hard without giving her a good clean for too long."

Magpie sighed. "That I have. There was no good place or time to care for her along the road. But I have to ride to Levrenn within the hour. How long until she'll be ready?"

"I'll find you another steed, sir."

"What about Tessera?"

The horseman shook his head. "You may push yourself like a machine, sir, but you can't expect a horse to run forever on no rest. She'd break her heart open for you and bleed out her last drop, but it's not fair to ask her, sir. She needs rest and care." The master ostler gave him a summing glance. "It would not hurt you at all to have the same. Unless the matter is urgent?"

Magpie grinned wryly. "No, and you're right. I'll go and be curried and eat my oats. I'll be much more presentable to my ladylove that way. If I can stay out of my father's path I'll go in the morning."

"That's wise thinking, sir," the master ostler said. With a sudden broad smile, he added, "I'm not supposed to know it, but the stableboys skip out work and nap on the hay bales back behind the tack barn just under the eaves. If another couple of bales happened to be occupied this afternoon I wouldn't be able to tell who it was."

Magpie laughed. "I may yet have to take you up on your hospitality, Master Covani."

He did not have to go to any great lengths to avoid his father. As it was a workday, His Majesty would be in the audience room or his private office all day, then dine in state, with visitors of rank, if there were any. Magpie felt fortunate to recognize on one of the closed carriages at the side of the stable yard the family sigil of a wealthy mine owner who lived in Breckon, the eastern province of Orontae, where his brother Ganidur was governor. That would keep Soliandur's attention firmly placed, and he wouldn't be on the lookout for an errant son.

Still, there was no point in taking chances. The castle was riddled with secret passages and staircases. He could reach his suite of rooms by means of a most aptly named privy stair, which led up to an ancient closet near his rooms that was now used as a storeroom. He sauntered casually along the western wall of the stone keep to a point behind the first guard tower and climbed up into the riot of bushes that grew along its foot. When he was sure no one was watching him but a few odd chickens, he popped a hand-sized stone out of the wall and pulled an ancient metal lever. He thrust his way through the thornbrake around the next buttress. A dark slit in the wall showed where the ancient door had come unlatched. With his fingertips he pried it open and slipped inside.

Once he shoved the stone door closed, he was in utter darkness. The lightfastness of the passage was an element for which he had often been grateful in his wilder youth. He felt to his right for the narrow stair that ascended sharply in between the outer and inner walls of the keep.

The way up was free of spiderwebs and dust. It had been cleaned and swept recently, Magpie was pleased to note, as he climbed up the steep staircase in the dark. The servants went along with the polite fiction that no one but the royal family knew where the secret passages lay. In fact, it had been Leweni, Covani's predecessor, who had shown this particular doorway to Magpie when he was a boy. He had used it ever since, first for the usual run of boyish escapades, later for more important ventures where an unheralded exit from the castle was called for.

The latter was the chief reason why his father could hardly stand the sight of him.

Magpie's sensitive fingertips found the rough surface of the door a step before he bashed his head into it. He felt for the padded catch, and emerged, blinking, into a small, dim, close stone room full of rolled mattresses and heaps of winter cloaks and blankets, all the things that were hidden away when they weren't needed. *How remarkably significant,* he thought, wading through a heap of musty feather pillows like knee-deep marsh mud and throwing up clouds of dust. He, too, was an inconvenient sight that many people were willing to conspire to keep out of his father's sight when he was not specifically of use. Until and unless Inbecca of Levrenn became his wife he was one of those needless items.

He cursed himself for being bitter, but it stung that he was unable to gain his father's regard. He understood that he was a reminder of how things had gone wrong. It was one of the reasons that he had found so many excuses to stay away from home over the past two years. If he had not loved his father and his homeland so dearly, he would have gone away forever. There were many places that would gladly offer him a home, and a world beyond them that he had not yet explored. Yet he had returned to this simmering pot, roiling with unhappiness under its seemingly placid surface, yearning for a time that had long gone, and a relationship with his father that had never been.

Orontae had now been at peace for two years. Three years before that, war had overtaken the country. Like any conflict, it came about for the most foolish of reasons: a misunderstanding about borderlands, the very Wilds that were part of his father's grand titles. Magpie had been educated since childhood to know the map of his homeland, which included the forests in the far southwest. They had traditionally been too remote to bother with, and remained the untrammeled province of dryads and elves for centuries, until recently, when trade by ship with more and more remote lands had begun to fascinate the rulers of Niombra. Merchants building ships found the tall, branchless conifers of Orontae's deep woods ideal for masts, and the heavy, ageless oaks suitable for ships' timbers. When the most accessible forests were logged out of decent trees, they were drawn to the virgin woodlands of the southwest. So, it seemed, was Halcot of Rabantae.

By the time Soliandur's woodsmen arrived to begin harvesting trees, half the forests had been stripped of all their best stands of wood. A few hapless workers still on site were arrested by guards and questioned. They had been hired from small villages not far from the woods, on the other side of the border in Rabantae, to cut the trees and send them downriver, to whence they knew not. To the investigators the destination seemed undisputed, since that river floated by Rabantae's shipyards, and word had come from traveling peddlers that trade in nails and ship's fittings seemed to have picked up there considerably.

Affronted, Soliandur had sent emissaries to demand why his old neighbor had invaded his lands and stolen his valuable timbers. Halcot had responded with an insulting message asking why Soliandur did not know the extent of his own most ancient kingdom. The forests were his, and he intended to exploit them as he chose. Soliandur sent back a curt message referring to the lord of Rabantae in thinly veiled terms as a thief. Less diplomatic accusations followed, earning responses ever more heated. Name-calling ensued, and every resentment and petty disagreement of the past thousand years had come bubbling up like the stink in a cesspit.

The two lands, for all that they sat side by side, historically had not had a peaceful relationship. Each thought the other was inferior human stock, a claim neither could bear out, since both the royal family and common folk alike had intermarried for centuries. The crossing between the borders was made as difficult as possible even for those who had legitimate reason to travel, involving presentation of papers, long explanations, and bribes that no one admitted to taking. Magpie had paid quite a few of those himself, and anyone who did not have the privy purse behind his finances had every right to resent their imposition, especially since trying to involve the authorities only increased the number of people to whom bribes had to be paid.

Both tried, without success, Magpie was glad to note, to involve the third noble kingdom of humanity, Melenatae, on his side. Neither could raise the interest of the elves, the werewolves, or the centaurs in the dispute. The dwarves merely ignored the emissaries, leaving the doors to their mountain halls locked and unanswered. At least it remained a battle of humans versus humans.

Ministers, distinguished by their skills in diplomacy, made the long journey between the capitals, braving weather, bad roads, wild beasts, and thieves, trying to smooth out the initial disagreement. Their efforts were without success. Halcot's woodsmen who attempted to return to the disputed forests for more timber were attacked, and two men were killed. Loss of income was one thing, but loss of life stirred the righteous indignation of all of the southern kingdom. Halcot sent a declaration of war.

Orontae had been ill-prepared for what Magpie had foreseen as the inevitable outcome. Terrifying rumors of secret attacks spread throughout the country. Guards had to be dispatched to keep peace in the streets while Soliandur decided how to respond. He called upon all of his ministers, including his court wizard, a man of foresight, for counsel. The king made numerous public appearances to quell fears, and managed largely by force of will to turn the people's attention to defending itself. They had a common cause and a common enemy, not nebulous forces attacking secretly in the night.

Once stirred to action, Orontae organized not only troops for the field, but a force of spies and information-seekers who operated through the office of the prime minister. Magpie enlisted himself with the corps. In his youth he had escaped from the royal court and gone about the countryside disguised as a troubadour who sang and played the jitar. In that persona, he was able to insinuate himself into the Rabantavian towns, even into the capital and the palace itself. He had gotten to know Halcot, even struck up a friendly relationship of sorts, as much as an anointed and crowned king would have with an itinerant wanderer and purveyor of news and entertainment. Halcot often called for private concerts for his family or himself alone. He paid well, so the traveling player was glad to oblige. He did not recognize in the man the child who had once played in those very halls during his father's official state visits.

Halcot was an old bore, in love with his own dignity, as he had proved once again in Olen's great room, but he wasn't a fool. From his first visit Magpie could tell he was troubled that the dispute had escalated so far. He refused to back down out of sheer pride, but was beginning to see that he had made a bad decision. Magpie felt rather sorry for him. In his opinion Halcot was more trusting than he should have been of a clever and witty observer who had the range of the whole castle during wartime. When he was not in the throne room or the grand audience chamber, Magpie sat with whoever wanted to talk, listening, never seeming to ask prying questions, but always leading gently toward garnering information on where the troops had been sent, what armaments they carried, and how long they had been gone. Magpie continued to make note of what he saw and overheard, but out of a sense of honor he refused to sabotage unguarded documents or change orders. He wrote and sang songs for those private performances to please the king, even making jokes with Halcot or one of his ministers as the butt, to take the king's mind off the war for a while. He often felt closer to the enemy lord than he did to his own father.

What had come after was in no way his fault or his doing. His allegiance never wavered from his cause. He had brought all this information home. It supplemented gleanings brought to Soliandur by other spies. All of the details confirmed the scrying of the court wizard, who was proving to be a true seer.

Magpie emerged from the privy room covered with dust and feathers just as a maidservant went by. She squawked with surprise, but didn't drop the pitcher of water she was carrying. He gave her a grin and unlocked the door of his chambers. They were as tidy and free of dust as the secret passageway, as if his mother had had foreknowledge of the exact moment of his arrival home. Gratefully, he stripped out of his dirty clothes and ran a bath for himself. There was no need to light a lamp, with the summer evening sun still pouring in through the unshuttered windows. He was tired of the glare, anyhow. Cradled in the porcelain bath full of steaming water, he remarked upon how little it took for civilized life to break down.

Magpie squeezed out the bath sponge and applied it to his face and neck. Grime rolled off his skin in layers. He had never thought that Nemeth had been much of a magician. His great workings usually failed. An attempt to bring rain to relieve a yearlong drought had been disastrous. Nor was Nemeth able to charm beasts, destroy insect plagues, or enchant weapons. It seemed that his greatest and heretofore untapped talent lay in clairvoyance, the ideal gift for an enchanter whose liege was pitted in a battle of wits with another. Too bad, though, that his father, disappointed in his enchanter's previous failures and distrustful of everyone, discounted almost everything that Nemeth told him after one incident, in which the enchanter warned him that advance scouts were avoiding lookouts by traveling through the old river tunnels. The king at once sent elite troops, only to find collapsed mine shafts, and no sign that anyone had passed that way recently. Again Nemeth pleaded for the king to listen, that there were other underground passages that the enemy was making use of. The king reviled him and denied his gifts. In vain, Nemeth had protested his innocence, saying that his seeing was true, and he was working on other means of defending the country. Magpie and Hawarti had defended the hapless wizard, who was no better at dealing with angry kings than he was with rainstorms.

Instead, Soliandur put his belief in information that had been bought from a traitor who claimed to be close to Halcot's general. They found out later that the man had been a spy in Halcot's pay all the time. They caught him and hanged him when the war was at last over, but it was too late for Soliandur. He threw too many men at too many points along the border, decimating his forces, and blaming Nemeth for each successive failure.

Two years after hostilities began, a herald had made his shaky way to the front line and surrendered to the nearest officer, and begged to be brought to the king without delay. He had a message of the greatest import from King Halcot. The Rabantavian king was suing for peace.

Soliandur took news of the surrender with grim satisfaction. Details arrived along with Halcot's chief minister who came to ask humbly for terms at the king's pleasure. It seemed that the most ancient of maps had been compared by the southern king and his ministers. They had realized their mistake. Halcot offered to halt the fighting and to to pay restitution, for their mutual benefit. Magpie believed that his intelligence was far better than Soliandur's, or that he paid more attention to it, and realized that little would be left of the two lands if the fighting went on for much longer. A proud man, he had swallowed his pride for his people. Soliandur drew up the terms of the treaty, demanding that Halcot pay tribute for twenty years and acknowledge Orontae as its master. That latter term Halcot would not agree to, but he accepted payment of the monstrous sum Soliandur demanded as weregild.

The war was over, but two years of battle had left Orontae scarred and, though few people realized it, near financial ruin. Soliandur had to try and rebuild a nation without seeming to need to. The king concealed from his people how much he hated the status quo, but he took out his anger on everyone close to him. To keep from revealing to the people how bad things were, Soliandur had borrowed heavily from the queen of Levrenn, his wife's cousin, and was paying it back mainly from the tribute that Soliandur had exacted from Halcot and new taxes levied upon an already groaning populace. Magpie knew all that had gone through his father's mind, and how devastating it was to a proud man.

It went without saying that the tunnels were found within a month after the end of the war. They were the course of underground rivers that had gone unnoticed for eons by any humans except possibly smugglers and a few children.

No one knew what had become of Nemeth. Soliandur had dismissed him from his service, for once and all. At Hawarti's urging he offered the angry wizard more gifts and a generous settlement, but to anyone who would listen he still said that Nemeth was to blame for their defeats. Nemeth had disappeared not long afterwards. The tower, from which they had heard angry shrieks, was still unoccupied.

A faint *snick* sounded in the next room, the noise of the door latch being opened very quietly. Before conscious thought took hold, Magpie's reflexes jerked him up and over the far side of the bath as silently as an otter. He wriggled across the floor toward his clothing and the daggers hidden in sleeve and boot. His father's antipathy toward him was known. It wouldn't be out of the question for a reward-seeking assassin to make away with the unpopular prince. While he had luxuriated in the hot water the sun had gone down, and shadow favored stealth.

On elbows and knees, he crawled around behind the bathroom door and peered through the hinge side to spy upon the intruder. Someone was moving around in his bedchamber, someone else who did not choose to light the lamps.

The door catch clicked a second time, again very quietly, and footsteps receded faintly down the corridor. Puzzled, Magpie crept to the end of the door and ventured a look around.

There was a note in his mother's handwriting: "Give Inbecca my love."

Chapter Twenty-three

hey were gaining ground on the Great Book, but not fast enough for Tildi. The gold dot on the map always showed it to be farther away than they thought it would be. The soundlessness of their passage through the air made it possible for the searchers to speak together while they rode. Lakanta narrated the features with which she was familiar, among them towns, rivers, and roads, adding funny little stories from her long experience as a traveling tradeswoman. As they had not fallen out of the sky, Tildi began to get over her fear of the heights, and saw the land unfold before her like a glorious tapestry. The map the schoolmaster had had in Clearbeck was a faint pencil sketch by comparison.

On the third day the trace on the map began to fade. It vanished entirely under the noonday sun, leaving them to seek about helplessly in midair. Tildi feared that the thief had managed to break the spell on the map, but it had only run its course. They landed in a field outside a huge farmhouse that was so much like Daybreak Bank that Tildi felt tears starting in her eyes from homesickness. Edynn had taken her briskly in charge and got her mind off past sorrows by insisting that she renew the map's spell on her own. To the relief and dismay of everyone, the dot sprang up again as bright as ever and as far out of reach.

Over the days that passed Tildi began to daydream about meeting up with the thief. She pictured Knemet as a handsome giant, with a black beard and bright golden eyes. In some of her dreams, the huge human handed over the book without trouble. In others, he started a war that consumed the whole world, leaving no one alive but her and him on a cliff. In order to save the world she must take the book and jump off, leaving him behind. She reached out to do it, and found herself falling, but she had never been so happy in her life. The sacrifice was worth it, because she had the book in her keeping at last.

No more demons had pursued them, but she viewed all clouds with suspicion since the first attack. Other things had harried them in the air, looking like snakes or deformed birds or shapeless blobs of flesh whose touch burned, but Tildi found it easier and easier to drive them back. Even Serafina had praised her growing skills with wards and protective runes. All of them kept a weather eye out for thraik. To Tildi's relief, the slimy, black-green creatures had not turned up again.

There was one bright spot, at least: since they were no longer tied to following the thief's tracks, they were able to detour for the night to more hospitable surroundings. Between them, Teryn and Lakanta had picked out the nearest habitation that had the chance of a decent inn or guest house and put down there, often to the open admiration of the clientele. Being able to sleep in a bed had done wonders for Tildi's morale. She was able to face the daily climb into the skies with resolve, if not outright enjoyment.

Edynn encouraged her further by helping her with magical studies. The wizardess was very tired when they landed in the evenings, but she insisted on squeezing in a little time for Tildi. In the Hourglass Inn, a picturesque spot in central Rabantae, they sat together over a hand-somely laid table in the corner of the main room beside a lively, crack-ling fire that was meant as much to cheer as to warm.

"There are so many disciplines of magic that you will be encountering over the coming years," Edynn said, as eagerly as a girl, leaning toward

Tildi. By contrast, Serafina sat back in the inglenook, her slightly hooded eyes staring at Tildi. The smallfolk girl tried over and over again to offer friendly overtures to the younger wizardess, but they were always rebuffed. "The biggest problem you will have, once this task is over, is deciding in what order you will want to approach each subject, or whether you'll want to learn some of them at all."

"I'd like to try everything I can," Tildi said. "I've had so little experience in magic that I don't know what I won't like."

Edynn leaned back a bit and gazed at the ceiling. "Let me see, there is Healing, Teaching, Naming, Making, Influence, Transformation, Psychometry, Weatherchange, Alchemy, Astronomy, Protective Magics— Olen has given you a good grounding in that, but you must learn to be less timid in its use—laws of Magic, Evocation, Invocation, and Trueseeing. Weather-witching is fairly common. Healers are also common. There are natural seers, but that is one of the rarest talents of all. Psychometry is useful. Contact with important artifacts can cause memories long buried in the item to surface, or give the seer insight into things happening elsewhere. This is a function of the Law of Contagion, in which that thing that touched another maintains a bond with it, no matter how distantly parted they are, and can cause things to happen to one part by using the other."

"Is that which makes the runes in the book change?" Tildi asked.

"No, that would fall under the Law of Macrocosm, in which, as you know, a small thing is tied to a larger thing that is identical to it. There is known to be dark magic that perverts this. It ties images to the humans they resemble. Misfortune that is visited upon the images also affects the person. There are dark analogues to all magics, I am sad to say. As a true rune is changed, the item it describes is also changed. We discussed this in Silvertree, you must recall."

"I do," Tildi said, turning her attention to her neglected plate, long grown cold. "I won't ask again. I'm sorry."

"Oh, no, no," Edynn said, smiling. "I'm only reminding you. I do not want to stop you asking questions. You should feel free to ask questions, as you did with Olen. I am your teacher, temporarily, until we have returned from our mission, successfully or unsuccessfully. I only remind you so you can tie together what you learned. The Great Book is a work for the ages, like the mountain halls of the First Kings, indeed, like our world itself."

Rin let out a mild sound. "*Sn-sn-sn.* Would not some of your fellow humans consider those words to be blasphemy? Natural phenomena are not to be compared with man-made."

"You are toying with me, Princess," Edynn said, with a humorous look at the centaur. "It could be considered so by some deep adherents to the Mother and Father, but most of what we wizards do question are all the elements of existence. You understand that what I say goes against those teachings, but only in a narrow interpretation. I believe, as you do, in Time and Nature as the architects of creation. And part of what Mother Nature has given us is the ability to question, so question I do. I must not refuse to use her gifts."

"And what do you think?" Rin asked Lakanta.

The little merchant threw up her hands. "I'm not what you call a normal adherent of human faith. Don't ask me!"

"Smallfolk don't approve of magic. It wouldn't matter if you had the gift, especially if you are a girl," Tildi reminded them.

"Nor is magic acceptable in every human culture. You should not have been afraid to use your gifts. Being a girl is not a disadvantage or a disgrace. You may put yourself forward. It is your responsibility. I know it's not the way it is in your world, but magic does not care if you are a girl or a boy, old or young, elf, dwarf, mermaid, human, or centaur, or any of the other wonderful permutations of life. It is power and therefore formless and without regard. It will not seek you out, nor will it spare you. If you have chosen this path, then you must understand that. That *is* your responsibility."

Tildi was impressed by Edynn's passion. If only Teldo could have lived to be there with her! Ah, but then she would not have been here with him. The apprenticeship would have gone to him, and he would be here with the page of the book, in the company of wizards and centaurs. She would have been at home in the Quarters, keeping house for Gosto.

"There is so much you can do with your skills. Talents are different between wizards, even members of the same family. I have many skills, but Serafina far outstrips me in Transformation. We are of similar skill in several other arts, including Healing. Weather-witching is a discipline I particularly enjoy, though I seldom practice it. There are too many natural repercussions one can suffer if one meddles too greatly with the flow of the climate."

"Olen is going to send me to Volek one day," Tildi said.

Edynn and Serafina exchanged glances. "Ah. Yes. I learned my skill with storms from him, but Olen is greater than Volek."

"He is?" Tildi asked, her voice rising to a squeak. "He told me Volek was the master of that craft."

"Oh, no. He's too modest. You could have done far worse than to apprentice yourself to Olen. You don't have to make up your mind where your talents lie. You'll find that out in a few years, and then you can decide if you will choose to develop that skill, or pick another field of study that interests you, whether you have a natural bent for it. You can still learn. You have the time. Once you begin to study magic, it stretches out your life. It is as if we put ourselves more in tune with Father Time, learning the slow pace of existence, and he gives us more of his precious gift in which to learn."

Tildi frowned, thinking of the book. "In the council, the wizards said that the Shining Ones lengthened their lives by changing their runes. Wouldn't wizards be at risk if the thief interferes with each of them?"

"That is what I believe," Serafina said severely. " It is much more than likely that we will be his first victims, as the ones who are most likely to be able to stop him. Only time will tell what his plans are."

"Edynn, would he be able to tell by reading each rune who is fated to live or die? Is our future written in the book? Does it say what is foretold to happen?"

"No, Tildi. It is only a record of what is now, if I can use the word *only* to describe the Great Book. The changes to the runes within run parallel to that which is occuring to the natural object, and no faster. It has no effect upon what is to come. As Olen told us all, it is only a tool. How you manage fate is up to you. For example, I know my fate. I have known it for years."

Serafina straightened up at once, aghast. "Mother, this is none of her business."

Edynn turned to her, the same mild expression of patience on her face. "But it is, daughter. If she is to be my apprentice, however temporary, it must be known to her. She deserves that." She put her hand on her daughter's, but turned to Tildi.

"You have the right to know, since you have been entrusted to me by Olen, that our time together may be limited. It is not that I have been deprived of a long and full life. I've seen several centuries come and go, like Olen. I have traveled widely, and enjoyed my time observing my fellow beings," she added with a nod to Lakanta. "I have been the adviser to kings and queens in three continents. I've served them in war and in the prosperous or thin times in between. In fact, until Olen summoned me to help gather rumors of the book's return, I had retired—to a lovely estate, the gift of my last employer, a very wise and ambitious merchant—to study magic and to raise my children."

"Children?" Tildi echoed, surprised.

Edynn dimpled, making her look younger than her daughter. "Yes. I have two sons, a general in a kingdom in Sheatovra and a merchant seaman, the master of his own fleet of ships. Serafina is my only daughter, and by far my youngest. I believe that she is also the one closest to me in temperament."

Lakanta let out a disbelieving chuckle, echoing Tildi's own thoughts, then assumed an innocent blue-eyed expression. "My apologies, honorable one."

"You must admit you are not seeing us at our best," Edynn chided her mildly. "It's been difficult for her. She has lived in the shadow of a famous mother all her life, and has resented it with the full force of an ambitious soul."

"Mother!" Serafina said indignantly. Her back went as straight as the fireplace poker. "I love and admire you dearly."

Edynn sighed and stroked her hand. "And that's the contradiction, of course. In time, you too will come to be respected and held in awe, for you are immensely talented, but only once I'm not here to be given all the credit. I do know all too well how she feels, Lakanta. I felt it with my father, who was more renowned than I will ever be. But I cannot do anything to change the way things are.

"I told you that the true sight is rare, Tildi. I do not have it. My ability to see beyond my own eyes comes to me through magical talent and long years of practice. When Serafina was very small we traveled over the sea to Tledecra with her brother. I met a fellow wizard there who was renowned as a seer. I was able to do him a small service. In exchange, he told me of his vision. He had seen me and Serafina together. In his dream, I walked through a door. When that door closed between us, he knew she and I would never meet again." Edynn smiled sadly. "I have had to tell her of the prophecy before we set out on this quest. I am afraid it has been preying on her mind ever since."

"Mother, please," Serafina said. Her proud chin was set, but Tildi could tell that she was near tears. "How can you talk about it so carelessly?"

"It might not come true, all the same," Lakanta said encouragingly.

"I must act as though it will," Edynn replied. "I have had the same dream since that day. There have been small signs within my vision to resolve any doubts that I have. I have had a long and fulfilling life. If the moment does come, I will go to my fate in peace, whatever lies beyond that door. Serafina, I count upon you to take charge of Tildi after that time, until you can return her to Olen's home. And, Tildi," she said, turning to the smallfolk girl, "take care of my daughter. I am grieved that you have had so many losses in your life, but perhaps you can help her learn to cope with just one. I hope neither is necessary, but you were entitled to know."

Tildi and Serafina eyed each other. Serafina looked as though having a smallfolk as an apprentice was far down her list of things she cared about. Tildi could tell she was quite frightened about her mother's pending disappearance. The knowledge changed how she felt about the abrasive young woman. She had sensed from the beginning that Serafina was frightened of something, and now she knew what it was. She was haunted by a vision of a tragic future. Tildi was deeply sympathetic. How terrible it was to know something would happen and never be able to do anything about it. At least the misfortunes that had come to her had happened without warning, not giving her time to fret about them. She turned to Edynn.

"I'm honored you have trusted me with this confidence, Edynn. I'll do my best for both of you, you know I will."

"All I ask is that you use this time we have together wisely, all of you," Edynn said.

Tildi gave Serafina a friendly look. The young wizardess withdrew into the shadows of her inglenook.

Nemeth slept badly. He had had visions of the alterations in the landscape that he had left behind him. Perversions of nature, unintended by him, but the inevitable result of the book's passage as it unlocked runes and accident altered them before the effect wore off. He did not want to see what he had wrought. He was responsible.

He had tried many times to scry the face of the person following him, but he or she was concealed amid a mass of faces, all of whose eyes stared at him. There was one face alone that he suspected of being the architect of the plot against him: a man with a long beard, so, likely, a fellow wizard. Seven faces, then fifty, then one again, all swirling in a gold cloud of runes. It consumed him that there was a whole world in pursuit of him. He had a purpose; why couldn't they leave him alone?

One dream in particular haunted him, a strangely shaped foot, toeless, near his head. He saw nothing else, but knew that person was a terrible threat to him. He, she, or it was one of the followers.

Nemeth woke up sweating, though the night was cool enough he could see his breath. The pursuers were not paying heed to his warnings. He must make them stronger.

Chapter Twenty-four

n the fashion of royal suitors for the last five hundred years, Magpie laid out his gifts on a piece of glorious, embroidered silk on the gleaming mosaic floor of the princess's receiving room, under the dis-approving eye of his fiancée, if indeed Inbecca, princess and heir to the throne of the Mother's Avatar on Alada, still was inclined to retain that title. He had been in that room many times over his life, but never before as a supplicant. He was aware of how well it had been designed to impress the eye of the appellants who entered, hoping for the princess's favor. The walls had been cut from sheets of agate striped brown and white, an echo of the image of a tiger, the mascot of the country of Levrenn. Patterns of pearls and semiprecious stones had been inlaid into the wall in fantastic designs that complemented the natural beauty of the stone. The pillars that held up the ceiling had a frieze of tigers' heads

with bright gold eyes all the way around. Magpie felt that they were glaring at him.

A quartet of court ladies, Inbecca's trusted friends and advisers, stood on either side of the room's two windows, as motionless as the chestnut-colored damask curtains that hung well apart, allowing in the brilliant mountain sunshine. The weather was almost unbearably hot, except in this room, where the chill was virtually wintry, or at least so he perceived. Nevertheless, he perservered, until he had everything arranged in a manner that even he had to admit was appealing. He looked up at Inbecca, standing at some distance from him, as enchanted as ever by her beauty. Where Magpie's skin was bronze, hers was silver. Her eyes were as blue as the faraway sea, and her hair, tied in three thick braids with silver bells on the ribbons, had the richness of cherry wood. Her white silk robes were embroidered with the images of tigers, and a huge tiger's eye gem adorned her silver belt. Her arms were crossed over her chest.

He did not find this to be a good sign.

"Did I ever tell you you look like the Pearl?" he said.

"And that is your apology, for going without contact for three entire months?" Inbecca said, frowning down at him. "Pretending you are a peddler and placing your goods as though I might want to buy something, such as a slightly used fiancé?" She passed by the clock, made with loving care by the wolf-kind of the south continent, who had a talent for mechanics; the tightly woven linen cloth nearly as transparent as glass that came from the Quarters; dwarf-made, decorated sweets that melted in the mouth, packaged in an exquisite carved stone box; even the lovely wedding necklace of delicately wrought gold from the centaur jewelers in Balierenn.

She looked bored, but Magpie had known her since they were children. She liked the presents, but she was pretending to disdain them to punish him. Still, she would have to be blind not to be impressed. These were the finest goods Magpie could find throughout Niombra. Inbecca touched the silver-and-enamel figurine standing at the end of the cloth with her toe. "That is rather pretty. Elvish work, is it not? How did you get *that?*"

"A favor from an elf marcher," Magpie explained, pleased. "The work of his favorite craftsman, a sculptor named Zimbro. He liked the songs that I sang to his ladylove. Said they were almost nondiscordant, for a human."

Inbecca's red lips gathered in an amused smirk. "He's right. You can almost sing. No, I tell a lie," she said, putting her nose up. "Your voice is the truest thing about you. It's certainly truer than your heart. Just when you ought to be here, wooing me with all your wits, you are riding around on that odd-colored horse of yours."

"Don't mock Tessera," Magpie said plaintively. "She's a good friend."

"I think perhaps I am jealous," Inbecca said, with a toss of her head that set her plaits jingling. "Since you would rather spend all your days with her, instead of me. If you gave her to me, I might actually believe you love me."

Magpie threw himself to the ground, stretching out his hands to her. "Take her, my heart. Take anything I have, if only you will forgive me."

Inbecca stepped in between his hands, her dainty slippers only inches from his nose. "I don't know whether I should. No offense offered, but I am not at all certain that I want to be tied to a dilettante, however ancient your lineage, in a creaking old kingdom that rumor has it is staggering toward ruin."

"It is not," Magpie protested, stung. He felt his face grow hot. How humiliated his father would be if he had heard that. She must indeed be angry to throw that in his face. "And I am no dilettante. I study hard at whatever I take seriously!"

Inbecca turned up her nose to look down it at him. "That's the trouble, isn't it? You don't seem to take any of the important things seriously. I do. I have been speaking with my aunt Sharhava. She wants me to join the Scholardom."

Magpie suppressed a groan. Sharhava, abbess of the Knights of the Word, had always struck him as far too serious. If she had ever shown any humanity, her stony demeanor would probably crack in two. Since their childhood she had been the rain shower that put out the bonfire of cheer, swooping down on them and their siblings, insisting that royal children did not amuse themselves like commoners. She had never liked Magpie, in either of his names. She was a further peril at this time, the very person from whom he must conceal the reason for his long absence. He picked himself up and pretended to dust down his clothing.

"You wouldn't throw away your realm for the sake of a group of misdirected wayfarers instead of marrying me," Magpie said casually. "Your mother has other daughters, but I know she is confident that you will be the best choice for queen after she departs."

"I don't know whether I want to do either," Inbecca said. "Neither of you offers me much in the way of blandishments, apart from trinkets." She put out her toe again and tipped the little statuette over. Magpie winced as it fell. It didn't break, which he took as a good sign. She went to stare out of the window. "I have been acting as Mother's proxy lately in several important matters. Statecraft leaves me little time for my own thoughts. I wonder whether I have time for a consort, or serious study outside my duties." She glanced at him, then engaged in a close study of her tiger's-eye bracelet. "Just because you have come back doesn't mean that I'm going to forget that you left. I am not a nymph you can trifle with and disappear from again. Perhaps if you reminded me why you think I should marry you I might take it under advisement. It would require many consultations with my ministers, but I believe that at least they have my best interests at heart."

Magpie took that as a softening of her fury, and cast himself on his knees at her side. "Beautiful lady, constant moon, I've loved you since the day we met."

"And you gave me an insect as a gift," Inbecca reminded him loftily.

He was surprised. "Are you still upset about that? It was a very rare bug, and I thought it was very beautiful, with those shimmery green wings and cobalt-blue eyes. It was magical, too. It could disappear and reappear."

"Well, it *was* magical," Inbecca acknowledged, "but it made me scream."

"That's right," Magpie remembered. "You hurt *my* feelings, and I know you hurt his."

Inbecca finally met his eyes. "I thought you were trying to torment me."

"Oh, of course," Magpie said lightly. "I thought it was more fun to upset you than please you. I was a little boy then." He did love her so, but letting anyone, even her, see the depth of emotion he felt for her was difficult for him.

"And you call yourself a man now, do you? Everyone thinks you're quite useless, the way you flit off from time to time, for no reason."

"I just go where fancy takes me," Magpie said. "The world is a fascinating place, you might learn if you ever set foot outside the walls for any reason other than official business."

"My brother says you're a fop. You don't deserve to be named after a hero like Eremilandur. He defeated a hundred knights. He killed the sorceror of Zirkali and freed the werewolves from their slavery."

"I . . ." Magpie began to protest. He was keenly aware that others had always made comparisons between the noted exploits of his famous warrior ancestor and the significant nothing that he had seemed to accomplish. In the meantime he had bred and broken champion horses, mediated disputes in his father's kingdom, played sports as well as he played his jitar, and prided himself on reading and understanding the books of history and philosophy that were allowed to gather dust in his father's library, as well as risking his life to spy during the war and go on missions on behalf of people he believed in, such as Master Olen, but he would rather die under torture than have to defend himself. Let them all think what they liked. He snorted disdainfully. "Perhaps he's right."

Inbecca looked cross not to have gotten a rise out of him with her taunt. "And you are so much unlike your brother Benarelidur. He's steady."

Magpie sighed deeply. "He's dull."

"How right you are," Inbecca said, merriment lighting her eyes and bringing out the mischievious touch of green in them. "I think it's a great pity that such a serious young man will be king. You would be much more interesting."

"Oh, no. Orontae would rise up in open revolt if I took the throne. Ganidur would make a better job of it than I. I greatly prefer the honor of being consort to Levrenn's future queen. If she would have me." He reached up to take her hand. Her expression turned from playful to tender. Magpie looked into her eyes and took a deep breath, summoning all the skill with words he had.

"Well, that's the way you ought to be, you irreverent pup, on your knees. No, don't get up. I like to see you that way." Sharhava, sister to the queen, strode into the room, her heavy blue robes swishing noisily around her legs like courtiers whispering. In her wake came two young men and a young woman dressed in livery of the same color. She was only a year younger than Queen Kaythira, but she seemed of another generation. She always wore an expression of deepest disapproval. "May I make you known to Lar Pedros, Lar Thyre, and Lar Colruba?"

"What is *she* doing here?" Magpie groaned.

Inbecca dropped his hand and went to kiss her aunt on the cheek. When she looked down upon him, the hauteur had returned.

"She's here so I have a witness that you showed proper atonement, and that you made me a promise. It's not because we are sister and brother princes that I accepted your word that we would marry."

"And we shall," Magpie assured her. She did intend to punish him.

Ah, well, he ought to be used by now to people mistrusting him, even Inbecca. "It's always been my dream that you would be my bride. If you will accept me, I would be the happiest man in the world. I will serve at your side or at your feet, whatever you choose."

"I want more assurance than that," Inbecca said. "We're old friends! I thought, after the war was over, that you would stay home for good. I was ready to give you my troth more than a year ago. I trusted you to be here at my side." Tears made her eyes bright. "Why couldn't you stay? Why didn't you send me word of where you were? During the war I thought you had been lost, time and again, when you disappeared off to who knows where? I suppose you're not going to tell me about where you have been all this time, are you? As an old friend, can't you confide in me?" She leaned toward him in appeal.

"I . . ." Magpie wanted so dearly to give her all the details of the great conference at Silvertree, but with Abbess Sharhava hanging there at her shoulder and her acolytes hovering near the door, avid to hear every word, he could not. "No, my dear, dear lady." Magpie bowed his head, not able to meet her eyes. Olen had been afraid to involve the Scholardom in the search for the book. Quite rightly, if they were all vultures like her. Mother and Father alone could predict what she would do if she got a scent of what he knew. "I went on a mission on my father's behalf. There is more going on than I can tell you at present. I've been asked to keep confidence."

"Is that all you can say? You would dare to put me off with a vague statement like that?" Inbecca's eyes filled with tears. She marched over to the window. Sharhava followed and put an arm around the girl's waist.

"There, child, do you see? Secular bonds do nothing to salve your soul. Throw them off. Join us. You can help to remake the world in excellence by aiding our search. You will get no true fulfillment in a pairing with an unworthy suitor like him. I see power in you, and strength of mind. You're a scholar with the heart of a warrior, the very embodiment of what it means to be a Knight."

Magpie could see that Inbecca was wavering. He had no intention of letting Sharhava talk her into such a foolish undertaking while she was feeling vulnerable.

"Unworthy?" Magpie demanded, rising majestically to his feet, and staring down his long nose at her. The effect, he knew, was somewhat marred by his tricolored hair. "You dare to call me unworthy? I am a prince of Orontae, of a pedigree longer than the River Arown!"

Sharhava eyed him. "Perhaps you are not totally without merit. At least you can keep secrets when you're bidden. You, too, would do well to undertake a serious occupation and stop wasting your life. I could find a place in the order for you, too. We will need every able body and willing heart." She looked him up and down. "We are less concerned about feeble minds. And that hair. It makes you look like a calico cat."

"What for?" Magpie asked, already dreading the answer. "Why do you need willing hearts?"

Sharhava looked triumphant. "Have you not heard the rumors? The book has come to light, prince of Orontae."

"Book? What book?"

"Why, the Great Book, you young fool. Have you not listened to me all these years? We have been receiving word that it has been seen, after centuries of being lost. We need to secure it for the Knights to protect!"

It felt like a physical blow to hear the Great Book mentioned by name, but he forced himself to remember that she had always talked about it freely, though no one else believed it really existed. It was only because he was so sensitive about carrying the knowledge he had that his nerves were jangling with every word. He summoned up the most supercilious expression he could muster.

"That book? That old myth?"

"It is not a myth, you uneducated whelp," Sharhava declared, matching him scorn for scorn. "It is a sacred tome that contains all the secrets of existence. Don't you see? This is a Creation-sent opportunity. We must have it."

"To do what? Have responsive readings?"

Sharhava looked at him as if he had no brain at all. "I do not have the time to correct the deficiencies of your education, nor of the knowledge of the faith you practice. This book commands all of Mother Nature's design. It is a tool that the knights have been seeking for centuries. It is vital that it come into our hands so that we can correct the outrages that have been perpetrated upon the human race."

"And what would those be?" Magpie asked.

"Werewolves," Sharhava said, with an open shudder. "Centaurs. Mermaids. These beings are not natural. We have it in the ancient writings that in the beginning there were only humans. Then a coven of wizards began mixing the species. This book was meant as a record so that right-thinking humans could one day undo the monstrosities and return the world to its pristine form, in all praise to the Mother and the Father. To that end we study what runes we find from the ancient times, but none of them contain the words of power that are needed to accomplish our goals."

Magpie felt faintly sick. To do away with centaurs and smallfolk with a stroke, as if they had never existed?

"Most respected abbess," he said, with great dignity. "You must be joking."

"Joking? Of course I am not. About what?"

"Several things. First, some of my very best friends are werewolves, and I resent the notion that you and your Scholardom entertain the notion that you can wipe them out."

"We don't intend to destroy them, merely return them to full humanity!"

"That will destroy them. Their culture is based upon who they are."

"Bah!" Sharhava said. "Culture. It's an echo of ours, that is all. Once they walk again in normal human form, they will forget about the aberration they have lived until now. All of us will be equal again, in the sight of Mother Earth and Father Sky! No more petty differences."

Magpie shook his head with exaggerated sorrow at the notion of "petty differences."

"Secondly, you cannot have it both ways. Either I am a useless wastrel, or I am worthy of joining the Knights of the Word. Which is it?"

The abbess goggled at him, her pasty face looking even more unappealing than usual. Behind her, Inbecca was staring at him.

"Thirdly, while I would never disagree with you upon your interpretation of our faith, you seem to find it allowable to question mine. That is . . ." he paused to think of the most insulting phrase he could use without resorting to bad language, "in bad taste.

"Lastly, you betray your niece."

"Never!" Sharhava's face turned from pale to beet-red. "I love my niece. I want only the best for her."

"Then why go against her wishes? She asked you here today to bear witness to my proposal of matrimony, an act that would cement relations between our two kingdoms, and bring both of us a great deal of happiness. I feel that it shows a lack of consideration when you seek to break us apart so that you can recruit both of us into the Knights."

"That is never my intention. . . . I have my niece's best interests in mind. . . . The well-being of her soul!" Sharhava sputtered.

Magpie bowed deeply. "As do I, I promise you. Now, if you don't mind, honored lady, you have interrupted an honorable proposal of marriage. May I continue?"

Inbecca glided smoothly from her stand near the window and glided over to tuck her arm into his. Her triumphant expression showed that while Magpie might never have won any battles that she knew of, he had just slain a dragon on her behalf. He hid his raptures, but he felt very pleased with himself. It was the first time in his life he had ever gotten the better of Sharhava.

"What about it, my aunt?" Inbecca asked. "Will you bless our union?"

Sharhava folded her hands together in her voluminous sleeves, and her face froze in an obdurate expression. "I see that I have little to say about this matter. You know my opinion of this man. You know my wishes are for your happiness. I believe that both of you would prosper in the Scholardom where your potential would not be wasted, as it would be in an ill-considered match. You are an adult woman, and you must make your own choices."

"Then I give her the opportunity to make one," Magpie said. He dropped to his knees and took Inbecca's hands in his. He looked up into her blue-green eyes.

"Inbecca, you are my friend and my beloved. I have traveled this world over, but I have never met anyone I wished to marry but you. Will you do me the incomparable honor of promising to become my bride, in the presence of Mother Nature and Father Time, and your most inestimable aunt?"

Inbecca squeezed his hands. Her lips quivered, and Magpie had the overwhelming urge to kiss them, but he waited patiently. "I will, dear Eremi. You will make a worthy consort. I accept your suit." She leaned over and gave him that kiss. Magpie closed his eyes to enjoy the sensation throughout his entire body.

Sharhava had no choice but to offer grudging congratulations. "May you be happy together," she said curtly. She gestured to her acolytes, who opened the doors for her. She sailed out of the chamber, and the doors closed behind all of them.

Inbecca glanced up. "Good riddance." She plucked at Magpie's hair with her fingers. "I can't wait until that grows out again. The stripes make you look silly."

"It will take a little time," Magpie said. "I no longer need the disguise. My days as a wandering minstrel are over. My last mission on my father's behalf is done."

"Good." Inbecca beamed at him. "You can stay through the arts festival, and unhorse all the others in the tournament as my champion. Let's go tell my parents right now." She pulled on his hands and he stood up, taking her into his arms. She looked up into his face, and he gazed down, enjoying her features at that angle. "Mother and Father have been waiting all morning. My father will want to make the announcements, and Mother can't wait to start making preparations for the betrothal."

Magpie took the opportunity for another kiss before they left the room. He was concerned about Sharhava's plans for the book, but it sounded as if she and the Scholardom really knew nothing about the book's whereabouts. There was nothing more that he could do to help it be found and restored to where it came from. That part of his life was over, and his new life was beginning.

He followed his bride-to-be toward the royal audience chamber.

Chapter Twenty-five

"I never thought that I'd be seeing leaves fall during Blackberry Moon," Rin said, looking down at the sparse trees below.

Days of flying had made Tildi numb even to the curiosity of an early autumn. They had been riding forever, it seemed, with the tiny dot of gold tantalizing them as it drew ever nearer. The thief was not moving as fast as they, but he was not impeded by having to help seven beings and seven horses to gallop on the air. Edynn was tiring at having to maintain the spell, all of them could see that, but no one could think of an alternative to their means of travel that would not allow the thief to escape. Their daily search was limited by how long she could maintain the spell that allowed them to tread the air. Neither Tildi nor Serafina was as adept at she, and could not take more of the burden on themselves. The dilemma was making Serafina more short-tempered than usual. It was inflamed further as they followed the thief's track on the map into the mountain country in between Rabantae and Levrenn.

That had all changed over the last few days, when the thief's track on the map led into the mountain country in between Rabantae and Levrenn. The air was as crisp as late autumn in the Quarters.

"It's a no-man's-land, and not much of anything else," Lakanta had explained. "Land's too poor for farming, and there's no grass for sheep. We peddlers avoid this stretch. No markets at all. Plenty of buyers both north and south of here."

"Bleak," Teryn said, as they set down in the widest valley. Her horse scrabbled to a halt on an oval of small stones, the most level surface visible. A narrow river meandered through the center of the winding gorge, surrounded by hardy scrub and a few windblown trees. Rocks had tumbled down the crevices in between the peaks, leaving heaps of ochre and tan rocks as large as houses.

"Oh, you should see it a month from now, when it really begins to get cold," Lakanta said, her usual cheerful self again.

"I'm cold now," Tildi said, feeling in her saddlebag for her cloak. It had been heavy to carry, but now she was glad she had gone to the trouble of carrying it with her. She spread it out as best she could to cover herself and as much of Rin's back as she could manage. When they first landed she thought she could smell rain, but now she was certain the watery scent in the air was snow. She sought about her with the leaf in her hand. The telltale runes had sprung into prominence on the steep walls of the canyon. Tildi basked in the warmth of their glow. Feeling as if she was closer to the book seemed to lessen the bitter wind that swept over them.

"He was here, then," Serafina acknowledged. "You can see why he chose it as a refuge. It's far away from any kind of civilization. No chance of an inn?"

"None at all," Lakanta said. "Our thief probably spent as uncomfortable a night as we are going to. We might be lucky enough to come upon a shepherd's cottage, but that would be all I'd hold out for here."

"We'll hope for that good fortune," said Edynn. She smiled, and Tildi was shocked by how pinched her face seemed. "We should ride for a while yet, to keep warm. It's too early to set up camp."

A solid wall of clouds had been visible while they were in the air. Tildi thought they looked like rain clouds, but she wasn't sure. There was little protection from the wind. Tildi pulled her hood down over her forehead. Rin shivered in her thin blouse. She took a pair of blankets out of the packhorse's bags and made herself a thick cloak.

"It is never like this in Balierenn," she said, from within her makeshift, dull-green hood. "If I had known I would be wandering glaciers in the month of Blackberries, I would have brought a much warmer cape. Alas, there goes the sun!"

The gray clouds arrived, covering the last of the blue sky. They brought with them an icy chill. The horses clustered close to one another for warmth.

"This is unnatural," Edynn said, worried. Her breath was white upon the cold air. "He knew we would have to come this way, and he has changed the weather. He has brought winter to this place, months ahead of time. The fool! There will be trouble. He'll cause a reaction the likes of which I cannot imagine."

If I had the book, Tildi thought, *I'd never change the seasons. Never.* She had been enjoying the sensation of being near the glowing runes again, but the link to the book was receding fast. She felt impatient. Why could they not go flying onward, forever, until we find its keeper?

Because the spell takes a lot of energy, her sensible inner voice scolded her. *You're tired, and you are responsible for only two of the steeds! And you don't even like flying.*

Edynn rode up beside her and placed a hand on her arm. She always seemed to know when thoughts of the book were overwhelming her. "Fight it, Tildi." A lessening of the longing came over her. She felt forlorn and resentful for a moment, then she realized she felt more like herself. She gave Edynn a rueful little smile.

Rin's flank twitched violently as they ascended the loose stone road that wound further into the mountains. At times they were cut off from sight of the sky altogether. The walls of the canyon were pitted with cracks and caverns, all of which looked to Tildi like hooded eyes full of malign purpose. She leaned close to Rin's back.

"I dislike being away from the sunshine," the centaur said, gazing unhappily at the looming towers silhouetted against the clouds. "I mistrust this land of stone."

"Oh, it's not so bad," Lakanta said, glancing around her. She wore a purple and blue cloak with a fringed hood that would have looked amusing on anyone else, but suited her. "Secure. Strong. We'll be glad enough of the caves if the skies open up, and I think that they will very soon. I only hope it's rain."

Tildi's cheeks and nose grew stiff with cold. She had wrapped her hands in her cloak to keep them warm. Serafina had fastened a fold of her pure white robe up across her lower face. Her long, dark eyes were restless, keeping an eye on the skies, and on the slanting shadows all around them. The cold was so terrible that Tildi began to drowse. She remembered fireside tales of maidens who wandered away into the snow, only to be found frozen and peaceful in the spring, as if they had only just fallen asleep. She fought with herself not to drop off. The dimming of the light didn't help. Evening was fast approaching.

"Shall we stop for a while?" Serafina asked, gauging her mother's strength. "We should eat something now, and make camp in a while. Is there any bread?"

"Honorable," Teryn said carefully, "we last purchased supplies three days ago, at that small guest house on the border of Levrenn. They did not have much, and what we had is gone. If you will take shelter here, Morag and I will hunt for some meat."

Serafina looked shocked. "Is there nothing left?"

"Nothing, honorable," Teryn said. She took their bows and quivers of arrows from the long pouch on the packhorse's side. "I apologize. I will make you a fire before we go."

"No, go," Edynn said graciously. "We are perfectly capable of that small task, and leave you to the greater one."

"Give me leave, little one," Rin said, lifting Tildi down. "This at least I can assist with."

She and the soldiers disappeared into the growing gloom. Tildi helped Lakanta lead the horses into the nearest stone mouth, a shallow cave formed by blocks of stone fallen off the mountain so long ago that moss grew on the rough surface. A thin shaft of light lanced down from a point over their heads where two of the blocks did not quite meet. The two of them left Serafina to look after her mother and went looking for wood.

As soon as they set foot outside their makeshift shelter, snow began to float down from the iron skies.

"Wouldn't you know it?" Lakanta said, shaking her head. A few crisp, white flakes fell off her hood. "We're to have no luck today." She and Tildi scoured the valley for a few hundred yards in either direction, but were able to find only an armload or so of thin, tough twigs and rough, dried grass. "And they're wet, too," she complained, setting the mass down in the stone circle Serafina had arranged. The two of them stood in the opening to brush the accumulation of snow off their shoulders.

"No matter," Edynn said, holding her hands over their offering. A flicker of light crept along the bottommost sticks, and spread slowly to the others. Tildi sighed at the welcome warmth. She pushed her cloak back over her shoulders, and held her hands out to enjoy the modest blaze. She was pleased that Edynn seemed to relax as well. Serafina, ever vigilant, kept jumping up to make sure the cloak covered her mother's shoulders, and that Edynn was as far away as she could be from the gusts that passed the cave entrance. None of them made conversation. Tildi was tired, and she was concerned about Edynn's state of health.

"It's this one," Rin's voice said irritably. "It is the only one with smoke coming from it."

The three hunters appeared in the doorway. Tildi looked up at them expectantly, but they held nothing in their hands.

"I apologize, honorables," Teryn said, almost shamefaced. "We have not been successful. Any beast with sense has fled from this unnatural weather. We need to get to better shelter, and soon." As if to emphasize her point, a gout of water poured out of the gap in the roof, and fell onto their campfire, extinguishing it. Morag jumped back, swearing, then muttered an embarrassed apology to the wizardesses.

"Well, that tells us it's time to leave," Edynn said, bringing her hands down onto her thighs and standing up. Her movements were stiff and hesitant. Serafina leaped to help her with her cloak and staff. "There will be a deeper cave farther on, and more wood. Come along, then."

They took to their horses again. Tildi sat on Rin's back, watching the snow mound up on the centaur's broad shoulders. It was falling even more heavily than before. Even if she had not known the source she would have realized it was not a natural snow. The group passed summer flowers that had frozen solid. Those were soon covered by thick flakes. As Teryn had said, the animals had fled from this place. They found tracks, outward bound from the valley. Those, too, filled quickly in and disappeared. The group kept together in a knot near the northern wall of the canyon, with Teryn in front and Morag bringing up the rear. They rode onward, feeling their way, unable to see anything against the onslaught of sharp-edged flakes. Tildi kept her head bowed. The chill invaded even her warm travel cloak, until she felt as if she had been turned to stone. Rin stumbled now and again as her hoofs slipped into the stream hidden below the snow.

"We can't see where we are going," Serafina shouted, over the hissing of the wind. "We have to get to shelter or we will die in this weather."

"Tell us a story to keep us going," Lakanta said. "Anyone. Anything!"

"I recall a battle we fought for my lord Halcot," Teryn began stoutly, trotting along with her back as straight as the polearm she held in spite of the heaps of snow mounting on her helm and her horse's rump. "A band of werewolves had made their way upriver from the south lands. There is a city just north of the seaport of Tillerton. They held it at bay, terrorizing the inhabitants. These carried silver amulets that prevent the spell that binds them from wearing off, so they were ravening animals all of the time. The villagers found half their cattle disemboweled and—"

"That's not a very soothing story," Lakanta said, interrupting her. "I'd almost rather fall asleep and die of the cold than hear it."

"Perhaps you know a better one?" the captain said indignantly.

"Perhaps I do!"

"We're out of food," Serafina shouted peevishly. "What about my mother? This weather is terrible for her. Do you know how many spells she is maintaining to preserve our safety? We must stop soon."

"To do what? There is no forage here." The captain turned to Edynn. "I am sorry, honored one, for the inconvenience. It will be remedied as soon as is possible. At present," she said, with a sharp look at Serafina, "there is no convenient inn to stop in and say, may we please have a bed for the night? And what's in the pot for supper?"

"I smell food," Tildi said drowsily, cuddled up against the cloth that rested over the pad of thick hair that ran down the middle of Rin's spine. It was more comfortable than any pillow she had ever used. "I smell roast beef and potatoes, and berry pie . . ."

"Nonsense," said Serafina. "Your nose is beginning to go to sleep. I will try to bring a spell about us and make it warmer."

"No, she's right," Rin said, flaring her nostrils expressively. "I am not hallucinating, and I smell it, too."

"It's a trap," Teryn said. "Another of our quarry's ruses to lure us to our deaths!"

"Perhaps not," Edynn said, essaying out of the folds of her cloak with her staff. "I do not sense enchantment here."

"It's probably dwarves, you know," Lakanta announced. "Dwarf burrows can be found in nearly every mountain range in the world."

"We could ask them for help," Tildi said hopefully. She was certain now that she smelled baking potatoes, and possibly roast chicken.

"Dwarves are," Lakanta said firmly and very loudly, "the stubbornest folk in the world. Almost all of them are bad-tempered, humorless gumps who would cut off their noses to spite their faces, who would eat a bag of sweets *right* in front of you and *never offer* you a one." Her voice echoed against the stone walls, but was soon swallowed up by the gale.

"The dwarves," Teryn said, annoyed. She made a dismissive gesture. "They care nothing for our mission. They will not care if we perish here."

"Let us try anyhow," Rin said.

"Oh, why not?" Lakanta said with resignation. "Just because they might not care for our task does not mean decency is beyond them. I have been through these parts many times over the years. They might be grieved, or at least annoyed, to find my corpse decaying upon their doorstep come spring, whenever our book thief lets it turn over into spring."

"How can you jest at the notion that we could die here within reach of help?"

The small woman regarded Serafina with sympathy in her eyes. "Child, I have been around a lot of years, and if you don't laugh, you cry."

She slipped off her pony's back and disappeared among the bare stones. The movement brought the packed snow on the rocks above tumbling down upon them. Rin stamped a hoof and twitched.

Teryn herded the rest of them over to one side of the canyon, under a broad stone outcrop that momentarily sheltered them from the snow. Tildi climbed down to let Rin shake out her blanket cloak. Edynn held out her hands. They were trembling.

"I'm not sure I can keep going, my friends."

"I can make a fire for you," Tildi offered. She held out her hand, and a green blaze burst out on her palm. She looked around for something to set it on.

"Don't use that, Tildi," Serafina snapped. "It'll attract more of our foe's lurkers. We are at a disadvantage in a fight at the moment."

"I am sorry," Tildi said, abashed at her impetuousness. "I forgot the wards." She drew them swiftly, pleased at her own expertise. Her experience had grown over the last weeks, and with it, her confidence. No malign creature would use it as a portal to harass them now. "This fire doesn't need any wood, you see. My brother used it to kill thraiks. It's just as warm as real fire."

"So I see," Edynn said with gentle amusement. Tildi set the blaze down on a nearby rock. The others gathered around it, glad of the heat. Tildi automatically felt in her pack, and came up with a dusty packet of tea.

"Would anyone like some?" she asked. Teryn couldn't hide the smile as she found the kettle among their luggage, filled it with snow and set it to boil over the leaping green flames. Shortly, steam began to rise. Tildi poured the tea and handed Edynn the first cup. The elder wizardess drank it gratefully.

"Whatever we may find after this," she said, "nothing could be as delicious as this little kindness of yours. Thank you, Tildi."

Tildi bridled with pleasure as she offered the hot beverage around. The compliment warmed her as well as drinking the tea did. Her nose thawed out enough to run, but she felt better. Once the tea was gone she filled her cup with hot water to hold between her cold hands and touch to her cheeks. Though the snow continued to fall just inches from her, she no longer noticed it as much.

Edynn bowed her head. "Friends, I am sorry. I apologize for my weakness. I did not foresee that our quarry would use the book against us. More fool I. He laid a trap for us, and we have walked straight into its snares. If I could have held out longer we might have been able to find a more hospitable place to stay. Now I fear trying to fly against this weather."

"It is not your fault, Mother," Serafina fretted. She paced up to the growing wall of snow at the edge of the lip of stone. The horses danced nervously as she passed them. Morag's eyes rolled with fear. She glared at him, making him step backward. At last she burst out. "Where has she gone? She has tried to turn us the wrong way ever since we set out from Silvertree."

"What are you talking about?" Rin asked sharply. "Lakanta is our true friend. She is trying to aid us. I hope she is not wrong, but I applaud her making the attempt."

The young wizardess's eyes were wild. "She's a spy. She's gone to lead the enemy to us."

"How could she? He's miles ahead of us."

"Then she is abandoning us. She knows where the dwarves reside, and she will live with them until this cursed storm goes. By then we will all be dead."

"In my home," Tildi said in her calmest and most friendly tones, doing her best not to sound accusatory, "we have a saying that the truth usually comes out in time. Why not just wait?"

Serafina could not seem to settle. Tildi now understood why she was so concerned, but there were no doors here to shut. It was not her mother's fate to die in these circumstances, so the chances were good that the rest of them would survive, too. Tildi knew well that there was no point in explaining her theory to Serafina. They simply had to wait, and watch her pace up and back through the melting puddles of snow.

After what seemed like forever, they heard threshing noises outside. Rin's sensitive ears went up as the horses' did, and the peddler woman appeared, walking very slowly because of the huge bundle in her arms. Teryn sprang forward to help, followed by Morag and Tildi.

"Easy there," Lakanta said. "The top one will slosh. I've already had a faceful of soup. Go on, now. Put that over the fire to warm up again. There's a deeper cave up ahead, one that will hold all of us. But that can wait until we've eaten. I'm starved."

"Where did you get this?" Serafina demanded as the others relieved the short woman of her burdens. Each of the dishes was beautifully made, either fancifully painted earthenware, or gleaming gold or gemmed silver. Tildi didn't care what they looked like, as long as the dishes contained food.

Lakanta grinned over the top of a covered platter encrusted with winking jewels. "There was a dwarf hall below our feet. I recognized one of the entrances back on the last turning but one. I thought that fallen scree looked as though it was too neat for Mother Nature to have tumbled it that way. You would not have noticed. You were not meant to have noticed it. They have been tracking our progress all this time."

"You mean you have been telling them where we are," Teryn said.

"Not at all. Here, take this. It's most of the knuckle end of a roast. And here is a cheese. These are dates stuffed with jam. Very sweet and very sticky. Ah, there, you can just lick your hand." She unloaded more packages from the capacious pockets of her cloak and handed them around.

"We mustn't eat this food! It might be poisoned," Teryn cautioned them.

"Don't be a fool and starve to death!"

"I can wait until we find a source I trust," the captain said stoutly.

"Ah, but can the noble lady here?" Lakanta asked, nodding toward Edynn. "You know that answer as well as I. That was part of the logic I used to get it, you see."

"How do we know the dwarves have goodwill toward us?" Serafina asked, more reasonably.

"Ah, now that is a good question," Lakanta said, and paused.

"Well?"

"I don't let this get out much," Lakanta said very hesitantly. "There are many good reasons, and you may guess most of them."

"What is it?" Tildi asked, becoming alarmed. Had her new friend a dark secret, as Serafina had accused her of having?

"I think I know," Edynn said with a smile. "They would not grudge provisions to a cousin."

Lakanta looked relieved. "That's it, you see. And you don't mind, though I think these two do." She nodded toward the soldiers.

"You're a dwarf?" Teryn asked in disbelief. "But you look like a human."

"Bite your tongue. In spite of what Olen told you that still doesn't make it a compliment."

"My apologies," Teryn said humbly. "This is a gracious feast, and we are grateful."

"Aye," muttered Morag.

"Indeed we are," Edynn agreed.

"Can we not go into the halls?" Serafina asked suddenly. "You can see how the storm is affecting my mother."

"No, no," Lakanta said, holding up her hands. "This is all the aid they would offer. Except for some blankets, and fodder for the horses, which you may find back there about a hundred paces. I couldn't carry them all the way and still keep the food from falling out of my arms." She nodded with her nose in the direction from which she had come. "They have fed you and given you what you need to survive. Consider that all you need. They like their privacy. Heavens, if every nosy traveler could just fall into the halls, then their lives would be over, as *they* see it."

"Come on," Serafina ordered Tildi. "We will follow her trail back to the dwarf hall. They will not refuse us shelter. You stay here," she said to Lakanta.

Tildi tucked her cloak tightly around her and followed the young wizardess into the twilight. At that moment the wind had died down. She followed Serafina's billowing cape around the bends of the canyon.

There was no difficulty in finding Lakanta's footsteps. The snow had come up to the middle of her thighs. She had plowed her way through, leaving twin trenches punctuated by deeper holes where her feet had pressed. Tildi inched along through one track, unable to see past Serafina.

The young wizardess stopped abruptly. Tildi cannoned into her legs and sat down in the snow.

"Curse them!" Serafina exclaimed.

"What is the matter?" Tildi peered around the woman's skirts at dark heaps to either side of the trail. "The blankets are here. And a bag of oats."

"And nothing else." Serafina flung out a hand at the landscape. Tildi did not understand what she was meant to see until she realized there was nothing to see. Beyond the piles of blankets the trail ended. The drifts of snow seemed untouched. "Did she rise out of the earth at this point, or do her dastardly relatives know the Cold Magic, and can call in winter at will, like our thief? What will happen to my mother?"

Tildi felt sorry for her. To think that she had ever envied Edynn the gift of the prophecy. Serafina could not see how her fear of the future made it impossible to enjoy the present. Shaking her head, she gathered up as many of the fallen blankets as she could hold, and stumped back along the narrow trail to where the others were waiting.

Teryn was still trying to make her case. "But do the dwarves not believe in our mission? They will suffer the same as we will if we can't get the book back."

"Of course they believe in it!" Lakanta said. "They can't bother to do anything about it themselves, but they believe in keeping their way of life safe, the way it's always been. That's why they've given us their best. Plus these lovely blankets. Oh, and see? There are linens in between. We shall sleep soundly and well in these. Best weaving in the world—except for what your people produce, my dear," she said to Tildi. "Ah, and look here. There's a hat for you."

"For her?" Serafina asked.

"Well, who else would it fit?" Lakanta demanded, holding up a wool hemisphere. "It fits across my palm, that's all. Unless you want to fit one ear into that, honorable lady, I believe it's a gift for Tildi. Yes, they're willing to give us whatever we need, but out here, please."

"No matter," Teryn said stolidly. "We'll make do with our own camp. Now that we have fire. And provisions."

Lakanta nodded extravagantly. "That is what I have been trying to tell you. Once we've had some good, solid food inside us, we'll see things in a much more reasonable light. Now, let's eat before everything gets cold!"

"I wish I could see the halls," Edynn said, as the guards reluctantly began to serve the soup. "I did once, long ago, before humans and dwarves fell out so permanently. They were beautiful. The carvings were worth a lifetime of study."

"I wish I could see them, too, Mother," Serafina said wistfully. "I wish we could go there together."

Edynn patted her fondly on the hand. "Now, child, you'll have your own experiences to tell your children about. Don't live through me. My stories are my gift to you."

Tildi was simply grateful for what she had at the moment. The stout pottery tureen holding the soup kept it piping hot until it was dished around in everyone's bowls. Tildi closed her eyes to breathe in the steam, partly to warm her nose, and partly to absorb the luscious aromas. What a lot she had learned how to do without in just a few short months! First her hair, then her home, then a roof over her head at all. Bathing had become an occasional luxury. But here she had food, lots of it, and it smelled delicious. She also knew a secret, one that made her new friend even more interesting a companion than she had been.

She opened her eyes to see Lakanta's bright blue ones gleaming at her. The dwarf woman winked at her and leaned close, her voice muffled by the roar of the wind at their backs. "Maybe some time I'll get you a tour, lass. But not these big bunglers. My kin don't want anyone bumping around and knocking the lamps askew. Not that even Rin is tall enough to touch the buttresses down below in this place," Lakanta added thoughtfully. "My heavens, I thought my homeland was a picture and a half, but that below us is a whole gallery."

Chapter Twenty-six

In the morning the party steeled themselves to riding out against the snow. The wind had not lessened, but the sky had lightened considerably with the rising of the sun. The footing had improved, as the snow had frozen during the night. Rin tested it gingerly and pronounced it suitable for the horses. Tildi renewed the spell upon the map. She felt forlorn as she saw how far away the book was. The thief was moving so fast that the dot flowed visibly on the broad parchment. He was still traveling north by northeast.

The dwarves were evidently in favor of the continuation of the quest. Outside the cavern where they had sheltered, covered dishes waited upon a flat rock. Lakanta was as astonished as the others. There wasn't a single footprint or disturbed wreath of snow to show from whence the generous bounty had sprung. Tildi squinted at the outcroppings of rock, trying to distinguish a door or a place of concealment, but she could not.

"There's no telling," Lakanta said, helping to bring them inside. "I called them stingy, so they're falling over themselves to be generous to us. I think they're just being contrary, but I'm grateful, no doubt about it."

Tildi, replete with a proper smallfolk's breakfast of hot porridge and sausages, felt as if she was fit to continue, though the snow was now pouring sideways past the door of their cave. Rin lifted her onto her back. Tildi bundled herself up in her cloak and one of the dwarven blankets.

"What will we do with the dishes?" Edynn asked with a glance at the pile of beautiful platters and tureens, looking like a treasure trove from a fairy tale.

"Oh, just leave them here," Lakanta suggested casually. "They'll come back for them when we've gone."

"I would like to thank them," Edynn said. "Is there a way I can do that?"

"Not personally. They don't want to meet you. If we accomplish what we have set out to do, they will consider that thanks enough," Lakanta said. "They won't help us directly, they've said that already, but they won't hinder, and they will not assist the enemy, though they believe, as we do, that he is already far ahead of us."

"Nevertheless, I owe them the gesture." Edynn rode out into the blowing storm.

"Friend dwarves!" she called out, holding her staff on high. "We are grateful for your hospitality. Thank you for sustaining us. Farewell! I will seek to repay the kindness if it is ever in my power."

"They'll just ignore you," Lakanta warned her.

Edynn turned to her. "No matter. They've saved our lives. I know I feel years younger because of their bounty."

The party set out at a near crawl. The wind was so harsh that Tildi only peeked out of her nest of woolen clothes now and again. The scene was nearly the same every time: a view of Rin's back, straining forward and half-covered with snow. Before them, the faint dark shape of Teryn, gamely leading them onward. Of the canyon she could see little past the pellets of snow that whipped by them. The canyon seemed to be narrowing, and the speed of the wind seemed to increase in response.

They stopped frequently to catch their breath and to rest the horses in one of the many overhangs that offered themselves in the sloping stone walls. As she was the only one whose fire was not immediately extinguished by the gusts and snow, Tildi was designated as provider of water for the steeds. The animals, whose eyes were crusted with ice crystals, drank thirstily. She patted the legs of the huge beasts with sympathy. She was grateful they were strong enough to help carry the party forward in the storm. If she had had to walk on her own feet, she would have quit after barely a hundred yards. Climbing down from Rin's back and gathering snow was heavy enough work. Her legs felt like lead weights.

Rin shook out her long hair, still damp but cleared of its crown of snow, and bound it into a single plait. Where her dwarven cloak didn't cover it, her striped coat was matted from the wet. "We are being blown backward a pace for every two steps forward. I believe it is growing worse by the hour."

"I am afraid you are right," Edynn said. "We must risk flying through the storm."

"Is that wise, Mother?" Serafina asked.

"I think it's worth the try. It's daylight. We'll never be stronger than we are at this moment. Every night we spend in this weather is depleting to us. We could freeze in our sleep."

"This is our enemy's intention," Teryn stated.

"I am sure you are right," Edynn said. "That is why we must take the greater risk and escape from here. If we can get a purchase on the air we can climb above the clouds. Once there we will be able to see our way again."

"Well, then why not?" Lakanta asked. Edynn turned to her.

"Because it is not a certainty that the spell will hold. One slip, and one of us can plunge to her death, and the others would never know it until we landed again. It will be horribly cold, much worse than anything we have experienced before. The storm clouds themselves will be enough to freeze us to death, and we have to go through them. There's no going around them. They could stretch for a hundred miles in every direction. I am in favor of going before we are too tired."

Tildi trembled at the idea of freezing or falling, but she took one look at the snow falling inches from them. "If we have a chance, I would take it," she said.

"We could die trying," Edynn warned them. "The winds could drag us back to earth."

Tildi swallowed deeply. "Then they do. It'll be a fast end, then."

"Much more preferable," Lakanta said. "If there's one thing in life I don't want, it's a long, painful demise."

"Lakanta!" Serafina exclaimed, shocked. The peddler grinned at her.

"I agree with Tildi," Rin said, rescuing the discussion, though she hid a smile. "It's much faster than trudging our way through the drifts. One way or another, we could die. Better to take the initiative again. This thief must not direct our lives."

Morag, on guard at the edge of the overhang, plodded over to Teryn with a flat brown object in his hands and a puzzled expression on his misshapen face. Before the captain could examine it, Lakanta beamed at him and raced out into the storm. She returned with a large woven basket covered by a bright-colored cloth.

"Luncheon, everyone," she said, setting down her burden against the wall. She shook snow off the cloth and laid it on the floor. From the basket she took earthenware platters edged with gold. They were filled with palm-sized, golden pastries. Steam rose, bringing with it a savory aroma. Tildi took a deep breath and sighed with pleasure. "Pies, ham and egg, by the look of them. Simple but filling. Ah, wine! May all creation bless them and their halls of stone. I think what our friend's got there is the desserts. Tuck in, now."

"They have been listening to us," Teryn said, eyeing the walls distrustfully, as she passed food around to the others.

"In that case," Edynn said, lifting her glass and enjoying the contrast of the brilliant red wine against the cold whiteness of the snow, "thanks again to our hosts."

"They may not welcome our presence," Rin said, "but they will facilitate our departure."

Tildi was surprised at how hungry she was. She had never had to travel so far during winter, and found it absolutely exhausting. Teryn and Morag took charge of the remaining food. They exchanged grim looks, which Tildi understood to mean should the thin times continue, they did not want to risk being caught without provisions again.

"The wind is coming directly from the quarter we wish to go toward," Serafina said, pointing at the gold dot on the map. "If we fly into its teeth, we could use the power to climb higher faster."

"Wouldn't it be safer to go with our backs to it?" Teryn asked.

"What does it profit to delay?" Rin asked, swirling her cloak around and fastening it over her shoulders and withers. "Let us try something. I'm tired of not seeing the sun."

Tildi recited the spell over her hooves and hoped for the best. They rode out into a solid mass of whiteness. On Edynn's signal, Rin kicked off from the ground, scattering a mass of snow around her, and cantered upward. Tildi peered over her shoulder. Ice crystals stung her eyes, but she didn't dare hide her face. She willed Rin to stay airborne.

The others disappeared in behind the blizzard's curtain. Tildi was chilled to the bone in the first few yards. There was no way to see how far up they were. She worried they would bump into the surrounding cliffs. Once Rin's hooves touched the stone, the spell would break. If they were not solidly on the ground, they could fall off. No one would see them.

Her face and hands stiffened painfully with ice. She tried to pay no attention to anything except the feeling of Rin's strong muscles under her as the centaur reached higher and higher. Snow mounded up so thickly upon them that Tildi had to clear her face to breathe. Every breath was a struggle. The frigid air hurt her lungs. The crystals banging into her skin felt like needles. She thought it was impossible to feel any colder, but it got worse the higher they went.

A gust of wind hit them head-on, and Rin stumbled. Her head went down, and they fell, turning head over heels. Tildi shrieked, clinging to Rin's cloak. Her hands were so numb. She thought she would lose her grip. Somehow she kept hold. Her legs flapped in the wind like a tattered rag on a fence. The centaur threw her head back and struggled with all six limbs to right herself. Tildi's stomach felt as if it had been left behind. Suddenly, she felt a thud. Rin paused, one foot raised. She scrabbled with her other hooves for purchase in the air. Tildi recited the charm to herself. Suddenly, they were running again.

Rin turned to look at Tildi. Snow decorated her long, dark lashes with diamonds. "Never say a princess of the Windmanes ever gave up a race! Let us see if we can beat the others to the sun!"

Tildi put her head down against Rin's neck and felt her surge strongly upward. Her ears burned with cold, but she heard a faint sound over the roar of the wind. Higher and higher they galloped. The pellets of frozen snow became sleet, then the sleet thinned into a freezing mist that seemed to surround them forever.

"Now!" Rin cried. Suddenly the mist broke around them, and they headed upward into blue, blue sky. The wind died away. The clouds beneath Rin's hooves looked like a dark gray quilt. She tilted her head back, pushing her hood off onto her shoulders. The snow and ice began to melt off in sheets of droplets. Rin sighed. "Ah, the sun."

As the circulation returned to her limbs, Tildi looked around her. The noise she had heard was Teryn. The captain cantered over the tops of the slate-gray clouds waving her sword in triumph. Her cheeks were pink and her snapping blue eyes aglow with triumph.

"Rabantae!" she cried. "Rabantae! Your enemies cannot defeat you!" Morag still looked frozen, galloping in her wake.

Lakanta surfaced, her purple hood and the perked ears of her horse shedding snow as they emerged. The little peddler broke into a wide smile, and she waved to Rin and Tildi as she rode toward them. "The best part of that journey was the ending, my friends. Where are the others?"

They waited anxiously until a bank of clouds half a mile distant began to roil and bubble like stew in a pot. At last, the mist broke apart. Serafina, her head nearly down on her mare's neck, cantered upward, pulling the reins of her mother's steed. Edynn was holding fast to the saddlebow with one hand, and her staff with the other. The jewel in the tip was gleaming dimly.

Her hood had fallen back. She looked exhausted, but she was otherwise unscathed.

"Good to see you, my friends," Edynn shouted hoarsely, her long white hair gleaming with ice.

"You, too!" Rin shouted, riding over to touch hands with the two wizardesses. Serafina unbent enough to clasp Tildi's hand with her cold fingers. "What an adventure! I shall have much to brag about at our next festival!"

Color returned to their faces swiftly under the warmth of the sun. Edynn pointed upward with her staff, and the rest followed her as she rode higher and higher. Tildi looked down. She was stunned to see what a small area was covered by the unnatural winter storm. It seemed to lap at the edges of the mountains that contained it like an overfull bathtub, but extended no farther. She felt in her pouch for the precious leaf, which she had wrapped well against the weather. It was dry and unscathed. She gave a sigh of relief.

Teryn sheathed her sword and produced her map. Edynn looked for the golden dot, moving to the northeast. She pointed her staff over the backs of the next range of mountains. "That way, my friends."

With a deferential nod, Teryn took point, spurring her horse. Rin fell into the pace behind her, and the others spread out at her sides.

Tildi glanced back. The storm seemed to be trying to follow them. The gray clouds crawled in their wake for a while, but appeared to collapse back into the ravine, too weak to follow farther.

"It will dissipate soon," Edynn told her. "We are free. Let us seek our quarry."

Chapter Twenty-seven

emeth was angry. He huddled in the woods close enough to an elven village that he could see a few of the inhabitants passing in and out of the soft grayskinned trees that they had hollowed out for houses, but he could not stop thinking about his pursuers. He was so much nearer to his destination, but the ones behind him had not gone away. They had ignored all of his warnings, even the catastrophic winter storm that he had conjured to turn them back days ago. They had had him on the run, when it ought to have been the other way around.

The voices in his mind seemed ever louder, especially that of Father Time. He was displeased and threatening retribution if Nemeth did not bring him the book. The tone distracted Nemeth, who was trying to formulate an easy means of stealing food. The irony was not lost upon him that he was capable of altering the climate, but not of creating a feast for himself out of raw ingredients.

Still, he had used the power of the book to improve his techiques. He sent an illusion to the mind of the slender, golden-skinned lad sitting on a stone, reading a book as he minded the spit on an open fire before his home, a tree hollowed but still living. Nemeth blanched at the sight of the domiciles in this village. They might have looked pastoral and pleasant to him once, but he now saw them as a cluster of prisons.

Not even aware that he was doing it, the boy made a quarter turn to the right on his seat, and continued cranking an invisible handle, never looking up from his book. Nemeth flicked a finger, and the spit rose vertically into the air. The meat on it divided in two—no need to be a hog about it—and one half of it sailed toward him. The rest of it returned to the spit. In the elven boy's mind Nemeth changed the image of the roast to fit its new dimensions. He would never remember that it had been different.

Nemeth let the chunk of meat hover behind him, dripping savory juices, until he had returned to the spot deep in the forest that he had chosen as his place of rest for the day. He had transformed bushes into a couch, which he covered with a blanket of silken leaves. This was surmounted by a living canopy from a slender rowan tree that let in a pleasant green light but would repel rain or too much sun. A cup of leaves held wine made from dew and berries that had gathered themselves together at his command. All these skills that he had seen in his fellow wizards that had eluded him all his life were to be found within the pages of the book. If he had only known how simple it was to bend the world to his will! The meat landed on a platter he had fashioned out of a stone, using the pattern of an exquisite dinner service that he found in the description of a castle in Oscora, then divided itself further, into dainty slices. Nemeth rested in his bower and commenced to dine.

He looked more at ease than he was. The voices continued to chatter in the back of his mind. Nemeth chewed his dinner pensively, dishes, meat, and haven forgotten. He just wanted his revenge, nothing more. These pursuers were refusing to give up the chase. He was but a couple of days' flight from his goal. They must not be allowed to follow him there. Every threat he had sent to deter them had been swept aside. They were relentless. Only death would stop them.

Once the thought had come out, Nemeth realized he had no choice. He had been pushed past reasonable alternatives. They knew where he was. If he had been a different kind of man he would have been able to raise an army of friends to help protect him against them. *I have no friends*, he thought angrily. No, he must raise a *force*. An army.

He thought of conscripting the elves in the village. They were crafty and tough fighters. But they had magic of their own. They might sense his intent and refuse to do his bidding. He could sense their thoughts, all concerned with mundane matters such as the weather and music.

Nemeth sought about him for a useful alternative, peering through the nearby forest for a likely creature to transform. The answer fell directly into his lap: a twig. He held it up. It had long, thin fingers, just like a hand. Nemeth smiled as he felt a stirring in it unlike any piece of wood he had ever touched. There was a voice inside it.

He reached for the book. It almost spun in his hands until he came to the type of tree under which he was sitting. The thin beech was *conscious* of its surroundings. Its pinkish gray bark concealed a lost brother of humankind. Well, they should become more human. Amid the individual runes for each tree he found the collective one that indicated all of this species within this forest. There were more than a hundred. He smiled. An ample number. He had played with wooden soldiers as a boy, the toys given him by his father, when the poor man thought he was raising a guardsman like himself. He was bitterly disappointed that Nemeth would rather try calling the rain than learning fighting stances, but the neighbors liked it, and Nemeth was encouraged to go on. He was apprenticed to a master wizard, and meant to go home after a few years as a trained weather-witch, but he never did. He wished often that he had. He would have avoided the humiliation he had suffered in Orontae. No, that would have meant he would never have had the book in his arms. He held the scroll tightly, feeling its perfection like silk that soothed his nerves. All had been worthwhile if he ended up with this treasure.

These would be his wooden soldiers. It would be so simple. He unlocked the rune and began to change a dot here, a stroke there. He reshaped their branches into thin, attenuated arms, each ending in a spear.

Around him the forest began to come to life. The beeches began to stretch and move, hoisting their shallow roots out of the soil. He felt their anger as they woke up, fury at all living and moving things. They sensed him sitting among them, and turned on him, reaching for him, stabbing at him with their re-formed limbs. Nemeth brushed aside the branches with a swift stroke on the page.

"You cannot touch me," he said. "I am your master. Furthermore"—he completed another small stroke, moving a gold line—"you shall not touch anyone else until I am ready for you to do so."

He sat in their midst as they shrieked and sallied at him. They were as impotent as his enemy. He felt sorry for them. It would be a terrible thing to be transformed against his will. He had done it to himself and hated it, but he had had no choice. *They* had no choice. These were his soldiers, and they would do his fighting for him. The living beeches did not understand, and threw themselves against the invisible barrier he had set around them. The ground shook with the violence of their anger.

"Hold your fury," he said, though he knew they could not understand. "Soon there will be an enemy for you to slay."

Nemeth waited. He knew that the followers were approaching, and fast. The merry voices in his head were drawing closer all the time. He must wait for them here. Once they were at the mercy of his army, he would be free to go about his business.

It happened sooner than he thought it would. The book was no longer alone. Another aura touched it familiarly. He felt jealousy welling up within him.

"How dare they?" he demanded, shaking the pillars of his forest seat. How *could* they? He had no true friend but the book. It must respond to him alone.

He knew the answer at once. One of the followers carried a fragment of a copy, just like the one that he had used to trace the book to its fastness.

It didn't matter. His toy soldiers would wipe them out. They came closer and closer, until the auras overlapped, began to join. It was almost too much for Nemeth to stand. He waited until the aura was at a level with him. With a wave of his hands, he set the trees free. They rushed away, seeking victims for their rage, leaving the jumbled floor of the forest empty.

In no hurry, Nemeth rose from his leafy bower and took to the air. There was no need for him to see what came after.

Tildi felt the change in the air as soon as they came over the range of low hills toward the dense oak forest. She knew the sensation well. It had been her constant companion during her trip north to Overhill. To a lesser degree, she had felt it in Walnut Tree and in the winter canyon days before. The leaf felt the master copy nearby, and dearly wanted to join it. Tildi fought being lost in the warmth of its presence.

"It's here!" she shouted to Edynn.

Edynn cantered silently toward her over the sky. "Are you sure?"

"He's down there somewhere," Tildi insisted. "We are drawing closer. Look!"

She pointed toward the sun. The angry gold orb in the sky bore a rune that flickered deep red.

Serafina blanched. "That is power beyond anything I have ever seen before. It's . . . excessive."

"I saw that on my way from the Quarters."

"And you didn't think it was strange?" Serafina asked, in a tone that made Tildi doubt her own sanity.

"Daughter, she had no experience then. Let be."

"Look there," Teryn called hoarsely. They all glanced down. A gold glimmer spread out over a crescent of woods below them. Tildi could distinguish not only the rune that said *forest*, but smaller words designating individual features. The rest of the group was now in no doubt. They were closing in on their goal.

"There's a village," Rin said. "Let us put down there. We will need help if we are to take our thief."

Unlike Walnut Tree or any of the human villages they had visited since leaving Silvertree, this place had an order that was pleasing to the eye as well as to the ear. Piping and the soft sound of harps melded in perfect harmony with the song of birds in the trees. Most of the elves lived in hollow trees, much smaller and narrower versions of Silvertree. Tildi even recognized that three of the domiciles were of the same species as in her former home. A few houses were of wood or stone, but these were so graceful in construction that they might have burgeoned organically instead of being made. Doorposts and window frames bore delicate carvings tinted with reds, browns, and deep greens, and living flowers twined everywhere.

Elves began to pour out of the graceful houses and tree homes long before the party galloped to a halt on a narrow green. Tildi looked at them shyly. Edynn's face lit up, and she swung off to meet a slender male with swept-back ears and very long black hair wearing a green tunic and pale gray trousers over light boots. The two of them looked so akin that Tildi had to bite her tongue to keep from asking questions about a possible relationship. The elves at Olen's home had been very touchy about it. Even allowing for the fact that their were backward, they were very similar to those of Edynn and Serafina. Tildi was acutely aware how strong the runes in this place were. She could see them everywhere here. The others, not as attuned as she was to the book, could not.

Edynn and the elf embraced and began to speak together. His people gathered around them. The conference was brief, as the forest denizens hastened off to their homes.

"Tildi Summerbee, my honor," the elf said, bowing to her with his hand over his heart. He knelt so that he was at eye level with her. "I am Athandis. Welcome to Penbrake. We have been warned of this very dangerous book by Lady Urestia, who was in the same council with you. I've been sending scouts out regularly to check for signs, but we have never found a trace. You are certain that the book is here?"

"In the woods," Tildi said. "It's a distance that way." She pointed. "I can see traces here, but off in that direction it's stronger than anything I have felt before."

"Do you think it not strange that he has stopped here? Can you tell me the reason?"

"I don't know. All I am sure of is the runes. Has anyone seen anything . . . strange?"

Athandis looked grave. "Not yesterday or today. The sensitives among us have reported an uncanny feeling, but no one has said they have seen anything."

"This man is dangerous, Athandis," Edynn said. "We must have a plan. It might take all of us—no, it will take all of us to capture him, but we must try. The book must be returned to safekeeping."

"I agree. My people have gone to collect weapons. They are also," he added, looking directly at Tildi, "versed in the natural magics. We will do our best. In the meanwhile, we will send messengers to the marchioness."

"Master Athandis!" A slender child came racing toward them. She came panting to a halt before the headman. She was half again Tildi's height, but could not have been more than seven years old, by smallfolk reckoning. Athandis steadied her, and poured gentle magic into her to strengthen her. The child gasped. "The forest! The forest is moving!"

The headman started to ask for details, but they became evident all too quickly. Tildi felt an onrush of power like the onslaught of driving snow. In its wake came the trees.

These were like no trees that she had ever seen, in any forest. Their bark was gray, their sparse crowns pale green, but their branches, sharpened to a point, waved and whipped of their own volition. In between cracks in the narrow, smooth boles she fancied she could see dark eyes glaring with hatred. What was worse was that they screamed. It was a high, thin sound that went through Tildi's brain like a needle. It was full of anger and pain. She was terrified, but at the same time, sorry for them. They were in pain like Morag was in pain, though he did not lash out.

A handful of young elves dashed out to meet the first wave. They brandished spears and bows. The first of the trees flowed forward on its many roots and knocked the foremost warrior flying. He landed on his back yards away. A couple of women in gray, knee-length tunics ran to help him. There was blood on his face.

The others regrouped swiftly. At a shout from the elven maid on the end, they all set the tips of their spears on fire. The trees recoiled slightly. The elves pressed their advantage, as more of them took up arms to defend. The gray boles retreated. Tildi watched in fascination. This is what the people of Walnut Tree meant when they said that the great tree had walked, but these were moving under their own power, and with their own aims.

Rustling on every side of the village drew the attention of Athandis and the visitors. More groves glided toward them, stabbing with their poinardlike branches. An elven woman in blue cried out as one thrust through her arm. Blood fountained, and the elf fell to her knees. Three of her fellows rushed in to form a circle around her until the healers could help her escape.

"Is this the work of the thief?" Athandis asked. He sounded far too calm to Tildi. The trees shrieked again, and she cringed.

"Most likely," Edynn said. "But this is his most violent transformation to date."

"Anathema. No respect for nature. We are their guardians, and they have been set loose upon us. I will see if we can calm them without rendering them harm."

"You're their guardians?" Tildi burst out. The elf smiled down upon her.

"It is why Penbrake exists, Tildi Summerbee. There are many such havens, all over Niombra. My father's grandfather was given charge of these trees when they were created, a hundred centuries ago. They think and feel, like we do. They are greatly troubled, though. You will want to take shelter in case I can't soothe them."

"I'll help you, Athandis," Edynn offered. She took up her staff. "Tildi, find yourself a place of shelter. I hope this will not take long."

A couple of younger elves took the protesting Tildi and Lakanta toward one of the houses. Tildi realized that it was a huge tree, not unlike Silvertree. In fact, it might have been a member of the same species, with its soft gray bark and pale leaves. Her guides boosted her up a rope ladder to a room some twenty feet above the forest floor that was clearly used by its owner as a study, with boxes of books and a big cushion for a chair. They brought her to an open window that looked out upon the clearing, and nocked arrows into the bows that they carried. The tips burst into flame.

"Just in case," one of them told her. "We will safeguard you, no matter what, but you can see from here."

The other set up a footstool for her. Lakanta stood next to her with an arm wound protectively around Tildi's waist.

It was a terrifying sight.

Edynn, Rin, and Serafina had joined the defenders. Athandis set the example, seeking to stop the creatures without killing them. As a tree reached for him, screaming its terrible cry, he brought his hands together with a loud clap. The tree stopped where it was as if cast in stone. Others came for him. He was stabbed again and again by many of his charges, but his calm never wavered. Dark blood stained his light tunic. Other villagers brought their talents to bear, paralyzing and soothing with the same patience as if they were caring for a school of unruly children.

Serafina was transformed from her usual sullen self to a swooping bird of prey. She moved behind the lines of elves armed with flaming spears, casting handfuls of light at the gray trees who pushed ahead of their fellows and threatened to overwhelm that far end of the village. When she struck one, it froze in place. Her mother was also paralyzing the attackers, but from a stance near a venerable copse of hazel. Teryn and Morag stood guard around her, fending off the attacking trees, but not damaging one unless it refused to yield. Soon they disappeared from view in the heart of a grove of trees that had not been there minutes ago.

Though they were mobile, the attackers did not move very fast. Rin wheeled and dashed among the shuffling trees, distracting them so the elves could do their work. A thin, wizened stick of a beech confronted her, stabbing at her with a dozen branches. One found its mark. Rin let out a shout of pain, followed by a stream of syllables that must have been an oath in the language of the Windmanes. She cracked her whip, and tied several of the limbs together. Then she turned on a single hoof and kicked the tree backwards with her hind feet. There was a tremendous *crack!* The trunk split lengthwise in two. The tree dropped backward, taking Rin's whip with it. It began to seep sticky red sap from its light interior wood.

"No!" one of the elves scolded her. He knelt by the fallen tree, a look of grief on his face, but it was no use. The baleful eyes winked out. Rin looked horrified.

"She got carried away," Lakanta said sadly. "Oh, that will haunt her, poor thing."

Athandis moved among the trees that had been halted. He touched one after another. Tildi could see that his face wore a troubled expression as he listened to each one in turn. She felt magic being used throughout the clearing. Its waves made her feel less frightened; she assumed that it had a much stronger effect upon its subjects. Other healers joined him, bringing their influence to help the trees.

It was not enough. The spell suspending their movement appeared to lose its strength only minutes after it was applied. One after another, the trees began to move again. One thick-trunked individual surprised the elven woman attempting to calm it, and walked right over her before she could get out of its way. The crunch of bones was audible throughout the glade. Tildi's stomach turned.

It became clear that the invaders were not moving at random. They had a purpose. To Tildi's horror, she realized that the wave of attackers was never-ending, and they all seemed to be converging upon the house where she had taken shelter. They were seeking her leaf of the book! The fact was not lost upon her protectors. The elf to her left drew back and loosed smoothly. The arrow pocked into the ground before the first of the trees. It glared up at him, and two of its branches reached for the arrow, snapped it in two, and cast it down. They began to shake the house from side to side. More joined them, until Tildi was looking down on a solid ring of gray branches, swaying like snakes.

"Back!" ordered her other defender. She and Lakanta were helped farther up in the tree. Before Tildi knew it they had pushed her out of a window onto a limb. It was wider than her shoulders, but it was still almost fifty feet above the ground.

"Oh, no," Tildi said, clutching the window frame. "I can't."

The elves didn't wait for her to consent. The first archer picked her up under his arm and ran surefooted for the nearest tree. An elf woman inside threw open her casement and reached for them.

Below, the trees shrieked at the attempt of their quarry to escape. Athandis and the others were pale spots of color in between the waves of gray. It was clear that his attempts to turn back the moving forest were failing. Tildi was yanked inside, hustled down a level to a handsomely furnished chamber a dozen yards across, and out of another window to a narrower limb.

They were outside the circle of trees at that moment. Tildi blanched at the endless waves of angry trees. The defenders were falling. Tildi let out a cry. She saw Edynn struggling in the grasp of a cluster of narrow-boled attackers. She froze a tree and turned to another, but by the time she did, the first one had come to life again, flailing its arms. Edynn pulled loose and let off another burst of energy. The trees shrugged it off and began to move away from her, heading toward Tildi's new hiding place.

"They are insane," said one of Tildi's defenders sadly, watching them come. "They have been hurt beyond saving."

"Don't say that!" protested his companion. The first gave him a look of infinite sadness. He nodded, and closed his eyes. "Athandis is grieved, but he agrees. Give them mercy."

Both elves drew their bows and set the tips of the arrows alight.

"What are you doing?" Lakanta cried. "They are living creatures."

"We are not powerful enough to change back what has been done to them," said the second elf. "They are lost. A fundamental alteration has been visited upon them. How, we do not fully understand. Poor things, they lived in torment for so long. We hoped that they could live in peace, but there is no hope of that now."

"Oh, you can't," Tildi protested, realizing what they meant to do, despite the danger the trees posed to her. "I'm sure something can be done for them . . ."

"Thank you for caring," the first elf said with a rueful little nod. "We are their caretakers. It is better if we are the ones to do this. Now, and swiftly."

They both loosed at the same moment. The fiery arrows struck two different trees, who brushed the missiles away as though they were stinging flies. They could not brush away the flames, however. The fire spread with remarkable speed. The trees recoiled, and the blaze spread from branch to branch, as others caught fire. The elven archers released arrow after arrow with blinding speed, setting more trees alight.

Tildi spotted Edynn. With terrible sorrow on her face, the elder wizardess held out her arms. The jewel on the end of her staff began to glow. Serafina assumed a similar stance. More trees burst into flame. Soon the entire grove was burning. It was swift, but a few of the injured trees staggered around, shrieking in pain. Rin and the guards hurried in to give as many of them the coup de grace. Tildi found herself weeping uncontrollably. Lakanta folded her into her arms and stroked her hair.

When it was all over, the elves and visitors stood in the midst of blackened trunks, smoke rising to the sky. Tildi was stunned to see that the oaks of the village were very little damaged. Those scorched patches of bark and stripped branches would heal. What would not be so easily healed would be the memory of the devastation of what had been hundreds of living things, reduced to charcoal. The elves held onto one another to grieve for their loss.

Tildi realized that she felt a loss, too, greater than her sorrow for the trees. The warmth she felt from the book had gone. The thief had fled.

Edynn, her usually spotless robes smudged and torn, emerged from the ruin on Serafina's arm. She spotted Tildi and beckoned to her. Tildi's protectors guided her down a spiral staircase and out into the glade. Rin and the guards came to meet them.

Athandis stood while healers bustled around him, closing his wounds, and cleaning the blood from his clothing. His dark eyes glowed like the eyes of the fallen race of trees. He hefted a spear and waved a hand over its end. The stone tip, which had been broken off in the fight, became sharp again, and the bindings tight. He gestured to all the elves who were still standing. "Now, my friends, we will go after the one who has tortured our poor brethren like this. He chooses to tamper with Mother Nature's children, but he has none of her loving-kindness toward her creations."

"He is gone, sir," Tildi said. "He went while you were trying to heal the trees."

The elf turned toward her, horrified. "You are certain?"

"She has a sympathy for the book," Edynn explained. "Surely Urestia told you of her."

"Yes, indeed, she did," Athandis said, grim-faced. "This wizard is cunning, and ruthless."

"He is," Edynn said. "More and worse could come out of this. Come, my friends. Let us mourn for our lost ones, and decide what we must do next."

Chapter Twenty-eight

Magpie awoke from a pleasant dream full of comfortable cushions, silken cloth, silken flesh, the silken feel of good wine pouring down his throat. He reached up to push the bottle away in order to take another kiss from those silken lips of his fiancée, and found it restrained by her hairy, scratchy hand. That wasn't right! He opened his eyes sharply and realized his hand was secured by a loop of heavy rope to the beautifully turned bedpost over his head. He tried to turn over to undo it with his free hand, and discovered that he couldn't because both ends were around the post, and the opposite ankle was also secured by an equally scratchy rope and tied to the bedpost at the other corner.

His elder brother Ganidur, arms folded in satisfaction, looked down at him. He was built along the same rangy lines as Magpie, but several inches taller, with big hands and feet, wider shoulders, and a long, humorous face.

"How do you feel this morning, Eremi?"

"What in the yawning abyss is this?" Magpie demanded.

"Father asked me," Ganidur began, with a kind of complacent smugness that made Magpie want to kick him, "to ensure that you did not get cold feet at the last minute and disappoint your fiancée. You will be at this engagement. You shouldn't be upset! After all, you didn't wake up in the cesspit the way you did to me on *my* betrothal day."

"That wasn't my idea, Gan," Magpie said indignantly. Then he paused. "Well . . . perhaps I suggested it," honesty compelled him to add.

"As I thought. Bena doesn't have the imagination for that kind of cruelty. I had to go to my loved one's ceremony smelling like ten days of the runs."

"You had a bath ahead of time," Magpie reminded him.

"As if that would do anything about an entire castle's worth of effluvia," Ganidur said with a snort. "The fact remains that you got to spend your betrothal night in your very own bed with your very own bedclothes and, I hope, your very own severe hangover."

Magpie felt his head with his free hand. "You have that right, brother. I feel as if a herd of centaurs clattered across my skull during the night."

"You're not far-off. There was a troupe of dancing girls. They were a bit on the equine side, I might say, but vigorous! I have to give them that. But this is all for Father's sake. I'm saving *my* particular revenge for your wedding night."

"Thanks for the warning. We'll be wed in a temple somewhere out in the wilderness, and you won't be invited."

"Nonsense. It's a dynastic marriage, and you won't have any choice in the matter. It'll be done with the full array of incense, prayers, chants, fastings, vigils, sacrifices, and everything that I can persuade the high priest to throw into it, because he knows just how very devout you are, because I have told him so."

"In spite of the fact that I shirk prayers whenever I can."

"I don't actually believe that," Ganidur said with an indulgent smile. "I know in what reverence you hold Nature. And I'm sure you have the same respect for Father Time. I'm your brother, remember? It doesn't matter what face you show to the world. I know what's inside you."

Magpie blanched. "Family can be damned inconvenient. Are you going to untie these ropes, so that I can get up and get my bath, or do I have to lie here and have everyone come to me?"

"You'd like that, wouldn't you?" Ganidur said, his eyes twinkling. "As it so happens, I personally oversaw all the preparations for your presentation. The horse is white. It has blue eyes, which means that it cannot hear any of the imprecations you're going to be hurling at the Powers in order to get out of your obligations. It's still a stallion, which you won't be if you are late to this. Father has set a whole troop of guards in order to see to it." Ganidur put a knee on the bed and began to untie the knots holding Magpie's wrist bond. They were at least triple knots. Magpie couldn't really see it from the angle at which he was lying, but the length of time it was taking his brother to undo them suggested it. Fair enough; with his habit of disappearing it was right of them to take no chances whatsoever.

His father was counting upon him. That fact alone would have made him behave. If they had only asked him he would have assured them that he would have done no such thing as disappear before this most vital ceremony. On the other hand, it would be unlikely that they would believe him.

"How's Elimar?" Magpie asked, sitting up and rubbing the red marks on his wrist as Ganidur walked around the bed to unfasten his ankle. As Magpie had surmised, the knots were complicated and numerous.

"He's well." Ganidur smiled at the thought of his six-year-old son, who was a special Nature's Child to Magpie. "Do you really mean to have him stand with you as your champion at the wedding itself? He's been practicing, and he can just about lift the practice sword over his head without toppling. I tried to have one made for his size, but he declared that he was going to lift the ceremonial sword for Uncle Magpie and nothing else."

"You know that Benarelidur still hasn't forgiven you for having a child first," Magpie pointed out.

"Six years to give his wife time—I think Bena had better admit that she's barren. Unless Nature remakes her in some way I am afraid that I or one of my youngsters is going to be the heir."

"It's an old and noble line," Magpie said with a sigh. "It must not die out."

"Then, hope for a miracle," Ganidur said simply. "For all that our brother was born elderly and is a stickler for rules in every way, and though he wouldn't mind exposing both of *us* upon a hillside, he does love his wife. He would never set her aside in favor of another, despite the fact he has no heir."

"Well, I have special prayers to be sent up before the altar," Magpie reminded him. "I'll send up a wish for her." Magpie had a soft spot for his brother's wife, who liked him despite Benarelidur's not seeming to very much.

Ganidur hauled him up with one mighty arm, set him on his feet, and gave him a slap on the back. He pushed him in the direction of the bathing chamber.

"There are eight servants in there, all waiting to scrub a different part of you, and eight more in the robing room across the landing. Have a lovely bath."

Magpie survived the cleansing ceremony with most of his hide intact and escaped onto the landing, leaving the servants behind to clean soap, perfumed oil, and water off the tiled walls of the bathing chamber, and made toward the robing room. His stomach rumbled. He ignored it. He was forbidden breakfast until after the betrothal service, when he would break bread with his bride-to-be, but it half killed him to inhale the smells of breakfast floating upward from the great hall, where his father was presiding over the morning feast with his early guests. No one really expected him to appear at the table. He was supposed to be robing himself and preparing to go and stand the vigil before the altar until his bride should appear, Father Time waiting for Mother Nature in all her beauty. Magpie smiled, leaning out of the window that overlooked the main courtyard. Inbecca was indeed beautiful. He looked forward to the two of them claiming each other. It was the fulfillment of his dream that had begun when they were children. If she could look into his heart at that moment he was sure she would be surprised at such a sentimental vision, but he hoped she would also be pleased.

The courtyard was full of carriages, wagons, and wains of every description. A few elegant closed litters had been pushed out of the way against the wall of the tannery. The horses were being curried by grooms preparatory to being turned out to pasture beneath the castle to make room for more guests' steeds. Heaven knows how many guests had already arrived on foot.

A young, dappled centaur, late for breakfast, shrugged on his ceremonial capelet as he galloped toward the door, wavy black mane flying behind him. His metal-shod hooves rang on the stones, striking up sparks. He and his companions had been accomodated in a stable that had been turned out and modified for guests. If Magpie had given his father more notice, a purpose-built structure would have been constructed. Instead, the ancient timbers were given a quick whitewash before chandeliers were strung from them, and dressing tables tucked into the hastily redecorated tack room.

The joining ceremony was important politically, and attended by the most solemn ministerial harrumphing. There was some opposition to it, of course. Most of the gossips said that Orontae was the one getting the bargain, not wealthy and secure Levrenn. Magpie had no trouble letting them think it. His brothers, not aware of his actions during wartime or after, both were convinced that Magpie has been wasting his time going around the countryside. He had come to terms with never being able to tell them he was doing as much work as they, yet had nothing to show for it. At least, the naysayers muttered, he would be making an advantageous marriage, and bringing Inbecca's dowry, which ought to be worth half the realm, with her. Since money was the last thing Magpie was interested in, he wanted to laugh in their faces. Instead, he deliberately went on looking like Nature's most foolish child, unaware of his good fortune or the people who made fun of him for it. The ones who mattered were his family.

He was sorry that Tildi and Edynn couldn't be at the joining ceremony. Tildi was such a fresh, interesting little creature. He would have enjoyed introducing her to his family, especially Ganidur, who would have spoiled her at once, and his nephew, who would have been thrilled to the skies to meet an adult who was smaller than he.

She would really have enjoyed seeing the ceremony itself.

It would have told her a good deal about how much humans and smallfolk had in common. Olen might be right or he might be wrong about the origin of the races of the world, but Magpie had been struck by Lady Urestia's speech. He had never heard an elf speak out so passionately on anything before. He'd had many lively discussions with them, but not with so much heat. They found *him* amusing, but they had respect for the elder humans like Olen and Edynn, and those who had attained wizardry. It meant that such humans as they were in tune with nature, much as elves were. It was a shame that humans had become so divorced from the very fact of their birth. And yet their entire faith depended upon those two vital elements of all: nature and time.

Magpie had often thought of these things while he was out on the road. It was funny to have the time and space to think about such things while at home. He never had time for such thoughts here. Usually he was so busy either following a task for his father, or keeping out of his father's way. Magpie reminded him of the loss that publicly was not a loss.

His mother, resplendent in a blue damask robe fastened up to the chin with silver buttons, came rushing out of the chamber opposite, and grabbed him by the arm.

"Eremi, they have been waiting for you for an hour!" she exclaimed.

"I'm sorry, Mother," he said, bending to kiss her on the cheek. "I was just thinking."

His mother shook her head. "You know, Benarelidur never thinks. In some cases I find that regrettable, but in terms of wasted time, you waste far more time upon such things than he does. And I don't see that it does you any more good."

This from the woman who had hired a classical philosopher as his tutor. Magpie opened his mouth to protest.

"I am joking, darling," the queen said. "Please go in. Everyone is arriving, and I wish you would give me one less thing to think about. Nature and Time bless your union, my son. I have been waiting for this ever since you two were children. You are meant for each other." She picked up her skirts to descend the steps. The young princesses, all in their new finery, bounded down the stairs past them, late for breakfast but still giggling. The youngest, Niletia, stopped to give him a big kiss on the cheek.

"I am so happy you are marrying Inbecca," she said, her brown eyes alight. "I like her."

"So do I," Magpie assured her. "You look lovely."

"Thank you for the dresses. We all like them." She beamed, and clattered off down the stairs after the rest of the girls. He smiled after her. She reminded him of Tildi. He would love to have told her all about the smallfolk girl, but while the party was on the trail of the thief, he had said nothing to anyone. He feared jeopardizing the safety of the party. He hated sitting in the midst of luxury while a group of women, admittedly two who were wizards and two who were accomplished warriors, went out on what might be nothing more than a fine journey, but likely to be a terrible hardship with a battle at the end that they could not win. He had to admit that he was jealous that he had not been included. Was it odd to wish to be in danger instead of safe at home?

"You don't think I'm a changeling, do you, Mother?" Magpie asked suddenly.

Lottcheva glanced back with a smile that reminded him of the winsome girl she had been when he was a boy. "Heavens, no, I was there when you were born. Your father showed up a few hours later after drinking with the council and asked, 'Is it here yet? Oh! Puny, isn't it?'" Her imitation of his father's bluff attitude made Magpie laugh.

"If he thinks I was puny . . . Mother, have you ever met a smallfolk?"

"Oh, yes, dear, of course. A delegation of them came to your father's coronation. I wasn't betrothed to him yet, but I was in his mother's court. They seemed uncomfortable at first, but they became an elemental part of the celebration afterwards, I do believe."

"Men and women?"

The queen tilted her head in thought. "No, just men, I think. Yes, that's right. It was rather fun to see them dancing with the ladies-in-waiting, barely coming up to the girls' waists. They were game, I must give them that. And good dancers, as well. Now that you mention it, I have never met a female smallfolk."

"They don't usually travel outside their homeland."

"Well, possibly not," his mother said thoughtfully. "If the men are so easily overlooked, the women must be small enough you would worry about stepping on them. You may ask them yourself. A contingent is expected from Ivirenn. They are coming upriver with some of the seafolk. Now, go get changed, please. You are expected at the temple, and it's well past midmorning!"

Magpie kissed her and went into the robing room.

Ganidur was wrong. There were twelve courtiers, not eight, awaiting him. The first two deprived him of his dressing gown and slippers before he'd set more than a foot in the room. He heard an embarrassed giggle, and caught a glimpse of a couple of blushing girls hurrying toward the upstairs before the door to the landing was shut. Magpie hoped his cheeks weren't burning. With the greatest of ceremony, the courtiers, all of high rank and conscious of the privilege they enjoyed participating in this ritual, led him onto a low dais and helped him into one garment after another, even moving his arms or legs for him. Magpie stared at the antique blue tapestries that lined the walls of the room and studied the history of his family while pretending he was a tailor's mannequin. First, smallclothes, of the finest silk. Plain, for which he knew he must thank his mother. He'd helped many a noble bridegroom on with his wedding clothes, and the embarrassing embroideries that were frequently doodled by loving hands onto the most intimate garments made great telling at the feast afterwards, when plenty of wine had loosened the attendants' tongues. Black silk hose and garters followed, with loose trousers over those. A thin shirt of the finest weave he had yet seen went on over his bare chest. He reached for the laces, and his hands were batted away by a solemn-faced lordling from the southern reaches of the kingdom.

"My mistake," Magpie said apologetically. No doubt territory had been staked out regarding each precious garment long before he had arrived, and he was upsetting the balance by attempting to dress himself.

"My honor," the lordling said with grave courtesy.

The light shirt was followed by a heavier shirt of glossy white silk, softer than water running over his hand. He sighed as the next, higher-ranking attendant fastened the high neckline with gold pins. The cloth cost more than a trio of fine horses, and in the summer's heat he immediately began to sweat into it. The embroidery on this shirt was exquisite: he assumed it had been done personally by his mother, his sisters, and his aunts. Yes, there in her kindness, his eldest sister had embroidered a motif of musical notes around the waist at the sides, where the belt would cover it. No one would know it was there but he—and of course, the twelve servants who robed him. But he appreciated the courtesy.

"Sigrun," he said to one of the young nobles, who was fastening on his left boot, when they were nearly alone, "would you undertake a small task for me?"

"Why, whatever I can, my lord," Sigrun said, in surprise. He was the son of a scholar-knight, who served a very different abbot than Sharhava. A young man of wit, he showed no interest in following his father into the Scholardom. He seemed to be very pleased to be entrusted with an errand.

"Here," Magpie said, fishing one out from the full purse that would shortly be fastened around his waist, "is a gold coin. Will you ensure that my jitar makes it to the celebration feast later today? I know that I am not supposed to be carrying anything except a bouquet of flowers and a full heart, but I have written a poem for my love, and I wish to declaim it to her at the feast, and I would prefer to accompany myself. On the quiet, I do not trust my father's lutenists. They were fine musicians . . . once."

Sigrun grinned. Everyone in the court had suffered through a festival or two or six at the hands of the king's minstrels. "I will, with good heart. If you will excuse the cheek, it's a pity you were born of noble blood, sir. My family would have been proud to have you in our household as court musician. I shouldn't say that. I beg your pardon, of course."

"I take no offense; in fact, I thank you for the compliment." He showed Sigrun where the jitar was stored, then was chivied back to the official dais to go on being dressed as though he was a life-sized doll.

Well, he'd done what he could to ensure that *he* would enjoy the feast, if nothing else. Obediently he let the next lordling fasten on the handsome belt, with plates of black onyx trimmed with gold. Between the music and Inbecca, good food and wine, he could put up with a great deal of ritual nonsense, dull speeches, and tasteless toasts from his friends, not to mention railing against his uselessness from his father on one side, and his profane character from Inbecca's terrible aunt Sharhava on the other.

That woman was poison, he thought, holding his arms up to make way for the purse of gold at his hip. What she had been telling Inbecca on the day he had returned he had no idea, but she had gone too far in trying to convince Inbecca to cast off her earthly bonds and join the Knights. Magpie was forced to admit that he had not been much help, disappearing on and off the way that he did. What else was the girl to do? She had intelligence, talent, skill in all the courtly arts, drive as well as extraordinary beauty, yet the man to whom she was planning to tie her life was never there. He could hardly ask a woman of her dignity to go out on the road with him, as much as he enjoyed that life, because she would not enjoy it. She wouldn't find peace in the service of the Scholardom, either, but her aunt would convince her that it was for a holy cause.

Yet again he wondered where Edynn, Serafina, and little Tildi were at that moment.

The final garment arrived, escorted in the hands of no fewer than four high-ranking courtiers. Some clever soul, a thousand or so years ago, and certainly by now dead, so that Magpie could not take revenge upon him, had come up with the proper symbolic presentation of Father Time for prospective grooms who were about to take their betrothal vows. Fortunately it would not be worn at the wedding itself. It consisted of a long robe that shaded from black at the shoulders, where it made even the healthiest complexion look muddy and gloomy, down through all the gray tones to purest white at the hem, where it could get dirty the very first time one walked across a dusty floor. This was bestowed upon Magpie with some ceremony, as well as the traditional overbelt of solid gold that represented the imperishable circle of time.

Everything he wore was as symbolic as it could possibly be. All the ornaments that followed were of stone or glass. There would be no wood, no leather, no bone, no other metal on his symbolic, exterior self. He wondered if Time was ever as personified in every groom and every priest, or in every young person stepping up to the altar for confirmation, acknowledging for the first time those twin forces that were greater than himself, greater than anything that had ever lived, that commanded his everyday life. And if Time and Nature did exist, anthropomorphic, what had they thought of what some of their creations had done ten thousand years ago, when the Makers had perverted what they had set in motion. Magpie might have, if he was with Olen and for the sake of argument, stated that if a creature or thing existed, then it was natural, and Mother Nature could not object. The priest of the temple was an old, old man sorely lacking in a sense of humor or any sense of exploration. He had not risen to his present state of dignity by entertaining concepts that were not written down in the book that stood upon the altar longer than anyone could remember. Magpie promised himself he would not start any religious arguments or cause any trouble. This was Inbecca's day, and he was there to serve her.

Magpie surveyed himself in the mirror, turning this way and that to get the full effect. In combination, just purely from a fashion sense, it looked completely ridiculous. Magpie wanted to laugh, but his attendants were conscious of their own dignity, so he kept his amusement to himself.

"Highness, would you like to open your presents now?" inquired a slender courtier with the rare dark red hair of the northwestern province adjacent to Levrenn.

That was evidently his honor, to preside over the opening of gifts.

Magpie allowed himself to be led to a table, where the redheaded courtier stood ready to hand him whichever box he pointed to. The table itself was an object of great antiquity, used only for occasions such as weddings and birth celebrations. It was made from a single piece of translucent white stone. The base was carved as a succession of puffy white clouds supporting the wide, polished top in which was set a brilliant golden sun. The carefully arranged boxes of white and red in the center of the table on top of the sun were gifts from Inbecca's family. He knew at once which items were from her. The smooth goblet carved from pure carnelian, with the symbols of both Orontae and Levrenn, the eagle and the tiger, intertwined on one side, was just the kind of gift she would choose. It was exquisite, the red agate as pure of color as if it had been painted by an artist. He hoped she would be pleased with the gifts that he had sent to her, including a box made from Silvertree's own wood, shed branches that were a gift to him while he had been wandering in the garden. He knew the tree—He? She?—thought that he moved too quickly for a thoughtful being, but had never refused him admittance to any part of the great building except the wizard's quarters, where the doors always seemed to unaccountably stick fast, even when he picked the locks.

"My thanks for your assistance," Magpie said, with a courteous nod to the redheaded visitor, as the last of the parcels were dealt with. By custom, most of the gifts were given to the bride, as the representative of the creative force of Nature. Chances were that Inbecca's home was being filled up with beautifully wrapped parcels, silken bags, baskets, containers, and any number and type of celebratory livestock customary during this event. He was glad he didn't have to make polite chatter over a sow and piglets, or try to keep a straight face at some of the offerings he knew would be forthcoming.

The importance of the ceremony meant that not a few of the guests who had been at Olen's secret conference would be coming to the betrothal. He wondered if he should behave as if he had seen them there or not, since he had been there in his guise as Magpie. Wouldn't that be a surprise to King Halcot, who did as yet not know his true background, and probably did not believe Olen when he used Magpie's honorific to try and make him behave. More fool Halcot. Olen knew more about the royal houses' heredity and their genealogy than they or any of the kingdom heralds did. Magpie assumed it was mainly because the wizard had lived through quite a bit of it. Olen had never said how old he was, but Magpie would not have been surprised if he was the father of one of the Makers of the Great Book. Still, as much as Magpie would have enjoyed seeing the dignified king react to his favorite fool marrying the heir to the throne of another country, the matter had to be breached, and Hawarti promised to speak to the king privately before he attended the ceremony. It wasn't fair to surprise and possibly embarrass him in public like that. Halcot might, and quite rightly, take the appearance of a former spy in a place of honor as a dire insult.

Magpie shut the lid on the final parcel, and turned back to the hovering courtiers. He forced himself to smile warmly at them.

"Gentlemen all, I thank you for your service, in the name of Father Time. I must now go. I look forward to greeting you after the ceremony."

They all seemed to breathe a sigh of relief as he released them. The battle for supremacy was not quite over. Magpie watched in amusement as they jockeyed for position to leave the room according to their order of precedence. Sigrun, carrying the jitar, tipped him a wink as he departed behind them, last and least, but the only one Magpie thought was worthwhile.

Inbecca's party was probably arriving within the capital city even now as Magpie began to make his way toward the temple. It was pure cheek on his father's part to insist upon having this ceremony in the temple of his homeland, instead of the one in Inbecca's country. She was the crown princess, and Magpie was only the third son of an impoverished king. But Inbecca's mother had a little bit more kindness and was inclined to grant her friend and former rival that one honor that he craved, knowing what he had suffered in recent years.

The sun was moving ever higher. He must go.

Chapter Twenty-nine

Nemeth hurtled through the chilly air above the clouds, faster and faster, until he had nearly left his breath behind him. He wanted to put as much distance as he could between himself and the violated forest. The voices in his head were joined by the spirits of the altered trees. They cried out, wondering why they were suffering. Nemeth had no answer but that of his expedience. They must dispose of his enemies so that he could remain free. He would apologize if he could, but his need was greater than theirs. Time had been lost. He must hurry. The distance left to cross was so small compared with what he had already traveled. If he rose high enough he could see the tops of the gleaming white mountains. Among them lay his goal. So close. So close!

He meant to ruin the world. He was almost looking forward to it. It had done him no good. He would have his revenge. All of those people, their homes, their lands, would cease to be! He had long waited for the chance to change the painful reality of his existence, and it had come to him.

Nemeth the Nameless they had called him, unworthy namesake of a long-ago wonder-worker. Humiliation had been thrust upon him, time and again. He had been Soliandur's good adviser. If only the fool of a king had listened, he could have had a much more powerful hold over the enemy to their south. They could have driven the intruders away and had a sound victory, with honor and glory for all. Instead, Soliandur signed a namby-pamby peace, with terms as poor as if the enemy—who was losing!—had written them to his own advantage—which he did!

Nemeth had sworn to the king that his visions revealed that Soliandur was being influenced by the enemy's wizard. He had seen it as clearly as he saw his own surroundings. Hodylla must have guided the king to place his troops and ordnance to the Rabantavians' advantage, so that more of the Orontavian army had been lost. Soliandur had laughed at him in open court, stating that no wizard had a hold on him. Nemeth had been disgraced and finally sent away from the court. Halcot, who had surely given the order for Soliandur's subversion, was pleased to make Nemeth's dismissal part of the "lasting peace."

He had been cast out. No position of honor, no comfortable retirement to look forward to with grand estates as he had always assumed he would have, when one day he chose to retire from active court life—which would have been never! Hadn't these stupid conditions proved they needed him for now and always? But *they* said he was a fool. His predictions didn't come true. Well, of course not—when he revealed the future, they changed what they had been planning to do, so those foretellings could never come true. He gave them the fate they would have had if they had not changed their path. *They* said his magic could not withstand the force of the enemy's mage. Not true, *not* true. He had been betrayed by his own assistants, and by others who spied upon him—did not the ruler see that his own court was infested with traitors? To Nemeth's humiliation, he had not. He should have known: he was the one with the true sight.

Having been so publicly disgraced meant that no other monarch would ever sponsor him. No amount of hastily given gifts or apologies would suffice to assuage him. The courtiers told him to let the insults go. The memory of them would pass in time, and kings would once again clamor for his services. Nemeth knew that was not true, and the sycophants were only saying those things because they feared him. They seemed sympathetic in person, but he knew they talked behind his back. They, too, deserved to be punished. The only solution he would accept was to wipe them out, all of Orontae. It would be the last act of his pathetic life. But that required a Great Working, one they claimed he was incapable of performing. Ah, perhaps *then*, ah, then but not now.

The pursuers behind him could never have suspected that he had begun as they did, with a single curious fragment of parchment. It had been a gift from Soliandur himself. The king had delivered the tool of his eventual undoing into Nemeth's very hands.

The first clue. Yes, he could see it now—if he closed his eyes—burning like a brand in his mind's flesh. A portion of a book. A leaf a yard or two long, pages that had been cut out of the middle of a scroll, with some interesting symbols on it, unfamiliar words drawn with an intricacy that hadn't been used since the world was young. Nemeth had studied runes, like every apprentice wizard, but he had never seen any like these. A curiosity, that was all the ruler had believed it to be when he tossed it to Nemeth as a sop, a magical item that scorched the bearer's hands like fire. It was so beautiful that it tempted the unwary to pick it up to look at it, then exacted its revenge. The fragment was meant to take away the sting of the first great insult, the humiliating public accusation of incompetence that Soliandur had made against him. Nemeth had crept away, chastened, to his tower, clutching to himself the scroll and the knowledge that he had been right.

The scroll did indeed burn, but not so brightly as Nemeth's curiosity. From where had such a thing sprung? How old was it? Who had made it? What was it for? His vision led him to the next discovery, that the runes of an object became prominent when the page was placed near it, like a candle illuminating objects on a dark table. An accident showed him that he could break those runes, and make one thing into another when the pages were close. What a treasure for a wizard who had never had much skill at Transformation, or even Healing! He experimented with anything that came near him, always in secret, mainly because his experiments were almost always failures. He had not the knack for detail needed to make the transformed items work.

Curiosity led him to find the next clue, there in the very realm, a most aptly named chapter of the Knights of the Word. Their archive contained a rich source of information, telling him that there was an ancient book of great power that lay buried and guarded far away. He realized that his possession must be a portion of it. If he could do such wonders with a fragment, what miracles could be wrought using the entire tome? He was convinced that the rest of the magical tome, if he could find it, would contain the information he needed to learn how to do true transformations.

During the long months of the war, he scryed for his king by day, but at night he researched the location of his goal, the rest of the book. He tried to help his nation in the war effort by harnessing the talents of the page and attacking the troops on the ground, but it had not been enough to make a difference, and it was not appreciated by Soliandur, who continued to chide him for his ineptitude. At almost the same time that he had discovered the whereabouts of the Great Book, Soliandur dismissed him from his service. Nemeth had tried to tell himself he did not care. He had a more pressing task ahead of him. He had to possess this book.

It lay far distant from Orontae,—but ah!—it would be worth the seeking. His research in the chapter house had led him to believe that the book was capable of undoing all of existence. At that time he was bitter enough to vow that he would rather see the end of all rather than go on being humbled and taunted the way he had been. So be it. He promised himself he would show these sad, deluded fools he was no bungler, just at the last moment before he wiped them out.

The journey had been hard for one who had seldom had to walk a mile under his own power, or shield himself from the elements. Revenge, the lust for it, kept the urge, the impetus, the goad to his back, alive in him when pain, privation, and frustration would have once turned him back. He admitted he had been a weaker man when his ordeal began. He considered all these setbacks as further stairs he had climbed as he overcame each by each. Ah, the satisfaction he gained as he rose higher in strength, thanks to his king's gift.

He had through sheer determination reached the place where the Great Book resided, a mountain fastness guarded by fierce beasts and myriad spells. He could feel the power of his fragment's mate calling to him through the very stone itself. He had begun the climb, heedless of the rocks and grass on which his feet and hands slipped. He pulled himself upwards by sheer will.

The first guardians, stone beings of indescribable beauty and great antiquity, had risen from the earth itself at the mountain's base, and had warned him to turn aside or they would be forced to kill him. Nemeth realized that these had once been human. He was determined that they would not stop him. They knew the power of that which they guarded. What they could never guard against was that part of the book that still existed in the outside world. His fragment showed him their runes. They were vulnerable to him—him! The pathetic seer of Orontae, the deluded fool, the weakling. He pleaded with them, assuring them that he did not want to destroy them, but they could not stand between him and his goal. At once, he had been driven to his knees with pain. He knew they were fools. If they had been wise, they would have killed him on the spot. Instead, they gave him a chance to strike back. Nemeth had been shocked into action. Without another thought, he had reached into the first creatures' runes, and unlocked them.

The stone wizards had cried out as they crumbled into the dust they should have been centuries before. Nemeth had continued upward, and more guardians challenged him. Winged lions rose from plinths and flew down at him, claws at the ready. He tore them to pieces. Dragons, sphinxes, giants, and others followed. Nemeth was in a trance at the thought he was so close, and felt no fear at their approach. He must pass them. Therefore, they must die.

They were far from defenseless against him. The dragons alone were accomplished wizards as well as dangerous creatures. They drove him back down the mountainside, wounding him, terrifying him. The book called to him, blinding him to his fears. What did it matter if the dragons could wipe him out with a breath, or sphinxes slice his body into five pieces with one swipe of a taloned paw? He had greater magic than they. These, too, he changed. Their bodies could no longer support life.

They realized what he was doing in a moment, and attacked, hoping to kill him before he could finish his spells, but many were already dying. The winged lions fell at once, roaring so loudly that their voices echoed for miles down the valleys.

They mustered their forces to bring him down before he could kill all of them. He did not like to think about the battles, which were bloody and terrible. Fighting the pain and fear, he had struck against his enemies, filling the air with nightmares until they couldn't tell if they were fighting him or one another. Subtly, under the cover of chaos, he broke them, ripping out their hearts, tearing off their wings in midflight. He could still see the guardians in his mind, withering as he twisted their symbols and shouted words of destruction. They died, crying out for mercy. Their bodies twitched and smoldered upon the mountainside for days.

Once they all lay dead, Nemeth realized what he had done. He huddled in a fearful heap under the shadow of a boulder, out of the sight of his victims. He waited and watched for days—or was it months?—until the feeling of the Great Book, so near to him, almost drove him mad with longing. No more guardians came to challenge him. He climbed the mountain.

Once again, the fragment gave him the key. No door lay hidden to him, since the runes of concealed passageways illuminated themselves at his touch. With his seer's skill he deduced how to open the mystic locks that caused the stone doors, each a hundred times the weight of a man, to roll aside and admit him. The enameled and gilded corridor rose until he stood under the peak of the mountain itself, and all the walls glowed with the golden glory of the Great Book at its heart.

He was not prepared for the beauty of the Great Book itself. It lay upon a pedestal inside a massive cavern, covered by a dome of perfect crystal. He realized upon comparing them that his precious leaf was no more than a segment of a lesser copy. The Great Book was whole and perfect, and he felt its power radiate throughout his entire body, a volcano compared to the fragment's simple flame. The latter, cherished as it had been, looked like a sad little rag. Still, it served him for one more task. It provided him entrée to the passage left, then sealed, by a long-dead wizard who thought no one would ever use it again. As he penetrated into the dome, the leaf rose up in a puff of smoke. Nemeth felt he might do the same. Just standing beside his treasured goal made him feel as if he might melt out of existence. The Great Book was more real than he.

His first attempt to touch it was painful, so painful he could scarcely remember how it felt. It took longer yet for him to be able to handle the Great Book freely. He forced himself to be near it, as agonizing as it was. He adored it. He felt his own rune burning within him, the fundamental description of his existence, and sensed its echo within the pages. Time meant nothing, since he was to achieve his goal. Willpower allowed him to alter himself slightly every day, painfully, a little at a time, until he was of a substance the book would permit to touch it. That final moment, when he lifted the Great Book in his arms and embraced it, was the happiest of his life. In itself, obtaining the Great Book would have been enough, but he knew that it was also the ultimate means of achieving his goal to destroy Orontae. Nothing in existence could stand before it.

Then, he had carried it away, confident that no one alive could have done what he did.

Ahead of him, the rounded shapes of the mountains and clouds gave way. Before him, glinting in the sun, lay his destination. Oron Castle—first stronghold of the first kings of Orontae—had been abandoned for more than a thousand years, yet its shape resonated with the force of the personality of those long-dead rulers who had pulled their unruly, nomadic people into a civilization that was the envy of the rest of humanity. A road, still navigable after millenia, wound through the mountain passes to six sets of double gates. The gates were long gone, the metal stripped for other, long-forgotten purposes, but the stone pillars, majestic in size and form, guided his flight to the outer walls. Oron stood on a plateau among peaks with a unique view that revealed the great, fertile valley, a thousand miles wide and many hundreds of miles long, that was its first settled province. He stayed high enough that the farmers working the fields below would not spot him. No one would have an inkling of his presence.

A scream interrupted his thoughts. He looked up to see the sinuous shadows of a dozen thraik. His heart pounded frantically in his chest. They must not see him! He clutched the book and made ready to fly down into the rocky landscape spread out below.

Then he laughed at himself. Of course they did not see him, he realized, as the oily, black monsters cast around the sky in vain. He thumbed his nose at them. His spell prevented them from having more than a hopeful impression that he and the book were there. They sought in vain.

There, on their worthless, horrible bodies, were their runes. It would be so easy to slash them in half. Let them fall wailing to earth, unaware of who had been responsible for their doom! He drew back his hand, preparing the stroke.

No, wait a moment, he thought, with a fierce grin. *Let them live.* They could not see him, but they surely could sense the ones who followed him. He sensed that the trees had not been enough to defeat his pursuers. Let *them* face the thraik.

Go that way, he urged the hovering shadows. He sent them an image of the forest. *What you seek is back that way.*

The thraik dithered a moment longer, then shot through the air, heading southwest. Deeply satisfied, Nemeth watched them go.

The castle awaited him like a returning conqueror. He set down lightly in the high courtyard and turned to survey his new domain.

It was surprisingly intact, despite not being occupied by anyone other than shepherds, bats, and curious children for more than a thousand years. A few hardy mountain trees had grown up amid the cubes of stone, pushing some up at angles and cracking others. Pure white moss spread over the remnants of colored plaster and mosaic tiles on the walls, which towered high and lonely against the backdrop of the mountains. He did not refer to the book for the images he wanted, because it would only show him what the castle was like now. But each rune of the tumbled stones aided him in harkening back to the way the castle was in its glory. In his sight he saw the grand city the way it had once been. Every one of the white towers sparkled in the sun, pennants flying from their conical roofs. Every outer wall was well-built enough to withstand any incursion. The oldest chambers had been hewed into the face of the cliff itself, but in later years as the court had grown, the castle had spilled down the face of the mountain like wax dripping from a pillar candle. He saw it in his mind. Fluted arches rose above the flagstone roads that ran among gracious apartments, galleries, workshops, nurseries for the many children, tilting yards, even a study or two for wizards. Balconies and terraces overlooked the successively lower levels like kindly nursemaids watching over beloved children. The lowest level was like a fortress, with a circle of walls so wide three men could walk on them abreast between guardhouses that could each hold a hundred soldiers, armed with cannon and crossbow. In fact, in five thousand years the castle had never fallen to attack, and the stones themselves were proud of that.

Below the castle, the remains of the city of the Oros lay jumbled like a child's building blocks. If he felt like it, he might turn his attention to it later. In the meanwhile, he claimed the castle for his own. Proudly, he marched through the thirty-foot-high doorway into the great keep itself.

"Good bones," Nemeth said, running his hand possessively along the carved stone pillar that held the roof more than sixty feet over his head. The ancients had been master craftsmen. The traceries like lace that spread out from the top of each pillar were actually carvings that were deeper than his hand was long, and many were still intact. "You have kept your trust all these years. You were abandoned, unwanted. Now you belong to me. I belong here!" he cried to the empty ceilings. His voice echoed away into whispers. By then, Nemeth had turned to making his new realm comfortable.

With an act of will he restored the stones using their old runes, which he could see almost superimposed upon the runes the way they stood. He held the book to his chest and watched while the blocks and sheets of unimaginable weight glided slowly around him. Row after row relaid themselves, crunching into place as the mortar, long crumbled to dust, packed itself into the crevices and filled in behind with plaster. Shadows crept from wall to wall, but Nemeth still watched the past revive itself. More dust flew up in spirals, repainting the frescoes and gilding the traceries around high, pointed windows that filled again with colored glass. Banners dropped from the ceiling. He did not recognize most of the devices. The lordlings who had earned them were long dead and forgotten.

Above the rear wall of the chamber, the ancient standard of the Orontae kings started to form. Nemeth dismissed it with an angry wave. He would not fly the cursed Orontavian flag. They no longer deserved that. He would make his own. His standard would show the beloved book in all its beauty. He forced the particles of the discarded flag to become a banner, ivory white for the parchment, with the outline of the book picked out in gold. It was a shame none would ever see it but him. He rebuilt the grand doors, shining, coppery wood bound with bronze polished to a bright gold. He caused them to remain open so he could see the country.

From the dust that was all that was left of all the palace furnishings, he restored to existence chairs, tables, sculptures, tapestries, carpets, and upon the latter a line of thrones that arose nearly in the center of the room. No humans had left their dust in this place. They had all departed alive and in peace. Nemeth was glad. He wanted to be alone with the book and his intentions.

The seven white thrones had been carved of a pure white wood whose grain was finer than skin. The backs rose into fanciful flourishes as though they had been drawn by a master scribe's pen along the side of a manuscript page instead of a carpenter's plane. Nemeth chose the center seat. It had been the first king's. It would not be his seat, though. He made it rebuild itself as a raised table for the book, and settled his precious burden onto it. He was glad to give it pride of place. The seat to its right was his. He felt humble and small as he took it. His ancestors had bowed down before it.

"Now," he said, turning to the book. He held his breath. The book seemed to know exactly what he wanted. It spun under his hands until it revealed its chosen page.

It was filled with but a single rune. In the archaic tongue, it read, "The Land of Orontae, which Comprises of its Diverse Parts . . ." Lovingly, Nemeth traced its outlines, which showed the entire country in a single symbol: every person, every horse, every acre of land. Such was the skill of the long-lost Shining Ones that he could almost see them in motion, going about the day's tasks, all unaware that they were being watched from above. It would be wrong to use this one, for where he stood was one of Orontae's diverse parts, and he wanted to enjoy his revenge, for a while at least. He unrolled the book farther, to where the book began to enumerate each of the geographical elements. Every mountain had its illustration, as did every river and every tree. It was the book's delightful magic that he could hold the scroll under his arm, yet it had an infinite number of pages, each describing a nearly infinite number of items.

He surveyed each feature with a delighted interest, as if he was sightseeing. Orontae was a handsome country, with picturesque rivers, broad valleys and forests, all surrounded by its share of the ring of mountains that protected the three noble kingdoms. He ran his finger over the rune that depicted the valley at the front of the old castle. That would be a good demonstration that he could see with his own human eyes, not his mind's eye.

Nemeth hesitated, then laid his hands on the edge of the page. He hated to think of what he was about to do. It was sacrilege to harm something so beautiful, but he had no choice.

"I am so sorry," he whispered. He tore out the rune and held it in his fingers. It seemed to pulsate, shocked, like a heart torn out of a living body. He felt like weeping, but he could not stop now. He kept hearing the derisive voice of Soliandur in his mind. His need for vengeance overwhelmed his sorrow and shock. It would not go away until the treacherous king was dead. "*Tal.*"

The fragment of parchment and the rune upon it burst into flames. Nemeth watched it burn almost all the way to his fingertips, then dropped it to the floor, where it smoldered to black ash. He sat and stared at the gap in the page, the perfect page, and felt as if he had ripped out his own heart and was bleeding into his lap. He loved the book, and he had hurt it. Tears dripped down his cheeks.

Beyond the doors, rumbling commenced. Nemeth gathered up the book and walked out upon the courtyard to watch.

In the valley below the lowest of the six sets of gates, the ground was heaving. Trees rocked and bounced until they fell over. Cracks opened in the earth all the way around the valley to the feet of the hills on either side. Suddenly, Nemeth felt an outrush of hot power that blew back his thinning hair and plastered his robes against him. He spun and crouched to protect the precious book in his arms. Blazing arms of fire surrounded him but did not consume him.

When he turned around again to look, the grass and trees were gone, as had the earth for yards beneath them. Fine ash filled the air. The blackened, raw stone edges of this new chasm seeped with water from a half-dozen interrupted underground streams. Nemeth looked down at it, disappointed. He thought that if he destroyed the valley that the land would wash in on either side like waves filling a trough. It had not. He would have to do that himself. He looked down at the book in dismay.

"I thought you were my ally!" he shouted.

It did not answer. He carried it back inside to decide what he must do to make the rest of Orontae disappear.

Chapter Thirty

he white horse was waiting for Magpie in the courtyard. It was so well trained that the reins lay on its neck yet it did not move a muscle until he stepped up into its plain black saddle and touched his heels to its sides. He wished he could have been riding Tessera, but the skewbald mare had been stabled out of the way, possibly even under lock and key, to keep him from indulging the fancy.

Magpie trotted out, the shaded robe flapping around his shoulders. He was not at all surprised to note that peddlers had set up their wares on either side of the road that led from the castle to the temple, all the better to catch people who might want to mark the occasion, this regal and sacred event, by putting a couple of coins into the hands of crafters who had made souvenirs to commemorate the day. There were cloths, hastily and badly embroidered, with his name, Inbecca's, and the date.

In fact, the woman behind one of the trestle tables was still sewing another cloth on a treadle-driven machine as he passed.

He thought the greatest piece of cheek was the peddler who was selling rabbits with the bride's and groom's names painted upon each one, depending upon gender, of course. The gesture was obviously meant to wish them fertility and a long happy life together. The notion made him grin. Still, he was a king's son, and speculating upon the fruits of their love seemed more forward than usual. He made a mental note to send one of the servants back to buy all of the rabbits before Inbecca saw them. He intended to free them if they were wild caught, or bring them to the palace kitchen yard as company for the chickens and geese if they were domesticated.

In spite of his reluctance about rites and ceremonies, Magpie loved the old temple. It genuinely felt as if it had been built on a holy spot. The temple occupied a raised oval of land on a tortoise-shaped hill, the highest occupied point in the kingdom, just slightly higher than the castle itself. It was lower than the original castle, with which it also was aligned. The old castle had been unoccupied for thousands of years, ever since the population of Orontae had outgrown the arable land in the valleys below it between the bands of mountains to the north, and they had gained access to better farmlands, those which he could see spread around him like a green-and-gold quilt.

As youths he, Benarelidur, and Ganidur had often explored the ruin, before Bena got to be so officious. It was more than two hundred leagues away, behind the first low crest of mountains, beneath the crest of the volcanic peaks that still smoked now and again. In the history, that valley was supposed to have been where humanity arose in the beginning of time, but Magpie suggested that perhaps it was the first safe place that humankind found to raise children and crops, away from the terrible beasts that threatened them in the more open countryside. The other two noble kingdoms also laid claim to the origin of humankind. Now he had to consider the elves' claim, so Magpie had to admit he did not know at all what was really true.

His horse blew through its nostrils as it began the long climb up the steep slope of the temple hill. The path had been strewn with white flowers. He hated to scatter them before his bride arrived to see how pretty it looked, but there was no safe way to avoid them. It was his task to mount to the temple alone. No doubt more servants, or townsfolk would be along to strew more appropriate flowers once he had passed.

He guessed that the flower-scatterers were concealed in the woods that rose on either side of the wide, paved road.

The temple, devoted to Mother Nature and Father Time, the forces of nature, was a tall, gorgeous structure of white, glistening granite that stood a hundred feet tall at its peak. Taller temples had been built across the land, but none had so magnificent or so holy a setting.

The earliest decorations on the temple walls were primitive and painted, which had always puzzled him, since the makers clearly knew how to make something beautiful, with the angles that caught the rising and setting sun of each major seasonal change. Perhaps they weren't human as he knew humans in the present day. That observation had often gotten him a clout from Bena, who was tired of hearing that kind of blasphemy from his indiscreet youngest brother. In their language, Nature and Time were also known as Ahmah and Abbah. In Inbecca's, they were Breetah and Huwer, two names he needed to begin getting used to for his future life. In Halcot's land they had other names, and he bet that in the Quarters the little smallfolk called their creators something different yet. But Magpie knew they were all the same, for how could Time and Nature be anything else? No statues had been made of them, for it was considered presumptuous to try and give a single face to the two avatars, but sculptors had filled the formal gardens around the spirelike building with perfect images in stone, wood, and metal of Their creations: birds, animals, trees, fruit, fish, and, of course, humans. Magpie glanced to his left for his favorite, a woven stone arbor of roses, among which real roses intertwined in season. It was full of red blossoms, which Magpie took as a good sign for his betrothal.

The temple was virtually empty when he arrived there. He had a rare chance to admire the beauty of the interior space. From a polished stone floor to the arching ribs of the ceiling, the temple formed a gently rounded teardrop. The pillars supporting the roof were carved in the semblance of oak trees, complete to gilded acorns peeping out from between the leaves. Between the buttresses of the walls were niches dedicated by past kings and queens of Orontae for favors such as victory in battle, good harvest, or the safe delivery of children. Vases of flowers and garlands of faded ribbon decorated these small altars, and plaques of every material and nearly every size climbed the walls for twenty feet above them, thanking the Mother and Father for their blessings. Above the dedications, colored windows reached another twenty feet. These were depictions of beauties of nature, such as fields of wheat, flowers native to Orontae, deer and wolves, wild birds, and domestic animals. Magpie had always been fascinated by the two windows nearest the altar, which were dark blue glass speckled with silver-and-gold glass constellations and comets. Behind the altar itself, the wall was one enormous window, crystal clear to allow the congregation to see the natural countryside beyond.

For the day's celebration, thus far only the long wooden seats for the guests and the altar were in place, and, just inside the door, two pairs of shoes, green for Inbecca, and black for him. He changed out of the brand-new shoes he had donned at home, and slipped into the new pair. It was another part of the tradition. New shoes, never worn anywhere else, were to indicate the promise never having been made by him to anyone else in his life, to tread life's path with this one woman. He knew, with deep happiness, that he would like nothing better. He hoped that she thought so, too. He was concerned, during the time they had spent together after his return, that her aunt had gained her trust, and was undermining her interest in the upcoming marriage.

The tradition was for the groom, the personification of Father Time, to stand vigil before the ceremony as the temple was decked out, as if the origins of life were going on around him, under his aegis. It seemed silly to be doing it now, when the same procedure would be repeated all over again at the time they married, but it was tradition. He was supposed to be left alone, but in practice, as long as he did not stir from his position, friends and guests often came up to pass the time with him until the bride's party arrived at the temple.

Two acolytes arrived and spread a great cloth over the altar. It was green on the right side and black and white on the left. A third acolyte arrived with the Book of Beginnings. He wondered if the book on the altar was modeled after the Great Book that Olen had sent them out to find, or the other way around, and wondered what the priests would say if he asked them such a question. He wondered if any of the runes inside it were the same, if they had the power of creation that the Great Book did. Perhaps the scroll they sought was the origin, the inspiration, for the book of Time and Nature. Since he was on vigil, no one was supposed to speak to him. He had all the time in the world with his own thoughts.

Magpie had always thought it was a trifle odd that he never felt as if he belonged anywhere within the kingdom or anywhere else that he rode. The fault was not in any of the places; it was in himself. That was the true answer. One piece of irony pleased him greatly: in his black-and-white robe he was finally dressed like his chosen namesake, the magpie. He had always liked shiny things, and talking, and his brothers had tried to tell him not to sing because he had no more voice than the strutting bird. It was not true, of course, and in the days that the court lutenist still had an ear and a voice, he had taught Magpie to play the jitar in its many modes—plaintive, martial, merry, moody, teaching—and been glad of the pupil. When he had gone to his father to offer to gather information during the war it had been with this persona in mind, and since it was all over he'd found other uses for the traveling minstrel, preferring it to his dull and unloved persona of the unwanted third prince. No, that wasn't true; his mother loved all of her children. His father dutifully cared for Bena, his heir, and you could not help but like big, blustery, friendly Ganidur, but difficult Eremilandur, with his friends among the poachers, the craftsmen, and the herb women, who said what he liked, was more likely to be dismissed as lacking in dignity and consigned to scorn. Soliandur would not admit he would be glad to have the boy out from under his feet, but Magpie could tell he was.

Magpie knew a legend; he'd sung it often enough—that humanity had arisen in the land that now comprised the three noble kingdoms. The other races had, too.

In the beginning, there was supposedly only that one island of land, and that other lands rose up around it, and in so pressing against it, created the mountains that now ringed the kingdoms, until the rest of the world was made. Now, this sounded like a pretty conceit, as far as Magpie could tell, but it made good telling. At the north the humans arose. At the south the elves. At the east and west were the centaurs and dwarves. Somewhere in between the werewolves and smallfolk made their homes. The plains and the rivers within the circle were meant for them to divide and live in harmony. But of course, in the telling of the tale, relationships among the races deteriorated more and more, until only the human beings were left. And the elves moved into the forests. The dwarves moved underground. The undines slipped into the rivers, lakes, and oceans. And the smallfolk moved away entirely. And the centaurs merely tolerated human beings. And usually after a rousing rendition of this legend, he could count on a big horn of ale or good wine, and a gold coin to go away with.

Personally, he thought the notion that the elves had made humans as a joke remarkably funny, but he'd surely be shown the door of a pub instead of getting rewarded for telling the tale. What a pity.

Ahead of him, the green woolly mountains, the Old Man's Shoulders—though properly it should have been Old Men, for the hunched, rounded, knobbly peaks were numerous—were the near ones, probably the oldest, and the most worn down. He had to admit it did look like a concatenation of elders having a natter about the uselessness of the younger generation. Behind them, and a considerable way across a fern-filled valley rose the volcanic mountains, which were the product of the continent butting up against the old piece of land, if the legend had any basis in truth at all. The Scapes sent high tors reaching up to protect the ancient volcanic cones in their midst.

On the other side was another range, but that one could not be seen. Those were known as the Necklace. If anything had been meddled with by the Makers, it was the Necklace Mountains, for they were just too regular, like pearls on a string, to be natural. But that was questioning the forces of nature, and he must not do that, not here in the center of their worship. Behind those were the Combs, the narrow peaks that had been raddled by the endless falls of rain until they were thin ridges. Many avalanches occurred in that area. But it was the nearest two ranges that held the history of his people. In between the volcanoes and the woolly hills were the mountains where the first human fastness, the first kingdom, or at least the first capital of Orontae had been founded.

The temple itself had been oriented in the direction of Oron Castle, and the new castle had been fixed to align with both of the older build-ings. On a very clear day like this one you could just see the faint gleam from the remains of a flagpole that had been placed on the peak a hun-dred years ago by an ancestor of his who thought he would restore the old capital. But it proved to be too far from where the center of modern life ran. It was hundreds of miles distant, but with the trick of the light in the clear air and, as his philosopher-tutor had informed him, the lens of hot air rising from the volcanic cracks, it looked as though it was much closer. He had often thought of going back and putting a flag at the top of that flagpole, perhaps one of bright red. Then he'd come back to the temple and see how it looked from where he stood now. One day he would do it. He and Inbecca could go. It would be an adventure for her, and a chance for her to see his family's ancient holding.

Out in the distance, the volcanoes behind the two rows of mountains began to tremble, their movement visible even at this distance, a little imperceptively. The clouds of steam started to rise. How marvelous! There was going to be an eruption in honor of his betrothal. It seemed appropriate somehow. He wondered what symbolism the priests and In-becca's unspeakable aunt would glean from the phenomenon.

A fourth acolyte gave him a shy smile as he passed, carrying a gold-trimmed tray upon which reposed the tokens of the elements: a crystal bowl of water rimmed with gold and silver; a crystal box containing nothing at all, which was meant to represent air; and a very beautiful porcelain bowl that held a miniature garden, the semblance of earth; a sand painting on the top a special effort for the bride and groom. He caught a glimpse of the design as it went by, and approved of it. The image of tiger lilies was quite beautiful. No expense had been spared for the service or the celebration that would follow. The flask that represented spirit was of precious blue glass. The urn that produced fire—he had no idea how it worked. He assumed there was a trick to it. It was entirely possible that it did work by magic, though the priests surely called it something else. He had never managed to get one of the priests to tell him. He assumed that it was a secret protected by oath.

The priests arrived and began to set the objects on the altar to suit themselves. The female priest was an amply built woman of about forty with long, dark hair worn unbound under a wreath of holly. She had several children, two of whom were acolytes. Magpie wasn't sure which of the large cadre they were. The old priest gave him a look with one raised eyebrow that was half-reproof. He and the priestess were clad in simple white robes, belted with braided sashes of white, black, and green silk. They also wore necklaces, his of gold, the imperishable symbol of the Father, and hers of silver, to show the evolving nature of the Mother.

Magpie's foot went to sleep. He shifted to the other for a while.

If only the things that Olen had said about the book were true, and that centaurs were the product of humans meddling with horses, and that smallfolk were the product of humans and he could not guess what—shrubs, or rabbits, some other species that would make them as little as Tildi, and with those ears. Werewolves were obvious, as were mermaids and Tritons. And dwarves might be the product of human beings and stone, he assumed. Then were the beasts of legend something to do with those Makers? Did they use the great powers at their disposal to make them?

He knew there were symbols that were represented on the banners and badges of kingdoms and noble households that showed such things as griffins, gryphons who were half lion, half eagle; Pegasi; hippocampi; and all other manner of combined beasts that did not exist as far as he knew. He had never seen one, in all his many travels, and he knew no one else who had seen one, either, yet all the human combinations still existed. All he could assume was that the beasts who had been mutated and perverted either warred with themselves, unable to reconcile their dual identities, fought with other creatures and destroyed themselves, or merely realized that they were abominations and destroyed themselves or let themselves die out. They had more sense than the human combinations. He could tell from what Rin said that the centaurs considered the alteration to have been an abomination.

Right here, now, in front of the altar of Nature, he apologized on behalf of his species. Humans had a great sense of self-preservation. No matter what shape they took, they didn't want to sacrifice their own existence. That tendency must have rubbed off on the animals with whom the Creators blended their own kind. He wondered if it was an improvement or not.

Were there other human combinations that unaltered humans never saw, such as a half-human, half-mole, who lived deep underground, even below the mountain fortresses of the dwarves? Did they have sleepy, light-sensitive eyes and huge digging hands? Smallfolk were curious enough. He wiggled his numb foot inside his shoe and wondered what it would be like to be without toes. The smallfolk delegation arrived and came up to bow to him. He bowed back, pleased. They all looked like Tildi's kin, with curly hair and big brown eyes, as if they were solemn children. He thought of asking them technical questions about how they walked, then decided not to. They might take offense, and of all days he wished to please his father, not annoy him. He smiled, and got more grave bows. Were all smallfolk so humorless except for Tildi? He guessed that she was the exception to many rules. He had to think about it for a moment. He'd been in the Quarters several times over the last few years. Perhaps they were, perhaps they were not. They had a great sense of occasion, much more than he did, and were sober when they were supposed to be.

The acolytes were taking a long time to get everything ready. Two of the youngest, charged with filling the lamps that stood at the end of each aisle, seemed to be having trouble with the jar of oil. A trifle bored, Magpie fixed his eyes upon the mountains in the distance. The day was beautiful, a tribute to Inbecca's beauty. He started to compose a poem on the subject that he might set to music.

"Mmm, nipped out for a minute, did he?" a voice inquired. Magpie slid his eyes sideways. King Halcot, dressed in a velvet tunic of red and white, sidled up to stand beside Magpie.

Magpie turned to him, and was rewarded with an indulgent smile. Halcot had taken Hawarti's news very well. He didn't seem to be angry or disappointed in Magpie. What a relief! He offered the visitor a comradely grin. "Welcome, my lord. Who nipped out?"

"Well, the prince, of course," Halcot said. "Don't be a mountebank here in the temple. Show some respect for the forces of Creation."

"Of course, my lord," Magpie said, and straightened his back.

"I mean, you must be keeping his spot warm while he went off for a glass of resolve-stiffener, eh?" Halcot pantomimed taking a drink. "Or are you dressed up like that as a joke to surprise him?" He turned to glance around the vast chamber. "What's he look like? I'll tell you if he's coming."

Magpie's heart slid out of his chest and down into his ornate shoes. Hawarti must have missed speaking with Halcot. He *didn't* know. There was no avoiding the subject now. Magpie had to handle the matter by himself, without fuss. He hoped that he could. From the depths of his soul he drew a calm demeanor.

"Did you . . . did you stop at the castle this morning, my lord?"

"No, curse it," Halcot said, brushing at his sleeves. "We had trouble above the ford. The track was muddy—too much rain. The wettest summer I can recall in all my years. We were going to be late, so I directed the train to come directly here to the temple. My grooms are delivering our luggage to the steward at the palace. What business is it of yours?"

"My business is as your host, my lord," Magpie said very carefully. "I'm dressed up this way, as you noted, for the very good reason that I am the affianced awaiting my bride. I'm not holding anyone's place but my own."

Halcot frowned, engaged in mental calculus. "But your name is Magpie."

"It's not my real name, sir. I'm Eremilandur, third son of Soliandur. I welcome you here in the name of my father."

The equation resolved itself in a lightning flash of enlightenment. Halcot's eyes blazed with anger.

"What? This is an outrage!"

Magpie sighed and bowed his head. "It was not meant to be, sir. My father's minister was meant to speak to you about me when you arrived today."

"To let me get all the way here to Orontae, then discover that the minstrel that I allowed into my confidence for the last five years was the son of my enemy? Surely I was owed an explanation long ago!"

"Indeed you were, my lord, but was there ever a good time to bring up such a matter?" Magpie asked. "If I had come to you to make such a confession, you might not have believed me—or I might have ended up in your dungeons for what remained of my life."

"It would have been short and painful," Halcot said through his teeth. "*Why* was this secret kept so long?"

Magpie glanced at the other guests milling about the echoing chamber, and kept his voice low. "My lord, my involvement in the war effort was known to only three others, my father, the prime minister, and the royal wizard. My father wanted to forget about all the matters concerning the war as quickly as possible once it was over, and the matter was pushed aside, but it can be ignored no longer. This event is an affair of state. You must, of course, be invited to the betrothal of a royal prince, and you must, of course, attend. I knew it would be too grave a shock for you to arrive here without being given the full particulars. Lord Hawarti was supposed to inform you before you saw me here, and answer any questions you had. As you might recall, I did not attend the signing of the documents of surrender two years ago. My presence, and the ensuing explanations, might have opened the hostilities all over again."

"I doubt it," Halcot spat out. "It was all over, and we were the victors."

"Funny," Magpie said, raising his eyebrows. "I was under the apprehension that we were. After all, you are the one paying my father tribute."

"Hah! I'm paying less in tribute a year than I would pay for a month's worth of keeping my men under arms. But you," Halcot said, studying him intently. "You're a puzzle. Perhaps I should demand your head as a condition of continuing to send your father his tribute."

Magpie contrived to look bored. "As you will. My father would probably be glad to send it to you."

Halcot's whisper was harsh with hatred. "You traitor! You pretended to be friendly. All those songs you sang for me, the counsel you gave. All a charade while you spied upon me!"

"No. The songs were a genuine tribute to a king I felt was doing his best for his country and his people, and I never gave you bad advice," Magpie said. He felt a pain in his ribs. He looked down. Halcot had drawn his dagger and held it among the folds of Magpie's elaborate clothes. Halcot leaned a trifle closer, and a hot drop of blood ran down

Magpie's belly. The king was going to kill him. He was surely justified. But the war was over. He met the glaring blue eyes straightforwardly. "You may not believe me, sir, but it's true. I had respect for you, and I still do. To disrupt your effort was not my job. I was there to gather information, and I did. I served my father, my king, and my country. I will never be sorry for that. I am not a traitor to you. I gave you comfort when I thought you needed it. I hope it helped."

Halcot's face turned red. "You abused my hospitality, whelp. Why should I not push this blade into your heart and leave you for your bride-to-be to find?"

"I did, but consider: you won. We both know it. You won the war in all but name. Everything that I did was to no moment. I apologize for eating your bread and salt under false pretenses, but it *was* war."

"I should kill you."

Magpie felt the point dig deeper, and tried not to wince. "Go ahead. My father would thank you if you went ahead. Inbecca will get over me. She is worthy of better."

Halcot looked down at the concealed knife as if surprised it was there, and the pressure eased. "I do believe that you're telling me the truth. Soliandur would rather see you die?"

The truth hurt him more than the blade. "Oh, I am, my lord. Punish me if you will, in the name of your dignity. I do not care, but spare my father the reason, will you? Tell him you did it because I annoyed you. That's true, isn't it? He's suffered enough."

"Damn it, I know that!" Halcot snarled. "What I wouldn't give to go back . . . but it cannot be done."

The king walked a pace away, spun on his heel, and looked at him. "You don't lack courage, I'll give you that. No one who walked where you did could be a coward. By Death himself, I believe you would have let the knife slip in and died without uttering a sound, wouldn't you?"

It was then he noticed Magpie's pained expression, and glanced down at the silk robe, which was matted and stained. The king was immediately contrite.

"Have I injured you?"

"Far less than I've deserved at your hand, my lord," Magpie said flippantly. "Luckily it is in the black section of the robe. No one will see."

Halcot let out a short bark of laughter. "You young ass!" He paused to study Magpie. "I always liked you, you know. Your witty tongue brought some merriment into my household during some dark days."

Magpie gave him a slight bow. "I did know. You honored me by your regard, sir."

"Stop talking like a courtier. You are a prince, and for your father's sake, you ought to act like one, today of all days." Halcot's creased brow drew down thoughtfully. "I hardly remember you, though I am sure I met you as a child. I know the whole brood used to come in Soliandur's train when he visited me. Which one were you?"

Where he was willing to accept death in service to his country in war, Magpie was abashed to admit childhood sins. "I . . . er, I'm the one who broke the glass Tillerton chandelier in the great hall trying to get your son Stalcot to swing from it."

Halcot's eyebrows flew up, compressing the lines into a single crease. "You puppy! He said *he* broke it."

Magpie smiled at the thought of his long-ago friend. "Call it a conspiracy of silence between princes. We nobly took the blame for each another's sins, but that time it *was* my fault."

"Did he know you were spying on me?"

"I think he saw me once in my minstrel guise, with these streaks in my hair, but for old time's sake he passed me by, and did not ask for an explanation of my presence. I never involved him, and I tried to stay out of his way thereafter. Don't blame him."

Halcot paused for a long time, then met Magpie's eyes squarely. "I cannot forgive what has gone before."

Magpie bowed his head. "No. I couldn't ask that. But we are allies now, are we not?" He nodded toward the book on the altar. It greatly resembled the image of the Great Book Olen had shown them in his vision.

"Death take it, we are," Halcot said with a sigh. "Let that do as a place to build anew. Have you had any sniff of the damned thing? I've not seen a sign of it myself across my entire kingdom, and I hope I never do."

"Nor I," Magpie assured him. "Not in these many weeks. I will go on looking until we get word that the thief has been stopped."

"It's an affair for wizards, that's what I think," Halcot said dismissively. "Er . . . have you . . . I wonder, have you chosen a place to visit for your honeymoon? Many of my kinsmen keep good tables, and they would be glad to offer a villa in a handsome setting for a month's sojourn."

Magpie took a deep breath, even though it hurt. He had genuinely thought that he was going to die, and he had been given a reprieve. The relief was so great he could have laughed or cried. Halcot had shown the quality of his royal lineage and not only gave him his life back, he was offering him a kind of friendship. It was more than he deserved, and much more than his own father would offer an enemy in similar circumstances. He bowed.

"You are most kind, my lord. I shall put the suggestion to my bride. I believe she should choose where we go."

Halcot nodded, pursing his lips. "Wise, very wise. It makes for a more peaceful wedded life. Well, I'm dry from my long ride. You cannot leave your vigil. Do you care for a glass of wine? Oh, I am forgetting the fast. Forgive me."

Smiling, Magpie shook his head. "Enjoy it. My father keeps an excellent cellar."

"Yes, the vineyards of Persham Province are well known across the continent. Excuse me."

Laying his hand briefly on the young man's shoulder, Halcot withdrew.

Magpie let out a huge breath. He felt as though he had been given life anew. He vowed that from that very moment he would devote it to making Inbecca happy. Heaven knew she deserved better than she had had from him. He would also try more diligently to please his father, if that was at all possible. Perhaps grandchildren would soften the old man's heart. In the meanwhile, he could look forward to a grand feast, with dancing, some indelicate toasts to the bride, and plenty of slurs against Magpie's character, but he didn't mind a bit. He had a future to look forward to now.

Chapter Thirty-one

in was much subdued as they rode away
from Penbrake. Tildi had tried consoling
her, but Rin didn't hear a word she had
said. Tildi knew what it felt like to deal
with losses of loved ones, but she had
never killed by accident. All she could do was listen, and hoped her
sympathetic ear would give Rin solace.

"There was nothing else anyone could have done," Serafina kept saying. "They were broken beyond help." That was true, but it didn't make
any of them feel any better. To her credit, the acerbic young woman
healed their injuries, and left them to make their own peace with what
they had just left behind them.

The elves of Penbrake had set about clearing away the dead. Athandis
had led a ritual that reduced the remains of the devastated trees to a fine
black ash. Each of the elves had taken a pinch of ash between their

fingers, closed their eyes to offer a silent prayer and apology, then let it go. Tildi had followed suit, but did not feel any peace come to her. Neither, she suspected, had Rin.

A weather-witch had brought a light breeze that began to whisk away the heaps. By nightfall of the first day, those had been reduced by half. A few elves brought out harps and flutes and played soft music. That, more than anything else, had smoothed away the rough edges of Tildi's mood. She was dealing with twin griefs: those of the death of the trees and the loss of the book. It was so far away. She chafed for the next few days until Edynn declared that they could go on.

Edynn was much better following her rest among the elves. She no longer seemed as weak as she had been since their desperate flight began. The elven healers had clustered around her after the battle. Serafina deferred to them with little grace, but even she could see that they were more helpful to her mother than she had been. Tildi had enjoyed the feeling of the strengthening spells as the energy overspilled into the atmosphere around Edynn. Athandis had given the party a beautiful house formed out of a grand beech tree more than twenty feet across, with wedge-shaped bedrooms above stairs, and a large room in the base with ceilings high enough for Rin to feel comfortable. At first Tildi had felt strangely reluctant to enter into the tree home. She had examined the fear and decided it was groundless, but it was curious, since she had always loved trees, and had lived in Silvertree for months without qualms. Teryn was satisfied because the elves had replenished their supplies and then some, giving them preserved fruits, breads, and meats sufficient to last for a month at least. Tildi fervently hoped that they would not be so long parted from the book.

The book! She jumped, enough so that Rin glanced over her shoulder at her.

"What troubles you, smallfolk?" she asked.

"It's stopped moving," Tildi said eagerly. "The book, I mean. It's halted."

"What's that?" Edynn asked, trotting closer on the air. "He has stopped again?"

"I'm sure of it," Tildi said. "We're getting nearer by the moment."

Teryn circled around to bring the map over for Edynn's examination. The elder wizardess nodded. "It looks as if he has taken refuge in one of the ancient places. We may truly be dealing with one of the Shining Ones."

"I thought so," Serafina said, tossing her head with satisfaction.

Tildi didn't care if the young woman had come to the right conclusion. All that mattered was that she, Tildi, was going to be close to the book again. She patted the leaf in her belt pouch. Somehow she must persuade the Maker to let her touch the original. She wondered what kind of refuge Edynn meant. This was mountainous country over which they were flying. The green hills below them were rounded and homey-looking, with blue rivers flowing in between. The rows of stark peaks ahead looked much less of a haven.

A cold power intruded upon her happiness at the same moment a shadow flashed across Rin's back. She looked up, and her heart clenched with fear. A dozen or more winged monsters had come out of nothingness. The largest one shrieked, and the others answered. Tildi hoped never to have heard that cry again.

"Thraik!" Teryn shouted. The captain wheeled her horse in the air and cantered upwards, pulling her bow out of her saddlebag. Morag galloped after her, brandishing his polearm.

But the thraik had other ideas. They zipped easily past Morag's clumsy attempt to flank them, and outflew Teryn's desperate chase. Dropping into a spiral on the tip of one wing, the lord thraik circled down toward Rin.

"Get Tildi away!" Edynn called. She unbound her staff from the side of her saddle, and followed the soldiers. A bolt of white light exploded from the jewel atop her staff. One of the thraik cried out in pain. Serafina threw a ball of red flame that burst into the chest of the nearest beast. Its wings shut and it dropped like a stone through the clouds. Lakanta kicked Melune into a trot and headed directly for the lord thraik, a sturdy club in her hand. "Go!"

"They will not catch us," Rin vowed. "Hold tight, little one."

Tildi buried her head in Rin's mane as the centaur opened up her stride and streaked across the sky. She heard a gargling cry. One of the others had succeeded in wounding a thraik, perhaps mortally. Against the darkness of her closed eyes Tildi saw again the day on which her brothers had died. Teldo had made fire and killed a thraik, perhaps the first time in memory that a smallfolk had managed to destroy one of the winged enemy. Then . . . she opened her eyes with a gasp, unable to bear seeing the nightmare unfold yet again. They had taken her whole family, and now they were coming for her, at last. Tears filled her eyes. She had come so far. Why could they not let her alone?

The lord thraik burst into being immediately before them. Rin let out a yell of surprise and wheeled. Tildi shrieked with fear. It reached for her with curved talons.

"I can strike these without regret," Rin gritted. "Hang on." She planted her forefeet, and kicked out with her rear feet, catching the thraik in its chest. With a thin, tearing cry, it fell a dozen yards before it caught itself and flitted back to them, hissing. "That felt good! Come, child, can you aid our defense? Make fire! Do something!" Rin kicked at the lord thraik. It swiped at her and missed. Rin flicked her tail in derision and drew her whip. "Tildi!"

Tildi tried to pull herself together. She heard the thraiks' death call again and again. Edynn and Serafina must be accounting for some of the others. She must do her part.

"*Ano chnetegh tal,*" she hiccuped. She was almost too afraid to take her hand off Rin's hair, but a thimbleful of green fire erupted among her fingers. She jerked her trembling hand back for fear of setting her friend's mane ablaze. "There, you monster!" she cried, flinging the tiny flame at the lord thraik.

It recoiled like a snake, and the flame missed it, extinguishing on the wind. It glared at Tildi with its dried-blood eyes, and she saw again the rune in them. She now knew what it meant. It sensed the scent of the book on her.

"I don't even have it!" she shouted. "Go away! Leave me alone!"

The thraik screamed back. Others answered.

At that moment, it was struck from both sides by a blaze of white and a blaze of red. It sank, its wings windmilling for purchase on the air.

Rin ran for their lives. Lakanta came up on their flanks, kicking Melune into a gallop for all she was worth.

"We're outnumbered," she panted. "Look!"

Tildi followed her pointing finger. The lord thraik must have called for reinforcements. Dozens of writhing black shapes appeared over their heads. The cry of their master directed them to the fleeing centaur and her passenger.

"We can't fight them all," Lakanta said. "Go down. Now. We can take shelter. Hurry."

Thraik vanished from above. Tildi jumped as three of them appeared all around Rin. One slashed at them with a claw. Bright blood sprang out on Rin's dark skin. Tildi drew her knife and stabbed through the thraik's paw. It recoiled, almost taking her knife out of her hand. It hissed at her, winging close to bite. Rin rammed her shoulder into its neck, and kicked it. Lakanta did her part, smacking whatever part of a thraik that presented itself. The muddy eyes glowing with runes were all around Tildi. She tried to concentrate on making fire, but all she could see was Gosto's limp body as he was carried off into the sky. She stabbed wildly, not caring if she struck anything. The tears were a welcome curtain that shut out the sight of the greasy-skinned monsters.

"Duck!" Serafina's voice called from above them. Red balls of light began to shoot between the defenders and the thraik. The beasts she struck let out agonized cries. The white mare dropped into their midst. Serafina gestured imperiously. "Flee! I will hold them back!"

"Down!" Lakanta insisted again. "Follow me!"

The stout little horse cantered through the air toward the bank of a river. Lakanta landed and beckoned vigorously for Rin to follow her. Screams echoed around them, then receded in the distance. Tildi felt the thump as they hit the ground, but she didn't cease stabbing at her unseen enemies until a hand took the knife away from her, and two strong arms enfolded her. She blinked to clear her eyes, and discovered that they were in a low cavern. The thraik were out of sight.

Rin was holding her as if she was a baby. "Are you better now?"

"I'm sorry," Tildi said, and her voice trembled. She swallowed deeply, trying to get control of herself. "I just feel so small in this world."

"So do we all, child," Lakanta said, leaning over to pat her on the head. "So do we all. You had been holding up so well I had forgotten you're not as old as you act most times, but by the Father, you're just a chick." The two oddly matched females sat with Tildi until she pulled herself together. Tildi reached into her pouch and blotted her eyes with Gosto's cloth. She was grateful for their kindness, and for the small, tangible reminder of her brothers. In a moment she had regained her senses, and regarded her friends with concerned eyes. "Heavens, Rin, you need bandaging."

The centaur looked down at the blood staining her torn blouse, as if surprised to see it. "It's not as bad as it looks." She grimaced as she pressed the brightly colored fabric against the flesh with her palm. "It stings. Their slime feels unclean."

"Where . . . where are we?" Tildi ventured to ask.

"In a cave," Rin said. "Lakanta guided me in here. For what reason I can't guess."

"Getting us past those thraik," the peddler said absently. "Wizards are all very well, but they can't kill all the thraik in the world. They want you desperately, don't they?"

"They want the book," Tildi explained. "I know it now. They think I have it."

Lakanta nodded fiercely. "Well, they won't have you. We'll travel a road they can't find. That is, if I can make someone see some sense."

"Make who?" Edynn's voice echoed behind her. The two wizardesses trotted into the cavern. "The thraik vanished as soon as Tildi did. We are not interesting to them, I see. The theory seems to be proven. It is contact with the book or a copy that fascinates them. Make who? More of your kin?"

Lakanta clicked her tongue. She and Melune disappeared into the gloom ahead of them. All they could hear was her voice as she felt her way along. "Oof! These aren't strictly my kin. Ouch, that stone ought not to be there. Sorry, Melune, dear."

Thin, tearing shadows streamed past Tildi's cheeks and shoulders. She bent and covered her head with both hands.

"Don't worry, child," Rin said with amusement, stepping forward to shield Tildi from the flow. "It's only the bats."

Lakanta kept up a steady chatter in the dark. ". . . Mother and Father help me if I've chosen the wrong sort of cave . . . aha!"

Edynn rode up beside Lakanta and illuminated the jewel at the end of her staff. The white light cast a moonstone glow on a pair of double doors twenty feet high. They were made of bronze and steel, and cast to look like the stone wall of the cavern at a casual glance. Once Tildi examined them more closely, she could see that they were most artfully made, covered with dwarven runes and lightly etched pictures. She touched the image of a fox, so lifelike it seemed as if she was seeing one running away into shadow.

"I've never seen such grand doors," Rin said. Serafina let out a hiss and rode to the centaur's side. She pushed Rin's hand away and applied a handful of warm white light to the long wounds in her flank. "I should never have guessed they were here."

"You never would," Lakanta assured her. "They don't want you to." She rolled off Melune's back and approached the doors. Her knuckles made almost no sound on the metal, so she picked up a stone and knocked again. *Boom, boom, boom.*

The sound seemed to echo deep in the hillside, beyond the doors. *Boom, boom, boom.* They waited.

"It may take a while before someone deigns to answer," Lakanta said. "Make yourselves comfortable."

Rin had just set Tildi down, when the ground began to shake under them. Tildi grabbed for the nearest wall, but it was shaking, too. The vibration was not enough to upset her balance, but it made her feel very uncomfortable. It seemed to go on for a very long time, shaking loose moss and small stones that fell down on them from the cavern roof. Tildi threw her hands over her head to protect it. Was the world coming apart? The horses danced and whinnied in a panic, until Rin and Teryn calmed them. Morag shook his head and tossed it as if he was a nervous steed. Edynn, holding her horse's bridle steady, frowned.

"Is that the dwarves' way of telling us we're not welcome?"

"No," Lakanta said, alarmed. "It's a tremor, but it feels like none I've ever experienced."

An hour or more passed after the earthquake ceased. Once she had gotten over being frightened by the thraiks, Tildi felt sleepy. She sat huddled against the wall while the others chatted in low tones near her. A crunching, creaky sound woke her out of her doze. A bright wedge of light made her blink. The door was open.

A man had appeared in the doorway with a glowing lantern in his hand.

"Hail, cousin!" Lakanta said, going to meet him. Tildi studied him curiously. He was a stocky blond male a quarter the height of the door, with his long hair and beard in braids, just like the kindly peddler who had given her sweets and discussed matters so solemnly with Gosto, yet with a twinkle in his eye. This dwarf had no twinkle for them. He seemed angry to see them, and especially Lakanta.

"You cannot enter here," he said, waving a hand sharply. "Go away. Find another road."

"Now, cousin," Lakanta said smoothly, moving closer so that he couldn't shut the door without catching her in it. "Let us speak privately with each other."

"We have nothing to say, *towa-chira*." Tildi perked up her ears at the unknown word, and stored it up to ask about later. Lakanta seemed taken aback by it, but perservered.

"We can help one another. You don't want our people to suffer because you were too stubborn to listen. Just a few moments of your time."

"Well?" the dwarf asked peevishly. He set the lantern down at his feet. She leaned toward him, and they fell into conference. They resembled each other so closely that Tildi couldn't understand why the man didn't acknowledge Lakanta as his kin.

Even Tildi's sensitive hearing was not keen enough to pick up more than a few words as the peddler bent all her skills of persuasion upon the door warden. More than once they glanced over in her direction as she heard Lakanta say something about ". . . only guide who can follow. . . ."

"Doesn't matter," the dwarf declared aloud, folding his arms. He leaned forward so Lakanta was pushed back into the cave.

"Please," Edynn said, coming forward to appeal to the little man. She crouched so she was at eye level with him. "Our path above is cut off by the thraik. They cannot follow us here."

"That's right," Lakanta said. "That's why you must help us."

The dwarf glared at both of them, and had an extra glare leftover for Tildi. "I don't see the connection it has to us. We like our privacy, and you are interfering with it."

Lakanta shook a finger under his nose. "Fool! If we don't live to catch up with this wizard, then we can't stop the trouble he's causing! That was no ordinary earthquake, and you know it."

The dwarf rocked back on his heels for a moment and stroked his braided beard. "We've been discussing it. You may be right. The timing's all wrong."

"I know I am. When's the next earth tremor due in these parts?"

"Not for a year, and nothing of this magnitude for at least five."

"You know when earthquakes come?" Serafina asked, surprised. "Without magic?"

"We are kin to the earth," the dwarf said with dignity. "I have no need of your wizard tricks. I can feel the pulses in my bones. Very well. You may go through. Show me where you're going. I will arrange a path. You will stick to it, you understand? One deviation, and you can discuss your nosiness with the thraik."

"We will obey your strictures," Edynn said, bowing humbly. "We will need water. I apologize for asking this further favor. And fodder for our horses. You gave me hospitality once, long ago. I regret troubling you now, but so much is at stake. I hope you will understand."

The dwarf turned a speculative blue eye upon her, and studied her for some time. His tone was much mollified when he spoke again.

"There will be provisions. You will want for nothing. Wait here. I must make arrangements."

He took the map from Teryn and shooed Lakanta back. Edynn stood up. The dwarf pulled the door to. It boomed shut.

"Darkness!" Morag exclaimed. He started casting about. "The light is gone! It's gone!"

He turned about. The small spot of light that was the cave entrance caught his eye, and he sprinted toward it.

"You can't go out there!" Teryn said, springing after him at once. "Morag! Attention! That's an order! The thraiks will come back! Morag!"

Tildi looked after him sadly. Edynn came and rested her hand on Tildi's shoulder. "It is a great pity. Serafina and I have tried many means to cure him, but it is beyond us."

Teryn finally got the man to calm down and return to his place by the horses, and lit a lantern to give him something to concentrate upon. He was still wild-eyed by the time the door swung open again. Tildi could see the blue-eyed madness was on him.

"Don't anger our hosts," Lakanta warned him.

"I'm doing all I can with him," Teryn snapped, then recovered herself. Her look was now one of open appeal. "He is harmless to others, peddler. He is only a threat to himself. I, we, beg for your understanding."

"All right," Lakanta said, "but mind you keep a close tether on him. I've no wish to expose Tildi to those bat-winged monstrosities again. I told you she was in love with him," she said in a low voice to Tildi. Teryn's spine stiffened at the over-loud whisper. As they led their steeds over the threshold into darkness, they could both hear the soldier whimpering quietly to himself.

The lack of sight only lasted a short distance as the party felt their way down a smooth stone ramp. Lamps bloomed into a golden glow, first near to them, then more and more of them reaching out to light an infinity of darkness.

Tildi caught her breath as she realized that what she thought was a corridor was a vast hall. Silvertree was a small stick of wood compared with this endless gallery of carved pillars. Mansions and temples large enough to cover a city block in Overhill were hundreds of feet lower the height than the ceiling. There were no small buildings at all. Every dwarf must live in a palace. The masons and stonecarvers had to have hollowed out the entire hill, and more beside. Fanciful towers had been carved according to the markings in the stone itself, so that there were soaring turrets, with each floor a different hue. What looked like lace on the ceiling was a network of paths and roadways so far above their heads they did not look wide enough for a person to walk upon, but in proportion must be suitable for a cart and horses. A complicated and beautiful fountain of smooth red stone burbled gently in the square below where the company stood, its leaping waters catching and tossing the white lights around it.

The scratchings on the bronze door had only implied the skill of artists who had been allowed free rein of their imagination and skill within the doors that only dwarves would ever see. On the walls of these vast buildings were carved murals, ten times life-size, depicted dwarves engaged in their daily life: mining, carving, gem-cutting, cooking, caring for children, defeating elves and humans in war, administering law. The colors used to paint them were those that could be produced by stone pigments, but those included brilliant blues and greens, rusty reds, ochre of every shade, as well as pure white and black, and all ornamented by precious metals and stones. Tildi was enchanted by it all. The odd thing was that she couldn't see a single living person or animal anywhere. Even the door warden was nowhere in sight. At their feet was the discarded map, the single golden dot glowing almost as brightly as the dwarf lights. Teryn gathered it up.

"This dwarf hollow is more magnificent than I dared dream," Rin said. "It is bigger than some of the kingdoms in the open air! Happy is the day that gave us this opportunity. What a beautiful home your cousins have, Lakanta."

Glittering red lights winked into view, beginning at their right and left.

"We must not linger," Lakanta said hastily. "That's our guide. Follow me."

She swung up into Melune's saddle and guided the stout little horse down the ramp into the city. They were halfway down when the land began to shake again. The horses staggered from side to side. Tildi grabbed hold of Rin's shoulders in alarm.

"Mother and Father!" Lakanta exclaimed. "What is he *doing* up there?"

Chapter Thirty-two

 hustle and bustle at the rear of the temple told Magpie that Inbecca and her family had arrived. The assembled guests let out coos and exclamations of pleasure. He did not turn around. He was supposed to glimpse her for the first time as she came up to join him. The delicate strains of harp music began, accompanied by the rustle of several hundred people in their finest clothes sitting down. He held himself still, hardly daring to breathe, as he felt Inbecca approach him on silent feet and tuck her hand into his arm. At that moment he turned to behold her, and his heart pounded loud enough to deafen him.

She was as beautiful as Mother Nature herself must have been on that first day of Creation. Her deeply cut dress of purest emerald-green made her sea-colored eyes the color of beech leaves. Her cheeks were slightly flushed under her rouge, but she needed no cosmetics to enhance her beauty. Her skin was as pure and soft as silk. He had the urge to stroke her cheek and feel her press it against his hand. All her jewelery was of living materials. She had earrings and a necklace of pearl and amber, as well as ivory and amber bangles around her slender wrists. The silken belt around her waist gleamed with more pearls sewn into patterns for the Mother and for the country of Levrenn. Magpie was overwhelmed by longing and caring. He wanted to tell her how much he loved her, and how beautiful she was, but he was all too aware that the entire temple was waiting for them to begin.

Folding her hand into his, he guided her forward a few steps, to the end of the carpet of flowers laid down for them. On his right were her parents, and on her left, his. His mother was smiling with tears standing in her eyes. His father looked, well, not disapproving, which was all Magpie could wish under the circumstances. Inbecca's magnificent mother, Queen Kaythira, sat at the end of the row. She was an older, more dignified version of Inbecca, with a touch of white just beginning at the temples of her coiffed chestnut hair. The train of her ochre-and-white dress was sewn with her royal device, the tiger. She gave him a warm, loving look, but with a warning in it, as fierce as her kingdom's guardian. He knew what it meant: *Take care of my daughter.* Magpie intended that with all his heart. Her father, a tall, craggy-faced man with crisp black hair shot with white, held his mouth pursed, trying not to let it be seen that he was crying.

The couple stopped short of the great wooden altar. It was not stone, for it was meant to be made from an element of nature that showed the passage of time to the poor, short-lived human beings who worshiped here. He felt the timelessness of the moment, with everything perfect. He looked across the altar and out over the valley through the crystal window.

"Beloved of Nature and Time, Ahmah and Abbah," the male priest began, as the female priest carried the urn of fire around them, "bless this couple who take the first steps toward thy perfect union." He intoned words so ancient and familiar Magpie didn't have to think about them. The priestess put down the urn and picked up the crystal box of air. Each of the elements was passed around them in turn.

He stared out at the mountains. He stood with Inbecca and said the words, but his mind was suddenly not on his love. The mountains—the Scapes—appeared to be shifting. He felt, rather than heard a rumble of the earth moving. How could that be? Mountains didn't move. Did they?

"Did you see that?" he whispered to Inbecca.

"See what?" she asked impatiently. Magpie looked up and realized everyone, especially his father, was looking at him. He had interrupted the ritual. Magpie offered an apologetic smile to the priests. He must keep his mind on what he was doing. The honor of the kingdom depended upon him there and then.

"Do you, Inbecca, lady of Levrenn, plight your troth to this man, Eremilandur of Orontae, completing the sacred circle of creation with him and him alone, to the continuation of Nature throughout Time?"

Inbecca blushed. "That I do."

"Do you, Eremilandur of Orontae, plight your troth to this woman, Inbecca, lady of Levrenn, completing the sacred circle of creation with her and her alone, to the continuation of Nature throughout Time?"

"That I do."

"Take these rings and hold them in your palm, with her palm covering yours," the female priest began. Magpie felt the weight of the two small circles, gold and silver. "Promise that you will learn to love each another, being true until the day shall come when you will be joined eternally and inseparably as Time and Nature were joined at the beginning of creation. None can exist without the other, and are made complete by the other. Take this time between now and the wedding to contemplate your future together, for you are promised now in the presence of Ahmah and Abbah. As it is written."

The assembled all answered in response, "As it is written."

Magpie stumbled slightly over the words. He smiled down at Inbecca, who gave him a worried look. He squinted over her head at the window. A cloud, or something like one, brown-gray, like dust, rose from the Scapes. Like pulverized stone. In fact, two peaks that were the sentinels guarding the rear of the ancient castle seemed to have moved closer together.

That was not possible—except through the power of the Great Book!

From what Olen had said it was virtually limitless, as the rune changed the object. The thief was playing with the land, doing something unimaginable to it, probably one of the experiments that Olen had told them about. After ten thousand years of having it being out of his reach, the Shining One must have been aching to try out his magical muscles once again. Magpie shivered at the thought of being transformed for the amusement and edification of an inquiring wizard.

They had all been warned to look out for anything strange going on in the area, and to report it at once. This was more than merely strange. He must send a message to Olen. If only the kingdom had engaged another magician, the communication could have been instantaneous! But more important, he must find a way to warn Edynn. He thought of little Tildi. If this was the kind of alteration that could be wrought by the book, then she was in greater danger than he had dreamed.

He continued to make responses automatically according to the rite. Inbecca kept shooting him warnings, her green eyes sharp with annoyance. After the priest reproved him with a sharp "Hem!" that made the children in the second row of seats giggle, Magpie brought himself forcibly back to the temple and the moment. He was ashamed of ruining a day he had promised for Inbecca's happiness with what was mere speculation, and gave himself fully to the final parts of the ceremony. They exchanged the rings, hers of silver and his of gold, and he bestowed on her the necklace he had had made for her. She would wear it, except to sleep and bathe, from now until the wedding. He shared the traditional cup of wine with her, smiling at her with all the love in his heart. It was a special summer vintage that tasted of fresh strawberries and raspberries, a gift brought by Ganidur from Persham. Handfuls of grain and rosebuds were sprinkled upon them by the priestess, and the priest tied their hands together with a long scarf of green and white. As the priests chanted their final prayers to the Mother and the Father, Magpie offered the ritual kiss humbly, and Inbecca leaned forward to press her soft lips against his. The assembled guests cheered. The priests ended their chants with voices and arms upraised, bringing the rite to a joyful conclusion.

Crowds of people clustered around the couple, laughing and patting them on the back. Magpie was kissed by so many relatives that he lost count. He held tight to Inbecca's hands, trying to keep her from being swept away by the press of well-wishers.

"I love the box," she shouted at him over the happy din. "Is it truly from Silvertree?"

"It is," he said. "You like it?"

"I am doubly honored," she said, her smile making her cheeks dimple, as her father tucked her into a pale green cloak that enveloped her like a cocoon. "See you later!"

"Are you reconciled to me, then?" he asked suddenly, as if the last few weeks had not happened.

"Why must you ask stupid questions?" she replied. Then she was gone, surrounded by her parents and family, leaving him only with the scarf in his hands. Sharhava gave him a sour look as she departed. Magpie restrained himself from making a face at her retreating back.

"Congratulations, Eremi," the female priest said, coming around him to embrace him in her big, soft arms.

"You're a man at last," the elderly celebrant said, with a more playful smile than Magpie had thought the old man could muster.

"Perhaps," Magpie said, equally impish. "But all I can think is that now I can shed this ridiculous robe!"

He had the satisfaction of leaving the priest shaking his head. Impatiently, Benarelidur pressed in between Magpie and the priest, who retired at once to make way for the crown prince. He wore the slate-gray cloak of the heir, fastened with an enormous silver eagle brooch. "Congratulations, Brother."

"Thank you." They shook hands, Bena less than enthusiastically. His sister-in-law, Eliset, a slim girl whose thin brown hair looked prematurely gray, stood on tiptoes to kiss him on the cheek.

"I wish you both happiness," Eliset said.

"Thank you, my dear sister," he said. "I need all the blessings I can get."

Bena turned her away hurriedly, pulling Eliset with him. Their brother Ganidur breasted his way through the crowd with an eager six-year-old boy on his shoulders.

"He wanted to congratulate his uncle in person!" Gan boomed, swinging Elimar down. Magpie offered him a very grown-up embrace. "I hear you will carry my sword at the wedding."

"Yes, Uncle!" Elimar beamed. "I've been practicing. See how hard my arm is getting!"

Magpie felt the small arm held out to him. At that moment he caught a glimpse over the heads of the crowd of another gout of stone dust flying into the air in between the mountain ranges. He caught Gan's shoulder and turned him to see.

"Do you see that?"

Gan squinted "Clouds over the Scapes. So what?"

Magpie shook his head. He could be imagining it—but he was equally certain that he was not. In the past he had been accused of being fanciful, but now he was not. He had seen storms, and he had seen eruptions. This was neither. Someone was moving the geography around. The thief must have gone into the mountains with the book. This was only the beginning of what destruction could take place. He must tell someone.

"Oh, you looked so handsome!" cooed an ancient aunt, pulling his head down to her for a kiss. "That girl of yours is a fine one. You'll have many pretty babies together."

"Thank you . . ."

"Congratulations, my lord."

"Best wishes for the future. I bet you wish the wedding was tomorrow!"

"I cried. That's a good omen, is it not?"

Magpie thanked everyone, accepted hugs and kisses and slaps on the back, all the time trying to get closer to the huge window, but it was like fighting his way upstream.

Soliandur and Lottcheva came from the crowd on the left to embrace him with dignity. "You did well," Lottcheva said.

"What was all the stumbling about?" Soliandur demanded. "You've known that rite all your adult life!"

"Father, I saw—" Magpie began to explain, then realized he was the worst person to tell.

"Now, my lord, he was nervous," Lottcheva said playfully. "Weren't you, on that day?"

"Well . . ." The king gave his son a sharp look. "You will be better practiced for the wedding."

"Yes, my lord," Magpie said, bowing. He was grateful as his father turned away. A stroke of luck, he was making way for Lord Halcot! He would understand. "Sir!"

The Rabantavian king came over to clap him on the shoulder. "You looked well, at any rate. Must learn to speak up. Those of us only a few rows back could hardly hear your responses."

Magpie moved close to him, and kept his voice low. "My lord, can you send a message to Master Wizard Olen? I must go along with the arrangements for the rest of the day, but you are at leisure. As my ally, sir, can you do it?"

"What? A message to Olen? Why?"

"The mountains moved, sir. The book must be there."

A roar of laughter burst out behind them, drowning out Magpie's words. Halcot strained to listen. Magpie repeated himself, but Halcot just raised his eyebrows.

"What? Of course the mountains moved! It's a betrothal! The Creators are pleased to see you joined, boy. Congratulations!" He slapped him on the back. "Here come your friends. Father knows what they've got in mind for you. Best of luck."

"My lord, won't you arrange for a messenger?"

Halcot was already moving away, allowing the next well-wisher to make his compliments. He had not understood. Magpie realized he was the only one who comprehended the threat in what he had seen. The cluster of young lordlings who had dressed him that morning gathered him up and bustled him out of the temple door toward where the horses were waiting.

A grim-looking rider in long boots and a mud-stained cloak swung into the courtyard as Magpie went to mount his white stallion. The rider scanned the crowd, and his eyes rounded with recognition as he spotted Magpie. He slid off the splattered horse's back and slid to his knees at Magpie's feet.

"Prince, I bear a message from the wizard Olen."

"Olen!" Magpie exclaimed. "But how could he know?"

He couldn't. Magpie broke the seal and read the scroll's contents. He could almost hear the old man's voice: "My scrying tells me that you and the Great Book will surely cross paths soon, but only if you act resolutely. Do what you must! History will forgive you, for without your efforts, no history will be written hereafter."

"Thank you," Magpie told the messenger.

"I serve willingly," the man said. He tipped his hand to his hat, and leaped back into the saddle. He clattered out of the temple environs under the curious gaze of the betrothal guests.

In a worried haze Magpie bestrode the white stallion and trotted back toward the castle in the midst of a crowd that seemed to have swelled to include the entire population of the city. People were laughing, throwing garlands of flowers over his saddlebow, pressing gifts into his hands. Magpie waved and smiled, but his mind was two hundred miles away.

"All right!" Ganidur boomed out, as they reached the castle doors. He held up his long hands to halt the crowd. "He's got to go change now for the feast. Everyone let him be!"

With a grateful look at his brother, Magpie fairly ran up the empty stairs to his chamber. He shed his finery onto the bed, with little care for the precious fabrics and fine handiwork. He called for a page.

"My lord?" inquired the tawny-skinned young man in the eagle livery who appeared at the summons.

Magpie scribed down everything he could think of about the odd scene he had just witnessed, and sealed it into a packet. "I'm sorry to rob you of attending tonight's feasting, but this message must go at once to Lord Wizard Olen, in Overhill."

The boy's eyes widened. "Olen?"

"Yes. Ask for a fast horse, and tell Covani I told you it was urgent." He felt in the purse still on his hip, and gave the boy a gold coin. "You'll have more people grateful than you can count. Go, lad, go!"

"Yes, my lord!" the boy said, agog at the generous tip and the commission. He hurtled out of the room. Magpie heard him clattering down the servants' stairs toward the stables.

He locked the door of his chamber, not wanting to be bothered by valets or courtiers. He could dress himself. Over his head went the fine shirt and the chemise, and he stepped out of the silk socks and black trousers. He examined the finery that had been laid out for the evening's feast. It was all made of silk, too, in slate-blue, white, and gold, the colors of the eagle, with an apparel depicting the white-headed bird in flight in the center of his tunic front. Everything was well made and looked as though it would be a pleasure to wear, handsome and comfortable, though not for a long ride.

He chided himself the moment the thought came to him. He must not leave. What would Inbecca say?

But he might be the only one in the world, save for the thief, who knew where the book was at that moment. He had to locate it at once, and get word to those who could recapture it. Sending servants was out of the question; he had no right to put them into the kind of danger he knew existed there. If he succeeded in locating the thief, he must send alone to Olen, or seek where Edynn and the searchers had gone. They had to know. He had to know. His country, his world, and his ladylove, much as the action he was about to take would anger her, were all in the gravest danger. The power of the book, unleashed, could destroy everything he held dear. He must stop the thief from exercising it.

Putting aside his ceremonial garments, he found where the launderers had stowed his humble travel clothes and put them on. The money he would take, for he might need it, knife and sword. There was little time. Soon others would be looking for him, to serenade him down to the feasting hall, from which there would be no escape.

Hastily he made for the storage room, and ran down the stairs behind the secret door.

Inbecca would be angry, no doubt about it, but the book must be returned to its place. If that task fell to him, then so be it. He would find a way to wrest it away from its creator and bring it back to Silvertree.

He pulled his hood over his head as he entered the stable yard. The grooms were busy with hundreds of horses and dozens of carriages. With the sun high, his hood cast a deep shadow over his face, and no one troubled to look closely. He found where Covani had stabled Tessera. The mare nickered at him as he threw a cloth and a saddle over her back. He sneaked her out of the yard and into the pasture behind the buildings. Fortune was with him: no one recognized or challenged him. As soon as he was out of sight of any of the servants he knew, he hopped on her back and began to canter over the meadow toward the northern road.

Behind him, he heard hearty music join the din of voices and clattering hooves and boots. The feast would be beginning soon.

He had better be a long way away when his fiancée discovered he was missing.

"Forgive me, Inbecca," he said sadly, giving one final glance over his shoulder at the brightly lit castle.

The polished head table in the center of the grand hall was laid for two, but only one person sat there. Inbecca, in a gorgeously embroidered gown that had been begun for her the moment she reached her womanhood, and jewelry that could ransom a dozen nobles, sat beside an empty chair and half a trencher. She was annoyed and very puzzled.

The coarse wooden dish was a throwback to ancient ways, serving to show that the betrothed couple would hereafter dine together on whatever life brought them. At past ceremonial feasts, Inbecca had thought it to be a rather touchingly quaint tradition. The peasant's dish had been ladled high with cooked beans and grains, with an onion for flavor—the basic nutrition in their earliest state of civilization. At that moment, its ugliness and indigestibility were further insults to her wounded dignity. It was such a terrible contrast to the grand room, hung with priceless embroideries of blue, gold, and white that had been made over ten centuries. She felt as though the statues in the curtained alcoves around the grand chamber were all looking at her, judging her unworthy of consideration, from their historical perspective. She was further humiliated to have to look at the spotless white brocade tablecloths on all the other tables, which glinted with crystal glassware, gold and silver candlesticks, porcelain plates encrusted around the rims with gold and gems, all filled with the most dainty foods, cooked to perfection by Soliandur's storied chefs. Under the feet of even humble guests were gleaming, betassled carpets woven from a hundred colors of silk, whereas beneath her slippers was a matting of husks. Where was the one who was supposed to share the awful meal with her? Everyone kept glancing at her, their eyes full of pity. Eremi's habits were well known, and she saw many people whispering to one another. She could guess what they were saying, but she knew that they were wrong. He loved her, and he was devoted to their future.

Eremi's big brother Ganidur, upon seeing his brother late for dinner, had gone in search of him. He had returned to his place at the royal table opposite Inbecca's with a puzzled expression and raised hands. That meant that whatever had happened he had had no hand in it. Magpie had warned her that his family and friends were likely to play practical jokes upon him. Maybe he was locked up in a cupboard somewhere, to be allowed out in time for the speeches and dancing. Something had happened. He had been preoccupied at the ceremony, a matter she intended to take up with him in private at the earliest practical opportunity.

In the meantime, she tried to make the best of it. She ate her half of the simple food, then pushed the trencher from her. A serving man whisked it away and another brought her a pottery plate with a large grilled fish upon it. She had little appetite for it. She took a bite out of courtesy. The servers kept coming along with dishes that grew daintier in character, and on successively more elaborate plates. Subtleties in spun sugar and carved chocolate appeared before her from time to time, and the white-coated pastry cooks invited her with entreating expressions to try some. Each of them was made in a shape that was meant to flatter her: a marzipan tiger with jelly-green eyes, a wise, spun-sugar owl to symbolize her sagacity and wisdom, a chocolate gazelle that inferred her beauty. She broke off a bit now and again, and put them to the side of her plate.

It didn't matter how pretty or how delicious the successive dishes were. She could still taste the onion. It matched the resentment growing in her belly. Whoever had chosen to play a trick like this would be in deep trouble when she discovered who it was. Few of the guests in the room would now meet her eyes. Inbecca kept her spine straight out of pride. She was angry, but she would not show it. Inbecca leaned back slightly to accept the service of a begemmed silver plate with a roasted fowl arranged upon it.

"Where is your fiancé?" Sharhava asked, coming to hover beside her. She still wore the severe costume of the Knights, but in more sumptuous fabrics than her daily dress.

"Detained," Inbecca said calmly. "I expect him at any time."

"Hmph! I wouldn't bother looking for him. He's unsteady. He always has been. He's undoubtedly ridden off again on some fanciful expedition."

"Surely not, Aunt."

Queen Lottcheva came sailing toward them, resplendent in dark slate-blue trimmed with silver and diamonds, with her long, light hair wound in braids under her crown. "Good evening, Cousin," she said to Sharhava. She put a gentle hand down upon Inbecca's. "How are you, my dear?"

Inbecca gave her a pleasant smile that concealed her unhappiness. "I am well, thank you, good mother."

"Where is her groom?" Sharhava asked, in strident tones that must have been audible to the first three tiers of tables. "It is an insult that she should sit here alone, in the sight of all."

"Now, Aunt—" Inbecca began, then bit her lip. It was exactly what she was feeling. She should not stop someone protesting on her behalf.

Soliandur approached, appearing very ill at ease. He inclined his head to her. "Lady, I apologize on behalf of my feebleminded son. Evidently he has forgotten the importance of appearing at dinner tonight. This is not uncommon behavior for him, I am sorry to say."

"My lord," Lottcheva said, in gentle reproach. "All may not be as it appears. Why not send to his chamber to see what is keeping him?"

"I had already dispatched Ganidur. He says the room is empty. No one he asked has seen him."

"Perhaps he was taken ill. Has anyone seen the Lord Chirugeon?" Lottcheva asked, looking about. She beckoned to a lady-in-waiting and gave her instructions. The young woman walked hastily out of the room. Inbecca watched her go. She had not thought of that. Magpie had not looked completely well at the ceremony. If he was struck low by some complaint she would be angry with herself for doubting him.

King Halcot of Rabantae approached her table, and made an elaborate bow to her.

"A fine afternoon for your happy event, my lady. My greetings, my brothers and sisters," he said, offering them all a pleasant nod. "Where is Magpie? I thought he would have been here long since. We're already on the third course. The subtleties are very good, by the way. You should rejoice in your makers of sweets."

"His name is Prince Eremilandur," Soliandur said with some asperity.

"Surely it is," Halcot said amiably. "Such a lot of syllables in your names. Magpie is much easier to recall. I became used to it over the last few years. Eremil-what-have-you, it is. You know, he is a remarkable young man. I feel you and I would profit from a discussion of his qualities some fine afternoon."

"As you please, my lord," Soliandur said, more wintry than ever.

"I see experience has not mellowed you, my brother. A pity." Halcot returned his attention to Inbecca. "Where has he gone?"

"He is not here, Lord Halcot," Inbecca said, surprised at herself for not bursting out into a fit of temper or tears. She was even more puzzled. How had Halcot and Eremi become acquainted? Hadn't the two countries been at war? Did this have something to do with the long journey he had taken in the spring? Soliandur certainly seemed displeased about it. "I am sure he will be back any moment. I would be grateful if anyone can tell me where he has gone."

"Well, I doubt he's in the healer's room," Soliandur said. "I would wager he's gone down to one of the inns in town where he can get drunk with his low-caste friends." At a gesture, a handful of courtiers in eagle tunics were at his side. "Go search out the prince. Bring him back here at once. This is absurd of him, and I will not tolerate it."

Lottcheva went into a modified flutter, offering confident assurances, yet managing to look like a wild bird pretending to have a broken wing to protect her chick. Inbecca felt sorry for her. Her mother and father came to join her.

"Why, what is the matter?" Kaythira asked, putting her arm around Inbecca.

"Eremi is not here," Inbecca said simply.

Soon, the young men in livery returned. "I have searched his room closely," said one, a fine-skinned youth with dark red hair. "His betrothal clothes are there. His prized jitar is not where I expected to see it, but I cannot see anything else that is missing."

"He's gone a-minstreling again," Sharhava said, gloating. "There, girl, he thinks as little of you as that."

"Oh, no, highness," said another young man, a stocky fellow with thick blond hair. "The jitar is over there beneath a table. He asked me to make sure it was here for the feast. He had a new poem to sing to her ladyship." He bowed to Inbecca.

"How charming," Kaythira said, after reading a desperate look from Lottcheva. "He means to serenade you."

"I am delighted," Inbecca said delicately, "but an assurance like that does not put him here beside me."

"Find him," Soliandur said furiously. "He has gone beyond decency this time."

"It might be his friends who are to blame," Lottcheva said with a smile. "Let us be patient, my friends."

"Wait a moment," Halcot said, tapping his fingers into his palm. "He said something to me at the betrothal. Yes, I understand his words now. Sounded like nonsense at the time. He told me about the mountains. He said 'The book must be there.' And he asked me to send a message to Master Olen. He's no doubt gone to send a message. Yes, my lady, depend on it."

"He's gone to send it, or take it?" Soliandur asked.

"Not a nobleman's job to carry a letter, is it?" Halcot asked offhandedly.

"What about a book?" Sharhava said, picking up on his statement swiftly. Inbecca stared at the visitor with budding curiosity. "What do you know about a book?"

Halcot seemed to take in the habit she was wearing with a guilty expression. "Nothing that would interest you, my lady. Council matters. I beg your pardon, but it is nothing I can discuss outside chamber doors."

"You are a poor liar, my lord."

Halcot's face grew very red. "You presume much, my lady."

"I am an abbess of the Knights of the Word. I know what you are talking about. You do not have to disclose it to me. Where did he say it was?" Sharhava leaned forward avidly.

"You are in on the great secret then," Soliandur said in disgust, looking from one to the other. "A myth. A folly. It has nothing to do with my peripatetic son disappearing again. He has run away from his responsibilities again, as he has for years. This has nothing to do with legends."

Halcot shook his head, favoring Soliandur with a pitying look. "My brother, you have learned nothing in five years. I think I must know your son far better than you do. You miss the best qualities of people. This is the reason you lost the war between us in everything but name, and you are letting your anger eat you alive instead of coming to terms."

"You presume much upon hospitality, my lord," Sharhava said coldly.

"I rule here," Soliandur snapped at her, but he, too, eyed Halcot with dislike. Inbecca could tell that he still considered the Rabantavian to be an enemy of Orontae. She believed that Halcot was telling the truth. Soliandur seemed to recall the presence of Sharhava's sister and his fellow monarch all too late. Soliandur bowed to Kaythira. "Your pardon, my sister."

"*Your* pardon, my lord," Sharhava said smoothly. "Perhaps you are not familiar with the Great Book. Your time may have been spent upon other studies . . . ?"

"I know enough," Soliandur replied.

"Then you will understand that it is vital to find this book and place it in our custody, for the protection and the good of all humans, not placed back into a hole and hidden away where none can ever use it. And we would make the best use of it of anyone in this world, studying its powers."

"The book?" Kaythira asked Sharhava. "Your book?"

Another courtier came panting into the room, and bowed deeply to the king. "Highness, Tessera is missing. My lord Eremi's horse."

"Find him! Send riders out along all the roads!"

"He's gone after it himself," Halcot said wonderingly. "A remarkable youth."

"Just a moment," Inbecca said, rising and taking Halcot's arm. "Tell me, my lord, where has Eremilandur gone?"

Halcot met her eyes sincerely. "I believe he means to put himself in harm's way for the sake of us all. I assure you, it is a most heroic undertaking. I am surprised he did not tell you before setting out. Perhaps he left a note for you with a servant?"

"What kind of harm?" Now fear was warring with anger within her. "What could befall him?"

"Which mountains?" Sharhava interrupted. "I heard you mention them. What range? In what direction?"

"Nonsense, woman," Halcot burst out furiously. "I don't intend to aid *you* at all. I have seen the effects of this book of yours. Destruction can result from a mere copy of *one page*. I have seen it! You cannot control it. It must not remain at large. The collateral effects that its presence has are harmful. It must be placed back in the hands of wizards."

"The Scholardom can control it," Sharhava assured him, with a superior look down her nose. "Are you part of some conspiracy that would thwart us from achieving our greatest purpose? How dare you?"

"How dare *you*?" Halcot countered. "You would play with the fate of nations, to satisfy your curiosity? You have no idea what this book is capable of doing!"

"I assure you, sir, I do. I think you underestimate how well prepared we are," Sharhava said.

"I think that you overestimate yourselves. If the boy has gone after it, he is placing himself in mortal danger."

"The only danger he is in is of being disowned," Soliandur said.

Inbecca barely heard the argument going on around her. Eremi had gone, without leaving word for her, in the middle of their own betrothal day. He must have left on the spur of the moment, afraid to face her when he ran off. He knew about Aunt Sharhava's precious book. He had known all the time that it was real, and he had made fun of Sharhava to her face, calling it lies and legend. He had lied to both of them. Inbecca's temper turned from the so-called friends who might have kidnapped him for fun to her would-be bridegroom himself. How dare he!

"Well, my brother," Halcot said, very stiffly, "if the event is over, then I have no reason to remain. I thank you for the hospitality of your house, and yours," he added, bowing to Queen Kaythira. "Your very good health, my lady," he said, bowing to Inbecca. "I wish you happiness in your married life. It would seem I have more faith in your affianced than his own father. And to you, my lady, my thanks for our warm welcome," he said to Lottcheva.

"Will you not stay for the rest of the feast?" the queen asked, alarmed.

"No, thank you, my lady. I am sorry. I am honored to have been invited. Farewell." He bowed. He turned to Hawarti. "I trust you can have my horses ready by the time I am packed to go." He turned and marched out of the dining hall. His courtiers rose hastily, blotted their lips on napkins, and followed him.

"Stiff-necked old fool," Soliandur grumbled. He stormed away, followed by a swirling cloud of worried courtiers.

"Eremi is not a fool," Lottcheva said firmly. "Something terrible has happened, or he would not have . . . I can't believe it. I cannot believe he has gone running off after a . . . a book! He was so eager to join with you, my dear." Tears were in her eyes as she went to embrace the girl.

Inbecca flinched involuntarily as the queen put her arms around her. She wanted to be alone, not here in the center of a thousand people watching her suffer utter humiliation. That the friend and lover she had trusted all of her life could prove to be so false hurt her immeasurably. It felt to her as if the world was crumbling out from under her feet. She didn't know what to hold onto, what still remained true.

"Never mind, dear," her mother was saying gently. "Forget him. We will go home at once. You will take your place at my side. You'll have time to think about your future."

"And deal with old men and court favors?" Inbecca blurted out. To sit and think when her heart was torn in two was the last thing she wanted to do.

"This is an opportunity," Sharhava crowed. "Child, you have a marvelous opportunity to steal a march on your faithless bridegroom. Come with me. You can be a part of the making of history. The young man deserted you. You're free!"

"Yes," Inbecca said. "I am." Hot tears flooded her throat, making her sob out loud. "It's a good thing we never wed. No one at all seems surprised he has gone."

"I am," Kaythira said, regarding her daughter and sister with alarm. "I agree with Halcot. Eremi would not leave without reason. Inbecca, listen to me!"

"It is too late," her aunt advised her, her voice buzzing in Inbecca's ears like eager bees. She dabbed at the girl's streaming eyes with a cloth. "You are tied to him, before the powers of creation. Unless you renounce all secular ties and join the Knights of the Book, that is. That will free you from him."

Inbecca was so angry she pushed the heavy dish away. She ripped the precious wedding necklace from her throat, hearing the clasp bound off and jangle to the floor, and flung it down. If their vows meant so little to Eremi that he fled, then that twist of metal meant nothing at all to her. Links and gems went flying in all directions, but she did not care.

"I'll do it," she said.

"Good. Kneel to me." Inbecca slid down to the floor. What did it matter? She felt Sharhava's hand settle on her head. "In the name of the Words, from which Creation sprang, swear to me to protect the book of all things, against all harm, against all enemies, forevermore, forswearing all other earthly ties."

I swear," Inbecca said.

"Rise, Lar Inbecca." Her aunt helped her to her feet and kissed her. Her eyes were glowing with pride. "With your drive and intelligence we cannot fail to gain the ancient book in the name of the Scholardom."

"I know where he has gone," Inbecca said, fired with a new cause.

"During the betrothal itself he stopped and asked me if I had seen something. There was nothing behind us but the window of the temple. He must be going toward the mountains that are visible from there."

"I knew your intelligence would serve us," Sharhava gloated. "We ride north, then. Come with me." She signaled to one of the Knights in her escort. "Find her robes and insigne. Summon the others. We know where the book is, at last. Make haste! Eremilandur has several hours' head start on us."

"My child, stay," Inbecca's father said, holding her hands. "Don't throw away all you have in anger." Kaythira looked stricken.

"You heard her vow," Sharhava said, putting a shoulder between him and the girl. "She is one of mine now. You will be proud. She joins a worthy cause."

Inbecca marched after her aunt. She glanced back over her shoulder only once, to see the two queens standing forlornly at the small table, looking down at the ruins of her priceless necklace. Her worthless necklace. She was glad to have a new cause, and one that involved catching up with Eremi and giving him a piece of her mind.

"We ride at once!" Sharhava said to the others as they hurried alongside them. "We will overtake the boy. He will guide us, and we will seize the book in the name of all that is good! And we will set the world right!"

Chapter Thirty-three

akanta," Tildi said, as they rode through another of the awe-inspiringly silent streets of the dwarf hollow on their third day underground, "if it's not offensive, what's *'towa-chira'*?"

The peddler laughed, a little uncomfortably, her voice echoing off the polished walls. "Ah, you heard that, did you? Ah, well, it means 'one who goes outside.' They don't like it that my husband and I associated with outsiders. Dwarves don't much like the sun. I don't know why. I have never felt that way."

"I'm sorry," Tildi said.

"Ah, well, it's something we have in common, isn't it?" Lakanta said with a brave grin. "We're both different than those we were born with. It's just that your family didn't mind, did they?"

"No, they didn't."

"Do you see? You were lucky."

"Marvelous," Edynn said, shaking her head. The gallery through which they passed was carved from a red stone streaked with white. The sculptors who had shaped it had used the white sections as accent pieces in raised relief, so that one came unexpectedly upon very beautiful cameo portraits, or the image of animals or plants. At their feet were croplands, growing quite contentedly in the wan light. Even flowers flourished in pots and troughs at the doors and windows of the buildings. Tildi went to touch one, and discovered that it was made of a translucent stone. "These dwarves live like kings and queens, and few will ever behold these marvels."

"But you have, Mother," Serafina said. "When? When were you in the dwarfhollows?"

"Oh, long ago. Several lifetimes, really. I was fairly young. As then, they were not very happy to let me through, but I had good reason that benefited them, as now. I saw a grand gallery, all curtains of onyx, like honey and wax and flowing amber, where the dwarven kings hold court. It puts every human monarch's throne room aboveground to shame."

"You never told me about it," Serafina said, a little petulantly.

"Oh, child, there are only so many years for bedtime stories, then we begin to talk about the here and now." She smiled at her daughter. "Isn't that better than dwelling upon what happened before? That was such a long time ago. I much prefer to enjoy the times we are having now, together."

"This place ought to be a comfort to you," Lakanta added. "Not a door around."

Serafina scowled. "I don't need your pity, peddler."

"It's not pity, but a straightforward observation. I'd have been grateful to have my mother's stories around. Look at Tildi. Whole family swept away, and she hasn't let out a peep of complaint!"

Tildi felt very uncomfortable as the others turned to look at her. Edynn came to her rescue.

"That may not be the most charitable way to put it, Lakanta," the elder wizardess said. "Just as no two wizards come to the craft in the same way, nor do they learn the same skills in the same order, it would seem that the life choices also strike one when they will. To live for centuries, as most of us do, sounds appealing, but it doesn't sound quite as much a gift when you realize that you will spend much of it alone. I have children now, but Olen had his sons long ago, and their great-grandchildren were old men many ages back, but it was right for him to have his family then. For you, Tildi, it happened to you sooner than it did to most wizards. You experienced what comes to most of us eighty or ninety years into our studies. For that reason many choose not to cross the line into long life. Those who do learn that the cost of magic is to be prepared to tread the halls of power alone."

"You are not alone," Serafina said fiercely.

"No, dear, of course not," Edynn said absently. "We are together."

At last, Tildi felt she understood Serafina's possessiveness. To have her family swept away unexpectedly was a horrible shock. To know it could—no, *would* happen at any moment, must be unbearable. She gave Serafina a little more kindness than ever, making way for her when she wanted to see one of the dwarves' works up close, or making sure that she was served the nicest of the dainties that their unseen hosts left for them. The girl did not seem to notice, but Edynn did. She gave Tildi a kindly smile.

Morag kept turning around in his saddle every few minutes as if he could sense the hidden eyes upon him. Teryn rode stolidly on at their head, directing them toward the next passage indicated by the glittering red lights.

As the door warden had promised them, the visitors wanted for nothing. Tables laden with covered dishes and open baskets of fresh fruit appeared regularly throughout the day. The horses were not forgotten. Fodder, gathered from who knew where, was always gathered in nets at nose level for the steeds. At what was presumed to be night, they would come to a place where the red lights ended. Clearly, they were intended to go no farther. There pavilions had been set up for them, the cloth tents looking rather incongruous at the feet of the massive stone domiciles around them. Always, baths awaited them inside, the steaming water glimmering in the pale dwarf light. Always, they waited in vain to see anyone they could thank for the ongoing and seemingly limitless kindness.

"The greatest thanks we can give them is to leave here as quickly as we may," Lakanta explained, as she unsaddled her horse for the night. "They are helping us because they anticipate our service." Melune made her way beside the other horses who were drinking out of a trough cut out of a single piece of priceless topaz, just one of the ostentatious displays of wealth that gave a twinge to Tildi's modest little soul.

Tildi knew they were covering ground quickly, many miles a day.

Inwardly, she was impatient. She knew they were still far from the book's enormous aura, and she could not wait to feel it again. Edynn always sensed when the longing for the book became too great for her. The wizardess appeared at Tildi's side, no matter what time of the day or night, to cast the wards over her that kept her mind clear. Edynn would lay a hand on Tildi's head and intone a few words under her breath, always with a patient little smile. Every time, Tildi recoiled, annoyed that the wizardess would interfere with her communion, but the impatience faded away as the warding spell took effect. Tildi felt grateful to Edynn, and ashamed of her own behavior. If the feeling was that strong so far away from the book, what would happen to her when she was actually near it?

The tremors erupted again from time to time, making Lakanta mutter to herself. When they consulted the map over the dining table, Edynn frowned at the lines of topography, but when Tildi asked her about it, she shook her head. The book had not moved from that one spot at the north end of the country of Orontae. Their position was closer to that spot every night.

It was always warm in the dwarfhollow, warm enough that Tildi rode in a simple shirt, with her cloak and tunic tucked away in Rin's saddlebags. That made it all a greater surprise when on the morning of the fourth day she emerged from her luxurious tent into a gust of cold air.

"Someone's left the door open," Rin said. "Can we ask them to shut it?"

"I think that it is intentional," Edynn said. "I believe that our journey underground is coming to an end."

Tildi put her coat on over her shirt. Rin unfolded her cloak.

"I fear it is far colder out of doors," she said.

The others made ready to go, and mounted their steeds.

The red lights sparkled into existence, leading them down and around a broad, curving avenue. Leering heads spouting water from mouths, ears, and noses lined the walls. The water followed the same curve, leading into a vast underground lake. The cold air swept across its surface. Teryn had drawn her sword, guarding against any unexpected incursions.

The outflow from the lake preceded them down the slope, through curtain after translucent curtain of stone, each carved by nature, then enhanced by the expert hands of the dwarves. The light ahead grew brighter as they went. Tildi squinted against the glare. After days in near twilight, it was more than her light-starved eyes could easily manage. In time, she became used to it, and was delighted at the astonishing detail that the extra illumination provided. Stolid, squarish runes had been worked into a kind of tapestry, starting high on the walls, and playing in narrow columns down to the edge of the stream, with gems picking out year markers.

"On these is carved the history of dwarven kind in this area," Lakanta explained. "The oldest date I can see is about six thousand years old. They were friends to the humans here, but not in a very long time. The last humans left long ago."

"Ah!" Edynn exclaimed, as they rode into the next chamber. The stone draperies looked as if they had been picked up and just dropped by a playful hand. All of pearl, or amber, or honey, some were bunched, others swirled in a spiral, some lapped over one another like necklaces on a gigantic scale. "Serafina, this is it! This is the chamber I visited so long ago. Oh, my daughter," she said, her eyes fond, reaching over to pat Serafina on the hand. "Even a thraik may do someone good. I never thought to be able to show you this."

The young wizardess's eyes went wide, and she studied the room around her with wonder. Tildi could tell how much it meant to her to share this with Edynn. None of the others in the party said a word, not even the voluble Lakanta. This was a moment for mother and daughter alone. Tildi felt a twinge of envy, but in her heart she could not begrudge it to them.

"It is a marvel," Serafina said at last.

"What comes next?" Captain Teryn asked, as they continued downhill toward the next chamber. The light was brighter at the foot of the path.

"A series of lower chambers," Edynn said, "many domiciles, and beyond them the entrance to the dwarfhollow in the Oros river valley, a lovely place."

Tildi pulled the collar of her tunic up around her neck and shivered.

As was her custom, Teryn trotted ahead of them. They saw her halt, then hastily pull her horse to back up several steps. She threw up her hand.

"It has changed, honorable," the captain said over her shoulder, in her emotionless voice. Edynn and the others dismounted. "Leave the horses if you want a look. I don't think the ground's stable."

Rin kept Tildi on her back as she followed the others through the thick barrier. There were no lower chambers beyond the curtain of translucent white stone, nor domiciles or corridors. Tildi found herself overlooking a valley, but one that had been gouged coarsely, almost clawed, out of the earth. Whole glades of trees, some of them hundreds of years old, by their girth, lay tumbled like heaps of pins on the clay-stained slopes. At the north end, a huge cataract poured into the gorge, forming a murky, irregular pool at the bottom. Wind gusted through the gorge, whipping up the water's surface. At the south end, a broad swath of mud winding off into the distance indicated a riverbed, recently drained. Silver fish lay dead on the dark surface in between lank heaps of river weed. Edynn looked aghast; Lakanta stricken.

"It looks like a massive landslide happened here," Serafina said. "All those earth tremors resulted in massive avalanches. It's changed the course of this river."

"It couldn't be," Lakanta pointed out. "There's no fallen stone. It looks more like someone simply scooped up half a mountain and carried it away."

"Could the book do this?" Rin asked, her deep green eyes wide.

"Yes," Tildi and Edynn said at once. "And it seems," Edynn continued, "that it has. But why? Why destroy part of the dwarfhollow? What reason has he for tearing up this area? It can have no significance for him."

Behind them, the red lights winked out. The dwarves had led them to the end of their domain. Tildi found she was trembling, and not just from cold. Though autumn had come to this part of the world while she had been beneath the earth, there was more. The edge of the book's influence touched her. She felt wild happiness erupt within her. The longing was stronger than love or common sense. Edynn met her eyes, her expression kind but firm. Tildi deliberately stamped down the joyful sensation. It was not good for her, she kept telling herself.

"The book is not far away," she confirmed.

"But not close enough to cast runes all around us," Serafina asked. "Where is he?"

"Why did he come here?" Teryn asked. "There's nothing here."

"I have been in this place before," Edynn said. "In my dreams, perhaps, or in the distant past? Sometimes it blends together in my memory." Serafina looked nervous. "No, daughter, don't be concerned. It is real. Teryn, let me see the map."

"There are no villages or towns marked near here," the captain said, presenting the parchment for her perusal.

"Not now," Edynn said. "But once, there was the greatest city in the world, city of the first kings, Oron. From here, humanity spread to the five continents, but this was the first stronghold. Oron Castle is here." She touched the map where the gold dot lay. "It is, or was, north of here, in this pocket in between two mountain ranges, along this river. This is, or was, the River Oros." Tildi shuddered as she surveyed the horror of the valley.

"You believe that he is in the castle?" Teryn asked.

"In its ruins," Edynn said. "It's been uninhabited as long as I can recall, but there was quite a bit of the shell left. It is a logical place for him to have gone."

"Do we fly?" asked Rin.

"I do not want to risk the thraik. We must make our way along the ground. It is not that far."

"The map shows what roads are here," Teryn said, "but how will we know which way to turn?"

"Need you ask?" Edynn said, pointing off toward the north. Lightning exploded in the distance. No rain fell on them, but the sky was gray only a few miles to the east.

"The Madcloud," Tildi said, shivering. Knowing the destruction it could wreak, she feared to go where it was.

"Indeed," Edynn said. "And it isn't moving. It is attracted only to strong magic, and there is none stronger than the book. He is there."

Tildi breathed deeply, enjoying the essence that filled the air around her. "So is the book."

*T*here, girl, almost there. Almost there." Magpie patted Tessera's neck. Both of them were covered with sweat. His body was battered and exhausted, and he hadn't even been the one doing all the running. He felt terrible for his poor mare. She had galloped full-out for more than three days, never complaining. She was so high of heart that she had willingly run herself into exhaustion and started out fresh the next day, as if she knew how vital the mission was that he was upon.

No more spumes of stone dust led him, but he did not need them to guide him. He knew where he was going now. The Maker must be in the ancient Oron Castle. It had been built in the earliest days of the kingdom. Some said that a band of powerful wizards had created it for the first kings, and some had lived there for a while. While none were mentioned in the legends by name, Magpie was certain that it must have been the Shining Ones.

Wouldn't it make sense that he's gone to ground here? It hadn't been occupied by anything except bats and spiders for centuries. If Magpie was a ten-thousand-year-old wizard, he would find it the perfect place to set up a new kingdom. But why now? Why now?

Lightning lanced through the sky ahead. The clouds didn't look natural. They were slashed with strange colors and hovering in one place, instead of flowing along. It must be another one of the Shining One's displays of power. Magpie tied his hood tightly around his chin as Tessera carried him ahead into the light rain. He didn't know what he was going to do when he got there, but he must do something!

The horror behind him also set spurs to his back. The devastation was startling and completely unexpected. Land had been torn away like pieces ripped out of a loaf of bread. Villages and towns, he feared to think how many, had been wiped out of existence. The people, terrified and uncomprehending, streamed past him with their few goods on their backs, heading south toward the capital to ask for the king's help, but what could Soliandur do against one of the Makers?

The most terrifying thing that he had seen was when the Oros stopped flowing. He had seen it happen himself late the previous day as he rode through a village on the banks. The water, normally several feet deep, dropped lower and lower, until the riverbed was empty. People in the village ran into the sucking mud, chasing the receding water southward, begging for it to come back. They had been insane, but he would have been insane, too, if he had just seen his village's lifeblood ebb away. Fish flopped helplessly, boats and ships heeling over in the mud. What magic had the thief wrought to divert an entire river? And why had he chosen to experiment upon poor Orontae? Had it not had a difficult enough time in recent years? And where had the water gone?

He pulled up shortly to the answer to his last question as he crossed over the pass in between the Old Man's Shoulders. The valley ahead of him had been destroyed, dug out to the very roots of the mountains. He could see the two halves of the Oros on either side of the chasm. A new lake was forming. He was relieved that the Shining One had not stopped the river altogether. That problem would solve itself as soon as the water level rose to the top of the gap. The river road was gone, but that was a minor consideration. Magpie and his brothers had ridden that way in past years and knew all the passes. He turned Tessera away from the stinking, roaring gap, and headed toward a side road, more used by deer and wolf than human beings.

A thraik screamed overhead. Small wonder, for strong magic was afoot. It paid him no attention, for which he was grateful, and vanished into the air like a candle flame being snuffed out. He hoped that he could catch up with Edynn and the others. He would warn them . . . of what could he warn them that they would not have observed already? He hoped he was not too late. He hated to think of what could have happened to poor little Tildi.

Three days' ride had given him plenty of time to think about the folly of his action. He was no magician, but if one more sword or set of wits could help Edynn to defeat the enemy and take back the precious book, then he would give his all.

He heard the sound of hoofbeats, and pulled Tessera back behind a tree as wide as she was long. It sounded like women's voices! He urged her forward onto the path and hailed them.

Before he knew it, he was on his back with a soldier in full armor sitting on his chest, and another pointing a spear at his throat. Captain Teryn, her face sunburned and windburned, ripped back his hood. Rain poured onto his face. He sputtered.

"Prince Eremilandur, what do you here?" Edynn asked, from under her white hood. She looked amused. Probably she had had some mystical signal he was here, one she hadn't bothered to share with the Rabantavian guards.

"Prince?" Tildi asked, her little face puzzled. "I thought he was a troubadour."

"A useful disguise," Edynn said. "He has been traveling the countryside on behalf of Olen and the rest of us of the council. I believe he even followed *you* once, to Olen's very door, but he is a prince of this land we are currently traversing. Get up, please."

"Thank Mother and Father you're safe," he croaked. The wizardess signed to the captain, who got off him and helped him to his feet with one strong pull. "I rode to warn you." He brushed water off the front and back of his cloak.

"Of what, young man?" She beckoned him forward. The male guard had hold of Tessera's bridle.

"The mountains have been moving," Magpie blurted out. "I could see them all the way from the temple, two hundred miles from here. I sent a message to Olen, but who knows how long it will take before someone comes." His sense of humor stuck a finger in his ribs and made him confess to the ridiculous. "I galloped here in hopes of intercepting you before you went looking for some ancient, all-powerful wizard reclaiming his own. I believe I know where he is."

"And where is that?" Serafina asked. She, too, looked refined down to the essence within her, brave, determined, but still of a sharp, impatient nature. The journey must have been hard. He was most shocked by the changes in little Tildi. She was preoccupied, not sunny and optimistic as she had been in Silvertree. Well, neither would he be, if truth were told, with a multicolor rainstorm pouring down on him and the greatest enemy in the world behind the castle doors.

"Oron Castle. It's a ruin, but a big one. A man could live there almost comfortably, even in weather like this."

"So we had already surmised," Edynn said. "There's little other shelter in this area. We have been making our way there since this morning. The roads are difficult."

"I can guide you through here. I have been there many times. I want to help. You would be horrified by what he has been doing to the land. Hundreds, maybe thousands of people have disappeared. I fear they are all dead." In as few words as possible, he described the catastrophic destruction that he had left behind him. Tildi looked sick.

"How could the one who went to the trouble to describe each of the forests and valleys in such loving detail crush them out of existence so casually?" she asked.

"He is destroying things at random," Edynn said, with a grim face. "He must have gone insane. Thank you for offering your service, highness. We will be glad of your help, though I do not know what any of us can do now. We must try."

Magpie hoped that the Shining One's whims would be stayed until after they had reached the castle. The rains made it difficult to see far ahead, but he was on his own ground. The top of the castle was already coming into view, the flagpole on the top of the derelict tower at the fore, acting as a guide to him. Something about the tower was different, though it was hard to tell in the driving rain. Magpie took a turning that led to a side path, which eventually let out into the yard for what in ancient days he thought were the kitchens. It wound upward and upward, until they were above the level of the trees. He could see not only the new lake into which the Oros was flowing, but some of the damage beyond the Old Man's Shoulders.

"Look!" he shouted through the rain. The centaur carrying Tildi twisted her lithe body around, and let out an audible gasp. Edynn and Serafina looked aghast. At this height the ruin of the valley was entirely visible, even through the rain. Mountains had been sundered, leaving a raw wound of exposed layers of rock. Smoke rose from the forests that had fallen. Birds of prey circled and called, looking for any dead that lay hidden in the wreckage of Mother Nature's beauty. They turned away. Magpie thought he could see tears on their faces. He led them upward toward the castle.

The side path was still largely intact, though sharp-bladed yellow grass grew up through the gigantic flagstones in the wide, walled pathway. He changed direction frequently, avoiding holes and stones too tilted for safe passage. Rin stayed at his side. The others followed close behind him.

"Remember," Edynn said, holding her staff aloft, "we are vulnerable now, but we are even more vulnerable when the runes appear. He must know we are coming. Take care. I expect a first strike at any moment."

Chapter Thirty-four

emeth sat in his throne with the book before him, surveying the rune that indicated the castle itself. He had been preparing to choose his next target of destruction, until he felt that *she* had arrived. He was frightened. The pursuers had defeated every one of his efforts to deter or dispose of them. They had won through, and now they were here, outside, preparing to enter. He studied the runes and let them guide his intuition.

At last the fog that had hidden the company of pursuers from view lifted. There, in his mind's eye, was his threat! Not the tall wizardess with white hair, who looked familiar to him, nor the strong warrior in the armor of Orontae's enemy, Rabantae. No, it was the little creature in the woolen cloak, sitting like a flea on the back of the long-haired centaur: a female smallfolk. She was the bearer of a fragment? How could she be?

It should have burned her to her bones. Yet his sight never lied. She was the one to whom he was tied. She wanted the book. He knew in the depths of his soul that she had come to take it away from him. His nerves were already sorely tried by the Madcloud, hovering overhead like an uneasy conscience. He had tried several times to destroy it, but the rune eluded his efforts. Some wizard in past times had so altered it that no matter what he did to it, it only seemed to increase its power. He was forced to leave it alone, though it shook the castle towers with its thunder and threatened to drown him in an endless deluge. The coming of an intruder with as great a claim to the book as his upset him. Should he flee?

No, he thought, straightening his back in the high white throne, *this is my kingdom now*. Every rock, every tree answered to his call. They would come to his aid if he chose. He needed guardians of his own. They must not be human at all; his army of trees had failed miserably, and he deplored the death of innocent creatures. They must not have any vital organs to thrust a sword into, or to feel mercy toward an opponent. Only magic would suffice, unemotional and absolutely obedient to his will. He unrolled the book slightly to find the nearest source of materials. There was his serried force, lying in graduated ranks. They would surprise the intruders. He began changing the rune to suit his purpose. The harsh sound that erupted from the level below was loud enough that he could hear it in the throne room.

What was that?" Rin demanded, as they bounded from stone to stone in the last loop of the switchbacks beneath the castle walls.

"A grinding noise," Magpie said. "I don't know what is causing it. The drawbridge engine fell apart centuries ago."

"It might be back together by now," Lakanta said, "seeing as he has repaired nearly everything else."

"I feel magic stirring," Edynn said, holding up a hand for silence. She and Serafina readied their staffs. Teryn and Morag urged their horses to the head of the party, swords at the ready. Tildi drew her knife, but she stayed close against Rin's back. Lakanta had her club, but she had also gathered a large sack of stones.

Teryn called for the others to halt as the road widened out. She rode ahead, leaving Morag to guard the company behind the last stretch of wall, then spurred back almost at once. Silently, she beckoned to them, patting the air so that they understood they should make their way slowly. Rin nodded. They crept ahead, emerging into the castle's side yard.

The rain was so heavy Tildi felt as if she would drown when she gazed upward, but she couldn't stop looking. The first things she noticed were the runes. The book was so near that everything was illuminated with its own name, blazing in brilliant gold. She looked down. She wore hers, too, over her heart like a badge. She had not seen it so since she was a small girl, when the leaf first came into the Summerbee household. At the time she had accepted its appearance without question, as all small children do to strange things that come without explanation, and thought it was pretty. Now she thought it sinister. Anyone, at that moment, could change or kill her, and she could do little to stop them except retaliate in kind if she was faster. The thought made her shiver.

Forcing herself to think beyond her fears, she could not help but admire the castle itself. It was beautiful, all made of smooth white stone, and huge, bigger than many of the towns through which they had passed, a city in itself. Outbuildings, like those around Silvertree, huddled within the high, thick walls, servants ready to respond to the will of their master, the great keep. It reached straight up over their heads, a massive rectangle ending in four turrets from which strange banners of white and gold flew. In the rain she could not see their device. One fork of lightning after another illuminated the castle walls in a series of bright bursts.

"How different it is," Magpie breathed, as each stroke revealed more beauties. Mosaics, their colors bright and alive, offered elegant designs that sprawled and burgeoned around each angle and each window frame. Statues of armed warriors loomed from recesses, sending a warning to any would-be invader to stay away. He felt their power. They were so well made that he could pick out likenesses in the faces to members of his family and paintings in the royal gallery. "It never looked like this. It was a shell. This is a work of art."

"This is how it was in its glory days," Edynn said. "I have seen the illustrations in ancient books. Oron Castle was the wonder of the world. Beings of all races worked upon its construction and ornamentation. Our thief has reconstructed it exactly."

The Madcloud did not seem to like people ignoring it. A stripe of blue lightning blasted out of the sky with a deafening boom of thunder, and knocked one of the banners off the tower, along with the stone pillar on which it had been mounted. It plummeted to earth behind the keep. The crash of its landing made the party jump.

"Where is he, Tildi?"

Wordlessly, the smallfolk girl pointed a finger at the tall tower. She could feel the other waiting for her there, with the book. She wanted it more than anything in her life. It would not matter to her if the other killed her, as long as she could touch it before she died.

"Good girl," Edynn said. She put a hand on Tildi's head, and the longing passed. Tildi relaxed, and realized she was miserably wet. "Where are the stairs?"

"This way," Magpie said. They left their horses in the yard, and followed the young man. He led them up onto a broad courtyard lined with tubs of growing vegetables. Huge, blocky stairs of white granite led upward around the outside of the square tower to the next courtyard. Teryn and Morag signed to the others to keep well back, and began to climb toward the next level.

The moment they put their feet on the steps, the lowest stair rolled upright, knocking the two guards flying. Tildi screamed. She saw the stones' runes changing as they rose up on end and began to take on definition. Legs, arms, and a blocky torso with a terrible, square head with twin gouges for eyes and a slit below for a mouth.

The slit opened wide, and emitted a terrifying bellow.

Teryn did not hesitate at all to take on the new enemy. She rolled up onto her feet and charged at the giant, sword raised. She struck it across the midsection. The metal clashing emitted sparks, but left no mark at all. Teryn gawked, but swung around in a circle and aimed another sweeping blow at its knees. It raised one bricklike arm and smashed at her. Teryn raised her shield just in time. It spread out the force of the blow, but Teryn staggered backwards from the force. Morag leaped and thrust with his polearm at the gap between the creature's body and head. He managed to drive the thin blade into the gap, and levered downward. The head popped off, and the creature stopped moving.

"That did it!" he shouted. He leaned down to help Teryn to her feet.

Behind them, the next highest step was turning into two stone monsters, and the next one, three. Magpie cried out a warning to Teryn. The guards turned at bay. Magpie plunged in, sword raised, and just managed to parry one of the new creatures from striking Teryn on the head. It missed, and roared its frustration. The guards joined him in trying to knock its head off. Rin galloped forward to help. Her chosen weapon, the whip, was less than useless against stone, but she turned and kicked at the nearest monster with her rear hooves. She managed to dislodge the right arm of one, and knock the leg out from under another. The disabled stone beasts still crawled after the moving prey, but Lakanta plunged in, battering at the fallen ones with her club. The company made progress in decimating the ranks, but more and more came on.

"This is more our task, daughter," Edynn said. She and Serafina pointed their staffs at the stone giants. The gems at the top glowed. Spheres of red and white fire hurtled toward the creatures. Where they struck, the granite slagged and melted. Edynn concentrated her spells on the legs, working to immobilize the giants.

Tildi stared dumbly. She was afraid to get anywhere near the creatures. Their fists were larger than her whole body. She stared at the runes aglow against the white of their square bodies. How had he altered them into moving beings? How did he know what to do? Could she turn them back into steps? She had only seen Olen perform an alteration of a rune once, when he changed the candle and made it explode. Transformation lessons were not going to be until later in the year.

But she knew what the rune for a stone looked like. Like hers, their runes were unlocked. She saw the parts that were different from the word for stone. She reached out as if she could touch the rune of the nearest giant, who was fighting with the minstrel-prince. *Stone,* she thought, stripping away the other characteristics with her fingers. They resisted, as if she was breaking candles apart. *Stone only!*

To her astonishment, the creature froze to a halt, its huge fist raised in midair. It lost definition, its features disappearing into the bulk of stone. Magpie gawked at it for a moment, then looked around and saw the smallfolk girl with her hands outstretched.

"Whatever you did, Tildi, keep doing it!" Another stone giant threatened him. He leaped out of its way as it struck the ground with its huge arms. The floor shook.

Could she do it again? She must. More giants rolled down from what had been the staircase, landing on the floor with a tremendous *boom!* The defenders did their best to keep away from the newcomers, who already outnumbered them two to one. The wizards could not keep up. Every time Serafina or Edynn made one stop moving, three more came behind it.

"Behind you, Serafina!" Rin reared up and kicked at the giant with her forelegs. It staggered backward half a pace, then strode up and knocked the centaur flying with a single backhand blow. Rin flew across the floor in a tangle of limbs and long hair. Serafina spun and pointed her staff at the beast. Its face slagged, but it kept moving toward her. Tildi concentrated on the creature that had hurt her friend, hoping she could repeat the success of her first try. Its rune felt tangible to her. She began to break pieces off it. The monster seemed to sense the attack and turned toward her, arm raised to strike. It froze. Tildi stared. It had worked!

The lightning struck down at them, striking in between defender and foe alike. Tildi tried to concentrate on the next beast, but the giants had noticed her now, and turned to move toward her. Instead of mere holes in their faces, she thought she saw strange, bulgy blue eyes gazing at her. They terrified her so much she lost all thought of reshaping them. She turned to run away. More of the giants were behind her, reaching for her, closing off her escape. Tildi dodged to the right and left, looking for a way out of the shrinking circle of stone. One giant raised its arm.

Edynn's cold fire melted the arm before the blow fell. Tildi took the opportunity offered, and ducked behind it while it tried to turn its inflexible body to use its good arm instead. One of its fellows slammed it in mistake. She gasped, feeling stone chips raining down on her. She hurried to get near one of the wizards. She could not be lucky like that always. They must hit her sometime, and it would take only one blow to kill.

Edynn beckoned to her. She was fending off four giants by herself, but as Tildi neared she started to form a wall of wards with one hand. "You at least must survive. Get behind this shield."

"I can help," Tildi said, though her voice was choked with fear. Edynn shook her head.

"We are too outnumbered. Keep the wards intact. Save yourself. Only you can rescue the book." She pushed Tildi into the shining silver cage and went back to her work. The giants noticed the smallfolk girl, and lumbered over. They raised their enormous hands over their heads and brought them down in a tremendous blow upon the top of the little shelter. The entire room shook. Tildi cowered, shielding her head, fearing that any moment they would crush her. Edynn did not let her down: the magic that protected her was more powerful than the one that gave life to the giants. Pieces broke off their arms, but they kept trying to break through. She huddled in a ball on the ground, too frightened to concentrate on changing their runes.

"Here! This way! Hurry!"

Tildi looked up at the sound of strange voices. From around the corner of the building, a man in blue-and-white livery jumped up on top of the wall. He surveyed the site, and beckoned to whoever was following him. A host of men and women in the same garb came running, wielding swords and war hammers.

"Anathema!" boomed a woman with a round, pale face and strands of chestnut hair peeping out from under her soaking wet blue coif. "Destroy the creatures!"

Magpie hissed with pain. He had dodged the wrong way when the giant he was fighting swung its arms at him. It had taken him full on the shoulder. It felt almost crushed to pulp. Wincing, he squeezed his fingers. They closed, though the movement cost him agony. Not broken, thank the Father. Lucky it wasn't his sword arm. He hopped back and forth, trying to get an opening where he could move in and stick his blade under the thing's chin. His sword was almost too light for the job, but he'd decapitated one of the giants already. He had never seen anything like these creatures. They looked like toy soldiers made by someone who only had blocks of soap to work with. The sword threatened to twist in his wet hand. With his teeth he tore loose a piece of his sleeve and used it to wrap the hilt. Better. One of the giants swung at him. He ducked, and the thing's hand slammed into the castle wall over his head.

Behind him, he heard cries. A male voice that he first took for the guard made him look up. Through the rain he spotted a flash of blue and white. To his horror he saw a strange man dressed in the livery of the Knights of the Word. He groaned. How could they be here? The first one beckoned, and an entire chapter's worth of knights came pouring into the courtyard, with Sharhava at their head.

"Help us!" Rin bellowed.

Sharhava gave the centaur a look of pure disgust. She wouldn't turn a hand to save what she saw as an unnatural species, but spotted the natural humans threatened by the stone giants, and made a sign over her head. The knights spread out across the courtyard, wielding sword and hammer or ax, and waded into the fray. Magpie felt relief. With the Scholardom's help they might be able to fight their way inside and find the book.

His eye was caught by one of the newly arrived fighters. Near the wall was a shapely figure that he would have recognized if she had been wearing a sack. Inbecca! The set look on her face when she spotted him watching her told him all he needed to know. The knights had followed his trail all the way from the castle. No time for the inevitable argument now. They were fighting for their lives.

Teryn and the others shouted instructions over the roar of the rain to the knights on the best places to strike the stone giants. A lucky thrust from her blade sent the head of one monster tumbling across the flagstones. A cry of acknowledgment went up, and the fighters began to angle for a position to take down the rest, all the while trying not to be crushed to death by the behemoths. It was not easy going. The giants seemed unmoved by the rain and lightning, and did not care which of the intruders they attacked. Magpie fought against one after another, shifting until he was striking away at the same monster as Inbecca.

"What are you doing with her?" he blurted out. "Why did you join the Knights?"

"What choice did you leave me?" Inbecca asked, flailing angrily at a stone simulacrum twice her height. She looked dignified and fierce, in spite of wearing a habit too large for her, and dripping with rain. "I was disgraced before the courts of five nations! Sharhava offered me a way out with honor."

"I'm sorry," Magpie said lamely. A stone hand as large as his head swung, and he ducked. A bolt of red energy blasted over his head and the hand melted. He pulled Inbecca back to avoid the steaming droplets that dribbled to the ground.

"I do not care," Inbecca said, between gritted teeth. She pulled herself loose and glared at him. "All we want is the book. Where is it?"

Magpie pointed at the castle. "One of the Shining Ones has it. He caused these creatures to come to life. We have to survive to get it."

"Then we shall," Inbecca said, with a furious look at him. "After that, you and I will part *forever.*"

His heart sank. That was not the moment to convince her otherwise, though. The number of giants seemed to grow endlessly. The defenders found themselves being herded backwards toward the corner of the terrace. Two knights died as the press of stone monsters closed in on them, flailing with their enormous limbs. Another was caught by a stroke of bilious green lightning that met an upraised sword. The knight stood still for a moment, then toppled, his habit on fire. The giants walked right over him in pursuit of living quarry.

Magpie leaped up on the wall over which the knights had come. He looked around for Tildi. He saw the smallfolk girl trapped in a corner. Four of the giants were beating against a cage of light in which she had taken sanctuary. The light around her was growing more feeble by the moment. He leaped down again, and thrust his way through the crowd of giants. He levered the head off the nearest one, then hammered at the others until they noticed him. The distraction was just in time. Tildi's protection faded to nothingness as soon as they turned away from her. With a grateful look she dashed toward the two wizardesses. Magpie ducked blows from the circle of attackers, then made a face at them. They lumbered toward him, arms out.

He ran back to the waist-high wall and leaped over it, looking for the path down into the city. The giants followed, more slowly but as inexorably as an avalanche. Instead of climbing the wall, they smashed at it with their hands and walked through the gap. Magpie changed directions and ran over the flagstones.

A burst of white light whistled past his ear. He flattened on the terraced pavement and looked up. Edynn stood over him. She threw another bolt. The centaur was there, too, kicking at the attackers. She had a bloody wound on the side of her head. The blond peddler woman laid about her with her club. Her braids had come undone, leaving her round face surrounded by lank streamers of hair. She was doing surprising damage to the giants for her size. Lakanta gave him a companionable grin.

"We'll take as many with us as we can," she said. "I fear we're making little headway, though."

"He can increase his army almost infinitely," Edynn said.

"Can't you stop him?" Magpie asked. "You're one of the most powerful wizards in the world."

"Our powers are not balanced as long as he has the Great Book," Edynn said. "I can buy you some time, I believe. This will call for the most desperate of measures." She glanced behind her. The defenders were being herded toward the castle doors. "Can we open those?"

"Consider it done," Rin said. She leaned forward onto her front hooves, and kicked out powerfully to the rear. The ornate doors flew open behind them and banged against the walls. Inside was a vast room, empty but for a few statues. The company and the knights began to move inside. At Edynn's signal, Teryn picked up Tildi and carried her into the castle hall.

"Go," Edynn said, raising her staff and knocking back another giant. "Hurry, inside!"

"One thin door won't keep those stone monsters out," Rin declared.

"I will keep them back," Edynn insisted. "Inside!"

"No, Mother!" Serafina shouted over the rain. Her eyes went wide with fear.

Edynn smiled at her, her long white hair plastered to her head. "We cannot deal with all three menaces at once. He can keep us out here infinitely, creating more and more giants, until there are none of us able to challenge him." She reached up to touch her daughter's cheek. "We all have our tasks, Serafina. This is mine. I may be wrong. We may all be wrong. Let it be so."

"Please, Mother, let me stay here with you," Serafina begged.

"They have no chance without you," Edynn said simply. "Tildi has no chance. You must stay with her. Help her. Teach her. *Now*. Now is your time. Hurry!" She pushed Serafina's shoulder, urging her inward. The majority of the giants had not yet reached them with their slow gait, but they soon would. Magpie gently urged Serafina to follow him. She pulled loose from his grasp, refusing to leave her mother's side.

"Get everyone inside!" Edynn called to Sharhava. "Keep out as many giants as you can!"

The abbess made a spinning gesture over her head. "Scholars! Into the castle!"

The knights disengaged from their opponents, and made for the castle door with alacrity. Inbecca passed him, but Magpie did not follow her. Serafina was not going to go without help. Edynn appealed to him.

"Aid her now," Edynn said. "The book must be secured. You have my thanks, prince and minstrel." She turned to Serafina and looked deeply into the girl's eyes. Her stern expression melted. "Ah, my child. I love you. Until the end of the world, remember that."

An unseen force pushed Magpie and Serafina away from her as an entire company of giants lumbered up the ramp toward Edynn. The girl stumbled, and Magpie helped her to her feet. She rushed to get outside again, but the white-haired wizardess waved a hand. The massive doors slammed shut, leaving them in darkness.

"No!" she screamed. "Mother!" She threw herself at the huge double doors and pounded on them. Magpie pulled her away. She was weeping. Rin threw an arm around her and spun her about.

"Your task is here now!" the centaur exclaimed. "We are not free yet. Act! Do not waste time. She will buy us time."

Serafina's eyes were wild with grief and anger. She sought about her.

They lit upon Tildi, who huddled, soaking wet, against the inner wall of the keep in between the two guards. "You! This is all your fault! If not for you, I could be there with her! She did this all for you. As usual, I receive no consideration!"

Tildi stretched out a hand, offering the girl sympathy. Serafina glared at her, and returned to trying to open the double doors. She raised her staff, and red flame rolled from its jewel, outlining them, trying to burn through her mother's spell. The red light went out almost at once.

"No!" she cried. Rin shook her by the shoulders.

"Accept that she has done it for all of us, silly girl," the centaur snapped. "Now, hurry! We must not waste the sacrifice! We still need to save all of existence! The thing we must do is up above, not out there!"

Outside, they heard hammering, banging, and the inevitable howl of the Madcloud. Suddenly, a loud wailing noise rose over all and echoed down the ruined valley.

Tildi's heart went out to Serafina. They both had reason to grieve. She had come to love Edynn. The wizardess had shown her kindness and protected her.

In a moment, she knew that the prophecy that Serafina had worried about for so long had come true. The longing for the book came back in full force, and she felt she had to be with it or die of sorrow. All of the protective wards and spells that Edynn had cast to protect her were gone. She must maintain her own sanity now.

Outside, it was silent except for the roaring of the rain. Serafina pulled herself upright and shrugged off Magpie's and Rin's supporting hands. Her face was a mask of grief, but she had no time to mourn. The threat was not gone, nor was their task yet completed. Her hands trembled as they sought for something. Suddenly, she levered her wand at one of the giants that had pursued them inside. A burst of red light brighter than any she had created before burst from it. The stone being wailed as it slumped into a heap of glowing lava.

"Upstairs," the young wizardess ordered grimly, as the others gawked. "Let us finish this now."

The great hall was like a huge, hollow box that stretched up at least sixty feet. A flight of marble stairs spiraled around the inner wall and disappeared through the ceiling. Serafina led the way to it, staff and chin held high. The guards flanked Tildi to protect her in the melee going on all around them. The head of a stone giant came flying off and landed with a crash on the floor. Tildi jumped back, but followed resolutely. Not another moment must separate her from the book.

As they neared the staircase, the lowest step picked itself up and stood upright. Teryn and Morag left Tildi's side to stand between it and the entire company. Being made of marble, this giant was thinner and lighter than the granite beings, but it looked just as menacing.

"Ah, Father," Lakanta groaned. "Has the man only one idea in his head?"

Serafina didn't hesitate. "Tildi, flight!"

Tildi snapped out of the daze she was in. She threw off the sodden cloak, and brandished her knife. The words that she had recited so many times on their journey came easily to her. Rin stretched a long arm down and put her on her back. Magpie raced after them and leaped onto the centaur's back, clinging with his knees.

"You presume much," Rin said with a snort. But she took a tremendous leap and bounded into the air.

Serafina bespelled the guards and herself. Lakanta jumped up.

"Come on!" she shouted to Tildi. "You're going to need me! Do I have to go get my horse?"

Tildi pointed the knife at her and chanted the spell again. Lakanta hoisted her skirts in her hands and stumped up the air after them. The first of the stone monsters made a grab for her, but it was too slow.

As they cantered through the air toward the hole in the ceiling, one of the knights bounded up the stairs over the awakening giants. She leaped after them and grabbed onto Magpie's leg. He hauled her into his lap.

"You're not going after the book without me," Inbecca said firmly.

Chapter Thirty-five

It was deadly silent in the room above the hall as Rin's hooves touched down neatly on the woven carpets that covered the enormous floor. Tildi gazed around her at the fine furnishings, the gloriously colored windows, the polished, painted walls, but her attention was riveted at once by the man who sat in one of the white thrones set in a row, staring at her. He had the bulgy blue eyes she had seen in the stone giants. He *felt* familiar. Though she had never seen him before, she knew him, but it was not a comfortable feeling. He moved nervously, as if he was going to jump up and attack her, or run away. More important, she knew the object on the altarlike table to his right. It was the Great Book. Tildi breathed. There had never been a more beautiful thing made in the entire history of the world! She began to walk toward it, unable to think of anything but touching it at last. It looked exactly as it had in her vision of the scriptorium where he and his fellow Shining Ones had made it except . . . except . . .

"How dare you?" Tildi demanded, halting, tears springing into her eyes at the torn pages, the gaping holes ripped in the perfection of the white parchment. It almost seemed to her to be *bleeding* into the air around it. She couldn't see the pieces, nor could she feel them anywhere. "How could you harm it?"

He turned bleary, red-rimmed eyes to her. "I had no choice." The book's spindle seemed to rotate in his right hand now. "You do. Leave now. Leave, or I will wipe you out of existence."

"How could you destroy something that you worked so hard to make?" Tildi demanded. "It took you years of your life! And why did you send the thraik to kill my family? They were simple, hardworking people who never did anything to you at all! Why are you making them attack me? You have the book!"

The face that turned to her was full of pain. "I didn't send them," he whispered. "He did. He wants it back. I hear him all the time. I cannot escape him. I hear him now. Do you want to know what he says? 'Bring it to me.'"

"You did," Tildi insisted, her hands in fists. "All of my brothers, torn apart by those *monsters!* You are responsible for the deaths of my whole family!"

"No, Tildi," Magpie said, over her shoulder. "He didn't do any of that. This man isn't one of the Shining Ones."

"What?" Serafina demanded. "Who is this?"

Magpie laughed bitterly. "It's our poor, damned, deluded magician, come home to kill himself. Why couldn't he just drink himself to death on our best brandy? We paid him enough to fill this whole valley with it."

"Nemeth?" Inbecca asked, in disbelief. "That old fool who ruined you?"

"He didn't ruin us!" Magpie shouted. "My father did! There, the dire secret's out." He tightened his lips. "We've all been trying to cover the shame of it for years now."

Inbecca's haughty expression vanished, and her blue-green eyes were full of sympathy. "Oh, Eremi, I am sorry."

The tired eyes of the man in the chair seemed to focus upon the minstrel. "Eremi? You?"

Magpie turned a sincere face to him, and kept his voice low and calm, almost as if he was singing a lullaby. "Yes, me, Eremilandur. We were allies once, Nemeth. Won't you listen to me?"

"You treated me like a fool! I knew! I told the truth."

"I know you did. I defended you. Hawarti defended you. My father . . ." The words clearly cost Magpie an effort, but he got them out. "My father is a fool. He would not listen to anyone, and has to live with his regrets."

Nemeth sputtered hysterically, "He thinks he can pay for his failures, and send us away, and no one will know." The pale man leaned forward. "You are different."

"Yes," Magpie said, edging smoothly closer to him. "I believed you. But you have a great treasure there."

"It is mine," Nemeth said, laying a possessive hand on it. "What I do with it is my business, and no one else's."

"Please," Tildi said, appealing to the wizard. "It doesn't belong to you. Please, let me take it. It has to go back where it belongs. You don't know the harm you are causing with it."

"I do know," Nemeth said, transferring his insane gaze to her. "It is Soliandur's punishment for destroying my life. He betrayed me, then humiliated me. I will not stand for that." He lifted his hands, and the book seemed to spin of its own accord. "He should not have made a fool of me before everyone in court! I served him well."

"But the people who lived on the land you destroyed," Magpie said, "they didn't harm you in any way."

"They belong to him," Nemeth said. "He cares no more for them than he did for me. He has plenty of *peasants*." He spat out the word. The blue eyes gleamed with madness. "I believe it is time to take something he truly prizes. Perhaps the castle itself!"

"Please don't," Tildi said, greatly daring. "You could hurt so many people. You must not betray others just because you have felt betrayed."

The eyes glared at her. "You dare! You who left your past behind, who ran away from offers of honorable marriage? You, who've abandoned your modesty. Look at how you dress, smallfolk. You still keep the relics of your past, but you can never go back. The others would be ashamed of you. It is all here!" He slammed his hand down on a page. "What are you doing outside the Quarters, dressed like a boy?"

Tildi felt as if he could see through her to her backbone. Tears sprang to her eyes. All of the progress she had made, the belief in herself that she had built up in the company of wizards and minstrels, crumbled away. She was again a smallfolk girl, defying convention. She would be shunned for this! She bowed her head.

"I had to go. You don't understand."

"You are a runaway!"

"A wizard's apprentice," Magpie countered, his calm voice over her head.

Nemeth blazed at her. "Stolen! You lied to get where you are. It's all here." He pounded the book.

Magpie chimed in. "Then all the things you have done are there, too, Tildi. All that you are is more than a girl from the Quarters. Think. Don't listen to him. He can read your heart. It's his gift. He's using your fears against you. Don't listen."

She looked up at the young man. He grinned at her. "You're even braver than I am. I couldn't go apprentice for Olen. He's too conservative for me."

"Olen. Yes." The wizard leered at them, a smug, superior smile. "You left to become a spy." He spun the book to yet another page. "A spy, up to no good. You are tied to this place. I have felt scrutiny from here. They must stop looking at me. I hate being spied upon. *Ano chetegh tal!*" Fire sprang from his fingertips. Tildi suddenly recognized the sign at his hand. It was Silvertree! He must not burn Silvertree! Beside it was another rune, *man, magic, green eyes*—Olen! Tildi leaped for the book. Nemeth flicked his fingers, and she went tumbling backward, struck by an invisible fist. Teryn picked her up and set her on her feet. Tildi felt her bruised cheek. The book—she must save Olen! She raced toward the man in the chair. The captain and Morag lifted her off her feet and held her back.

Magpie waved his arms, trying to attract the wizard's attention. "Nemeth, stop!" he shouted. "Leave them alone! They're not the reason you're angry."

"No," Nemeth boomed, pausing and turning his full gaze upon Magpie, as the flames burned in his hand. The lightning outside seemed to echo his word. "It is Soliandur. You, you are his flesh and blood! He will see how I take my vengeance."

He thrust out a burning finger and began to draw in the air. Magpie began to protest, but his words were cut off. He fell to his knees. To Tildi's horror, a rune overlay Magpie's. His hands thickened until his fingers disappeared in pads of flesh. The young man's narrow face lengthened, and his teeth curled out like tusks. Magpie cried out. Knobs of bone punched through the fabric along his spine, and his rib cage shrank until his breaths came in pants, starved for lung capacity. He lay on the floor moaning. Nemeth drew himself up. "I will do the same thing to Soliandur. He will suffer before he dies."

Tildi stared at him. She was horrified at the transformation, but not as much as Teryn and Morag.

"You!" Teryn exclaimed, gazing at the wizard in the chair. "You're responsible for killing my soldiers!"

Morag, his eyes glowing blue with madness, leaped for Nemeth. He almost reached the wizard, but Nemeth threw the handful of fire at him. Morag dropped to the floor and rolled to one side, avoiding the flames. Teryn closed in on him, too, thrusting at him with her sword. Nemeth created more fire, and threw it at her. She dodged and kept coming. Nemeth seemed to panic. He seized the book.

"Do not come near me! I will burn all of Orontae at once!" he cried. "Rabantae will be next!" The soldiers froze. The book spun again, until it revealed a page with one huge rune on it. He took hold of the edge of the page.

Tildi could not let him harm the book again.

She ran toward him, reaching for the book. Nemeth whipped his hands upward, and a circle of flame appeared around his throne. Tildi windmilled to a halt, surrounded by a dancing fire that moved outward. The soldiers retreated. If it touched her, it would destroy her. The book needed her.

Though Edynn was gone, she seemed to feel the wizardess with her still. She knew, too, that she was Teldo's sister, not just a faithless wretch who had run away. She was Olen's student, Magpie's friend, and Edynn's apprentice. Those thoughts gave her confidence. She reached deep into herself and made the wards that Olen had taught her.

"*Fornai chnetegh voshad!*" The silver lace formed stronger than she had ever managed to make it. The flames had no chance against the protection spell, and broke apart. She glanced back at Serafina, who smiled at her and urged her forward. The young woman aimed her staff at the wizard, and a bloom of red fire flew at Nemeth. He batted at it, and it dissipated. Serafina kept the barrage up, moving closer. The others followed, closing inexorably inward toward the thief.

"So you are a wizard," he said furiously. "A wizard and a spy! I am beset by enemies! You shall not take the book from me!" He created handful after handful of fire, his movements growing ever more wild. Flames flew everywhere.

The shield protected Tildi. The tapestries over his head were burning, now, and the rugs were smoldering. Rin let out a loud bellow as a gout of flame landed on her mane. She beat it out, and charged at Nemeth, blood in her eye. The wizard cringed, snatching the book off the table and holding it to his chest. He reached out at her, his fingers twisting.

"*Voshte!*" Serafina cried. Silver lines wound themselves around Rin, covering the rune.

"That will not stop me," Nemeth barked. He started to wind through the pages. He must be looking for Rin's rune. He would kill or deform her, the way he had done to Magpie, the way he had harmed Morag and Teryn's soldiers. She must take the book from him so no one else would get hurt.

Morag hefted his polearm, and threw it at Nemeth. The wizard shrieked as it struck the wooden throne above his head. He clapped the book shut on the page he was perusing, and threw more gouts of flame at the oncoming soldiers.

"I must . . . I must stop you," he muttered. "The book is mine. It's mine!"

Rin reared up and battered at Nemeth with her forelegs and snapped at him with her whip. The lash struck him across the face. He fell back, his forehead bleeding. He flung up both hands, and Rin tumbled back-ward. Lakanta and Teryn closed in from both sides. Nemeth sent them flying, too. They rose up and charged him again. He rolled up the book, and gathered himself, as if preparing to leap out of his seat. He tucked the book under one arm. Serafina moved from side to side, covering him as if with a crossbow. Nemeth watched her eyes, poised to spring as soon as he could. Teryn took him by surprise, bounding forward with her sword on high. She chopped down. Nemeth shrieked. Blood spurted from his shoulder. He waved both arms, and Teryn flew backward help-lessly until she struck the wall. She slid down bonelessly. Morag went to her rescue. Serafina fired another blast of red fire at him.

Tildi saw her opportunity. She rushed toward the wizard, arms out. He met her charge with an outstretched hand.

"Not so fast, little one," he hissed. Tildi danced to a halt. With a sick feeling she knew what he meant to do. He was going to alter her rune, as he had poor Magpie. He must not!

"*Ano chnetegh tal!*" she cried. The green flames sprang into being. She threw her fire at Nemeth. He flicked his fingers, and the flames curled into his palm. Instead of sending it back at her, he shrieked. The green demon-fire refused to leave his hand. It clung to his skin. He shook his arm, hoping to make it fall, but succeeded only in spreading it to the hangings on the wall. Tildi feared for the book. It must not be harmed!

She sprang forward and grabbed hold of a corner of it. The parchment burned horribly in her grasp, like the first time that she had touched the leaf, but many times worse. She wondered if she would die from it, wondered if her limbs were withering like Halcot's hands. She must prevent it. *Go past the pain*, she told herself. *It's no worse than a scald from a cooking pot*, even though her teeth were clenched so hard she feared she would break them. With an act of will, she took hold with her other hand. Both curled with agony, but she would not let go. She had the book at last!

Nemeth wailed as his precious book slid away. He must get it back! He had only one hand to use now, for the green fire would destroy it. He held fast to the spindle, chanting the spell to surround the small female with a ring of fire that would consume her. He would take the book as she burned to death. The spindle slipped out of his fingers, out of his reach. The little girl turned to crawl away from him. He threw himself after her and seized her foot. The boot came off in his hand, and he found himself looking at the strange, toeless little foot of his vision. At that moment he knew he was doomed.

"Give it back to me!" he bellowed, as the book disappeared into the web of flames that surrounded him.

Tildi defied him. She wrapped herself around the scroll and huddled over it, holding to a patch of bare floor. She sensed that the book hurt, too, from having been torn by Nemeth. It wasn't exactly intelligent, but it was alive. They soothed each other in the midst of the battle. She was no longer hungry, thirsty, or tired. She had the book. It made her feel profoundly happy in spite of the pain.

The castle shook around them, and she heard the clatter of more stones falling off the roof. The Madcloud overhead was taking its vengeance on the people inside. It must go away. She thought about the vast, multicolored cloud, and surrounded it in her mind with a cage of wards, as Olen had taught her. Enclose it, and send it far away, into the eastern seas.

There was a sudden silence overhead, and Tildi knew that the book had made it true. The Madcloud was gone. *So this was what it was like to have infinite power over the things of the earth*, she thought. She was glad to have experienced it once before the fire killed her. The heat made her gasp. Any moment she was going to run out of air. She would be ashes moments after that. Only the fact that she had been wet to the skin had prevented her and the book from being roasted, but she was dry now. The flames were licking at her sleeves. Over her head she heard shouting and scuffling, followed by a wild scream of pain. Tildi trembled.

After what seemed like hours a hand reached through the flames and felt around until it located her collar. With a powerful jerk, it pulled her free of the circle of flames and all the way to the far wall. Tildi took a deep gasp of breath. Lakanta pounded her on the back.

"Your arm," Tildi panted. "It's not even burned!"

The dwarf gave her meaty hand a casual glance. "Fire doesn't affect me same as you, my dear. We're part of the earth, you know. You've got it! Good girl!"

Tildi unrolled the scroll just a little. It was agony to handle it, but more manageable now. She felt as if she had never loved anything as much as the book. It seemed that it liked her, too, curling up to caress her hand. She welcomed the pain, because it felt good at the same time. The book made her happy. She looked at the page where Silvertree's rune was scribed. Olen was still well. She was glad to have saved him. She must save all of her friends. The book would help her to do it.

"Give it back to me!"

Tildi looked up. Nemeth was on his feet now, lurching toward Tildi. He threw a handful of light at Serafina. His spells no longer seemed as powerful, without the book in his hands. The young woman clearly saw that she had an advantage. Her staff emitted an enormous ball of red light that surrounded the wizard. He staggered. He was angling to get past the soldiers, to get to her, to retake the book, but he was growing weaker by the moment. Tildi clasped it to her. He must not have it!

Rin interposed herself between Tildi and the charging wizard. She rose up, her powerful hooves flailing. Nemeth let out a terrible cry, and went down before her.

"Leave me alone!" he shrieked. "Leave me alone!"

"Get back," Serafina ordered, as Teryn and Morag closed in upon the fallen Nemeth. "We have defeated him. The book is ours."

"No," Morag said. "It is not over yet." His eyes glowed as blue as Nemeth's. He stepped forward with his sword raised, a dark shadow against the dancing flames of the burning tapestries.

"Don't," Serafina pleaded. "He's beaten now."

"It is justice," Teryn said, holding the wizardess back with her sword. "But we will never be able to help Morag if he dies."

"Tildi will," Teryn said firmly.

Lakanta covered Tildi's eyes to shield her from the sight, but Tildi heard the blow. Nemeth let out one final scream. Tildi dissolved in tears.

"I didn't want anyone to die," she said.

"I know, child," the peddler said, patting her on the head. She looked down at the book in Tildi's lap. "Look at that! Isn't it fine? No wonder my husband thought he could sell scraps of it. But we've got it back now."

I have it, Tildi thought. *Nemeth loved it, but it's mine now.*

She was shocked at her own thoughts. She did love the book, but her entire purpose for coming along had been to obtain the book, to safeguard it so it could go back to where it belonged. Edynn had sacrificed her life for her. Olen would be disappointed if she did anything else. She pulled herself together, though it wrenched at her heart. The book would go back to where it belonged. She would be able to enjoy it for a time, but she would see it set in a place of safety where it would stay for all eternity, where no one else could harm it or tear out its pages. Edynn and Olen, and Teldo, too, would be proud of her.

Serafina came over to her at last. "Well done, Tildi," she said, crouching down beside her. She took each of Tildi's hands in hers and concentrated. The gentle warmth healed some of the raw, burning sensation that handling the book had caused.

"It's glad I have it," Tildi said.

"It's just a thing," Serafina said. "Just an object. A beautiful and precious one, but it has no consciousness."

"It does," Tildi insisted. "I hear it."

The young wizard turned Tildi's chin so she could look into her eyes.

"Tildi, listen to me. You hear the things inside it. They make a great harmony that pleases you, because it is complete. It's the world."

Ah. The world, complete in her lap. She felt all of its ills as well as its joys. To think that a girl from the Quarters would have such an opportunity. Tildi felt somewhat unsteady, trying to assimilate all of what the book's acceptance of her meant, but for the moment, she knew that it was all right for a girl from the Quarters to possess the greatest treasure in all of Alada.

She looked up at Serafina. "I can't read these runes. Will you teach me?"

Serafina looked at her distrustfully, and Tildi knew she was recalling the promises that both of them had made to Edynn. She nodded slowly. "Yes. I will be your teacher now, until we can get the book back to its haven, and I have brought you safely back to Olen."

"Thank you," Tildi said simply.

"Help me," a woman's voice said. "Wizard, can you help him? He is dying!"

Tildi looked up. The young woman in Scholardom livery sat near the remains of the thrones. She held Magpie's head in her lap. She appealed to them.

"Can you do anything?" she pleaded.

Tildi felt terrible. She had forgotten about poor Magpie. She and Serafina went to him. The deformities looked even worse than she had thought. His eyes were bulging out of his sockets, and his skull depressed painfully over the forehead.

"Tildi," Magpie croaked, his voice as hoarse as his namesake's. He looked up at her, surveyed the scroll under her arm. "You have it. Can you fix me?"

The room was suddenly full of men and women wearing blue-and-white livery. The big woman in the elaborate habit let out an exclamation of horror.

"Lar Inbecca! Stand to attention! Remember your duty!"

The girl ignored her, and focused upon the smallfolk. "Do you know the magic to restore him? I know he must be in the Great Book. All of us under the heavens are."

Tildi rolled the parchment on its spindles, searching through the largely unintelligible pictographs in search of one that meant *Magpie* to her. She finally found one, but it matched the one that glowed upon his chest. Tildi saw the goodness inside the prickly, playful exterior, and knew it to be a disguise. She blushed suddenly. She knew too much about him. She looked at Serafina.

"That's why we swear apprentices not to reveal the secrets of our craft, Tildi. It's not our place to divulge all we know."

Tildi studied it closely, and turned to Magpie with sincere regret. "I can't do anything with the one written here. This shows your rune the way you are now, not the way you were."

The deformed hand unlatched itself from the girl's, and felt in the pouch at his belt. It emerged with a slip of parchment folded between two of the padlike fingers. He proffered it to Tildi. She hesitated, but the hand shook insistently. It was the rune she had drawn for him that day at Olen's house.

"Oh, I can't," Tildi said.

"Please," the girl begged her. "Little one, whoever you are, help him."

"You saw how he did it," Serafina said, with the gravity of her mother. "Concentrate, Tildi."

Tildi seemed to hear voices coming from the book, wizards from all throughout history, speaking to her as though she was an equal. She did not feel the equality, but she must not let down poor Magpie, who had written her a song.

"Draw it for me again, little Tildi," Magpie said, his tongue thick in his misshapen mouth. "Ironic, isn't it, that I came here to keep you from harm, and you end up having to doctor me? If it doesn't work, then please give me the coup de grace. Think of me as a chicken for the pot."

"Stop saying those things," Tildi begged him. "I'll start thinking about chickens, and who knows what will happen?"

"I'll get feathers," Magpie said, and began to laugh. That hurt, so he started choking.

"Lie still," Serafina said severely. She drew wards around them, enclosing the four of them in a sphere of pure light.

Tildi studied the image, trying to memorize every detail. She closed her eyes, doing her best to ignore the golden rune on his body, seeing in her mind's eye only the faint black line on the parchment. Olen had taught her the basics of rune manipulation, but this was more serious than anything she had ever done. She raised her hand and drew it in silver on the air, willing it to take the place of the other. She must do it exactly right, or Magpie would die. She felt warmth exude from the prone body beside her.

A loud groan made her open her eyes. The rune on his chest was now the same as the one on the parchment. She had done it! Magpie lay on the floor, admiring his hands. They had returned to their normal shape, long and slim with blunt-tipped fingers. He scratched his ribs experimentally, then beamed. He sprang to his feet, and knelt before Tildi.

"Well done, Tildi! You are a wizard among wizards. I'll sing your praises at every feast from now until my last day!"

Tildi smiled back shyly. She felt another presence at her shoulder and looked up. The guard Morag stood there, his eyes returned to their normal color. He bowed to her humbly.

"Can you fix me, too?" he asked.

Tildi shook her head sadly. "I have no rune for you," she said. "But I will learn how, I promise."

Serafina came to lay a gentle hand on the guard's shoulders. "Now that we have the book, many things will be set back to rights."

The abbess Sharhava in blue and white regarded them with a sour face.

Tildi gathered up the book and embraced it, the pain less now than before. She was surrounded by her friends, and she was halfway to finishing the task set for her by Master Olen.